D0379948

Swimming
Kangaroo
Books

The Silk Palace
Swimming Kangaroo Books, September 2007

Swimming Kangaroo Books
Arlington, Texas
ISBN: Paperback 978-1-934041-42-0

PDF 978-1-934041-41-3
Other Available formats: MS Reader, HTML, Mobi (No ISBN's are assigned)

LCCN: 2007929840
British Library Cataloguing in Publication Data.
A catalogue record for this book is available from the British Library.

Cover art by Berin Uriegas

 This book is a work of fiction and any resemblance to persons, living or dead, or events is purely coincidental. They are productions of the author's imagination and used fictitiously.

Also by Colin Harvey

Vengeance

Lightning Days

The Silk Palace

by

Colin Harvey

Swimming Kangaroo Books Arlington, Texas

This book is for my parents.

Dramatis Personae

Bluestocking: A scholar.

Prince Casimiripian (Cas): A provincial ruler of the Karnaki Empire, under whose protection Bluestocking travels

Halarbur: His servant

Arial: The Prime Minister of Whiterock.

Jasmina: His wife

King Redoutifalia: The King of Whiterock

Queen Juliophelana (Ana): The Queen of Whiterock

Princess Evivalesinan (Evi) : Their eldest daughter: High Priestess of the Church of Brighannon.

Princess Lexnovoswartoner (Lexi): The King and Queen's second daughter; affianced to an Emir of the Western Alliance.

Princess Cavendsilperisha (Cavi): The King and Queen's youngest daughter, affianced to Prince Casimiripian.

Talaben: The Emir's vizier, and Lexi's protector.

Myleetra: Grand Witch of Whiterock.

Copel : A librarian

Aton: An itinerant peddler

Chapter 1

The Silk Palace perched in the end of year sunshine high atop Whiterock, all great grey battlements and fluttering pennants, invulnerability made manifest.

Now it was out of sight of the riders below, even when they craned their necks. Many of them rode leaning outwards, away from the massif, as if oppressed by it. Rearing heavenward from the flat grasslands, the white rock seemed to fill their world, their long column snaking round its massive bulk. It wasn't completely white, but speckled with impurities and moss. Over the millennia, trickling water had cut tiny vertical riverbeds into the rock, and elsewhere sporadic outcroppings bulged overhead. Once they rode so close, Bluestocking reached out and scratched a flake off and licked it. Her finger tasted bitter.

"It might be poisonous," Halarbur said.

As always when he was around, Bluestocking couldn't help thinking, *Does he know?*

The Prince's valet rode with hands holding up the reins as if to show her how to grasp them. His thinning grey hair was combed forward and chopped in a bowl shape. As usual, his square face gave nothing away. For all that, she sensed disapproval; he never called her by name or title. As if he knew that she wasn't all she pretended to be.

"Then I'll be ill." Her tone dared him to argue with her, but he looked away.

Above the caravan, delta-winged gliders quartered the open sky away from the rock, riding the rising thermals, their mage-pilots weaving their defensive web of spells. The sun was high in the sky, finally breaking through the clouds, and Bluestocking's spirits lifted with its warmth. She wrung out her jerkin's rain-soaked sleeve.

A shadow passed overhead. Unable to stifle a cry of surprise, she flinched.

The other riders guffawed. "She shrieked like that time Pasceb goosed her," Luer wiped her eyes between fits of laughter.

It was all Bluestocking could do not to scream at them. To show she wasn't scared, she ostentatiously craned her neck, leaning so far back in her saddle that she almost toppled from Fourposter's back. She looked down at the ground, where countless hooves had churned the mud to a quagmire and shuddered at the thought of falling into it.

"My apologies, Milady," the officer leading their escort said in his barbarous language, while the glider vanished as suddenly as it appeared, "on behalf of that idiot."

They rode together for a few moments, and he cleared his throat several times as if his voice was rusty. "Do all Princes in the Karnaki Empire have ladies-in-waiting who speak our tongue so well?"

If that's an attempt to strike up a conversation, it's a decidedly clumsy one, she thought. She wondered whether he was mocking her, or the Empire, or both, but accepted the question as serious. "I'm no lady-in-waiting. I'm from the Karnaki Imperial Library, to translate the Scrolls of Presimionari." She took pleasure in watching his eyes widen, and he gestured northwards, as she'd seen them do before; clenched fist in front of the eyes, palm forward, fingers splaying open. She said, "Prince Casimiripian kindly offered me an escort from Ravlatt," and added, "That's a city in the Empire."

"Your name's Bluestocking, Maestress?" He used the formal name for scholar, clearly impressed by her mentioning the scrolls, but he mangled her name badly, pronouncing it Dzahrmin*ah*, rather than Dzahrmin*i*. *You're only being pedantic again,* she thought. *You shouldn't let it irritate you.* It was easier thought than done.

"It is."

"Doubtless named for your dzahr eyes," he grinned, openly flirting as he mangled the dialect word for 'blue' to unrecognizability, "or your garments."

She blushed. "A Bluestocking is a female scholar, who attends The Woman's University," she said crisply. "My father knew what he wanted for me from the day I was born– a good education." A lie of course, but this oaf would never know that.

Prince Casimiripian rode up. "Are you all right, Bluestocking?" He lifted his lightweight helmet and wiped sweat off a freckled forehead below cropped brown hair. His cheerful countenance had changed to a concern so exaggerated that he might have been a travelling actor. She was unsure whether it was genuine, or whether, as she suspected of his courtly manners, he was mocking her. He seemed not to hear the other rider's sniggers.

"I'm very well, thank you, Majesty." *Go away!* she thought.

"I'm glad to hear it, my dear," the Prince said, faintly emphasising the last two words. "If these yokels frightened you, I'll have them flogged. They need to learn manners."

The officer said, "I'll signal the pilot to maintain an appropriate distance."

"No need, Majesty." She realised with a sudden rush of compassion that the Prince was probably more nervous than anyone in the caravan. *It's not every day that he finally meets his intended bride,* she thought. "It wasn't the pilot's fault. I was wool-gathering."

Softening, he said, "No doubt thinking about your books." He made them sound as exotic as a Cimetrian dragon from the arctic wastes. *To an outdoorsman, I suppose they are.*

"No doubt," she said to his back– he'd already spurred his great grey stallion back to his place near the head of the line. She sneaked a look at their escort's officer; he was white-faced and trembling with rage or fear. "I'm sorry about what he said."

The officer hawked up phlegm, and spat. "No need to apologise to me. A Prince can say what he likes."

To fill the lengthening silence, she said, "The clouds seem very regular. Does the king regulate the weather?" Ask stupid questions, Sister Lucretia once told her. The old woman thought all men drank liquor morning, noon and night, and beat their women for pleasure, but Bluestocking knew her own intellect intimidated many men, so for once it seemed sound advice.

He was silent for so long that she didn't think he'd answer. Then, "The King has most of his wizards working the weather; says it keeps them out of mischief. They stand along the North wall of the palace like a line of black crows, waving their arms, and chanting their nonsense. Most rain falls at night, but they've got some schedule that means it always rains some time during the day. Mostly on that side." He gestured northwards again.

Despite herself, she giggled. "He'd hate all that untamed weather where I live. We have few mages. Most are busy squabbling amongst themselves, or working for rich folk, but the ones we have try to move passing clouds off their patch onto another's. Some clouds bounce round like ping-ping balls."

"That's the Empire," the soldier scoffed. "This is the free Kingdom of Whiterock." He quickened his horse's pace slightly, and rode away.

"No use trying to engage these peasants in civilised converse," Halarbur said.

Before she could snap an answer, an Imperial guard distracted her, saying, "How are we supposed to climb it? There isn't a step anywhere."

"Perhaps," she said, "there are hidden tunnels in the rock." She added, quietly, so he wouldn't hear, "As long as we don't have to climb it, I don't care."

They had their answer soon enough.

***

The caravan had stretched out. Fifty Imperial guards and twice as many hangers-on, all mounted, escorted the Prince. The troops had their own horses, fake bat-wings and serpent's tails to scare the enemy in battle, while the camp followers had 'borrowed' mounts, old nags mostly, or shared them with the baggage. For every rider and horse were two mules, laden almost to collapse. *By an Imperial Prince's standards,* Bluestocking thought wryly, *he's travelling light.* Their hosts had provided another fifty troops at the border, nowhere near as grandiosely decorated as the Imperial mounts, but the curving horns collared to their horse's heads made them nearly twice as tall as without them.

The Prince had rejoined them. "Where do the people who work in the Palace live?"

"In the warrens beneath, Majesty."

They've tunnelled into the rock, Bluestocking thought. *Perhaps that's where the famous Silk Spiders are?*

In the distance were a score of what Bluestocking thought were spherical buildings. They were the strangest things she'd seen since the Floating Towers at Lake Mairain. When they drew close, Bluestocking saw people scurrying around the structures. Each globe was taller than ten tall men. The globes were huge spherical bags, each painted like a playground attraction in gaudy reds, blues and yellows, while beneath hung a basket, crammed with people, moored to steps leading down to a gantry.

Several men guarded each gantry. They moved away from one, untethering the basket. The huge bag rose gracefully and, to Bluestocking, terrifyingly, up the side of the rock. Each basket was held tight on its course by a thin wire that ran skyward from the scaffold at perhaps fifteen degrees from vertical. Bluestocking's gut knotted with fear. She could see no other way of reaching the summit; and could not possibly sit in such a contraption without dying of terror.

"We'll be able to get off these damned nags soon," one Imperial soldier said to another. "Think they'll have cock-fights here? I missed them in Langedor. Typical of His Nibs to leave so early we'd need to bed down by sunset."

"I can think of better uses for cocks than fighting," one of the comfort women said.

*I've never **heard** someone leer before,* Bluestocking thought.

"Away with you, woman!" The soldier said, laughing. "D'you never think of owt else?"

"Only money," the woman said, "And drink."

Bluestocking studied the nearest of the huge bags.

A long metal tube poked up into the gap at the bottom of the bag. An attendant stretched up and dropped something into the tube. After a few seconds, a blue-white flame blazed out of the top of the tube with a whoosh, visible even through the thin material of the bag. It looked so hot that for a moment, Bluestocking thought it would set fire to the bag.

Oh, she thought. *Balefire; that's how they do it, of course, no ordinary flame would burn bright, and strong enough. I suppose the bag's safe– they must practice constantly to perfect the dosage.* A mantra ran through her head– *you can do this, you can overcome your fear; you can do this.*

As they reached the gantry, the lead riders dismounted, handing their reins to attendants, the troops nuzzling their mounts goodbye with an affection that surprised Bluestocking and climbing into the baskets. One after the other, those behind followed, until it was Bluestocking's turn. She could put it off no longer. She dismounted, stomach hollow, her knees weak. She licked her lips.

"Are you all right, Milady?" asked the man taking Fourposter's reins.

"I'm fine," she snapped. She rubbed the horse's nose.

"We'll look after him, fear not."

"I–" she nearly admitted her fear but, voice quavering, said instead, "Is it always so busy?"

"This time and the morning rush are the worst times of day, when all the travellers are on their way. The King's decree; all travellers through the kingdom must pay a tax. The only place they can pay is at the Sheriff's office." The man's ruddy face split into a grin. "Which is only open an hour before curfew. Shame that, all they travellers having to stay over and pay a night's lodging."

"There's no other way up the mountain?" There, she'd asked it.

"T'other way's worse," the man said cheerily. "Sit in a sack with holes cut in the corners to take your legs, and get hoisted up– or down. The Poor Man's Rise, they call it. The rope has a habit o'breakin', but 'cause they's only pauper's takin' that rise, no one cares too much. You'll be fine," he said gently, patting her shoulder.

The prince called, "Bluestocking! With me!"

"Majesty?"

"We're in the first basket," he said, and grinned. "The sooner we leave, the sooner we arrive. Come on! Halarbur, you'll fly with the baggage afterwards."

"Majesty," Halarbur bowed, his face impassive as ever. His gaze flicked over Bluestocking with what she was sure was disdain. *At least he won't be there to see you make a fool of yourself,* she thought.

An attendant helped her to climb into the basket. She reached out and fondled a stray piece of fabric hanging down like a talisman. "Silk," someone said, and she nodded.

Amongst the crowd she thought she saw– "No, it can't be!"

"Bluestocking?" Casimiripian said.

She laughed nervously. "I thought I saw someone I knew, Majesty."

"From Ravlatt?" Casimiripian said. "Unlikely."

No, further east again, she thought. "You're probably right."

Soon a dozen of the prince's people and two locals packed into the basket, all men except for her.

"Shut your eyes," the man said.

Bluestocking half shut her eyes and looked away as the man dropped a ball of straw into the tube. He mumbled a spell and the straw, which had been soaked in an acrid concoction, burst into flame with a hollow **whoof**! Spots of light danced in front of her now-closed eyes.

A second attendant held onto the basket, reciting a string of what Bluestocking guessed were wardings. Elementals weren't the only predators in the skies; a dozen people rising slowly would feed an afreet nest for days.

"You can open your eyes now," their host said. "Take a look around you. You'll have a magnificent view."

She knew that she shouldn't open her eyes; if she did, she'd see how far they had to fall. In her mind's eye she saw the basket break, her body tumbling to splatter on the ground. She opened her eyes anyway and nearly fainted. The Kingdom of Whiterock lay below her, a green patchwork of trees, fields and buildings, and animals and people scurrying about.

"Look," the attendant said.

From this high, Bluestocking could see the road on which they'd ridden since leaving Langedor at first light. Following the muddy road, she was sure she could see the nominal frontier-post they'd crossed just before mid-morning. The frontier was too long to fence and required too many men to guard. But protocol demanded they enter at the wooden hut with its twin flags of the Empire and the Kingdom and join the waiting honour guard sent to escort them to the Palace.

Beyond the frontier post, the serrated peaks of the Northern Spine were hidden in a wall of drizzle, but Bluestocking still felt their monolithic presence dwarfing even the white rock.

South of an invisible line, farmers worked in gentle spring sunshine, tending the green domes of mulberry trees that lined the hillsides in artificially straight ranks. Beyond those gently sloping hills, the Southern Spine rose more gradually than its Northern half, but these mountains were even higher, and distant snow-capped peaks reflected the sunlight. Where sunshine and rain jostled for supremacy, the ground steamed in a line creeping northwards.

"Are those tents?" The Prince pointed at a sprawl of canvas around the foot of the southern side of the rock.

"Aye, Majesty," one of their escort replied. "Fairhaven. Pretty deserted at the moment, but much more crowded during winter. Where most of the slaves live. The freeborn workers and their families live in the town opposite. Northside."

"Fairhaven, eh?" The Prince said. "I'm surprised you let them live on the nicer side."

The outrider grinned, showing rotting stumps for teeth. "It's only nice in the daytime, when most of them are out working in the fields. At night, when the King's decreed it's their turn to be rained on, they wail and moan and beg The Gods to stop pissing on them."

"Look," an Imperial Guard gasped, pointing. Bluestocking looked.

Now they were higher up, Bluestocking had a better view of individual clouds, and their movement toward the storm, which crept northwards at walking pace. The wizard's magic would hurtle clouds at dizzying speed from where nature had allowed the breeze to carry them to slam into the main mass. Tiny lightning flashes sparked off the impact. Sometimes the rain fell as white drops; Bluestocking had been caught in a hailstorm soon after entering the Kingdom. It had only lasted thirty seconds, but she still felt the sting of the stones on her arm.

Where the clouds had been before, the air rippled and eddied, seeking equilibrium. For a moment she thought she saw a face and wondered if an elemental had become entangled. Probably not, she decided. They'd have exorcised it.

A vortex of spinning air circled over the rock in a whirl of blue and white; the still-point, drawing energy from the clouds' movement. Around it the sky was a mottled grey, as if it were fevered from all the activity.

She looked from the cloud to the focal point of the strangeness. Even though they still had to look up, from up here it was easier to see the top of the rock and what was actually a small walled city that sprawled across the plateau.

A reed in the wicker floor snapped, her stomach lurched and stifling a scream, she clutched the nearest support- the Prince's arm.

"Be calm," the Prince said. Wincing, he prised her fingers away, leaving livid imprints on his arm. "It's nothing to worry about."

Bluestocking felt her face burn as a trickle of liquid ran down her thighs. She was acutely aware of it and was convinced that everyone around her would smell it.

"Why do you all make that gesture when you look northwards?" the Prince asked the pilot. He referred to the hand-opening gesture she realized and knew he meant to distract her. For a moment, she could have kissed him.

"It's asking the Gods to stay on Mount Halkyan, Majesty," the second attendant said.

"Your gods live there?"

"They do, Majesty." There was a long pause, and the man asked. "Is it true? That your gods live among you all year round?"

The Prince said. "Of course. It seems strange not to have them here. We miss them, but they don't travel well. At least you're spared foreign gods visiting you."

"Amen," the pilot said.

Bluestocking made herself open her eyes again. Taking deep breaths, she stared at the rock, trying not to think about falling. She prayed: *Nangharai, Mother of the Gods, let me walk on solid ground, and I'll light you a candle every night again.* Of course, Nangharai wouldn't listen. Even if Bluestocking's prayer carried all the way back to Ravlatt, why would the goddess heed the prayer of someone who'd turned her back on the gods?

"Blue," the Prince said, so quietly she almost missed it. "Blue, take my hand. No one will know." She looked up at him, then away from the pity in his eyes, but took his hand. "Look outwards," the Prince said as gently as to a skittish colt. "Look across, not down."

Gripping the basket with her free hand, Bluestocking made herself look northwards. The rain had cleared, revealing the nearest peaks of the northern Spine stabbing the bright blue sky.

"You could gallop across this Kingdom in a day on a fresh horse," the Prince said. "So small, yet a fulcrum for the world."

He's right, she thought, glancing westwards toward the distant hills shimmering in the afternoon sun, toward the easternmost of the ragbag caliphates and emirates that made up The Western Alliance. *I wonder if it's true that they're all fanatics and madmen, and the greatest threat our empire has ever faced.*

The Kingdom of Whiterock provided the only lowland crossing of the Spine Range that separated the Empire and the Alliance. Other passes required that the traveller overcome altitude sickness, bitter winds, snow and the risk of snow-trolls sending avalanches down onto the unwary.

Looking back, beyond the waist-high tumuli that they'd ridden past earlier, a faun ducked for cover. "Not a house to be seen," Bluestocking muttered. She watched the peasants bowed double over rows of cabbages stretching into the distance, probably all the way to the marshes at Llamarghesa that were the Kingdom's Northern Frontier and separated it from the mountains. "If they all live in those tent-towns, it must get very crowded."

A sudden gust caught them; the basket wobbled. Bluestocking redoubled her prayers, just in case the priests told lies and the goddess listened even to heretics.

"Milady," the Prince said. "You must loosen your grip, unless I'm to be in the care of a physic for the next few weeks." He added, "And I swear I do not jest."

With a huge effort, she loosened her grip. He grimaced in relief. Despite her terror, she almost laughed. "I'm sorry," she whispered.

He sighed. "No matter."

They cleared the outer wall that ran around the lip of the rock. *Now if this thing collapses,* Bluestocking thought with grim humour, *I'll only have a short fall before dashing my brains out.*

"I dare say you'll be pleased to get there, won't you?" The Prince said softly.

She nodded, tears prickling, suddenly homesick for relief from three weeks of shared rooms in lodges or taverns, and respite from the noise from the next room of the comfort women's grunted, groaning couplings with the soldiers. While her room had often been bigger than her rented chamber back in Ravlatt, there'd been no privacy or peace with the paper-thin walls.

The rope tautened and they were reeled into a huge open square in front of the palace, full of soldiers in gaudy uniforms whose helmets gleamed in the sunlight. The basket was hauled to rest against a gantry like those on the ground, wooden planks ten feet above the cobbled expanse. Hands reached in, and the Prince pushed her forward. "Take the lady first," he said.

Out of the corner of her eye, Bluestocking glimpsed a wizard performing an invocation.

She stood unsteadily and gripped the hand of the man nearest her as if she were drowning and he were a lifeline. He helped her down the steps to the ground, saying, "There, there. No need for tears." His kindness almost undid her, but somehow she stayed on her feet, reaching down to touch the cobbles for reassurance that they were real.

"My name is Ariel," the man said. He was a rotund little figure with a mouth slightly too wide for his features, which gave the impression that he was smiling all the time. His eyes protruded, and his tongue flicked in and out. An ornate cap only partly covered sandy hair. A huge gold chain hung round his neck over his dark robes.

As the others disembarked, Bluestocking looked up at the walls of the citadel. In front of them, a small group watched the new arrivals. The Prince led his group forward.

At the front of the waiting group, a giant of a man towered above the others, robes trailing on the floor. Square-headed with a bull-like neck, red-gold hair tumbled in curls to his shoulders, while his short beard was flecked with grey. Below a simple crown half-covering his forehead, wide-set eyes studied them, passing over her in an instant, dismissing her as unimportant. In that instant, she felt the King's terrible, restless energy and his willpower that changed the very course of wind and rain. The moment passed, and once again he was simply a big man lording it over a tiny backwater.

The King bowed from the waist. "Welcome to Whiterock, Prince Casimiripian."

The Prince seemed taken aback. He paused, as if collecting his thoughts, then laughing bowed too. "A short, simple, yet elegant greeting, your Majesty. I'd prepared a long flowery response full of pomp and wind. Instead, I'll simply say that I'm very pleased to be here."

The King nodded a half-dozen times, then grinned, his teeth whiter and more regular than any Bluestocking had ever seen. "Well said. There'll be enough time for speeches later. We're simple people here, slow of thought and direct of speech." He threw open his arms. Casimiripian hesitated, but stepped forward into the King's bear-hug. Lifting his hands, he patted the King's back.

Beside the King stood a dark-haired woman, only as tall as his shoulder. Her face was pinched, thin and sour-looking. But when the King touched her arm, she looked up at him with a tender look that transformed her face. The King said, "My wife, Queen Juliophelana."

"Majesty," the Prince bowed again.

The Queen curtsied and said in a lilting voice, "Call me Ana, son-in-law to be."

Ana? Bluestocking thought. *They talk as if they're mere commoners*!

"Let others worry whether shortening their names erodes their status," the King added. "Life's too short; we know who we are. We don't have to parade our names to remind us."

"Then call me Cas," the Prince said with a nervy laugh, and Bluestocking wondered how much that concession cost him.

A large, pug-nosed woman stood to the King's right, looking, Bluestocking decided, as if she could smell something nasty. The King introduced the Prince to, "My eldest daughter, Princess Evivalesinan. Evi is High Priestess of the Church of Brighannon."

The Princess boomed, "The main church of Whiterock."

To Evi's right stood a slightly younger woman who shared her father's red-gold hair but whose features were more delicate. "The Princess Lexnovoswartoner," the King said. "Lexi is betrothed to the Emir of Blackwater."

Lexi never took her eyes off Prince Cas except when he kissed her hand, when she closed them. "My fiancé's ambassador, the Vizier of Talaben," she said in a low voice and waved vaguely at her left shoulder, behind which stood a bronze-skinned man. His nose was a hooked beak, and the fierce eyes which scanned them all in turn were set in a face whose triangular shape was emphasised by a white, pointed beard. His left arm, which was slightly withered, hung at an awkward angle.

To Lexi's right stood a girl with Queen Ana's dark complexion but the King's open features. "My youngest, your fiancé," the King said. "Princess Cavendsilperisha. Cavi."

"Majesty," the Prince knelt at her feet.

"Arise, Your Majesty," Cavi said, laughing. "May I also call you Cas?"

"You can call me anything you want, Cavi," the Prince said, standing up.

"You'll be tired from your long journey," the King's voice boomed over the breeze. "But before we retire, we'll stroll around the castle walls and show you our surroundings."

They followed the Royal party up the path from the square, through the main gate into a shaded antechamber. Inside the walls was another courtyard, but rather than cross it, they turned right. Something small and dark scuttled into a doorway, but when they passed there was nothing there, although the door had stayed closed.

A little way along the corridor they climbed up one, two, three and even a fourth flight of corkscrewing stone stairs up to the grey stone battlements. On the way they passed a chanting mage who glanced up without pausing in his ritual. "He's strengthening the fortifications," Cavi explained. "Those who would harm Whiterock constantly try to undermine us."

Looking around at the fields laid out below the gap in the walls in a pastoral scene of apparent tranquillity, Bluestocking wondered whether everyone in Whiterock believed in invisible enemies and whether or not they were paranoid.

They stood on the very walls themselves, with only a thin chest-high lip of stone between them and infinity. Bluestocking's heart hammered both from exertion and sheer terror.

Turning to her, Cas murmured, "Bluestocking, please walk before me."

With a thin smile, Bluestocking obeyed.

The wind up here tore at their hair, plucked at their sleeves. Despite the warm south wind, it was cold; Bluestocking shivered. Cas murmured to one of his men, who wrapped his cape around Bluestocking's shoulders. She mumbled thanks and looked up to see Cavi watching her. She felt the flush rise up her neck.

A shape flashed close by. There was a flare, a shriek and the sound of frying bacon, and she saw the amorphous, semi-transparent shape of an elemental impaled on the palace's invisible defences.

No one seemed concerned. "I thought that we'd start here," Princess Cavi said, smiling. The King seemed happy to let her do the talking now. "This whole edifice," she waved vaguely around her, "is just the latest layer of skin on a scab dating back centuries." She added, "The other reason for taking you on this little tour is that it's a good excuse to indulge another of our guests. Lexi and I believe that Daragel doesn't see his homeland often enough."

"I have her Majesty's beauty as consolation," the vizier replied with a flash of brilliant white teeth in his bronzed face, bowing to Lexi. "And helping to look after both her and my Prince's interests is a great solace."

"The other reason," Cavi ignored Daragel's flattery, "is that this is probably the nearest Cas has been to the alliance. True?"

The Prince nodded.

Daragel said, "You see, Majesty, we are mere mortals, nothing to fear."

Cas smiled acknowledgment.

"There it is," the Princess waved at the distant hills, now partly obscured in low clouds. "The Alliance of Free Rulers. The Western Alliance, as it's known in the Karnaki Empire. It has almost as many names as there are Kingdoms, Emirates and protectorates within it." She added, "Please correct me if I talk nonsense, Daragel."

"I'm sure that won't be necessary, Your Highness."

"Most of the territories beyond are semi-desert," Princess Cavi said. "The people there believe in letting the gods dictate their climate or if you echo their beliefs, in letting Mother Earth choose when to water the soil. If we allowed this to happen to Whiterock, we'd have weather similar to theirs."

"Do you believe that this is a good thing?" Cas asked. There was a sharp intake of breath from someone nearby.

"What I believe is unimportant," the Princess said, smiling, putting a finger to the Prince's lips. He looked dazed.

Cavi resumed. "The palace walls are made from stone quarried from the Southern Spine. Stone from Whiterock, while moderately hard, wouldn't withstand siege engines. We've had peace for centuries, but the palace predates our tranquil times. Let's walk around the battlements."

As they walked, Prince Cas whispered, "Are you all right?"

Bluestocking nodded, gripping the inside wall of the battlements. "I'm ...all right," she waved her free hand to emphasize the word, "as long as I'm away from the outer walls, and I have something to hold onto." She was exaggerating how safe she felt– the wind was like a siren song, plucking her toward the wall– but she didn't want the pity of strangers.

Bluestocking grew increasingly restless at their snail-like pace. Preoccupied with the scrolls, her thoughts turned to The Great Library. Even deep within the Karnaki Empire, scholars knew of the vast trove of books, manuscripts, scrolls and letters that comprised the greatest repository of knowledge in the known world - Whiterock Library. She wanted to be at those books with a gnawing hunger that grew minute by minute.

Toward the southern end, they passed an open square. The Prince asked, "What's there?"

"Gallows Square," Cavi said, and the subject was dropped. Even the small town where Bluestocking had grown up had its Gallows Square.

At last they returned to their starting point.

Cavi said, "Let's go below."

They descended the steps and went indoors. "Are we near The Great Library?" Bluestocking blurted. No one answered. *I'll find it on my own, then,* she thought.

As they passed a side corridor, Ariel had Bluestocking separated from the others and taken down it by a page. "These are your quarters, madam. There wasn't space for you to be with the Prince's party, so we put you in this block."

"Where do I go to pay the tax?" Seeing his puzzled look, Bluestocking added, "I thought that all travellers had to pay a tax?"

Ariel smiled. "You needn't worry about that." He threw open the door for her, and his footsteps receded down the corridor.

Bluestocking pushed the heavy door shut with her foot. "Well, I'm here at last," she said to the empty room.

Her jaw dropped.

Chapter 2

This isn't a bedroom," she muttered, perching upon the huge high four-poster bed, "it's a silk-sheeted warehouse." She thought, *the **bed** is bigger than my chamber in Ravlatt.*

Drapes and throws festooned the room, softening the harshness of its dark polished wood. Sketches of deer, horses and a hippogriff hung on the walls. The bed was soft, and it was with a conscious sense of virtue that she made herself climb off it and study the map drawn in ink next to the room's only window. It told Bluestocking that the country outside was Thamwesh, part of the Western Alliance.

The room was hot, so she removed her jerkin, still soggy from the earlier rain, stared in the full-length mirror at her wind-burnt face and blue eyes and decided that she looked no worse than usual. She ran her fingers through her hair, blonde streaked with premature grey, cut short to level with her ear-lobes in a futile attempt to keep it tidy. She practised a smile, revealing the gap in her top teeth the Prince professed to find so appealing.

She walked into the next room, which was barely three paces wide by four long and as tall again. The floorboards had been polished until they were treacherous to stockinged feet. Two upright wooden chairs with upholstered seats flanked a small table, all stained mahogany to match the colour of the floor.

She shook her head in wonderment. "The gods only know what they've put the Prince into." She grinned. "Unless I've got his rooms, by mistake."

Someone knocked at the door. "Yes?" she called.

The door swung open, and clutching her travel-scuffed sack stood a skinny youth in the same red and gold livery as the Whiterock soldiers. He said, gazing at his feet, "Yer bag, mum." He turned away, still not looking at her.

"Wait!" she called. "Can you show me where the Library is?"

He shook his head, looking anxious. "Don't know where it is, mum. I'm supposed to carry the bags, mum."

"Is it up here, at the top of the palace?" Bluestocking asked patiently as if he were an idiot child.

He shook his head again, looking as though he might burst into tears at any moment. She allowed exasperation to creep into her voice. "Where are you going now?"

"The courtyard." He looked happier at being able to actually answer her.

"Then I'll walk with you."

***

After he waved airily in no particular direction and said, "The library's that way, mum," they parted, and Bluestocking was soon hopelessly lost.

She'd learned that she needed to descend several levels. Each was slightly narrower and gloomier than the one above, but fortunately all ended in a sun-lit open square.

At one point, she passed a group of pilgrims. "This window commemorates the battle between Brighannon and the Dead God, Ralac," their guide intoned in a bored voice.

While she walked, she puzzled over the familiar face down at the air-bag station. His clothes, a long coat with many pockets from which tools and geegaws protruded, marked him as an itinerant peddler. She was sure that she hadn't seen him in Ravlatt, or on the way here. So she must have seen him before she entered the nunnery. *Don't panic,* she thought. *He'll probably only stay one night. It'll be another three weeks yet before you're supposed to leave Ravlatt to return to the nunnery. And **that** journey's another four weeks.* She'd worked it out before accepting the invitation. Seven weeks should be enough for her to either make such an impression on the King that he'd petition the Gods for a pardon or for her to fail miserably and slip away into obscurity.

Without warning, she emerged onto a brawling, densely crowded street with walls several times a tall man's height that made it even more claustrophobic. There was an astonishing variety of races here, fair like Bluestocking, copper-skinned like Daragel, a few with epicanthrically-folded eyes, and even a couple of black-skinned people who had presumably travelled down the Spine from their tribes in the far north, all of whom were testament to the importance of Whiterock's position as a cross-roads on the trade routes.

Most of the crowd, though, were pallid, short and stocky; many stared at her open-mouthed. Bluestocking reeled at the stench of cooking odours and sweat, bad breath, flatulence and stale excreta.

The noise echoing off the walls was constant and almost overwhelming. Hucksters bellowed from each corner from underneath conical hats, "Get yer lucky charms, ladeez and gennelmen! Jilted by yer lover? Cheated by yer neighbours? I've got everything yez need! Whether it's dragon's feet, four-leaf clovers, a unicorn's sweat, or the bones of a saint, you can change your life right now!"

Others sold vegetables, clothes, a puppy, even a set of knives. Despite, or perhaps because of the buffeting, Bluestocking felt at home for the first time in months. *For the first time since the prince took his 'interest' in antiquarian texts*, she thought.

She had backed out of a doorway, her arms full of scrolls– common, ten-a-kopleck texts used to establish whether students had the makings of scholars or were just wasting their father's fortunes– and collided with someone who trod on her foot. Lunging for her now-scattered armful, she swore, ending with, "clumsy cretin."

The man, who she suddenly realised wore an imperial uniform, yanked her head back by her hair.

He stopped at a drawl. "I wouldn't do that, captain. Unless you wish your next posting to be cold, wet, and very uncomfortable."

Her face aflame, she crouched down, picking up the scrolls. As she gathered the last, a pair of ornately stitched boots stood directly in front of her. She stayed down, but the boots didn't move. At last the drawl said, "Can I help you with those?"

She muttered, "No, thank you, My Lord." He obviously was a lord, if he could threaten a captain. Slowly, hoping that he would get bored and leave, she looked up into the smiling face of the Lieutenant-Governor of Ravlatt, Prince Casimiripian.

She groaned inwardly, but managed to stammer an apology to the glaring captain.

"Don't worry," the prince said, smiling. "But it usually helps if your eyes face vaguely in the direction you're going. What's your name?"

"Bluestocking, Majesty," she said. So the lie that she lived became treason.

Now someone jostled her, snapping her back to the present. "Watch it, Dollymop!"

Another man, brown- robed with a thin face asked, "Do you need sanctuary, young lady?" Beneath a few strands of hair, dandruff sprinkled his shoulders. "Throw yourself on the mercy of Raesh, and you'll be spared when the unbelievers are swept away!"

She backed away from the fanaticism in his eyes and trod on a foot.

"Milady?" The woman's pockmarked face was lined with three vertical scars on each cheek and was blacker even than those Bluestocking had seen on the levels above, darker than the face of anyone she'd ever met in the Empire. Her front teeth were missing, but for all her ferocious appearance, she seemed friendly. "Are you lost?"

Bluestocking nodded. "I'm looking for the Library."

"Follow me," the woman said. "It's not a good time to be down here." She added, turning, ponderous as a wind-galleon on the steppes, showing her heavy pregnancy, "We'll drop my shopping off first. My rooms are close by. Though they'll not be as grand as you're used to, you'll be safe enough."

"I'm sure they'll be fine," Bluestocking said, smiling thinly. "I'm very grateful."

"I'm Mari," the woman said. "I'll put my arm around you now, to make sure we aren't separated."

"I'll carry a basket. I insist," Bluestocking said over Mari's protests. "Or you'll need three arms. When's it due?" She nodded to the woman's bulging belly.

"In about two months, mayhap less," Mari said.

"They say if it shows at the front, it'll be a boy. Is that your belief, as well?"

Mari nodded. "The seers say it's a boy."

Together, they shoved through the crowds. Bluestocking even found time to look at the small kiosks jammed full of produce on either side of the street. In one hung onions and other vegetables. In another, flies buzzed around great cuts of meat. Bluestocking wondered absently, *What huge beast yielded them?* She'd seen few animals in the fields.

"Watch that some pickpocket doesn't lift your purse," Mari said.

"They'll be disappointed," Bluestocking laughed. "It may sound foolish, but I never brought it with me." She'd grown used in the Prince's company to not needing to bother with trivialities like cash. Everything was provided, as if by magic. *I must learn to stop thinking that way,* she thought. *That way lies dependence on him. And now, here I am without a single kopleck on me. Helpless as a new-born!*

"Must be nice to not have to worry about money." Mari radiated unspoken disapproval.

"I have no local scrip. Is Karnaki currency acceptable here?"

Mari laughed a short sharp bark. "They'll take any money here, my dear."

They needed ten minutes and another flight of steps to reach Mari's rooms. Bluestocking grew increasingly anxious at the stares and glares of the locals. A man spat at their feet in passing, drawing curses in return from Mari. On what turned out to be the last street, she noticed that people shied away from the walls, but there were too many to see why. Until the crowd parted for a moment and Bluestocking saw a long, thin snout, a verdigris-stained copper collar that scraped against a stone neck as it moved and mean little eyes. "Stranger," the creature hissed, sounding as if its teeth were loose in its mouth. "Beware." As Mari tugged her along, Bluestocking wondered whether it was warning the locals against her, or vice versa.

Releasing Bluestocking, Mari reached into the folds of her long skirt, producing a bunch of keys to unlock the door. She grimaced. "This will be nothing to write home about by your standards."

"It's very nice," Bluestocking said, adding, "honestly."

While Mari unpacked fruit and vegetables and a brick-like loaf of bread, Bluestocking said, "What did you mean when you said it wasn't a good time to be down here?"

Mari let the silence hang for a few moments. "Last night's was the third death in a month." She laughed mirthlessly. "The old goat that fell over the body nearly died of fright." She chopped the laugh short and added, "Don't misunderstand me. People down here are no angels; but whenever the local lads get out of hand, someone will give them a little tap to the back of the head and knock some sense into them."

Bluestocking nodded. "Everyone knows everyone else, so there's little crime, is that right?"

"Exactly! Unless somebody wanders off their own patch into another, like you have. And word soon gets out who's done the deed. But since someone found the second victim a week ago– a young boy with his throat cut, dumped into one of the middens– everyone's become a little twitchy. Some say that it's because of the royal visit. Others have their own ideas. But whatever the reason, people are scared. Scared people do silly things, especially to strangers." Mari searched Bluestocking's face. "May I speak honestly?"

Bluestocking nodded.

"If you return unharmed, that'll be all the thanks I need." Mari said. "I want to get you back without a knife in your back and without seeing some lad's foolishness leading to the royal guards driving my neighbours from their houses at dead of night." She added with a smile that was probably meant to be reassuring, "Now sit yourself there. I'll be back in fifty heartbeats."

A few minutes later Mari returned with a bedraggled crone with tattoo-covered arms. The women ushered her out, Mari again putting her arm around Bluestocking. They led her up the levels, the old crone muttering constantly. Mari said, "It's a spell to disguise you. To a casual glance, it looks as if we're moving a basket of washing."

Their journey was uneventful until they reached the library. "Damn!" Bluestocking rattled the handle of the locked door and knocked.

"You there, woman!" A male voice rang out. "What brings you up here?"

Bluestocking wheeled around, and realised that the guard was talking to the crone. He hadn't noticed Bluestocking. She interrupted. "They were showing me where the library was. I'm sorry if I brought them somewhere I shouldn't have. It's my fault."

"Who are you?" The man's tone was guarded.

"Bluestocking. I arrived today with Prince Casimiripian of the Karnaki Empire. You know who he is?" Without waiting for an answer, she plunged on. "Your Prime Minister invited me here to translate the scrolls of Presimionari. I got lost on the way, and these kind ladies took pity, and showed me to the Library. Unfortunately, it seems to be closed."

"It closes at four hours after the noon," the guard said, mollified.

"I didn't know," Bluestocking said mock-sweetly. "And you are?"

"Overly cautious, Milady," the guard said. "I didn't see you there, and if I had, of course I would have understood." He flicked a couple of small coins at Mari and the crone. "Thank you."

The crone pocketed her coin, but Mari looked as if she wanted to throw hers back at him, though she took it.

Bluestocking touched her arm. "Thank you. I mean it sincerely."

Mari nodded, smiled thinly, and went.

"Is there not free passage in Whiterock?" Bluestocking said. "No one warned me there were restrictions on people's movements."

"Commoners and slaves are allowed up above this point," the guard said. "This is a free city. But they must have a reason, and the higher the level, the better the reason."

"Well, Sir Overly Cautious," Bluestocking said. "You'd better tell me how to return to my rooms."

***

Bluestocking opened her door. "Who are you?" she asked.

The girl removing Bluestocking's clothes from her travel-bag looked up.

Bluestocking almost stopped breathing. The girl was beautiful, black-haired and thin-limbed. "Well?"

The girl's voice was low, husky. "My name is Kyr," she said, in a thick local dialect.

"Ke-er?" Bluestocking repeated.

"No, Milady. Kyr. One syllable: As befits a slave." Her lips were painted a dark pink matching the ribbons in her hair. She wore a white smock beneath a plain black jerkin, with a thick leather collar and metal clip around her neck. She knelt at Bluestocking's feet, her own poking out from beneath the smock. They were filthy, with a mole showing through a rare clean patch of skin. "How would you like me to serve you?" Her eyes were the darkest blue that Bluestocking had ever seen, almost black.

"Is there a bath here?" In the little towns and villages where Bluestocking had grown up, baths were considered weakening, but the sisters had inculcated her to believe cleanliness to be synonymous with godliness, and on arrival in Ravlatt, she had discovered the luxury of bathing.

"Of course, Milady. We're quite civilized." Kyr looked up, then ducked her head again, but not before Bluestocking glimpsed a look that jolted her to the core. There was mischief in Kyr's eyes, wantonness, and a knowing look that verged on mockery.

"Then I'll have a bath." Bluestocking drew away.

Kyr padded into the next room. From it issued a mighty groan, followed by two loud bangs and a slow, rhythmic clanking. She returned. "It will take a few minutes, Milady." She resumed unpacking Kyr's bags.

When Kyr finished, she picked up the sword and looked for somewhere to put it. "You're a warrior, mistress?"

"No." Bluestocking laughed. "The Prince suggested I learn to use one. I think he believed it might be dangerous here, so he had his servant teach me the basics. We finished the lessons last night."

Kyr put it in a drawer. "Your bath should be ready now." She led Bluestocking into a small chamber with floorboards partly covered with rugs and panelled with dark-stained wood.

A marble bath that looked big enough for a whole family stood on four great copper feet shaped like bird's talons. Tendrils of steam rose from it. Kyr felt the water, and ran the other tap. "It'll scald you, else."

She added, "I'm to disrobe you. Unless in the Empire you bathe fully clothed?"

Bluestocking raised an eyebrow, but Kyr seemed serious. *I'd rather remove my own clothes,* she thought, but shrugged. "Do I just stand here?"

"Yes, mistress." Kyr unbuttoned the front of Bluestocking's tunic. Bluestocking was acutely conscious of Kyr's fingers, and as if drawn by gravity, looked slightly down again, into her eyes. Kyr looked up, seemingly innocent, and Bluestocking felt her stomach flip over. "May I slide this off?" Kyr reached around Bluestocking so that the slave's breasts pressed against her. Kyr's hair smelt faintly of cinnamon. Her body though, reeked of sweat and sex. Close up, one jaw-line was dotted with spots. Bluestocking swallowed, allowed her blouse to slide off. Kyr stepped away, and Bluestocking remembered to breathe.

Bluestocking dipped her toes into the water, then climbed in. She was unsettlingly aware of Kyr humming.

As the slave watched her bathe, Kyr said, "Shall I scrub your back for you with a soapstone?"

"That sounds…interesting," Bluestocking said doubtfully.

Kyr picked up the rectangular stone from the windowsill and rubbed Bluestocking's back, gently at first, then more vigorously, her right hand pressed flat against Bluestocking's back, her palm holding the soapstone, while her fingers on either side of the stone brushed against Bluestocking's skin. She gripped Bluestocking's shoulder with her free hand for purchase; Bluestocking felt Kyr's warm breath on her neck and experienced an uneasy mix of excitement and queasiness.

"Lean back," Kyr murmured, and pushing Bluestocking's shoulder, changed the hand holding the soapstone. She worked it down Bluestocking's forearm and back to her clavicle, in slow, small circular movements. "Is that nice?" she said. Bluestocking looked up to see her smiling down. Kyr worked it down from Bluestocking's clavicle to her breast, and her fingers brushed a nipple.

Struggling to breathe, Bluestocking pressed her buttocks against the base of the bath; parting her legs slightly, she bit her lower lip. Kyr stroked a nipple and her lips brushed the other woman's jaw. Her teeth nipped Bluestocking's earlobe and she whispered, "Is there anything else I can do for you, Milady? I'm your slave. I'll gladly do whatever you want." In the silence Bluestocking felt her pulse throbbing in her ears. Kyr whispered, "Anything." Bluestocking turned her head so that Kyr's lips touched hers. Kyr's tongue flicked and touched Bluestocking's top teeth.

In the distance something banged. One man laughed and another swore.

Bluestocking pushed Kyr away. "Get away from me!"

"I'm sorry," Kyr stammered, looking pitiful. "I thought you wanted me."

"Just get out of here," Bluestocking hissed.

Kyr fled, slamming the door.

Bluestocking thought she heard weeping, or laughter. She preferred to think that it was the latter. It gave her strength. Then her rage left like the tide, and she lay back in the bath, disgusted with herself, until the water grew cold, and her skin wrinkled like an old grape.

***

Bluestocking was dressing when someone knocked at the door, interrupting her daydream. "Yes?" she said in a small voice.

"It's Halarbur."

She groaned silently. "What do you want?"

After a long pause Halarbur replied too-evenly, "The Prince has sent me to fetch you. He wishes to escort you tonight. You hadn't forgotten that there's a welcoming banquet?"

"Of course not," she lied. There **had** been talk of it, but she'd assumed she wasn't invited. "Prince Casimiripian knows that ladies are always late," she said, resorting to a girlish flirtation she normally despised. "But I must look my best; which will of course take a long time. Perhaps he'll let me know when I should be ready?" *It's now, of course, you stupid girl,* she thought, but the ruse might buy her a few minutes.

"I'll speak to His Majesty." The acid in Halarbur's voice should have burnt through the door.

In a feverish whirl, she tried every piece of clothing she possessed, before finally settling on the second item she'd rejected, a plain black dress that showed off her figure, without looking gaudy, cheap or fussy. *Why can't I stay in the background?* she thought. *I don't want to meet nobility.*

She possessed no jewellery, necklaces, or bracelets; only an amulet in the form of Styris, a monkey god so ineffectual even the nuns who'd raised her hadn't objected to her buying it from an itinerant relic-monger. "But it is the Day of the Monkey," she said, after she'd checked the days off on her fingers, kissing its head, "so at least it's appropriate."

A few minutes later, she called, "Coming," to another knock.

She opened the door and stepped into the corridor. "Majesty," she stammered. "I'm sorry to keep you waiting."

"Don't be," the Prince said. "I needed a little tour of the Palace. Exercise aids appetite and digestion, so the wise men tell me." He looked her over with the sardonic gleam in his eye that she knew well. "You look wonderful."

A local pageboy led them and the Prince's guards through twisting corridors. Sometimes Bluestocking saw what might have been elves or imps lurking, and once a big, fat, golden spider scuttled up the wall.

They entered a great vaulted room to stand uneasily upon a dais overlooking a banqueting hall. Portraits of horse-faced women and smug-looking men lined the walls. Drapes in the corners formed red and gold waterfalls. The Master of Ceremonies boomed, "His Highness, Prince Casimiripian of the Karnaki Empire."

Looking both annoyed and sheepish, the Prince descended some steps in front of the dais. Bluestocking followed the bodyguards to where a group waited for them. The Whiterock royal family stood at the front, ringed by pompous-looking men in ermine and gold, plump women who held their men's arms while covertly studying their rivals, servants waiting for the signal to move into position and hard-eyed soldiers watching them all.

One of the others was a familiar figure. The King said to Prince Cas, "You've met my Prime Minister, Arial, son of Kylar of Demonda," and added, "His wife, Jasmina."

Jasmina towered over her husband. She was strikingly good-looking, but pancaked make-up couldn't quite hide her wrinkles. Her blonde hair was piled high, while the rings that bedecked the fingers the Prince kissed were even grander than her earrings. Cold grey eyes raked Bluestocking, who looked down. *No need to ask what attracted you to little froggy,* she thought. *Money and power.*

Someone of indeterminate gender stood nearby, stout, red-faced, with heavy jowls and pudding-basin haircut, wearing a migraine-inducing red, yellow and orange shapeless smock. "I present," the King said, "Myleetra of Ahern, Grandmother-Superior Elect of the covens of Whiterock." Bluestocking thought she heard a snort from Princess Evi's direction.

"Enchanted." Bowing, Cas kissed her hand.

"Your Majesty honours us with your presence," Myleetra said in an adenoidal voice, fondling hair which was the fine yellow of cornfields.

"I wanted to meet as many people as possible," Prince Cas said. "To get to know my fiancée's subjects." He added, "I present Mistress Bluestocking, one of the finest translators in the Empire." Bluestocking curtsied, face burning.

"You're the translator," the King said, impaling her with his gaze. "Come to spread the glory of our history to the wider world."

"Majesty," Bluestocking stammered, but he had already turned away.

"Ah, you're the scholar," Evi boomed from beside her. Bluestocking smiled, trying to look at ease.

"Is it true," Evi asked, "that you worship different Gods in this Empire of yours?" She leaned her face into Bluestocking's.

"We have different names for the Gods, but many of them look the same when you see the hieroglyphs on scrolls, Majesty."

"Highness," Evi corrected her absently. "Father is Majesty. The rest of us are just Highnesses. And you have a different calendar?"

Bluestocking made a non-committal gesture. "The days are named differently in some cases. You have no sea-creatures such as lobsters in your calendar, but you have others, such as the lion. The day-keepers simply wear a different garb on certain days. We have seven days in a phase and twenty-eight days to a moon, the same as you."

"But you have a First Day, not a Last Day, so there must be some imbalance."

"A little, but such things even out, Highness. And every fourth year, we have an extra day, the same as you."

"But on the last day of the year, not on the first, when we have our Free Day." Evi gnawed at her lower lip. "I must consult with the priests and the augurs. To a layman, these differences may seem slight, but to the educated–"

"They may be significant." Bluestocking had read of wars started over how many priests should perform a service, never mind the days of the year. She opened her mouth to speak, but Evi had gone again.

The King motioned them toward their seats. Bluestocking sat at one end of a long table beside Myleetra, opposite Arial and Jasmina. At the other end Cas sat with the royal family. Others watched from adjoining tables, hungry for power and influence. The waiters ferried platters to each table, weaving around each other, narrowly avoiding collisions.

Jasmina ignored her, which suited Bluestocking.

Arial said, "Should we call you Bluestocking, or just 'Blue'?"

Bluestocking swallowed. *Does he know something?* She said cautiously, "The King seems to prefer informality. I've no wish to give offence."

"King Redoutifalia is a visionary, but not everyone agrees with his views. Milady," Arial leaned forward intently, "Honesty offends no one, surely? Your reticence tells me you're a traditionalist."

And you called the King by his full name. She nodded.

"Then Bluestocking you shall be." Bluestocking sensed that she'd won his approval and was abashed to be so pleased.

"We revere Redoutifalia," Arial said gravely, "but even we, his staunchest supporters, fear he risks the wrath of the Gods for this heresy. Few religions in the Karnaki Empire, the Western Alliances, the other free cities, or here, agree on anything– save that a name defines its bearer's status and can only be changed by their regent, or divinity. How else are we to know someone's true place in society?"

"Unless they lie," Myleetra said. At his in-drawn breath, she added, "I don't condone malpractice, Arial, but it happens. You surely admit that? When such deception is exposed, it's never through divine hands, but always through mortal means."

Arial nodded, looking pensive. "Unless you believe that mortal means may be divine agency concealed."

"Perhaps," Myleetra conceded after a long, thoughtful silence. "But you must admit that while the King may be eccentric, he's hardly a heretic. We know who he is. He's not adding extra syllables to gain advantage, but dropping them. How can a man profit from claiming to be less than he is?" Arial nodded pensively, and Myleetra continued, "The Gods condemn those who deceive for profit, material or otherwise. All he's doing is extending the practice we all give to families and friends to call us by pet names, as surely you and Jasmina do at home?" She smiled, to soften the point.

Arial's face creased into a reluctant smile, heightening his similarity to a frog. "You're right."

In the silence, a woman further down the table said, "Arial, I believe we're summoned to a Retribution tomorrow." A little frisson of excitement ran round the table.

"Apparently so," Arial said. "He's a freeman trying to pass himself off as a better. As he's a freeman, not a slave, we've no choice; until the square is full, all freeborn must attend."

The woman said. "What fool thought he could get away with it?"

"Are you alright, my dear?" Myleetra asked Bluestocking. "You've spilt some of your wine."

***

For the next two courses, a juggler, a jongleur and a deliberately inept comedy-magician entertained them. Arial alternated between telling Bluestocking about Whiterock, which required only monosyllables from her, and asking about her background. That was the last thing she wanted, and her answers revealed little more than her polite noises to his statements. She kept thinking of the freeman who had tried to pass himself off as his better and the Retribution that awaited him, his family and any accomplices.

She sipped her thick red wine too quickly. "A local vintage," Arial said. "Grown on south-facing walls, wherever we have space. If you prefer a white," Bluestocking shook her head, "we have a much lighter grape from between the mulberry plantations and our border."

Only when Arial asked what she missed most from home, did Bluestocking start to relax. Once she drained another glass, she couldn't really understand why she'd been so nervous before.

"There's a large lake at home," she said, "almost an inland sea, sacred to many local cults. We used to visit on holy days. I learned to swim there. The nuns threw me in."

"We have a Lido here," Myleetra said. In answer to Bluestocking's puzzled look, she said, "It's a pool, surrounded by a stone deck for the bathers to dry on."

"And you use it?" Arial looked surprised.

"Yes! You should try it!"

"I don't really have time." Arial looked sheepish.

Jasmina blurted: "You can't swim anyway, so I don't know why you're even talking about it."

Arial's face took on a closed look, as if he'd drawn shutters down over his eyes. Not before Bluestocking had glimpsed sadness, disappointment and hurt.The conversation around them stopped dead, the others assuming a studiedly disinterested look. *What kind of love is it that needs to humiliate the one we love?* Bluestocking wondered.

She ducked her head and concentrated on chewing the stringy meat and mopping the grease off the wood with some unleavened bread that was as tough as the wood, and about as tasty. The other courses had been put in front of her and whirled away so quickly that she'd barely had time to do more than nibble at them. Already her head swam. Every time she took a sip, someone seemed to be at her shoulder, refilling her glass.

Someone said at conversation-stopping volume to Myleetra, "So what's the difference between your quackery and Princess Stuffy-britches?" *It must have been someone else,* she thought as Arial choked on his bread, *even you wouldn't be so rude.*

"My **quackery**," Myleetra said, "comes from within, whereas each church relies on its own god." She pushed up her sleeve, revealing an arm like a thick ham, tattooed with intricate designs. She pointed to a tattoo; "Strength." To another; "Endurance. Foresight. Invisibility. But **we** work our magic, not gods."

"You mean you're all atheists?" Bluestocking shrieked.

"If anything, we're all pantheists," Myleetra said. "Even omnitheists–acknowledging all gods, but unwilling to bend the knee to any particular one, so unable to call on them. Our magic is self-derived, so not prone to their whims." She added, "It's weaker than church-magic, but we believe our freedom's worth it."

"Do you have tattoos on your hands? Is that why you wear those gloves?"

Myleetra nodded. "But these are just the externals of who and what we are. There's as much within as without."

Bluestocking saw the uncomfortable looks on the other's faces. *Polite Whiterock society clearly doesn't talk about such things,* she thought. Common sense told her to change the subject, but drink-fuelled mischief made her ask, "Can anyone work magic?" She took another, deeper draught from her goblet, and a server appeared djinn-like to refill it. She giggled quietly at the djinn-imagery.

Myleetra shrugged. "Almost anyone. You need ability, as any skilled craftsmen does, and training, stamina and persistence. Most noviciates fall by the wayside within days of joining. They think they'll be able to work miracles straightaway, but get a rude awakening. We don't let them anywhere near magic until they've learnt humility and patience." She barked at Jasmina, "You wanted to say something?"

Jasmina shook her head.

"My wife and I," Arial said smoothly, "have chosen a different path, but we believe each must follow their own. Don't we, dear?" A spasm crossed Jasmina's face, and Bluestocking wondered if he'd kicked her under the table.

Suddenly, the door that they'd come through opened, and sounds of commotion drifted in from the corridor. A soldier reported to the King, who beckoned Arial over. Arial said to them all, "Excuse me everyone, a small inconvenience requires my presence." He crossed to the King's table, then soon after followed the soldier out.

Bluestocking drained her goblet and banged it down. "Sho," she said and stopped. "So," she said, slowly and carefully, "no one's gonna talk 'bout was happenin?" When no one spoke, she shrugged and yawned so wide her jawbone cracked. She stared muzzily at Jasmina who stared haughtily back at her and raised an eyebrow. "Wha'?" Bluestocking asked, "you looking a'?" Her head felt heavy and her stomach over-full.

"I'm looking at someone who can't hold their drink," Jasmina said primly.

"Least I didn't sell myself f'r a dowry." Bluestocking wished she could stop the room from spinning.

"No?" Jasmina sneered. "At least I **got** a dowry. You're here...why?" The last word stank of contempt. "Oh, yes, to translate some scrolls no one's ever heard of. And doubtless as the royal belly-warmer."

"You–!" Bluestocking made to lunge, but couldn't move. Every muscle, every sinew, screamed with the effort, but her arms, legs and torso were paralyzed. She heard a whispering to her right; Myleetra, forehead beaded with sweat, tapping one of her tattoos.

Someone further down the table said mildly, "I've heard of the Scrolls of Presimionari,"

Myleetra stopped chanting. "Come along," she took Bluestocking's arm. "I think you've had enough to drink, don't you?"

The paralysis had faded, leaving Bluestocking weak and drained. "I'm all right!" She tried to wrench her arm free. "Ow! Leggo! You're hurting me!"

"This is nothing," Myleetra hissed, "compared to what Prince Cas will do to you, if you shame him."

Bluestocking shook her head violently, swinging it from side to side. "Mustn't upset li'l Prince," she mumbled.

Myleetra staggered as she half-marched, half-carried Bluestocking to the door, wiping beads of sweat from a face suddenly bone-white.

"You'll right?" Bluestocking felt distinctly unwell and swallowed several times.

"Just fatigued from working that spell so hurriedly," Myleetra said. "One is supposed to prepare oneself for such an effort." She beckoned a servant. "The lady is tired from her long journey," she said. "Help her to her room."

The servant nodded and with a colleague helped Bluestocking out of the doorway.

The servants turned her the other way, but not before Bluestocking saw, further down the passageway, Arial and the soldier. They stood by a large box, its edges strewn with dirty laundry. A pair of women's legs poked from it, brown stockings rumpled and torn, one foot shoeless. There was something odd about the shape of the legs; though she couldn't quite work it out at first, it seemed to her as if they'd been almost...deflated.

She wanted to ask whom the woman was whose death was reduced to a few moments of inconvenience, but the servants marched her off.

The return to her room was a fragmented blur.

Chapter 3

Bluestocking awoke to the sound of the distant trumpeting of an unruly troll. Her head throbbed. Gingerly, she opened one eye, winced at the dagger of light that speared it from a gap in the heavy curtains and closed it again.

She tried to go back to sleep but couldn't keep the flood of images from surfacing: the other diner's shocked faces; turning into a wildcat when the servants had tried to undress her; abusing Jasmina and Myleetra; a glimpsed memory of Kyr standing in the doorway, mouth agape, then their bodies entwined on the bed. But that couldn't be real–she lay on her bed, fully clothed. That denied the reality of the disturbing dream with the androgynous figure.

She was startled by a tap on the door. Kyr entered, accompanied by a slave carrying a tray, crossed to the curtains and drew them. "Good morning!"

"Go. Away." Bluestocking snarled.

Kyr said, "Did we overindulge?" She took from the tray a tall glass of a frothy red liquid, and reciting a simple spell, placed it on the table beside Bluestocking. "Drink this. You'll soon feel better." She rummaged in the drawers, pulling out clean clothes.

"Did?" Bluestocking croaked. She tried again; "Were you here last night?" She sat up, tried the drink, which tasted mint-like, grimaced and drained the glass.

Kyr shook her head. "I was tucked up in bed, milady."

"So you didn't see me come in?" *Perhaps the memory was a false one after all, put there by some trickster imp,* she thought, and breathed a silent sigh of relief. *Thank you, Nangharai.* The irony of thanking a god she had effectively denied wasn't lost on her.

Kyr padded into the bathroom, and Bluestocking heard the sound of the taps gushing. She lay back, and closed her eyes, until Kyr started undoing her buttons. Suddenly it was difficult to find air to breathe in.

"Forgive the impertinence, milady," the slave said, "but you stink."

"Yes, mother." The tension easing slightly, Bluestocking followed the slave into the bathroom. Fortunately, the water wasn't as hot as the night before. She lay back, feeling slightly better since drinking Kyr's concoction and dozed while Kyr laid out her clothes.

She had a sudden fantasy of Kyr pressing her breasts into her face. She awoke, panting, to the sound of voices. As she climbed from the bath and grabbed a towel, Kyr returned. "That was Halarbur," she announced. "He said that His Majesty awaits your presence." She added, "I told him to come back later."

"Good," said Bluestocking dressing hurriedly, looking away from the slave. She was gratified to see Kyr's eyes widen, when she added, "I can be elsewhere when he returns."

***

The Great Library was high-roofed, with a huge window in the outer wall commanding glorious views of the Southern Spine. The broad lecterns– almost as wide as a man could open his arms– faced the window, as if to inspire the scholars when they looked up. This morning it was empty.

The Silk Palace

Books lined almost all of the internal walls from floor to ceiling, except for the door through which Bluestocking had entered and a small alcove in the corner opposite. The shelves ringed a room ten arm-spans by twelve, dotted with a half-dozen armchairs for casual readers.

The room was large, but Bluestocking was still disappointed; she'd expected a cathedral of books, but this room was small compared to the libraries in Ravlatt.

A man rose from the corner. He sported a spade-shaped beard and clean-shaven cheeks, and his eyes had filmed over with cataracts. His voice was a rumbling bass. "You must be Mistress Bluestocking. Welcome!"

"The pleasure is mine," she said. "You have the advantage on me," she added, smiling, "You know my name."

"I am Copel, Chief Librarian." His chuckle was like a small earthquake. "Chief of one." He led them to the chairs with the sureness of a man whose sight is completely normal. *Or,* Bluestocking thought, *with the sureness of a man who knows the exact location of every speck of dust, every chair, every book in this room,* "Be seated." A small table stood beside his chair. He said, "Will you take tschai with me?"

Bluestocking didn't really want to, but decided that if she refused, she might offend him. "Thank you."

A large metal urn and a charcoal brazier ringed by a firebreak made of stones sat in front of the alcove. Copel crossed to it and after a few minutes returned with a tray. Bluestocking moved to help him, but Copel said, "Thank you, I can manage." He poured dark amber liquid into two tiny cups and said, "Would you like honey or lemon, or will you take it as it comes?"

"As it comes."

Copel nodded approvingly. "Spoken like a true Rockman; you have taste. Too many nowadays pollute a beautiful drink."

The tschai was bitter and aromatic, with an astringent aftertaste. When she finished the drink, Copel took the cup from her. *How do you do that*? She wondered. She ran her tongue around teeth that suddenly felt covered with fur.

After some desultory small talk, he walked her to one of the lecterns. "I heard last night that you'd arrived." He shook his head sadly. "If only I'd known, I'd have waited for you. As it is, I came in early and removed the scrolls from their place of safe-keeping. I thought you would want to at least glance at them today."

Bluestocking joined Copel at the lectern. A knee-high wooden box as long as Bluestocking was tall sat on the lectern, filling its entire surface– it was also half as wide as it was long. The dark wood was engraved with runes that reeked of old, powerful magic. Her fingers tingled with the throb of its power, and the hairs on the nape of her neck lifted. A rusted hasp sealed the box.

"Are these runes ceremonial?" Bluestocking said.

"I'm not sure whether they're to keep the scrolls in or to keep prospective thieves out," Copel said. "You should never underestimate the power of magic, or of words. When you link the two, you magnify the power infinitely."

Bluestocking's headache had eased on the way down. Now it returned, but where before it had been a stabbing pain pressing vice-like on the temples, now a great weight squeezed the top of her head. For a moment she thought she saw a shadow cross the window, but then it passed. *Probably just a cloud,* she thought.

Copel uttered an invocation, more like a series of barks than human speech. The hasp sprang open. He unfastened the box.

Bluestocking looked down at the scrolls of Presimionari. There were five of them, yellowed with age, brittle, each bound with a ribbon, and tied by a chain to the box. An invisible choir seemed to be to singing in impossibly high-pitched voices, hurting Bluestocking's ears. Her headache worsened abruptly until she felt sick. As she reached down to touch the first of the scrolls, Copel recited another spell; the chain holding the scroll to the box loosened, and her headache eased slightly.

As she reached for the scroll, Bluestocking felt as if she were pushing against something. But then the resistance vanished. The scroll was of parchment, and its vast age seemed to be included in its weight. It was so heavy that it was an effort to lift it. She undid the ribbon and opened the scroll.

"The characters look similar to Old Karnaki," she said. "But then someone would have translated them by now."

"Indeed," the librarian said dryly.

The characters swam and blurred before Bluestocking's eyes. An occasional word looked slightly familiar. *It's as if they're alive,* she thought, *and don't want to be caught in any net of understanding.*

She heard voices outside, and as the door flew open her heart plummeted in despair. "Oh, no," she whispered. *Did you think you'd get away?*

Prince Cas looked flushed, and his jaw was clenched, but when he spoke– although it was clearly a great effort– his voice was calm. "I thought I'd find you here. Getting a quick look at your scrolls before we attend the Retribution, eh?"

"I thought there'd be no room in that that small space for me, Majesty."

"Then we'll stand outside the Royal Square, and listen."

We can't miss all those screams, whimpers, and pleadings for mercy, can we? she thought. "Majesty," Bluestocking stammered.

Prince Cas held up his hand. "The King has decreed that all freeborn will attend the Retribution. Is that not so, Master Librarian?"

"Indeed, Majesty." Copel bowed as Bluestocking followed the Prince out. "I was about to leave, myself."

***

The crowd were gathered in whispering, excited ranks on the way to Gallows Square, jostling for a view.

There was a tense silence between Bluestocking and the Prince as they added to the swell of commoners. Bluestocking knew that if she said just one wrong word, Prince Cas might lose whatever fragile grip he held on his temper. She thought, *you don't disobey royalty, you fool, no matter how amiable he seems; that's a quick way to have your head removed from your shoulders. No matter how desperate you are to avoid this circus.*

As they neared Gallows Square, the crowd started to murmur, their excitement growing by the minute.

The sky overhead was streaked with sickly yellow, while to the north lightning licked the Spine, and thunder rumbled in a single, low, continuous rolling boom. A variety of winged creatures– afreets, elementals and several broken-and-reassembled-badly-looking things danced on the air between Whiterock and the Spine. They seemed to be drawn to large gatherings, like malevolent children reduced to peering through the fence at a party. *The blood will drive them into a frenzy,* she thought.

The air had a just cleaned feel to it, tainted only by the smell of frying onions and roasting meat. Outside the Square, several stalls sold bits of meat of indeterminate origin, in all shapes and sizes, while another boasted a roasted pig on a spit. Bluestocking swallowed, her mouth watering, despite, or maybe because of, her hangover. Her stomach grumbled.

The stallholder grinned, showing several gold teeth. "Want some, mistress? Put hairs on your chest, this will."

"I'm not sure that's a good–" Bluestocking realised then that the man was joking. "I have no money," she said sheepishly.

"You're that foreigner, eh? Royalty never has money." He beckoned her nearer. "Well, my little cherub," he sliced off a slab of pork, and slammed it onto a piece of unleavened bread. "Don't you go telling no one, but here's some Whiterock hospitality. On me, Majesty."

Bluestocking was about to protest that she wasn't royalty but saw his grin again, and he winked and, waving away her thanks, turned to the next customer. She caught the eye of the waiting Prince. Despite his stern face, he raised an eyebrow and a corner of his mouth twitched in an almost-smile. She wondered if he'd overheard the conversation, but he strode on, his guards a battering-ram through the crowd.

She folded the bread in half, and bit into it. The juice dribbled down her chin, and something in the bread grated against her teeth. She sighed happily and allowed herself to be carried along with the tide of people.

Only one of the four entrances to the Square remained open. They were so late they had to stand at the back of the crowd, near the entrance.

Bluestocking became conscious of being watched. As the unsettling feeling grew, she looked around and saw, tucked away to one side just behind them, a wooden stand set against one of the walls. From it, the King and his family watched the proceedings. Lexi looked away quickly.

A little later Bluestocking caught Daragel smiling at her and felt a chill. It was the smile of a cat that has a mouse in its paws. He spoke to Princess Cavi, who glanced across at them and frowned.

Several militiamen bumped through the crowd to the Imperial retinue. "Come," Cas said, without stopping to see if she obeyed, and with a despairing sigh, she followed in the retinue's wake. *You will witness this,* she thought, *no matter how much you wish not to.*

They clambered up onto the stand. Cavi was lecturing Daragel about some historical event, but she broke off to greet the Prince with a smile and a clasp of hands, before darting an irritated look at Bluestocking. "I see you brought your pet."

"Royal command," Cas said cheerfully. "She'd never have got in otherwise."

"True," Cavi conceded.

Face burning, Bluestocking looked ahead at the stage. It was at the lower end on the far side, chest-high and almost the width of the whole square, so that from this far back, she could see it clearly.

The stage was dominated by a chopping block made from the base of an entire tree-trunk, a yard high and twice as wide, stained and pitted with old bloodstains. Behind the block and mostly obscured by it were a number of devices that Bluestocking guessed would be dragged out later.

At one end of the square in front of the stage stood the gallows tree, its topmost branches overtopping the walls around the Square. Its leaves had been plucked. Magic, together with powdered blood sweat and tears scattered around the tree's base, kept it alive.

Bluestocking had ended up standing beside Lexi. "Your sister knows a lot about your history," she said lamely.

"Doesn't she?" Lexi had intense green eyes that seemed to drink Bluestocking in. "Until now she has had few distractions, so book-learning is easy for her." She spoke quietly.

"You are not a great reader then, Highness?" Bluestocking said, making polite conversation.

"Call me Lexi." She laughed. "I've never read a book in my life. Dead, dull things, they seem to me. Not like you, I suppose? Isn't that why you're here? To read books?" *She makes it sound like a penance,* Bluestocking thought, but nodded.

"Are your quarters adequate?" Lexi asked, suddenly changing conversational direction.

"Perfectly," Bluestocking said.

"The slave we provided? She's met... **all** your needs?"

"Yes, thank you." Bluestocking thought, *you have a mind like a grasshopper, Highness.* She asked: "She's your personal slave?"

Lexi nodded. "Mine and Cavi's. We have our own slaves, but share her as well. We both need another slave sometimes, but not enough to justify one extra each. She's very helpful. If wilful at times." She smiled at some inner joke. "If she needs to be disciplined, do so. Sometimes I think Kyr needs to be reminded that she is a slave." In answer to Bluestocking's questioning look, she explained. "Those near power often gain authority by association. Occasionally we learn that Kyr has become a little too self-important. Nothing obvious, you understand?"

Bluestocking nodded with only half her attention while watching the crowd and the axeman sharpening his blade out of the corner of her eye.

Lexi chuckled. "Sometimes she's more like a pet than a slave; we spoil her terribly. She's very adept at telling my people she's with Cavi, and telling them she's with me. The gods only know what she gets up to then." She smiled at her inner joke again. "I often wonder if she provokes us on purpose, or whether she's simply wilful. I swear a girl shouldn't need as much discipline as she does." Lexi leaned conspiratorially toward her, again changing the subject abruptly. "What's he like? Prince Cas? Does he read books too?"

Now it was Bluestocking's turn to laugh. "I think the Prince would rather face a man-eating monster than a woman armed with a book."

"Oh," Lexi said thoughtfully glancing at Cas and her sister. "I suppose they won't talk about books. They say that opposites attract one another; perhaps his lack of affection for them will counterbalance her fascination. Still, it seems something of a mismatch, even if it is purely a political alliance."

It seemed to Bluestocking that Lexi was unduly interested in the Prince: whenever Lexi looked away, it seemed to be him that she was looking at. *But surely,* Bluestocking thought, *she has a fiancé of her own?* "Does the Emir read, Majesty?"

Lexi stared at her in surprise. "Heavens, no! He doesn't do much of anything except eat and drool over his harem." She glanced around, but Daragel seemed intent on Cavi's lecture. "I've only met him a few times. He's fat, and sweats like a pig." She giggled, and Bluestocking warmed to her; *She's so indiscreet.* "I'll do my duty when we marry, but it **will** be duty."

"When will that be?"

"Oh, no date's been set yet," Lexi said. The twinkle in her eye said as if she'd spoken out loud, *and it won't be anytime soon, if I have my way.*

"What about your older sister?" Bluestocking said. "She's next in line to the throne, surely? Isn't it unusual to find the eldest unwed or not affianced?" She added, "Are these questions impertinent?"

Lexi shook her head. "No, just blunt." She smiled. "You just say what's on your mind, don't you? I like that– too many people round here are too frightened to say what they mean. To answer your question, she's wedded to the gods. She renounced the world of the flesh for the spirit-world and with it her claim to the throne. But what she does now is just as important." Seeing Bluestocking's startled look, she added, "Just because we don't live in our god's pockets like you, doesn't mean they don't watch over us. And we revere them every bit as much as you do yours."

Remembering her promise to light a candle to Nangharai and how quickly she'd lapsed, Bluestocking said nothing.

At the far end of the square a little flurry interrupted their conversation.

At the other end of the stage was the speaker's podium at which stood a florid faced man with jowls that hung like a turkey cock's wattles. When he shouted, "Hear ye! Hear ye!" The wattles shook, and Bluestocking had to stifle a fit of giggles– the way she felt, they could easily turn to hysteria. She swallowed bile and shuddered. Feeling suddenly unsteady, she gripped at the nearest object for support– Cas' arm.

"Are you all right?" he hissed in a stage whisper loud enough to make heads turn.

Bluestocking nodded. "Overdid the wine," she whispered equally loudly and saw a few smirks among her companions. *Mustn't let them think there's any significance.*

"Gather now and witness The Gods' Retribution against wrongdoers," the crier bellowed from his stand, his voice echoing back off the walls, so loud that Bluestocking guessed that it was amplified by some means, magical or mechanical. A Nomenati wearing knee-length white robes with gilt embroidery followed him onto the stage. His cowl was, unusually, thrown back to reveal a young man with head shaven except for a plait hanging from the nape of his neck.

"You are gathered by the will of their representative, King Redoutifalia of Whiterock." the crier continued. He droned on while Bluestocking, her over-tired brain buzzing with dipthongs and ablates, and royal engagements, studied the crowd, who were waiting with the fixity of vultures willing their next meal to die; for the talking to be over and the action to begin.

A pock-marked youth, hands thrust deep in his pockets, joked with a gang who each hefted stones from one hand to another.

A pregnant woman, so big her time must be near, chewing on something bought from one of the sweet-sellers stalking the margins of the crowd.

An old man, racked by a coughing fit until his eyes distended.

A family of four passing a bag of sweets around, ordinary in every way, except that like the others, their eyes were feverish with the expectation of blood. "Bin two months," father mumbled. "Bout time us had a bit of fun."

To her right, Lexi and her family watched the stage, showing little obvious emotion, but the way Evi chewed at her lip and Cavi's nostrils flared as they studied the scene, showed that they were not quite as disinterested as they wished to appear.

A drum began to beat, asynchronously. Bluestocking's heart beat slightly faster. Guards led out two men from behind the stage. Their hands were manacled to a long chain that looped through collars round their necks. Bluestocking's mouth seemed filled with sawdust, and she licked her lips. The first man was unchained and led to the block.

The executioner stepped forward, hefting an enormous axe. He was naked from the waist up except for a hood over the upper part of his face. His muscular torso was beaded with sweat.

The crier bellowed something Bluestocking couldn't quite hear about a God's retribution. The wind picked up. The thief's hand was placed on the chopping block and his arm held so that he couldn't pull his hand away.

As the axe landed with a thud, the thief flinched, looked away and emitted a thin, shrill little scream. He was dragged away to a brazier behind the block, and the now blood-spattered executioner cauterised the wound. The severed hand left behind on the block was picked up by the executioner, who waved it at the crowd. Several people yelled with glee as the executioner shaped to toss it to them, before pitching it further back into the mob, which squabbled over it until fists flew.

As Bluestocking fought another bout of nausea, the second man was dragged forward. He struggled and fought, and the crowd emitted a single continuous growl, like a dog. Two more guards tackled him around the waist, and the whole scrum rolled forward. "I'm innocent!" he shouted.

"They all say that!" someone in the crowd bellowed back, to roars of laughter from around him.

"This is Nyos, found guilty by a tribunal of spreading defamation about Ectri," the crier bellowed.

"Who, by an amazing coincidence," a wag called out, "is a friend of Arial. What odds that the tribunal was stuffed with their friends?" Those around him silenced the wag with anxious glances at the stand where Arial stood.

The slanderer's head was placed in a vertical vice designed for the occasion. He still managed to move his head slightly. A guard pinched his nose until Nyos had to open his mouth to breathe; a pole with a white block at its end was crammed between his jaws. He bit on the block, but they forced his jaws apart by turning both pole and block.

Bluestocking's view was obstructed, but she'd seen similar punishments meted out enough times at home to know what was happening. A pair of pliers would be thrust into the man's mouth.

The crowd began jeering, and someone threw a tomato.

Bluestocking saw the flash of something bright in the soldier's hand, and with the jeers of the crowd turning to cheers, the knifeman turned and held up Nyos' tongue. His hands still bound, the slanderer was led away, with a soldier holding a rag to his bleeding mouth

Bluestocking swayed, feeling suddenly light-headed.

"Now comes the real villain," a shaven headed man near Bluestocking said with lip-licking relish. Someone hushed him, and he looked sulky, but fell silent.

The crier bellowed, "Hear this! Hear this! The man known as Avisohn, is accused that: He was born Visohn of Brammattra Apartments. He has falsified his position in society, given the gravest possible offence to all who know him by his false name; stands convicted of treason against our sovereign and has blasphemed against the Gods."

The Nomenati produced the name-stone from its ceremonial tray and recited the spell that would warp time back to the moment of the accused's naming. From out of the past a ghostly voice whispered, "Visohn."

A man Bluestocking had barely noticed before at the edge of the stage slumped and grabbed at one of the soldiers for support. *Visohn's accuser,* Bluestocking thought. *Destined to take the place of the man he accused, had the stone confirmed his name as Avisohn.*

Suddenly she saw her own fate and felt light-headed. She became aware of a whimpering from within a box near the crier's feet. It sounded like a puppy crying for its owner, but she knew what it was. The hair on the nape of her neck stood on end, but she was unable to look away as the box was opened.

A man was dragged from the box. It was he who was whimpering. He was bound hand and foot. Two soldiers lifted him, each taking an arm. Another gripped his hair and yanked his head back.

The crowd let out a low animal growl, an inhuman sound that made Bluestocking want to flee, but she couldn't take her eyes off Visohn.

The executioner poured a black treacly liquid into Visohn's mouth with one hand, while his other clamped around Visohn's throat.

"Foulbane," a man explained to the boy he'd lifted onto his shoulders. "If he swallows it, the knave will die a slow death."

Still holding Visohn's throat, the executioner forced the accused's head forward, then pinched his nose, so that to try to breathe, Visohn had to spit the liquid out. The executioner let go of his throat, and Visohn coughed and gulped for air.

Moments later, he began to scream, a high-pitched sound more animal than human. Bluestocking wanted to cover her ears, but dared not.

"See?" The father said to his son. "They just rinsed his mouth out. The itching is so bad, he has no choice but to bite his tongue out. It's bad; see how he bites his lips."

"You have lied and lied again," the crier intoned. "The gods demand we take your tongue so you can lie no more." The man writhed and wriggled, but in the grip of the soldiers, he had no chance of escape.

"The last sight the gods have granted you," the crier's voice faltered for the first time, "is to witness what you've done to your family. Bring them!" A woman barely past adolescence, carrying a young girl, perhaps a five-year old, was led forward. They both wore simple white shifts and a black ribbon around the neck. Both were manacled. A soldier prised the child away from the woman, and the child began to cry. "Avisohn!" the woman screamed. "In Brighannon's name, what have you done?"

Avisohn's eyes almost popped out of his head. He made frantic "aahing!" noises. The little girl was helped up the steps to one of the branches of the gallows tree, and a soldier popped a sweet into her mouth.

"Probably drugged," someone near Bluestocking said, and she longed to punch the face to which the know-all voice belonged. The mother, now crying freely, was bundled up steps to another branch. Nooses were placed around both the girl's and her mother's necks.

Bluestocking watched Avisohn's face as the steps were pulled away. At the first crack he let out a wordless cry and closed his eyes. Bluestocking had never seen such anguish seared into a man's face.

"You have tried to hide the truth from the sight of the Gods. In turn, they will hide the beauty of the world from your sight." The executioner lifted a poker, its tip glowing red-hot. Bluestocking shut her eyes and covered her ears, but Visohn's screams cut through her muffling hands as easily as the poker burnt into his eyelids.

Aware that she risked attracting the attention of the others, Bluestocking forced herself to open her eyes.

An attendant rubbed cream onto Visohn's scorched sockets.

"Once," the crier intoned, "a villain like you managed to still inflict himself on a woman. Never again shall this happen." A soldier cut the ragged cord holding up Visohn's leggings. Several people took a sharp intake of breath. Bluestocking felt the bitter taste of blood where she had bitten her cheek.

A sword as long as Bluestocking's arm was lifted, glinting evilly in the sunlight; a piece of silk was dropped, and the sword cut through it instantly. The crowd moaned.

An attendant painted in the gaudy colours and dress of a hermaphrodite lifted Visohn's penis, and two more soldiers gripped his torso, holding him absolutely steady, while another soldier placed the sword against Visohn's genitals. The sword barely seemed to move, but a gout of blood spurted, and Visohn's scream echoed around the square.

The hermaphrodite shoved a rag into the wound, struggling to push it in as Visohn writhed and screamed. "They'll put a tube in, if he lives, so he can piss," someone said, but to Bluestocking the voice seemed to come from a great distance.

"To ensure no retribution against the citizen who brought your evil to the God's attention," the crier said, struggling to make himself heard over Visohn's screams and the crowd's muttering, "your hands shall be made safe."

Nangharai, how much more is he supposed to take? Bluestocking thought, but she knew the answer.

She looked around at the blood-lust on every face– except one.

The Prince stood next to her. He said sadly, "I've seen too many of these events. Surely such villains know that they can't get away with it?"

"Perhaps the need to be someone else is so powerful, that it seems worth the risk." She shrugged. "Maybe he– oh, I don't know!"

He nodded. "If the girl had named him, she might have been spared."

"And maybe she wouldn't," Bluestocking said tartly. "Maybe she didn't know," she said, ignoring the glares from the other spectators around them.

"Didn't know?" Cas' voice dripped scorn. "Of course she did! How could she not know something like that?"

"Are you saying that you could never be fooled?" Bluestocking longed to wipe the superior smile from his face.

"Hush!" someone hissed, but Cas ignored them.

He said to Bluestocking, "Sooner or later, name-changers always give themselves away."

"Perhaps," Bluestocking said, feeling suddenly reckless, "she loved him enough to accept whatever happened to her. You've never loved have you, Majesty?"

"Don't be too sure," he said sadly.

"Have you ever loved someone so much, that you'd do anything for them? Even live a lie?" She swayed, feeling light-headed again.

"Are you all right?" the Prince asked.

She nodded. "Suppose?"

"What?" the prince said.

"He had done something valorous, something wonderful, they would spare him then, would they not?" She knew suddenly that for all her dreams, translating a bunch of old words was hardly going to be the stuff for which the Gods could forgive heresy, and her shoulders slumped.

"You look as white as snow. Not much longer now. They're almost done."

The soldiers had laid the now limp Visohn on the platform. His body was spasming in shock, but a soldier knelt on his chest, while another took his left arm, and a third took his right arm. The swordsman had exchanged his sword for an axe, which he lifted and brought down on Visohn's left wrist. The only sound Visohn made was a muffled sob.

Bluestocking noticed a movement on the edge of her vision and saw Myleetra, bobbing backwards and forwards, her lips moving to a recitation, stroking one of the tattoos on her arm.

The axeman walked around and lifted his axe high again, blocking their view

The blood roared in her ears, and everything seemed to be a long way away.

"And to ensure, lastly, that you shall stay and face your victims, those you have deceived," the crier bellowed, "Your feet."

Two more soldiers knelt on his legs. As Bluestocking looked away, a man in front of her seemed to separate into two, both occupying the same space. No one seemed to notice anything out of the ordinary. While one watched the spectacle, the other turned to her and leering, said with a wink, "You're next, name-changer."

The roaring in her ears grew louder, like a waterfall, and she slumped forward in a faint.

Chapter 4

Bluestocking floated in and out of consciousness; voices all around her, but though they were familiar– one very familiar– she couldn't quite work out who they belonged to. Someone lifted her up with a hand between her shoulder-blades, and vague shapes sharpened into faces. A woman said, "Drink this Milady. It'll make you better."

As she drifted again, hands grabbed her at each end and placed her on a litter. She heard a familiar man's voice (*Father?* she wondered) bellow, "Clear a space! Stand back, damn you!"

Background voices grumbled like the sea on a blustery day, "Seems the foreign bint couldn't stomach a Retribution," a man said. "Reckon 'em may be heretics."

"Quiet!" Father said. "Open your mouth again, and you'll visit the dungeons!" She slept properly then.

Awaking from a dream that had towards its end become erotic enough to make her cheeks burn in memory to small domestic sounds: the murmur of voices, the clink of cutlery, and a sour smell– but she shut that out for the moment, wanting for as long as possible the freedom from responsibility that sleep brought. With eyes still closed, she luxuriated in silk sheets, wondering if she was back in her own bed again. The direction of the sunlight was the same as when she'd awoken that morning, and for a moment, she wondered if she'd dreamt the whole thing. But she knew better than to believe that. The horror in Gallows Square was terribly real. She shook and thrusting a knuckle into her mouth, bit on it.

"Mistress?" Kyr asked, forehead furrowed in anxiety. Her red shift slipped down over her shoulder and she pulled it up but not before Bluestocking saw a livid bruise on her collarbone.

"How long have I been asleep?" Bluestocking asked.

"The whole of yesterday," Kyr said, eyes glinting, and her jaw worked. "We were **so** worried. I wondered if you'd ever wake up. The Prince called several times." She said with a thin smile, "I'm not sure that Princess Cavi appreciated his concern."

"Nonsense," Bluestocking said. She sniffed and changed the subject. "What's that awful smell?"

"Incense," Kyr said. "For your safe return." She added, squeezing Bluestocking's hand, "I'm glad you're alright."

"Silly," Bluestocking said, smiling. "I was probably tired from the journey and everything. I've barely slept for four days." Remembering the dream, when the androgynous figure had morphed into Kyr, she gently extricated her hand from the slave's. When Kyr pouted, Bluestocking said gently, "I'd like some water, please."

Kyr fetched it while Bluestocking sat up. When she finished drinking, she stared into space.

"Milady?"

Bluestocking roused herself and smiled. "I was thinking," she said. "Fainting in the square was just tiredness and excitement catching up with me."

And fear, she thought. But if she admitted that, then Kyr would know what she was afraid of. *Of ending up like that poor man, shut into darkness, unable to speak, to move, to talk, with only pain and fear and hunger for company.*

"I should have been at work two days ago." She used the headboard as a prop to clamber from her bed. "Not flitting around the Palace, attending Retributions. Fetch me some clothes, will you? Anything will do."

When Kyr passed her a blouse the slave held onto it for a moment too long. Her finger stroked Bluestocking's thumb.

Bluestocking jumped as if stung and snatched her hand away, refusing to meet Kyr's gaze.

"Mistress, be careful," Kyr said, lifting Bluestocking's chin with a finger and gazing into her eyes. "Nothing is as it seems here!"

Pulling herself away, Bluestocking buttoned an ankle-length skirt, and said, "What do you mean? You're the second person to say that in successive days."

Kyr walked to the window. "See this?" She reached up and pointed to a mark on the window frame. Her movements were jerky, like a badly-worked marionette. *As if she's struggling against something,* Bluestocking thought.

She studied the frame where Kyr pointed to it. The frame's texture was more like papier-mâché than wood. Bluestocking picked a fragment away from the frame with her nail and tore it apart. "What is it?"

"Silk," Kyr replied.

"Compressed into a laminate." Bluestocking nodded understanding. She strode to a bedside cabinet. "Wood, probably mulberry." Kneeling, she worked a loose floorboard up, swearing under her breath as she caught a splinter. She picked at the supporting joists beneath it. "Silk again." She gazed up at the ceiling, which looked at first like plaster and paper, but then saw the same patterned lines. "So floorboards, furniture and the bed-frame are made of wood," she said. "But the items less likely to the noticed are all made of compressed silk."

Kyr said. "Wood's so scarce they have to use something else. Silk's as common as air." She sniffed. "Mind you, if the King would let 'em grow trees for wood instead of fruit crops, there wouldn't be a shortage of lumber."

"I suppose if timber's difficult to find, you only use it where you must," Bluestocking said. She sat on the edge of the bed and shaking her head, looked at Kyr in wonderment.

Kyr looked like a dog that has successfully performed a trick. She said quietly, "Mistress, may I ask you something? It may seem impertinent, but it's not intended to cause offence."

"Sometimes I wonder about you, Kyr. It's almost as if there are two of you. Do you have a twin?"

Kyr laughed nervously, clearly discomfited by Bluestocking's answering a question with a question. "I'm sure if I'd sisters, mistress. Ma would've told me. No, there's only me."

"The day I arrived," Bluestocking said, "you were insolent and slatternly...well, whore-ish, to be frank. Other times, like today, you're sweet, and..." She waved her hands around, searching for the right word. She added lamely, "I don't know why I even wonder. I suppose I should treat you like the furniture."

"I can tell you've never had a slave, mistress," Kyr said. "Else you would. Any slave can tell a pawn from a master."

"If I had," Bluestocking admitted, "Maybe I'd know when to flog the skin off your back and when not to. What were you going to ask?"

Kyr blurted, "Has the Prince had you?"

"What?" Bluestocking said incredulously.

Kyr held up her hands. "I mean well, honestly!"

"Then," Bluestocking said, "explain slowly, and precisely, *exactly* how you meant well."

"Well," Kyr said. "I assume you has some feelings for him. He's always round here, mooning them big eyes at you. Either he's desperate, or there's something between you, and if so, you're in danger–"

"Enough!" Bluestocking put fingers to Kyr's lips to silence her, then snatched them away. "*How* am I in danger?"

"Princess Cavi," Kyr said. "She'll put up with a dalliance, but if it's serious..." She made a slashing gesture across her throat.

"There's no dalliance." Bluestocking sighed. "He amuses himself by flirting with me. I suppose I could have, you know..." She blushed.

"Milady?" Kyr said, grinning. "You talk like a virgin. Anyone would think that–" Her eyes widened. "You've never..."

Bluestocking shook her head. "I've never met the right man. When I do, I'll know about it. But it's not the Prince– at least, I don't think it is."

"So who keeps you warm at night?"

"I do." Bluestocking shrugged. "I don't need that kind of warmth."

The silence hung heavy.

"Don't you?" Kyr asked. She licked her lips, glanced down, then up coquettishly from beneath her lashes. "P'raps I do take advantage, mistress, but sometimes a girl has to take a risk and cheek a pawn, 'specially if they makes you melt inside, and you just wants to break through that barrier, so they sees what's possible."

"What in the god's names are you babbling about?" Bluestocking shook her head, laughing. "Barriers? Possible?"

Kyr took Bluestocking's hand and pushed it against the fabric of her skirt between her legs. Bluestocking snatched her hand away and slapped Kyr so hard it echoed in the silence.

Then Kyr shouted, "You're so...buttoned up!" The mark blazed livid pink against her white face. "You think Prince or Mister Perfick will just show up and sweep you off your feet?" She laughed scornfully, miming a pumping action with her arm and clenched fist. "I'm a pleasure slave. It's my job– when I'm not wiping their arses– to be whore or maiden for the men, or a man for the ladies. And the men who ain't sure." She took a deep breath, said more calmly, "I know how men are. So either let the Prince have you or complain to Cavi that he's pestering you. Then she'll know you're not blame." She sighed. "You go to the Library, milady. But look up from your studies sometimes. There's danger about, even for a tight-cheeked virgin, and no number of books will save you from it."

"I'm going to the library." Bluestocking almost kept her voice steady. "I expect you to be gone when I return."

***

The morning passed slowly in the almost-deserted library. Occasionally old men passed a half-hour warming up their freezing hands before leaving again. The other visitors all seemed to know where to look for what they wanted, although Copel would materialize anxiously to shepherd them around the shelves. The library reminded Bluestocking more of an exclusive club than a place of study.

Bluestocking had regretted her outburst the moment Kyr had left, but she found it unsettling being around the slave. She pushed it from her mind and gradually grew calmer, losing herself in her work, as she always escaped her troubles.

It was a strange text. The individual words made sense, but their overall meaning kept swimming away from her, as if the words wanted to thwart her desire to understand them. She made copious notes, corrections and scribbled amends to the corrections in the margins. Soon she had a small hill of papyrus on the lectern, her fingers were stained black with the ink, and her hair was tousled from running her fingers through it.

Her work ended abruptly with a hand upon her arm. She jumped.

"I'm sorry," Myleetra said, grinning, "I didn't mean to startle you. I wondered if you needed a break." She giggled. "Have you seen your face?"

Bluestocking shook her head.

Myleetra marched her over to a window, muttered an incantation, and the window clouded over, becoming an opaque silver.

The reflection's hair was a bird's nest of tangles, and her face was streaked with ink where she'd absentmindedly wiped her forehead. Bluestocking pulled a rueful face and muttered, "Nothing that some water won't take care of."

"Come to the temple," Myleetra said. "After you've washed, you can tell me how you're getting along."

Bluestocking shook her head. "I'll keep at this. It's driving me mad; every time I think I've got this language worked out, the meaning seems to slide from underneath me. It's like chasing smoke." She added grimly, "But I will decipher it."

Myleetra said, "As you wish. But if you need to take a break, you know where I am."

Bluestocking smiled and on an impulse, hugged Myleetra, who looked flustered and cast an anxious glance at Bluestocking's ink-smeared hands, which, fortunately, Bluestocking had kept well clear. "I never thanked you for taking care of me the other night, nor apologized if I embarrassed you."

Myleetra looked startled– then roared with laughter. Several men glared. One put his finger to his lips, but she ignored him. "I don't know when I last had such fine entertainment as at the banquet. You didn't offend me, and if you upset anyone else, well, that's a bonus."

Bluestocking shook her head. "I never want to feel as ill as I did the next morning. I've never got drunk before. I doubt I will again."

Myleetra said, "You learn not to drink too much, so quickly, and to eat before you drink." She left, lifting her hand in farewell. "I'll be in the temple."

***

From the position of the sun now shining through the windows, Bluestocking guessed it was mid-afternoon when she sighed, straightened up and looked round at a small noise, catching Princess Lexi sneaking toward her. Lexi muttered an oath. "Drat that floorboard! Myleetra said you were in here. Said if I crept up on you, you'd jump clear to the ceiling."

Bluestocking ostentatiously looked up at the high ceiling, raising an eyebrow. "Not quite *that* high, Highness. I see you have a...robust sense of humour."

The Princess giggled. "You obviously don't." She adjusted the shoulder of her dress. "Call me Lexi, for Brighannon's sake. You sound like one of those tedious courtiers, always bowing and scraping. Have you eaten?"

It was clearly an invitation. Bluestocking was momentarily wrong-footed by the abrupt change of subject. She thought, *Why is everyone so preoccupied with food? Do they do nothing except eat?* "No, but I need a break." She re-wrapped the scroll and took it back to Copel.

She gathered up her notes, tidying them into a single pile and turned to Lexi, who was craning her neck to look up at the top of the shelves, slowly turning her head. "How does he get the books down? Does he whistle or click his fingers? Or climb up there like a monkey?"

Bluestocking said, "He has a ladder on wheels that lock; see it there, tucked away beside that shelf?"

Lexi said, "I'd never have thought of such a device." She looked so awed that Bluestocking almost burst out laughing. Lexi added, changing the subject again, "If I ate pastries as often as I wanted, I'd be the size of the Emir." She puffed out her cheeks and widened her eyes. Bluestocking smothered a giggle. "So instead, I limit myself to special occasions. Like now."

"I count as a special occasion?"

"You do when it gives me an excuse," Lexi said, grinning evilly. "A new shop has opened, and the slave there is rather fetching." Her grin widened, before she grew serious at Bluestocking's shocked look. "A girl can look, as long as she doesn't touch. At least," she added, "this girl can."

***

They left the library, Lexi's guards falling into step behind them, shadowing them up through the levels toward the sun. Bluestocking felt like a mole emerging from underground. "If this is how I feel after a few hours, how do people feel who have spent their whole lives shut away?"

Lexi only shrugged. "Even peasants see daylight." For a moment, Bluestocking saw the citadel as a giant prison, and she longed to break the bars. The moment passed.

They arrived at the highest enclosed level on a long, wide concourse open at the end, with a railing for a barrier. In the distance, fields rolled gently up to the Southern Spine. Late afternoon sunshine streamed in, bathing people in a golden glow.

They stopped at a small cafe that had spilled out onto the thoroughfare, chairs penned within a roped off area. The proprietor rushed out, dusting down the chairs furthest from the shop and deepest into the concourse, fussing round like an anxious hen. Lexi spoke quietly to him. He said to Bluestocking, "This way, milady," and led her inside to wash.

Emerging, she saw Daragel, purple robe billowing over the rope, talking to Lexi.

Bluestocking hung back, not wishing to intrude, but Lexi's angry voice drifted across. "I won't be bullied into this. And I'm not some scullion to be accosted on the street. We've agreed on a time and place, endorsed by the Emir's advisers and our priest's interpretation of the portents. That it's later, not sooner is irrelevant."

"Highness, if you hadn't avoided me so much, I wouldn't need to accost you on the street, as you put it." Daragel's teeth flashed white in the sunlight. "I'll leave you to ponder our conversation." He caught sight of Bluestocking and bowed. "Mistress, you're recovered from your ordeal? Alas, travelling long distances does not always suit the ladies." He bowed, and left.

Bluestocking shuddered, and Lexi echoed her thoughts, "Horrid little man. When I marry, the first thing I'll do is make sure that Daragel is sent somewhere far, far away."

"Can you do that?"

Lexi shrugged. "What's the point of marrying the Emir, if I can't do as I wish?" She laughed. "I know they want me as a brood mare, but I'll get what I want out of it." She paused. "I assume that you heard the last part of the conversation, so you might as well hear the rest. Cavi announced her wedding date this morning. It's months before ours, and it's thrown Daragel into a blind panic, in case they produce a male heir before we do. So he's trying to bring forward my wedding date." She clapped her hands. "Good, the pastries are here!" They nibbled and sipped sweet fruit juices. Lexi chattered about inconsequentialities and people Bluestocking didn't know, while Bluestocking worried at the scrolls. Something Lexi had said had started her thinking.

Suddenly, Bluestocking sat up straight. "Yes!" She looked up at a clearly bemused Lexi. "I was trying not to listen to your conversation with Daragel, but I heard 'sooner' and 'later' and it set me thinking. What if the verbs had different tenses for different periods of time? So the immediate past and future have different endings from the distant equivalents. Some of the very remote tribes in the North Eastern wilderness have such oddities in their dialect."

"Do you know," Lexi said, "I understood perhaps a third of what you said?" She burst out laughing, then said, "You have no interest in feminine things, like sewing or gossiping. Even eating— for you, food is food, rather than something to be enjoyed. Yet I find you utterly fascinating!"

Lexi's enthusiasm was infectious. Unsure whether to be offended, Bluestocking smiled back. She bit into a pastry. Cream shot out of its side. "Mm, vanilla," she murmured.

***

Lexi came the next three days and dragged her away again to eat pastries at the café on the Royal Mile, as she had learned the concourse was called. By then, the novelty had palled, and frustration set in

"Look," Lexi breathed. "Here's Cas!" The Prince sauntered along with his entourage.

Bluestocking groaned inwardly.

"He's **so** good looking," Lexi breathed. "He flirted shamelessly the last time we met." She fiddled with a clasp on her long blonde hair.

"He flirts with everyone," Bluestocking said. Seeing the anger flit across Lexi's face, she added quickly, "These pastries are delicious."

Lexi ignored the diversion. "How did you meet him?"

"At Ravlatt University," Bluestocking said. "I suddenly seemed to bump into him all the time. When I received your father's invitation out of the blue, Cas mentioned that he was also visiting Whiterock. He invited me to travel with him. The chance to travel with a group was too good an opportunity to miss."

Bluestocking didn't mention that two days before, Sister Ida from the convent had visited to learn why Bluestocking had stayed a year longer than planned– and when she was returning to the convent. Sister Ida, who knew her true identity.

"Ladies," Prince Cas' honeyed tones interrupted them. "What a pleasant surprise. You're enjoying the afternoon sunshine?"

"Always," Lexi said, as Bluestocking shot him a thin little smile. "We were just talking about temptation and how to resist it."

"Indeed," Cas said, his grin predatory. "You must teach me."

"Oh." Lexi put her hand to her throat, fluttering her lashes "Did I give the impression I'd learned how? I was hoping that **you** could teach me." Her laugh was low and, Bluestocking thought, exceptionally dirty. Bluestocking longed to slap her.

"If you'll excuse me." Pushing back her chair, Bluestocking offered it to Cas. "I must return to the Library, Your Highness."

The Silk Palace

"Blue," he said. "We're all friends here. Please, call me Cas. You mustn't return to that dreary library. I believe that the little man has closed for the day. When I wondered past, looking for you– both–" he added, "it was deserted."

"Then I'll work in my rooms," Bluestocking said. "I must press on. Ravlatt University only agreed to a three-month secondment, and the journey and return takes half of that."

"We'll walk back with you, won't we, Lexi?" Cas said.

Lexi nodded, looking sulky.

They walked back in a silence that baffled Bluestocking. *Was it something I said?*

Lexi stopped and pointed to a corridor branching off from theirs. "I go this way," she said. When Prince Cas bowed and kissed her hand, she added, "Thank you for your company," and held onto his hand for a few moments. Bluestocking saw a look flash between them like a bolt of lightning.

Cas said to Bluestocking, "I'll accompany you to your rooms."

"No need, Highness."

"I insist, Blue. And it's Cas, remember?"

"Thank you, Cas."

On the way, the Prince hummed, but said little. Bluestocking said even less. When they reached her quarters, he told his men, "Wait outside. I'll check her rooms are secure."

When they were inside, Bluestocking said, "You see; no mad-eyed assassins waiting to slit my throat. You can rejoin the Princess. Whichever one you choose." She clapped her hand over her mouth but too late.

Cas seemed more surprised than offended. "Blue? Have I angered you somehow?'

"Your pardon, Highness," Bluestocking said. 'I'll have no complaints, whatever punishment you decide on."

"No, no!" the prince said. "No ducking behind walls of protocol! What's behind this outburst? Because I flirted with Lexi? I'll stay until you answer." He lay on the bed, staring at the ceiling.

"You flirt with *every* woman you meet," Bluestocking said. "I'm not interested in whether you're tupping her."

"Ha! By Rem's hairy hands you're not!" Cas sat upright. "What do you mean?" His eyes narrowed. "Every woman?" He looked so troubled that for a moment Bluestocking felt for him, but she thought, *harden your heart.*

She said nothing. There was nothing she could say without making things worse.

He said nothing, but watched her, with eyes like a puppy's.

"Bluestocking," he said when the tension was almost unbearable. "I don't know what I can say to convince you. All around me are people who bob and curtsy, who smile...then stab me in the back with words. You're the only one who doesn't behave as if my shit smells of flowers. When you think I'm a fool, you manage to let me know. I can't wed you, but a wedding ring isn't everything. But nor will I force myself on someone who doesn't want me. So, I'll ask you straight. Do you feel anything for me?"

For the space of a hundred heartbeats, Bluestocking tried to think of something to say.

"I think I have your answer," Cas said.

***

Normally Bluestocking liked to be alone, but when Cas left she would have given anything for a friendly face. Opening her notes, she worked on them until it grew too dark to see, and someone knocked on the door.

"Come!"

A slave in royal livery entered, bearing a candle with which he lit the lamps. Kyr followed, carrying a tray. Even a few friendly words from her would have been welcome, but Kyr simply placed the tray on the table. "Your dinner, milady." She curtsied.

"Do you have money I can borrow?"

Kyr stared at her, then glanced at the other slave. "Money?"

"Money. You know? You exchange it for things like food."

"I know what it is, but I don't understand why you want it."

"Could you get some, from say, one of the princess' retinue? Do it discreetly, though."

"I'll do what I can." Kyr lifted another tray, with the previous night's dinner uneaten.

"Now?" Bluestocking asked hopefully.

"I'll do what I can." She was gone before Bluestocking could thank her.

***

The next day after a perfunctory, almost brutal wash from Kyr, the slave placed a soft, slightly overripe pear in one of Bluestocking's tunic pockets, a slab of bread in the other. "Eat," Kyr said. "If you starve yourself, they'll hang me."

Bluestocking nodded and left for the library, carrying her papers under her arm, coins jingling in her pocket, food already forgotten. If it hadn't been for the dream she'd had the night before with its disturbing sexual overtones, and the impression that nothing here was what it seemed, she would have felt almost at home for the first time since leaving Ravlatt.

Today the Clock of Days bore a stylized lion's head. The Daykeeper nodded a greeting.

On an impulse, Bluestocking took a detour.

Halarbur opened the door to her knock, his expression inscrutable.

"I'd like to speak to the Prince, please," Bluestocking said, giving no hint of her inner turmoil.

"Indeed?" Halarbur's voice was studiedly neutral. Before Bluestocking could snap a reply, he added, "I'm afraid his Highness is not available. Would you like me to pass a message to him?"

"I'll write a message," Bluestocking said. Halarbur passed her a sheet of vellum, a quill and ink pot. She scribbled a few words, folded the sheet over and gave it to Halarbur.

***

She spent the morning in the library, occasionally sensing Copel's eyes boring into her back. Once she concentrated, though, he faded from her thoughts.

"The God, demigod, or is that power?" she muttered. "Lifted the shield? Or is that cup? Oh, sod it!" At last she stopped and straightened, pressing both hands into the base of her back.

"Can I be of any assistance?" Copel appeared at her elbow.

"Not unless you have the gift of tongues." Bluestocking's laugh was a short, sharp bark. "Three days, and I'm barely past the first paragraph. I suppose it will get quicker, as I get used to the language, but it's painfully slow at the moment. It's like something is giving the words the power to swim away from memory."

"Do you think that's possible?" Copel asked.

"I doubt it," Bluestocking said. "I'm just moaning. Take no notice of me."

Copel said, "If I were you, I would consult one of the churches, or the covens, depending on your beliefs."

"I may do that," Bluestocking said, to humour him.

The doors flew open, and a pair of brawny men marched into the Library. "You are Bluestocking?" one of them asked. Bluestocking noted absently his five o'clock shadow. She nodded.

"Princess Evivalesinan will see you now."

"Will she?" Seeing that Copel was about to speak, she said quickly to cut off any argument, "I'll take a break and hope my eyes un-cross."

Evi's rooms were, unsurprisingly, the largest Bluestocking had seen yet in Whiterock– probably the size of a small palace in their own right. Not only was she the eldest daughter, but she had the dual role as leader of the 'official' church to fulfil. Nonetheless, Bluestocking also suspected that Evi was mindful of her status and keen to flaunt it.

"I have spoken with my advisors," Evi said without wasting time on small talk. "They tell me that while it isn't heresy for an outlander to study the Scrolls of Presimionari, it's doubtless ill-advised."

Bluestocking opened her mouth, but Evi pressed on, "Nonetheless, His Majesty sanctioned this invitation, and for the moment we will accept your presence. You will report to me each day at sundown with your progress. We will then assess whether we will petition the King to revoke your invitation."

"Your Highness is very...thoughtful," Bluestocking said levelly. She was about to continue, but Evi said, "You may go," and left the room.

Walking homeward, Bluestocking decided in the end that it would be best to simply ignore the summons for as long as possible and if Evi decided to complain, to argue her case via Arial, who had issued the invitation in the first place. She suspected that she was caught in the middle of some ongoing struggle between the Princess and Prime Minister, but didn't want to become any more involved than she had to.

She had no conscious intention of going there, but she rounded a corner and looked out over Gallows Square.

The Gallows Tree was festooned with the victims of the last Retribution, each hanging from a different bare branch, swaying in the breeze like wind chimes. Surprisingly, there were no guards present. No one to witness, or to try to stop a kindly passer-by from acting on a whim. *Perhaps they're changing shifts,* she thought and then shrugged. Why didn't matter.

Visohn hung by the arms from a forked branch, an armpit over each bole. His head lolled forward, and at first she thought that he was dead. Then he coughed. Incredibly, with every limb amputated, he still lived.

"I brought you food," she whispered, removing from her pocket her breakfast. Though it wasn't a very practical gift, somehow she felt moved to this small act of defiance.

She climbed onto a lower branch and said, "Open your mouth." When he did so, she took the pear and squeezed it as hard as she could so that a trickle of juice ran into the ruined mouth. He made a noise that might have been gratitude or pain– it was impossible to tell which– and pressed his stubbled cheek against her hand, like a dog seeking comfort. "More?" He nodded slightly, no more than a dip of the head.

She broke up the remnants, pushing them into his mouth. He coughed, and she whispered, "Sorry." He dribbled, a small stream mixed with blackened blood, which she wiped off her hand onto the tree. "That's all there is," she said, and he whined, a small keening sound in the back of his throat.

"How could you do it?" she said. "That's what they were all asking, in that mob. As if you'd butchered babies and eaten them. But it's so easy, isn't it? A small fib here, another one there, and suddenly you're trapped in your own lies."

Somebody shouted from across the square. "I think the guards have seen me," she said, and added, "I'll come back if I can."

She clambered down from the tree, and rushed from the square, her heart beating wildly and ran straight into a familiar face. The peddler she had seen when climbing into the balloon. "I know you from somewhere, don't I, mistress?" The words were said innocently, but a small gloating smile played around his lips.

"No, I don't think so. You mistake me for someone else, perhaps."

The smile didn't reach his eyes, which remained watchful and heavy lidded, but before he could speak, someone else cleared their throat.

"Mistress Bluestocking?" The young man and four soldiers accompanying him wore royal regalia. He stared at the peddler and lifted one eyebrow a fraction, enough to make the peddler slink away. "Was that man bothering you?"

Bluestocking wavered; if she said yes, the peddler would be expelled, possibly executed, unless he babbled an accusation, hoping to earn clemency. That would make her situation even worse. "No more than they usually do," she said with a smile.

The young man smiled back, but it seemed to require a great effort. "Princess Cavendsilperisha has told me to escort you to her. Would you come this way?" It was a question that had only one answer.

The soldiers ringed her. Their walk was brief and brisk, with people quickly moving out of their path.

Bluestocking was ushered into a high-ceilinged, marble-floored room. The Princess looked up from a scroll. "Please be seated," she said gravely. "You're comfortable? Your rooms are adequate?"

"They're excellent, thank you." This continual solicitousness was starting to weary her.

"Your work progresses well?"

Ah, the other main topic of conversation, she thought. "Slowly, I'm afraid."

The Princess nodded slowly and produced a familiar piece of vellum, "Do you expect to be here much longer?"

Bluestocking swallowed and said in a thin, tight voice, "I have to return to the Empire in, I would say, about three weeks or so."

The Princess didn't open it but instead recited from the vellum, "I'm sorry I couldn't give you a satisfactory answer to your question, but I hope that you were not offended and that we can remain friends." She studied Bluestocking and said flatly, "What question did my fiancée ask you?"

Bluestocking said nothing.

"Answer me, damn you!" Cavi slapped Bluestocking across the face with the letter.

"Has the Prince not told you?" Bluestocking couldn't keep the tremor out of her voice, but anger gave her courage. "Your Highness, you could have me killed as easily as I can swat a fly. But if he hasn't told you, then I won't. It's private."

The Princess stared, her face the stark, pale white of bone, her eyes narrowed to slits. She swallowed, said, "As you say, you'll be gone in three weeks. Until that time, you will stay away from my betrothed."

"You had best instruct your...betrothed...as well, Highness." Bluestocking shook with rage and fear but somehow managed to stay seated. She was sure that if she moved, the guards would seize her.

"I think," Cavi said with a ferocious smile, "that I can sort that out." Taking a deep breath, she continued in a steadier voice, "If you value your life, don't be foolish. As you say, I could arrange for you to be killed, and no one would dare question me."

Bluestocking almost argued, but common sense prevailed, and she nodded. "May I go, now?"

"Please do," Princess Cavi said, turning back to her reading. In her left hand, she screwed the letter into a ball.

The same young man who had escorted her there showed Bluestocking out.

She glared at him. "How did the Princess come by a private letter? Did you search the Prince's quarters? Perhaps you search his rubbish?"

The young soldier looked away but said quietly, "Perhaps the Prince gave it to her. Or his man. However she came by it isn't my concern. Go now," he murmured. The threat in his eyes as he turned to her chilled her to her marrow. "Before you suffer an accident."

Chapter 5

She strode away, still shaking, unable to think straight, walking at random, until she was calm. She decided that more than anything she needed a friendly face. Walking down several more levels, she ended up on a narrow alleyway with a window-slit at one end. Farther along wall-mounted torches burned feebly, their light casting shadows where there were no objects to be shadowed.

Bluestocking paused at a doorway, hesitating.

An unfamiliar voice called from within, "Come in, child."

The woman who had spoken was elderly, her skin so wrinkled that the tattoos on her body were indecipherable. She sat just inside the entrance to a marble-floored vestibule on what looked like a canvas chair. A single lamp on a flat surface cast barely enough light to illuminate the woman's face, while the rest of the vestibule was dark apart from one wall illuminated by a solitary concealed lamp.

A painting of an old man hung on the wall. His luminous cloak reached all the way to the snow-covered ground. On the cloak were painted in blue-green all the continents of the world. He seemed headless, although Mother Moon could have been his head instead, hovering close by his hand in the inky black backdrop. His two feet peeked out from beneath the cloak like claws, marring the perfect symmetry of the snow.

Dragging her eyes away from the painting, Bluestocking said hesitantly, "I'm looking for Myleetra."

"She is...engaged," the old woman said with a faint smile.

Bluestocking turned to go.

"She won't be too long," the old woman said. "It's a risk you run, calling on her at home. Local people stop us on the street. They all know their local witch." She added, "Your accent is not native, is it? Your name is?"

"Bluestocking."

"I wondered if you were she. In that case, I'll show you through. Follow me."

She led Bluestocking through a door at the back, hidden in the gloom, into a room more suited to a romantic fantasia. While brighter than the vestibule, the lamps still cast only a subtle lighting. Thick sheepskin rugs, probably fake– made of the ubiquitous silk– covered the walls. Several small statuettes showed couples, and even groups, intertwined in acts that made Bluestocking's cheeks colour.

A chaise-longue covered with thick red fur dominated the centre of the room. It was draped with clothing that looked familiar.

In the corner of the room a chain hung from the ceiling. At the end of the chain was a tripod. Myleetra stood naked on tiptoe with legs apart, her arms stretched up, her wrists manacled. A woman knelt at Myleetra's feet with her back to Bluestocking, her face buried between Myleetra's thighs. Someone else stood behind Myleetra, half hidden by the witch. From the muscle definition Bluestocking guessed it was a man.

Bluestocking's hand flew to her mouth. "I didn't mean to interrupt–"

"No! No need to go!" Panting, Myleetra pointed to the chaise-lounge. "Sit there a moment!" She turned her head, and said to the man behind her, "Undo those manacles. And you," she said to the woman still kneeling, "get up."

The girl stood and looked directly at her. It was Kyr. The similarity to the dream made Bluestocking take a step backward, and she felt the heat rise to her face.

Myleetra's fat face split into a lascivious grin, and Bluestocking saw malice in the woman's eyes. "Wise people claim that exercise gives health. They don't say what form the exercise should take."

Rather than look at Kyr, Bluestocking glanced at Myleetra as the fat woman pulled her robes on, covering the livid red weals on her breasts, then looked away. Trying to keep her voice as unemotional as possible, she said, "And what do your partners gain, apart from becoming healthier?"

"A sense of virtue," Myleetra replied.

"I thought that chastity was a virtue," Bluestocking said.

Myleetra chuckled. "Only because their gods don't want their followers to have more fun than them." She grew serious. "Where do you think we draw our power from? And what even better reason for those dreary dullards to hate us? We witches have all the fun that's denied them!" She turned serious. "Is this a social visit, or can I help you with something?" She said to Kyr, "You can go now," and the slave turned away. Bluestocking thought she looked dazed.

Before Bluestocking could speak, Kyr murmured, "Good night." Bluestocking noticed how small her pupils were, and reaching out, scraped something from the side of Kyr's mouth. It was soft, gelatinous, and bitter-smelling. Kyr didn't move.

Bluestocking looked away and paused before answering Myleetra, "Not surprisingly, I'm struggling to translate the scrolls. I have the feeling that the difficulty is as much magical as linguistic. I wondered if you had a spell that might help me."

As Kyr left, the muscular young man followed her out without speaking.

Myleetra raised an eyebrow. "How much do you know about magic?"

Bluestocking tore her gaze away from the departing slaves. "Not much," she admitted.

"I thought so," Myleetra said. She fired a question at Bluestocking: "Why do we work magic?"

Bluestocking thought for several moments. "Because we can?" Her guess wasn't entirely serious. Myleetra looked disappointed. "I don't know!" Bluestocking said, exasperated. "Because it's easier than doing things the hard way?"

"Wrong, wrong, wrong!" Myleetra stared at her and sighed. "This is the first question we ask noviciates. Few of them get it right, either. In fact, using magic for mundane tasks is harder than doing them by hand, so we use it for things we can't do any other way. But the world and the heavens are continually fighting against us using it. Every time we work a spell, we diminish the magic in the world. One day it will all be used up– unless as some scholars insist, there is a secret heart to the world from which we draw it– and when the magic is used up, the gods may well no longer exist. Who knows?" She smiled sadly at Bluestocking.

Bluestocking said, "I understand languages but not magic."

Myleetra thought for a moment and then said, her thoughts taking another direction. "Lay-people always think that as soon as they have a problem, they can run to a witch, and all their problems will disappear with a snap of their fingers."

"So you can't help then?"

Myleetra leaned forward. "I want you to understand *why* I may not be able to help you. Magic is a mood, a word, a thought, a deed, a place, but above all, a time. Some spells, like the one I'll perform for you, only work at particular times; they are influenced by the phases of the moon, the sun and the tides." She held up her hand. "Yes, we're thousands of leagues from the sea, but there are tides within the stones, as well as within water."

Rising, Myleetra beckoned Bluestocking. "Let me show you something," she said. She picked up a shapeless mass of crinkly parchment, vaguely skin-coloured, and draped it like a cape across her shoulders. It had legs that bumped at the back of Myleetra's legs, and arms that hung down, covering Myleetra's own.

Bluestocking thought, *It looks like a human body emptied of all its contents.* "What's the material?" she asked and as Myleetra turned on her a chilling smile, realized that she knew what it was. *How could you be so stupid? It's human skin!* To cover the stretching silence, she asked, "Who is– was it?"

"Her name was Plotolep," Myleetra said, smiling. "She's my predecessor. Just as my skin will be removed and cured by my successor. So we live on, through those who follow in our footprints."

Bluestocking flinched when Myleetra came near her, but the other woman said, "I'll not hurt you."

Bluestocking said, peering, "Your tattoos look tinged with red."

"They are red," Myleetra said. "Instead of ink, we use sanctified blood. My own blood, magicked to create more magic. You remember how I told you at the dinner that most novitiates fall by the wayside within days, weeks or months of joining our order, or one of our related orders? But the real culling doesn't begin until we start the sacred tattoos, based on our own blood, drained over the nights of a full moon and mixed with that of a grand-mistress of one of the orders. Thus is power and talent made manifest." Her eyes glinted in the torchlight with delight and menace.

"Come with me," she said, and lifted a curtain to reveal a concealed doorway. Against her better judgement, Bluestocking followed her into another, even smaller room, so bare of furnishings that it was little more comfortable than a prison cell. The only furnishings were a cupboard mounted on the wall at eye level, a miniature tree, a table and a chair, which Myleetra motioned Bluestocking to sit upon.

From the cupboard, Myleetra took and placed several objects on the floor near Bluestocking's chair. Bluestocking saw a little chalice, a small bowl of salt, a larger bowl, containing water and lastly, a plate of small cakes. From the folds of her tunic Myleetra took a small dagger and cut a sprig of greenery from the tree.

In the silence Myleetra sat cross-legged on the floor and closed her eyes for a time. Then bending forward, she picked up the plate and offered the cakes.

"I'm not hungry, but thank you," Bluestocking said with a smile.

"Mushroom cakes, harvested from the caverns. The silk spiders aren't the only things of value down there," Myleetra said, then urged, "Take one."

Bluestocking ate the cake, which was almost tasteless. She had started to feel nervous and excited. *If this translates the scrolls,* she thought, *I'll empty the plate.*

"Now, my dear," Myleetra said, "fold your hands in your lap, sit with feet flat on the floor, and push your back straight against your chair." Bluestocking did as she was told. "Now, take five breaths, each one very slowly, and let them out, taking your time and relaxing as completely as you can."

Myleetra looked down at the floor and also took several deep breaths. After a long silence she said, "I want you to imagine that you are a part of the chair. The chair is part of the floor. Its legs grow down into the floor. Can you imagine that?"

"I think so," Bluestocking said. Her body was starting to feel heavy. To have moved her and the chair would have taken a hundred men or more. But she felt completely relaxed, as if all her cares had faded away.

Myleetra climbed to her feet with a cracking of her joints and slowly began to pace about the room. She took the little dagger, and pointing it, made a circle in the air around them both and the items on the floor. She touched the water in the bowl with the tip of the dagger, murmuring something. Then she touched the salt with the dagger's tip. With the point of the dagger she tipped a little salt into the bowl of water, and murmuring softly, stirred seven times.

Taking the bowl, Myleetra sprinkled water seven times into each of the room's four corners. Taking a tiny glowing coal from the brazier, she murmured something and placed it in the water. She inhaled the smoke rising from the water, muttering softly. Again she went to each of the four corners of the room, making little signs.

"You're moving clockwise," Bluestocking found the strength to murmur through her lassitude. "Do you always move clockwise?" The whole ceremony was interesting, and she didn't want to miss it by falling asleep. Asking the question helped keep her awake.

"For this particular ceremony, yes. Hush, no talking." Myleetra circled the room yet again, making another little gesture.

Finally, Myleetra called, "Air, earth, fire and water! Hear this summons from your daughter!" She sat cross-legged on the floor again, visibly exhausted.

Nothing happened for a very long time.

Then Bluestocking realised that she felt slightly different. When Myleetra had told her to imagine herself as part of the chair, she had experienced a slight downward pressure on her body. Now she could feel the chair's legs pressing into the floor and the floor connected to the walls, in turn connected to the huge white rock, could feel a connection all the way down to the base of the world. She could feel the rocks and soils of the earth, as if it was part of her very flesh. Cool, damp, musty, but nourishing. But she could not move. *I'm a part of Whiterock now,* she thought. It didn't bother her.

Now her consciousness moved up through the rocks as if she were swimming to the surface. Now she was part of the caverns with the silk spiders in it. Ugh! Suddenly they seemed repellent, threatening. Upwards again, and she felt the tramp of feet on the lowest floor; again, upwards and she was in the library walls.

She felt herself moving, not only through stone but through the pressed silk of the shelves, into the first box. She felt like the sun on a hot summer's day, the power contained within the scroll burning her, as if she'd spent too long lying out of doors.

She felt a faint tickle of comprehension, as if understanding was almost within her reach, but still it eluded her, a little fish swimming clear of her fingers.

She could feel something else was there as well. Huge and old, aware of her, but she was insignificant at the moment. But it was unhappy– no, it was furious, frustrated and pent-up.

It is not time yet.

It pushed her away, and her consciousness swam, back through the shelves, through the rocks, up into the chair.

She opened her eyes and wondered how long she had been asleep.

"I had the strangest dream." She yawned. "What happened?"

Myleetra shook her head and smiled, but looked sad. "Nothing," she said. "It's as I feared. It isn't time to work the spell."

With sinking heart, Bluestocking asked the obvious question. "When will be right?"

Myleetra studied her nails. "Not for another twenty-four days. Three days into the New Year."

Bluestocking lowered her head. "Too late," she whispered.

***

Up above, narrow thoroughfares were lined on each side by stalls selling roasted ground-nuts and other delicacies and were crowded with revelers, the congestion made worse by clumps of spectators and jugglers, stilt-walkers and fire-breathers.

"Bluestocking!" A familiar shriek cut across the crowd. Bluestocking turned as Lexi hugged her. Bluestocking just stopped herself recoiling from the smell of wine on the Princess's breath. "It's good to see you out and about! Come, walk with me," Lexi commanded.

They passed Arial, who was talking to a pair of militia-men, making urgent gestures. When he saw them, he stopped and smiled and made a little bow.

"Odd little man, isn't he?" Lexi said.

"I think he's very nice," Bluestocking said and added, "but I don't really know him."

Bluestocking allowed her mind to drift while Lexi steered both the conversation and them, the crowds so dense they were slow to part. As always, it seemed to Bluestocking that Lexi wanted to talk mostly about her sister and Cas. And how she talked!

Bluestocking, who had quickly grown tired and frustrated, almost snapped at her several times, but just managed to keep her mouth shut. *No sense in alienating two royal sisters,* she told herself sternly several times.

When the crowds had thinned and the curfew bell tolled, Lexi hugged her again and said, "Come round tomorrow night." She giggled. "By royal command."

Bluestocking smiled tiredly and stifled a yawn. "I'll do that," she promised

She staggered home and, exhausted, kicked open her door and threw her papers on her bed.

"Mistress?" Kyr appeared from the bathroom, cloth in hand. She wiped her forehead with her hand and crossing to close the door, grimaced, so faintly that Bluestocking almost missed it.

"What's wrong?" Bluestocking asked, when what she really wanted to ask was, *What were you doing down with that witch?*

Kyr smiled tightly. "Just a headache. Tail end of *that* time."

"I'm sorry," Bluestocking said. *Do you mean something different by **that** time?* "Do you need to lie down?"

Kyr looked stunned and seemed lost for words. Then she shook her head. "'Tis only a headache." She added, still struggling for words, "but thank you for your kindness, milady."

"You are allowed to look at me." Bluestocking added, "You don't offend me by existing, you know." She smiled, to remove the sting from her words, and Kyr smiled back, wanly.

"No one's ever–" Kyr broke off, at a loss for words again. "The princesses, to them I'm just a possession, like that chair. You wouldn't ask your chair if it needed to lie down, would you?"

"No," Bluestocking said, watching Kyr intently.

"I mean, I'm very grateful, and thank you, milady."

"What news on the murders?" Bluestocking asked, to ease the awkward silence.

"Have you heard the latest gossip?" Kyr said.

Bluestocking smiled, but shook her head and said nothing of Mari, merely hoping that the woman was all right. She kept quiet, knowing full well that this would start Kyr talking. The murders, together with snippets of gossip from around the Palace, were the main excitement in Kyr's drab life.

Kyr leaned forward, "Apparently, the murders are the work of a foreigner," she said, licking her lips.

"Yesterday, you said that the killings were done by a local," Bluestocking said innocently. "The day before, that it was one of the royal family gone mad and their identity kept secret." She raised an eyebrow, and Kyr shrugged.

"That was then," she said and, undeterred, elaborated on the theories about the unnamed foreign agitator of unknown origin.

The one good thing about her banal chatter, Bluestocking thought, *is that at least it relieves me of the need to answer her. Or to even* ***think*** *about anything;* for which Bluestocking was profoundly grateful. She sighed and massaged her temples. "Sometimes it feels as if my head will explode," she complained. Kyr began to rub her head, making soothing noises.

Bluestocking stared at the plate that Kyr had put in front of her, as if noticing it for the first time. "Who pays for the food?"

"What?" Kyr said, frowning in puzzlement.

"I *said,* who pays for the food?"

Kyr said, "The royal household, of course. You're a state visitor. Your visit was agreed to by Arial, and the King concurs with everything Arial agrees." The way she said it, Bluestocking might have been a foolish child asking why the world was flat. It just *was*. Everyone knows that, her tone seemed to say.

"Oh," Bluestocking said. *If Cavi wants me thrown out,* she thought, *she could presumably have arranged it, simply by cutting off my food. Couldn't she?*

"I'll run you a bath, and put some salts in it," Kyr said. "They'll help you relax."

Ah, yes, Bluestocking thought. *The inevitable bath.* It had become a comforting ritual.

Every night Kyr undressed her with heart-stopping slowness, standing so close that Bluestocking's breath caught in her throat. Tonight Bluestocking looked away. *I wish you wouldn't stand so close, and look so longingly,* she thought, but Kyr's behaviour was sufficiently innocuous that Bluestocking couldn't say anything without appearing foolish. And she didn't *really* wish it anyway.

But that last thought was getting too close to her dreams to be comfortable.

Every night since arriving, Bluestocking had dreamed. The difference was that unlike any she had ever had before, these dreams had gradually unfolded, as if she were participating in a story. At first superficially innocent, the dreams had become increasingly disturbing as they had grown ever more graphic. The last few nights they had been absolutely drenched with sex.

Initially the mystery figure with her in them was androgynous. After several nights it took on the physique of a hooded woman. When– the next night– the woman threw back her hood, there was only smoothness where a face should have been. Slowly, night by night it took on distinctive features, until it was Kyr who straddled Bluestocking's bound body, making her arch her back in ecstasy.

In her nocturnal visions, they writhed together, bodies slick with sweat, on beds, and tables, even on the carpeted floor. Sometimes they bathed together and coupled in the bath, taut-nippled, hair water-slicked, other times they waited until after they had emerged.

Her nocturnal visions were disturbing and left her so highly charged that her fingers seemed to have no choice but to slide between her thighs and search for her clitoris. Her breathing getting ever-shallower, she sought a relief that would not come.

Tonight Bluestocking lay back, letting the tension ooze away. The bathroom filled with steam, and the water was as hot as she could stand it, burning her skin and assaulting her nerve endings. She laid right back, allowing the day to drain away.

She became aware of Kyr watching her as she lay back. Once she would have blushed, but now she simply stared back, feeling the heat rising in her.

"I'll help you dress," Kyr said huskily.

Kyr was unusually clumsy, but Bluestocking didn't complain once, even when Kyr pressed her hand against Bluestocking's breast. Instead Bluestocking stared deep into Kyr's eyes, refusing to give the slave the pleasure of thinking that she was scared, instead issuing a counter-challenge. To her delight, Kyr eventually buckled, and looked away.

"I'll see you later," Bluestocking said as she left the bath. Once outside, she leaned back against the wall and exhaled deeply, trying to stop her hands from shaking with desire.

***

"I was just coming to see you," Bluestocking said, smiling.

"I am honoured," Lexi curtsied. "A visit from you three nights in a row."

"If it's a problem–"

"Don't be silly! Of course it isn't!" Lexi half-scolded her. "I'm going to see a play. Do you want to go as well?"

"I can't," Bluestocking said. *Since I quarreled with your sister, any invitations from Whiterock society have mysteriously dried up.*

"Why not? Come as my guest."

Bluestocking shrugged, trying to find a way of saying it.

"Nothing to wear?" Lexi asked. "I'm sure I've got something that'll fit you, we're about the same size, after all."

"I *can't*," Bluestocking said, scuffing her foot along the ground and staring down at it. She could feel Lexi's gaze, could sense the princess' growing perplexity and annoyance.

"Can't, or won't?"

"Can't," Bluestocking looked up, bit at her lower lip, then said, "Please don't look at me like that! You're about the only friend I have here!"

Lexi's annoyance vanished as quickly as it had appeared. "Whatever is the matter?" Her eyes widened. "Is it Cas? Has he done something?"

Bluestocking shook her head. Taking a deep breath, she told Lexi about her arguments with Cas and then with Cavi.

Lexi boggled; there was simply no other word for it. "He told you he *loved* you?" As usual, Lexi put her own individual interpretation on what she was told.

"Of course not!" Bluestocking snapped. "He asked if I felt anything for him– as usual, there's no feeling for anyone else but him, in his world–" she stopped abruptly. She had been about to say, "like all royalty," but just stopped in time.

"It doesn't sound as if he feels anything for Cavi," Lexi said, smiling. "So he's marrying purely for politics, not love." She shrugged. "It's a shame he can't find a woman as useful to him as Cavi, and who he could love." Lexi pressed her hand to Bluestocking's shoulder. "I'll see you later." 'She smiled, clearly wanting to reassure Bluestocking. "Don't you worry about them."

Bluestocking thought as Lexi turned away, *There speaks a woman who has no idea of reality. Who's never had to worry about the consequences of upsetting someone far more powerful than her.*

***

"Good morning, Bluestocking."

"Oh, Arial. I was miles away!"

"I'm sorry I startled you. Where are you going so early?"

"The Library," Bluestocking said, "as always."

"A strangely tortuous route."

Bluestocking smiled and shrugged. "I like to look at the day-keepers on my walk to work. It's not like Ravlatt, where they're dotted at random amongst the populace." She added, explaining, "There, any daykeeper can be used by a passer-by as an oracle."

Each day, as the bear had given way to the gopher and in turn to the snake, the various day-keepers on duty had changed the combination of coloured banners festooning the Day-House, and a different line of petitioners would gather at first light to ask their chances of success in a venture, or what qualities a child conceived or born on such a day would have. Here they were given their own little square, Ur Atan N'ur Kalgaxz– The Place of The Days– with a fancy little faux-stone hut (doubtless made of the ubiquitous silk, Bluestocking guessed wryly) which groups of churches took a day in turn to maintain, depending on their god's affiliation to the day in question. *Although,* she thought, *every day there seems to be someone attending from the church of Brighannon. How long before they outlaw other churches? Would the peoplace accept it?*

Instead, she said, "From here I like to climb up to the top levels for a glimpse of the sky, then circle the Palace walls on the way to work. Would you care to join me?" By watching the changing of the days,

Bluestocking eased a little of the loneliness and sense of being far from home that she'd felt since arriving and more importantly, she kept a sense of how long she had until the end of the year.

Arial peered at the drizzle from under the awning and shuddered. "I fear I'd only slow you down. You walk this way every morning?"

Bluestocking nodded. "It helps me gather my thoughts before starting work."

Arial watched the other people scurrying from shelter to shelter. "The place is buzzing with activity." He added wryly, "I'm *not* usually up here– or anywhere else– this early, as you may have guessed."

Bluestocking nodded, still pre-occupied. "You encounter everyone up here on top of the Rock. From the almost statuary guards on official buildings, the wall of wizards working the weather, shamans divining their oracles through strolling couples— such as Cas and Cavi– to clerks and merchants hurrying to appointment."

Arial shivered. "Why would anyone want to walk in this weather?"

"It's the only time I get to see the daylight," Bluestocking said. She laughed bitterly. "Even so, one day is very much like another." She added quickly, "Please don't think I'm criticizing your King's ideas. But in Ravlatt, I'm used to harsh winters that give way only with grinding reluctance to a short spring. Some days there is cold, clammy grayness, such as you have here." She sighed wistfully. "But also clear, bitterly cold nights that turn into days of fierce bright winter sunlight. Here, it's always the same: Rainy mornings and dry afternoons." She rubbed her forehead as if she had a headache.

"Bluestocking," Arial touched Bluestocking's arm. "Do you think you might be working too hard?"

"Probably," Bluestocking admitted, then with what was clearly a desperate attempt at cheerfulness, pointed at the horns stitched to the day-keeper's head-piece, "I thought today was the day of the Wolf?"

Arial shook her head. "No, it's the Bison."

"That explains the horns," Bluestocking said, and her shoulders slumped. "Less than two phases to New Year." She sighed. "Arial, could I ask for your help?"

"Ask," Arial said.

"I have had a…disagreement, I suppose you would call it, with two of the Princesses."

"Two?"

"Evi is…uneasy…with the idea of my translating the scrolls," Bluestocking said.

"You know," he said with the ghost of a smile. "It's not a good idea to offend these ladies."

"I'm learning that," Bluestocking said and sighed. "But I don't think I'm going to be able to finish the translation by the end of the year. Can we– would the King agree to me staying beyond the New Year?"

Arial shook his head. "I'm sorry. I'm fighting to keep you here even that long." At her look of panic, he held his hand up. "Don't worry. The King has agreed that you can stay to the end of the year, but beyond that…it wouldn't be politic to push for an extension at the moment."

Bluestocking blinked back tears, and as she turned away, Arial reached out and squeezed her shoulder, but she simply said, "I'd better get to work. The Gods be with you." She cut short her walk and descended the steps back down through the levels to the Library.

However, she never quite reached her destination. Instead, as she was opening the door, a voice cut into her train of thought.

"Princess Evivalesinan wishes to see you," the messenger said.

She was about to argue when she had a thought. She produced from within a pocket the substance she had scraped from around Kyr's mouth. "What is this?" She waved it under the messenger's nose.

He recoiled, eyes widening. "It's *Skrai*," he said at last, looking uneasy. "Where did you get that from?"

"And what is Skrai?"

He frowned. "You don't know? But you have some..." he seemed to come to a decision. "It's a narcotic. It saps the will, rendering the taker extremely pliable. Used in certain cults that my mistress would like to, ahem, end. Where did you get it?"

"Please pass my apologies to your mistress. I will be unable to meet her today–"

"But–"

"—tell her that what detains me concerns this," Blue said.

Chapter 6

The days avalanched through the latter end of Thirteen-month toward the end of the dying year, now only ten days away. The land gradually warmed as mid-winter edged toward spring and the renewal of the world, but Bluestocking barely noticed it, except subconsciously, as she needed to wear one layer less of woollens to walk outside.

Two evenings after meeting Arial, Bluestocking strolled again with Lexi and tried not to think about the passing days.

Bluestocking was unsettled by the constant sense of things moving in the shadows, so common-place here that no one even seemed to notice, let alone comment on it. High in the sky, a gibbous moon had waned past the first quarter. The evening air had a just-washed feel to it. "It wasn't scheduled to rain so late today," Lexi said and added complacently, "Daddy will use someone's guts to make garters."

They rounded a corner, and Cas strolled toward them, deep in conversation with Cavi, their heads bowed toward one another. Their guards were a discreet distance away, yet close enough if needed. They looked up at the same moment, and the colour drained from Cavi's face. "Sister." She pointedly ignored Bluestocking.

"A nice evening for a walk," Lexi said. "Good evening, Cas. Are you well?"

"Very well, thank you," Cas said with a smile that faltered. "Bluestocking, how goes the translation?"

"It goes," Bluestocking said, equally coolly.

They passed without anyone breaking stride. When they were out of hearing, Lexi said, "Poor Cavi."

"Why?" Bluestocking said. "I'd have thought her in quite an enviable position."

Lexi studied her nails, holding her hand up to the light of a brazier. "She's changed from how she was before he came. She's in love and so scared of losing him that she's become almost– oh, I don't know, it's so hard to explain."

"Like a shadow?"

Lexi shook her head. "It's as if she's a different person at times: when he's around."

Something in the comment set Bluestocking's mind racing, but she knew that worrying at it was futile, so she made herself think of something else. What sprang to mind was Kyr. That was only a little less uncomfortable, so she asked, "Where do you want to go?" to distract herself.

Lexi said, "I have a bottle of dessert wine begging to be tasted."

They strolled back to Lexi's quarters, which took up enough space to lodge a hundred families. Lexi treated Bluestocking like a sister, but the sudden distance between Cas and herself had taught Bluestocking to be careful, so she guarded her tongue even as she smiled at Lexi's prattling.

All the time as they walked back to Lexi's chambers, Bluestocking kept trying not to think of Kyr. There was something in Lexi's comment about her sister being someone else that would help with her translation. If she could manage to keep mulling over irrelevancies, she might suddenly receive the sort of revelations that followed long periods of ignoring what she really wanted to think about. It was as if the Scrolls were shy creatures who disliked being ignored.

"Sorry?"

"I said, how are you getting along with Kyr?"

"Very well," Bluestocking said, "generally." She regretted the last word the moment she said it, thinking, *Lexi's probably the kind of owner who believes a good thrashing's the answer to every problem.*

"Generally? Not all the time?"

"It's like, she's two different people," Bluestocking said. "Most of the time she's sweet, and caring, and wants to serve me as well as possible."

"But..."

"There've been a few times when she's like someone else." Bluestocking saw Lexi's eyes widen. "She's an arrogant... well...slattern."

"I'll speak to her," Lexi said grimly.

"Please don't," Bluestocking begged. "Let me sort this out."

Slowly, Lexi nodded, and changed the subject with her usual abruptness. "There was another murder last night. Papa's going absolutely mad, talking about making curfew earlier, limiting exeats and other over-reactions."

Bluestocking was glad that she hadn't voiced the sinister yet ridiculous thought that she'd had several times; that Kyr's moods seemed to alter just before and after the killings.

***

"She really said that?" Bluestocking giggled as Lexi nodded solemnly and then also burst into giggles. The room was taking on an uneasy pitch, and remembering her first night in Whiterock, Bluestocking placed her hand over her glass when the slave tried to refill it.

A long, contented silence settled over them. Bluestocking said at last, "I should be going. Another long day in the library awaits."

"Kyr will walk you home," Lexi said. "With a couple of guards," she added, over Bluestocking's protests. "I'm not having you end up dead in an alleyway, 'cause you were so proud, woman! It's an order!"

"Aye, mum," Bluestocking snapped a wobbly salute, and they burst into giggles. "Thanks," she said awkwardly.

"For what?"

"I'd have gone mad these last few days without a friend like you," Bluestocking said.

Kyr appeared in the doorway. "Majesty?"

Lexi said, "The lady will need assistance getting home," then burst into giggles again.

Kyr helped Bluestocking put her cape on and buttressed her as they weaved along the corridor.

"You can go now," Kyr told the guards when they reached Bluestocking's suite. "Come on." She suddenly sounded weary. "Into bed."

"Are you coming?" Bluestocking said.

"Mistress, you're drunk–"

"And you're a slave," Bluestocking said, "but I'll be sober tomorrow." She blinked owlishly. "Sorry. Not nice thing to say."

"No," Kyr said, unbuttoning Bluestocking's dress. Humming, Bluestocking ran her finger down Kyr's jaw. "Mistress, when I said you were drunk it was a warning. Don't do something that you'll regret."

"The only thing I'll regret," Bluestocking said with the careful precision of a drunkard trying to sound sober, "is if you don't stay with me tonight."

Kyr kissed Bluestocking's finger as it rounded her jaw, then bit on it, hard enough to make Bluestocking gasp but not enough to break the skin.

"Do you want me to beg?" Bluestocking asked throatily.

"It would make a change," Kyr said coolly, "from me begging. I seem to remember a similar conversation."

"So it's revenge you want?"

Kyr shook her head. "Only for you to be absolutely, *absolutely* sure."

Bluestocking put her hands on either side of Kyr's face, staring into her eyes. "I'm sure." They kissed, gently at first, then fiercely, until they toppled over in a heap.

***

Bluestocking awoke from deep sleep to a profound sense of disorientation. She had dreamed that she had seduced by Kyr. She blushed at the memory of their bodies entwining, arching in time to a tempo of tongues and hands exploring, blood pounding, tides of lust surging and roaring and ebbing and rising again and again, until they were too exhausted to go on. She blushed at the thoughts but smiled, too.

In her dream, she had imagined that she had slept, but half-awoke to a little rush of cold air as Kyr climbed out of bed and drew back the curtain to gaze out of the window. The moon had been hiding behind clouds, but then it peeked out, and instead of Kyr, something monstrous but ill-defined stood in the window for a long time. Bluestocking couldn't work out whether it was its shape or its dimensions that was so wrong. It turned and stared at her, but then the moon went in, and it padded back across the floor, and it was Kyr that climbed back under the covers.

A chink of half-light shone through a gap in the badly-drawn curtains. It was a little noisier than usual outside her rooms, and at the same moment as she realised that she must have slept late, she rolled over and found herself staring into Kyr's wide-open eyes, which gave no clue to her thoughts.

"Oh," Bluestocking said, "it was no dream, then." She smiled shyly and snuggled into Kyr's armpit, nuzzling her gently. "Morning," she whispered and slid lengthways against Kyr.

"Morning," Kyr said, her voice hesitant.

"What's the matter?"

"Nothing," Kyr said, voice flat.

"Tell me what's the matter." Bluestocking ran her nails down Kyr's flank, making the slave shudder.

"I wondered..."

"Yes?" Bluestocking said. "Tell me," she urged with a smile.

"I wondered if you regretted last night..." Kyr said.

Bluestocking shook her head and kissed Kyr's cheek, then ran her tongue along the jawbone.

Kyr said slowly, "When we get dressed, we go back to being mistress and slave."

Bluestocking shook her head. "Not now. Not after last night."

"Yes, now," Kyr said savagely. "The minute we leave this room, I must behave differently."

"But in here." Bluestocking touched her breast, "and in here, you're my lover. As much my owner as I am yours."

"You say that now, but you'll change," Kyr said. "You have no idea of what it's like to be a slave."

Bluestocking thought of the Sisters of Beatitude, of mornings scouring cold stone floors while it was still dark outside. Her laugh was a raven's caw. "Don't flatter yourself, Kyr." She regretted the harshness of her words the moment they were out of her mouth. *Too much like mistress to slave,* she thought, and added softly, "I didn't mean to sound so cruel. But you mustn't think you're the only woman who's ever known slavery."

"And you would?" Kyr asked incredulously. She hooted derisively, then added, "It's all right for you, mistress, with your airs and your soft hands and your right to keep your legs crossed when you want to. Have you ever wondered where your next meal was coming from? Or why that nice man or woman has suddenly turned into a ravening beast?"

"There are all sorts of slavery," Bluestocking said, remembering the petty cruelties that even the humblest noviciate could visit as a free-woman on a slave– especially a gifted, precocious slave.

Kyr seemed not to have heard her, retreating instead into memories, her eyes taking on the distant, slightly unfocussed look of someone lost completely in the past. "I can only just remember Momma, as a vague blob of warmth and comfort. Any security I might have felt vanished– like a man's promise when he's had his way– when her master sold me off."

Bluestocking reached out and touched Kyr's cheek. The slave flinched slightly, then saw the hurt look in Bluestocking's eyes and kissed her lover's hand before continuing.

"Since then, from the time when I could walk, I've had men and women alike sticking things up me and in me. Don't misunderstand, mistress–"

"–Bluestocking–"

"—Mistress," Kyr emphasised. "Sometimes it's good; I love to have a man inside me, all big and hard. Better still when it's a woman. I love the way we move together, and when it's your tongue slippery-sliding inside me like a little eel, that's best of all."

"Was that what that other night was all about?" Bluestocking hadn't dared mention that other night at Myleetra's until now. She had wanted to ask Kyr so many times why the slave was down there. "Down at the witch's–"

Kyr stopped her with a finger over her lips. "I'm a pantheist, see?" Her accent grew broader as she grew more excited. "Witches ain't like them church-y folks with their airs and graces and, 'don't you put that thing near me, husband.' All witches wants is fucking and sucking and licking, and I," she finished with a huge, demonic grin, "*love* it!" She leaned back on her haunches, and Bluestocking stared at her, open-mouthed. Kyr wiped her eyes. "I've never admitted that to anyone until now, see? How much pleasure I get out of seeing hoity-toity lords and ladies reduced to my level by what I can do to 'em."

"Oh," Bluestocking said, but Kyr rattled on, "This woman once borrowed me off the princesses. She wore thigh high leather boots and carried a riding crop everywhere, even though there are no horses up here. That should have given me a clue. If I hadn't guessed when she asked them– *very* carefully– whether there was anything they didn't want her to do to me."

"Kyr, please." Bluestocking tried to cover her lover's mouth,.

Kyr pushed her hand away. She said, "I want you to understand what it's like, what I'll go back to when you've gone. I'm not just saying this to shock you or make you feel sorry for me. I don't want no cheap pity. But you must understand." She gazed at her, pleading, and Bluestocking nodded.

Kyr continued, "The princesses looked at one another and shrugged. Cavi said, "As long as she comes back to us unmarked, with no serious damage, you can do what you want– she's only a slave, there are plenty more like her." Lexi said, "Just keep any marks out of sight," and turned away." Kyr pressed her lips together and wiped her eye

Bluestocking placed her hand over Kyr's mouth. "Now listen to me," she hissed. "I am not the princesses, nor that woman. I am me. You understand?" She kept her hand over Kyr's mouth and urged, "You understand?"

Kyr nodded, and Bluestocking removed her hand. "I want you to call me Blue, when we're alone here. Will you?"

Kyr said, "Yes, Blue." She sounded so contrite that Bluestocking burst out laughing. Bluestocking kissed her, and Kyr responded exultantly.

"What would you be, if you could do anything at all?" Kyr asked dreamily.

Bluestocking ran her finger down Kyr's side. "I'd be exactly what I am," she said, "a linguist."

Colin Harvey

"Not a warrior, or a wizard, or a queen?" Kyr asked playfully, stroking the arm that rested on her chest.

"I might have said that before I came here," Bluestocking said, "but I've seen too much of them at close quarters to think that they get any more out of life than I do– on good days. Days like today."

"Yes?"

"Well, last night, anyway."

Kyr giggled. "Flatterer. I bet you say that to all the girls."

"What girls?" Bluestocking stiffened. "You don't think I make a habit–"

"I was teasing." Kyr pressed her finger to Bluestocking's lips and kissed her breast.

"Sorry." Bluestocking's breathing caught as Kyr stroked her nipple.

"You wouldn't be a queen or a priestess?" Kyr asked wide-eyed, seemingly amazed.

"No," Bluestocking said between gasps. She took a deep breath and added, still breathily, "They eat, sleep and crap the same as the rest of us, my love. Don't get fooled by the wrapper, it's what's inside that counts."

"Like what's inside…here?" Kyr asked.

Bluestocking whimpered. She said, fighting to keep her breathing even, "What about you? What would you be? If you could be anyone or anything?"

"I'd be, a…queen," Kyr said, her own breath starting to catch.

"You already are."

"What?"

"A queen," Bluestocking said, then kissed Kyr, long and languorously, and harder and harder. When they came up for air, she added, "You're my queen, anyway."

"Oh, my darling," Kyr gasped, "you say the sweetest things." She kissed Bluestocking again, and they stopped talking while they made love.

When they stopped, Bluestocking almost told Kyr about herself, but even as she opened her mouth, Kyr slid down the bed, and the moment passed. "I...don't...regret...a thing," Bluestocking gasped, and added, "There." Any thoughts she might have had about telling Kyr vanished. Afterwards she slept again.

***

When she awoke, she was alone. She dressed quickly and hearing the clock-tower, counted the chimes. "Ten hours," she muttered, grimacing. Snatching an apple, she munched as she pulled the door shut behind her, nodded at the guard stationed at the end of the passage and headed straight for the Library, acutely self-conscious of the huge smile that she wore.

When she arrived, Copel placed the scroll-box on the last free lectern. "The Library's busy this morning," she said, thinking, *at least he can't see your idiotic grin.*

Copel cocked his head to one side, bird-like. "You sound happy this morning." He added, "Our patrons don't work over the year end, so they're finishing off before the break."

"You're not closing the Library?" Bluestocking asked sharply, her smile vanishing.

Copel shook his head. "I have no interest in staying at home." He left her to her work.

That morning Bluestocking found it hard to concentrate. She kept thinking of Kyr, wondering what she was doing, remembering the night before, or fantasizing about later, no matter how sternly she reproached herself to concentrate on the task at hand.

Eventually the scrolls elbowed her lover from the forefront of her thoughts. She immersed herself in translation, worrying at their meaning, losing herself in a world of verbs, gerunds, perfect and imperfect tenses. Lost herself so completely that when a shadow fell across her, she didn't even notice at first.

"What?" Bluestocking said. Then, "Oh."

Evi stared down at her. Her face was obscured by shadow, but Bluestocking got the impression that it wore little friendship, sweetness or light.

"You've disregarded my instructions," Evi said.

"Highness—"

"I have decided," Evi said, "that you shouldn't be here. Your translation of the scrolls is sacrilegious."

"What? It's sacrilege to seek knowledge? To spread the words of your God?" Bluestocking was incredulous and inadvertently raised her voice. Several other scholars lifted their heads in unison.

"Your lack of respect shows exactly why it is dangerous to allow an unbeliever to study the scrolls!" Evi shouted. She made a visible effort to control her temper. "Think on it. Words are weapons. With a name, you give and maintain status. With words said in the heat of the moment, you can start or end a love affair. With a spell, you can cause an avalanche. These meaning of these texts is lost to us for a reason–"

"Because language has changed," Bluestocking said.

But Evi waved her interruption away as if shooing an insect, "—because the gods do not wish us to understand them. Would you give poison to an infant to play with?"

"How do you know that they are dangerous, if you don't know what they contain?"

"Because I know the history of Whiterock, and I know what has happened to the last four meddlers who played with these texts over the last several thousand years. Think on it. Show some respect, child."

It was Evi's calling her "child" that did it. *Don't lose your temper,* Bluestocking thought, but it was as if the instruction never reached her mouth. "The only disrespect being shown is by you to a scholar who's been invited by the King and Prime Minister."

"If I have anything to do with it, that invitation will be withdrawn by this time tomorrow!"

"Go ahead and try!" Bluestocking shouted back. "I'll see you dead before a brat like you drives me away!"

"Ladies!" Copel's whisper interrupted them, as he laid hands on their arms.

"Shut up, old man!" Evi stormed out of the Library.

Copel shrugged, as if to say, *What can you do with someone like that?*

Bluestocking took a deep breath, and sat down, shaking with anger. The readers in the Library, all men, stared at her open-mouthed. She glared back at one old man until he looked away, then glowered at another. By the time he looked away, the others had got the message.

Still, her concentration was broken. She stuck at her task for a little while longer, but finally gave up, shaking her head. Presenting the scroll back to Copel, she said evenly, "Sometimes you get a day when nothing goes right. You just accept that it's a day wasted."

Inside though, she felt differently. *I'm so close,* she thought. *It just needs one more moment of inspiration and the pieces of the puzzle will fall into place. I need to find somewhere quiet, where I can think undisturbed.*

Her emotions told her that she should find Kyr, but the dispassionate, analytical mind that usually held sway over her emotions knew that minutes wasted now could prove precious at the end of the year. Much as she longed to hold her lover, to pour out the hurt that she felt from the quarrel with Evi, that constant sense of grains of sand falling into the bottom of an hour-glass was greater.

As she left the Library, she deliberately didn't think about where she was going, but instead walked at random.

And ended up in Gallows Square.

She realized with a guilty pang that it had been several days since she'd visited; time just passed so quickly.

She took deep breaths to calm herself. All the way to the square, she had been conscious of side-long glances from passers-by, in a way that she hadn't since she'd first arrived. *You're being foolish,* she thought. *No one here worries about who you are.*

Except that you've just threatened the eldest daughter of the King of Whiterock, a sly little voice warned her. No amount of calm could deny the damage she'd done to any chances of gaining an extension. *Stupid girl,* the inner voice chided. *That's two of three princesses you've offended.*

The square was quiet, but not as deserted as previous occasions. A couple of lovers strolled arm in arm on their way to somewhere else. A lone soldier stood on guard, and a peddler lugged a sack on the far side of the square.

Bluestocking shuffled aimlessly past the gallows tree, which was now empty and approached the lone guard. "What happened to the heretic?" she asked. "Has he gone?"

The guard nodded. "He died two days ago. You a heretic spotter?"

Bluestocking shrugged. "I've never seen one before," she lied easily.

The guard nodded. "Not much to see. He was more like a maggot than a man, after they cut his arms and legs off. He pretty much gave up living at the end. Funny. For a while, it looked like he'd make a fight of it, and live past the ten day mark– that's the record for a heretic."

He nodded to a platform on the other side of the Square that she hadn't noticed before. "He's up there."

Bluestocking squinted at Visohn's decaying body, where several crows picked at moldering tatters of flesh.

"I'm finishing my shift," the guard said, winking at her. "Let me buy you a drink."

Bluestocking smiled as demurely as she could. "No, thank you, sir."

"Oh, well." He sighed. "I'll leave you with him," he nodded at the platform.

The square soon emptied. Although occasional locals taking a short-cut still hurried through, apart from the corpse, Bluestocking was alone. It suited her. She was able to once again run through what she knew of the language of the scrolls, from which she suspected the modern dialects of the lands around Whiterock were bastardized corruptions.

Some time later, a pair of battered men's boots appeared at the top of her vision.

She ignored them at first, but they didn't move. Eventually she looked up.

"Hello, missee," said the peddler she'd seen when she had first arrived. His eyes glinted brightly, his discoloured teeth bared in what was probably meant to be a friendly smile.

Too late, she managed to summon the power of speech. "Do I know you?" she asked coolly. "Why do you disturb my thoughts?"

He shuffled from foot to foot, the bright bird-like eyes never blinking, the teeth still bared until she began to wonder if he was lack-witted.

Just as she began to think that she'd worried about nothing, and made a simple peasant into a bogey-man, his next words removed any illusions she harboured. "I know you, Blue," he said, his accent clear enough now. Pure Katstevya Province, in the Far East– where she had grown up. "That is yer name ain't it? But I'm figgerin' it ain't what ye call yerself nowadays. More like 'Mistress Bluestocking,' hey?" His laugh was a sighing wheeze. "Took me a long time to place ye, but I never forgets a face. Helps me remember them that owes me money and to dodge me creditors." He laughed his little wheezing sigh at his own joke. His smile faded, and she wondered how she'd ever thought him a simpleton. "I'm reckonin' it'd be a shame for a fine young girl to end up at a Retribution, don't ye?"

"I have no money," Bluestocking said.

The peddler shrugged. "Get some."

"I can't! I see no one but a slave every day. My food and lodging are taken care of."

"That's yer problem, missee." He studied her.

She stared back, warily, like a mouse that knows the cat is about to pounce, but doesn't know which way to leap to safety. "What's your name?"

He smiled, and the image of a cat became so strong she half expected to see a mouse's tail poking out between his teeth. "Why? Ye going to work some devilish spell on me?"

"Hardly," Bluestocking said. "Even I know that name spells are the easiest to work, but easiest to counter. Are you afraid to tell me?"

The peddler's eyes flashed. "A girl with spirit. That's good for when ye have to sell yerself to raise money." He laughed nastily. "Ye looked shocked. Not so cocky now, are ye, missee? Just my little joke. The name is Aton, by the by. Ye'll need to get used to my sense of humour." His accent softened again. "I'm sure you will in time." The threat was implicit. He wasn't going to settle for a single payment but keep bleeding her until she had nothing left. "You got 'til tomorrow night to find one hundred crowns." He was no longer smiling.

"I won't need it," Bluestocking replied, equally grimly. "I don't have any kind of money, no matter how small."

"Mayhap I'll take payment in kind?" Aton leered. He flinched, dodging her slap just in time. "Ye'll regret that!"

"Not as much as you will, if you ever suggest that again!" Bluestocking stormed out of the square.

***

She wouldn't go back to her room yet, she decided. She needed to calm down before she saw Kyr again. The villain had almost managed– no, he *had* managed– to taint the day. She felt unclean. Besides, she had the feeling Kyr wouldn't understand. She would suggest that Bluestocking give herself to him. It was, from a slave's perspective, the logical thing to do.

Instead she walked around the palace walls, taking deep breaths, gradually growing calm again.

Until she saw Prince Casimiripian walking straight toward her, deep in conversation with one of Princess Cavi's retinue. *He hasn't seen me,* she thought, and stepped back.

Too late. He looked up, and for a moment Bluestocking thought he might speak, but he glanced at Cavi's man then looked through her as if she wasn't there.

"Good afternoon, Your Highness," she said loudly, but he ignored her. Instead he said to his companion as they passed, "So, tell Princess Evi that Cavi will not be at home, but will speak with her later."

Bluestocking shrugged, but boiled with anger. She sat on a wall, gazed out over the countryside stretching back to the Empire and fought back a wave of homesickness.

You need to start mending bridges with these people, she thought. *It's unlikely that Cavi will talk to you, but you could try. If that fails, pass a message through Lexi, apologizing for your outburst.*

She sighed heavily, and climbing to her feet, set out for Cavi's chambers.

***

The corridor leading to Cavi's quarters was empty, the usual guard absent. Stomach churning, she walked to the great double door and rapped loudly.

No one answered, although, listening carefully, Bluestocking thought she heard the faint sounds of careful movement inside the doors. She knocked again, and waited.

There was still no response, but she heard another faint shuffling sound. She muttered, "For the God's sakes, if you're too scared to answer the door, at least have the sense to keep still."

The door opened a crack, and an old woman peered out. "She'm not in, Madame." She shut the door before Bluestocking could speak. *At least that explains the shuffling sounds,* Bluestocking thought. *Poor old girl looked almost too infirm to move.*

Bluestocking turned away. She walked perhaps a half dozen paces, when she heard a faint noise, so high pitched it was almost beyond the range of human hearing. But she had sharp ears. It sounded like the release of some kind of pressure from a container.

She walked on.

Bluestocking heard some voices behind her but didn't hear what was said, although one sounded like the Princess Evi.

She turned and saw a soundless flash of light ripple across the corridor. Immediately afterwards a burst of flame billowed outwards, and then came a dull roar.

Chapter 7

As a child Bluestocking had once seen a picture mirror. It showed an unnamed god sitting on a throne at the summit of a mountain, judging the first of a throng of mortal pilgrims who were climbing an impossibly long flight of steps toward it.

A novitiate cleaning the picture rail had caught the mirror, and it had smashed on the floor. The girl had been despatched to find a pan and a broom and eventually returned to sweep up the fragments, grumbling all the while.

While she was away, young Blue had sat and tried to put the fragments back together. None of the pieces had fitted, but the child had spent happy minutes playing with them.

The days after the balefire blast were like that. Nothing quite fitted together. Bits of those times seemed to run into other ones, while whole chunks seemed to vanish.

First fragment:

Bluestocking muttered, "If the Old High Tongue is the root from which today's languages derive, then why is this so bloody difficult?" She tore at her hair and mumbled, "The eagle flows out of the copper kettle? Fly, not flow? Unless..." She scrabbled amongst her notes and sighed. "I thought I had it then."

She'd been working since first light, sitting on her bed, Kyr curled up on the other side. It had been easy for Bluestocking to slide out from between the sheets without disturbing her. As soon as she thought it would be open, she headed for the Library.

She stared into space, remembering what Lexi had said about Cavi; *it's as if she becomes a different person at times*. The words rattled and rolled in her head. *At times...different.* She muttered, "What if the meaning of the word changes at particular times? Where is it?" she opened the scroll and copied what she was looking for down laboriously, then carried the scroll back to its box.

She took another scroll and sat down, working her way down through it, shaking her head from time to time and opening her eyes wide, as if trying to re-focus them. She looked up at a slight noise and realized that she was no longer alone. Several other people had arrived while she was distracted.

Her finger tracing the words was half-way down the scroll, when she stopped. Her eyes widened. "What if, instead of ***chiri***, the eagle, it was ***chira***, the western tongues for snake? The snake flows out of...wait a minute!" She worked her way back through her notes. "On the same basis, ***sionpen*** is an amphora, not ***sionpan***, the copper kettle... there's something here, something... something..." She rummaged through her notes on the creation myths of Whiterock and let out an excited squeal. One of the other readers swiveled and glared at her, and she hugged herself.

Second fragment:

The wall opposite the fire collapsed, and someone screamed. It seemed to go on and on, rising in pitch and volume until without warning, it stopped.

The ensuing silence was broken then by a low sobbing.

Bluestocking stood rooted to the spot, unable to go back to help, unable to go forward. She heard someone shout, "The Princess is in there. In Brighannon's name, get her out!"

Something that might have once been human crawled out into the corridor. It lay flat on its belly and pulled itself along with its arms to a small symphony of whimpers. When it raised an arm, blackened skin hung from it in delicate lace-like filigrees. The insignia on its tunic identified it as one of Cavi's retainers.

She should have gone back to help; that would have been the charitable thing to do. But even the suffering that Visohn had endured in Gallows Square paled compared to this unfortunate creature's torment. It turned toward Bluestocking, even though it couldn't possibly have seen her with those sightless white eyes. Bluestocking must have made a noise, or it must have sensed her movement.

She turned around and almost walked into Princess Cavi, whose rooms were behind her at the heart of the explosion.

"Gagh," Bluestocking said and swayed but managed to stay on her feet.

"What are you doing here?" Cavi asked. "What's going on?" She looked toward her rooms and stiffened. "Evi!" she shrieked. She shouted at one of her guards, "My sister was waiting for me in there!"

Third fragment:

"Will you be alright on your own?" Kyr asked, bustling around Bluestocking's chambers, putting away clean linen and tidying cups and plates into a pile.

Bluestocking nodded. "The Library's closed, so I'll work here on my notes." She was close now, she could feel it; the impatience was building within her until she was ready to explode. At first the manuscripts had seemed to fight her, but now she had the thought processes behind the scrolls gripped between her teeth, and she was damned if she was going to let them elude her.

Colin Harvey

She realized that Kyr was talking to her. "Sorry?"

Kyr smiled. "I said I'm sorry I have to leave you. But Cavi and Lexi are agreed for once that everyone should be present to prepare for the Memorial." She sighed. "I never liked her. Not that it matters more than a handful of dust to most folk whether a slave likes you–"

"It matters to me."

Kyr smiled. "–but I wouldn't wish such an end as that on anyone."

A fourth fragment:

Night had fallen by the time the Prime Minister finished interrogating the others and had worked his way around to Bluestocking. Tension and suspicion hung thick in the air with the dust from the collapsed wall.

The King had arrived, grim-faced, and insisted on looking over the scene, and no one had been allowed to leave while he did. Lexi and the Queen had arrived a few minutes later, and Lexi had to be escorted, weeping, back out on the supporting arms of her mother. Then Daragel arrived and waited just a few yards from Bluestocking, until the King beckoned.

"These are grave days, Majesty," Daragel said after they had exchanged the bare minimum of civilities. "Speaking frankly, a killer who has now murdered four times with increasing frequency and impunity is loose. You cannot guarantee the safety of your people."

Bluestocking was stunned at Daragel's insensitivity. Perhaps this was how little life– even royal life– was valued in the Western Alliance. Perhaps Lexi was right in wanting nothing to do with Daragel's people.

"Careful, Daragel," King Redoutifalia growled. "Bad enough that I must endure a killer's insolence without yours as well."

"Majesty, Princess Lexi will soon be an Alliance citizen, and I must protect her, even at the cost of my life."

"You think I don't care about my daughters who still live? Not only the one I've just lost?" For a moment the King allowed his grief to show, and Daragel paled and stepped back.

"Of course you do. I regret having to seem callous–"

"Aye, callous is the right word."

"But my duty is to the living, and Lexi is my country's future. Unless you can guarantee her safety, I must take precautions."

"That sounds like a threat."

"Can you guarantee her safety?"

"Enough!" The King raised his hand to strike Daragel. All around them soldiers tensed, but Daragel never moved. The King lowered his hand, and they relaxed fractionally.

"I could have you slaughtered on the spot. No one would lift a finger to save you." The King's voice was a gravel rumble, barely audible.

"My Emir would send another to replace me. One who was equally prepared to give his life for her." Daragel never looked away, even for a moment. "Unless you wish to break off the engagement between my master and Lexi. The Emir would surely consider that tantamount to a declaration of war."

"I said enough!" the King roared. "I will not tolerate this!"

"Forgive me," Daragel said, "but whether our emotions are bruised is irrelevant. We both have a duty to our people, surely?"

The King nodded, eyes narrowed.

"Then I'll ask again. Will you swear by Brighannon as to the safety of your daughter?"

"Daragel." the King whinnied. "No one can absolutely guarantee anything!"

Bluestocking thought, *invoking Brighannon was a masterstroke. Even the King balks at lying under oath to a god.*

"Of course a rock could fall on her," Daragel said soothingly, relaxing slightly. "Or lightning might strike her. But from the hand of this killer," Daragel leaned forward, striking the moment like a cobra. "Can you in Brighannon's name absolutely guarantee her safety?"

The King didn't answer but looked away.

"Then I must ask the Emir for guidance," Daragel said, his voice sad, unaware that Bluestocking watched him like a hawk. For a moment– and it might have been her imagination– she glimpsed a momentary smile. He added, "I'll send a messenger spirit."

Another fragment:

Bluestocking punched the air. "Yes!" She twirled round and round in the air. She stopped, smiling sheepishly at a small group that were talking to Copel but staring at her. It was typical of her luck that both Cas and Cavi were among the half-dozen people in the group. Lexi gave her a small wave, and Bluestocking smiled back.

She returned to her work, occasionally drumming her feet on the floor with excitement. Even Cavi's presence couldn't quite dampen her elation. After a few minutes she stopped and carried the scroll back to Copel. "I'm going to need the first one again, I'm afraid," she said.

"Does your work go well?" Daragel asked.

"It goes extremely well," Bluestocking said, bouncing up and down slightly, while she waited for Copel to return. "I discovered this morning that the characters in capitals mean something completely different from the same words in small letters." She wouldn't normally have exchanged two words with Daragel, but she had to speak, the excitement was welling out of her. She half laughed. "Not very interesting to anyone but a linguist, I suspect."

He smiled. "It's interesting to see the effect it has on you." He bowed. "I'm pleased for you," he added, and for the first time Bluestocking found something to like in the man.

"Does this mean you will be leaving our little kingdom by the agreed time?" Cavi had clearly been listening. Her voice was studiedly neutral.

"I hope so, Highness," Bluestocking said. "Oh, I do hope so." She returned to the translation and was soon oblivious of the others.

Another fragment:

"If you had seen the look on Daragel's face when he backed the King into a corner," Bluestocking said, "He was trying to look all concerned, but the oily snake couldn't hide his smugness. If the King hadn't lost half his wits with grief, he'd have caught that triumphant look. Whatever he's planning, it won't be anything that will do Whiterock much good."

Bluestocking swallowed and stared into space, and Kyr asked, "Was it really bad? The interrogation?" They had both carefully avoided talking about it until now.

"Just a little chat," Bluestocking said, staring into space. "Nice and friendly. They understood, they said, that I just happened to be in the wrong place at the time, but would I tell them what my argument with Evi had been about? Of course they didn't think I had anything to do with it. What would a citizen of the Empire want with killing the King's eldest daughter?' She shuddered. "All nice and friendly, but they led me past the cells, so I could see what it was like in there. And they made sure that I could hear the screams and whimpers of the prisoners." She thought, *it feels as if the world I thought as solid as the rocks I stand on is suddenly no more firm than a wisp of smoke.*

"But they let you go," Kyr said, cradling and stroking Bluestocking's head. "That's the important thing."

Bluestocking nodded. "Promise me," she said, "that you'll kill me, rather than let me face that again."

Kyr shook her head, "Oh, no. No, don't talk like that, my love. You're free now. Put it out of your mind."

"Promise me."

"I'll get you out, somehow. But I couldn't kill you."

"As long as you don't leave me there, kill me, free me, do whatever you have to do. But don't leave me to face that alone." Bluestocking buried her face in Kyr's shoulder.

"As long as you promise me the same thing," Kyr said. "I'm not as brave as you are. But I know I could face almost anything, as long as I knew you would come to end whatever torment I was facing. Will you promise me the same, my darling?"

"I promise," Bluestocking said.

Kyr stood, ready to leave.

"I think I'm the only person in Whiterock not invited to Evi's funeral," Bluestocking said. "Not that I'm bothered, honestly. Everywhere I go, as soon as I open my mouth, and people realize that I'm a foreigner, I start to get sideways looks."

"People are just a little jumpy at the moment," Kyr said. "Things will calm down in a few days. They'll make a few arrests, and things will go back to as before."

Bluestocking wasn't so sure. For the last two days she had felt the pressure of people's gazes; aimed not just at her, but at any strangers. Two vagrants had been strung up by enraged acolytes of Brighannon for not genuflecting as they passed the Church doors. It seemed that conversations stopped in mid-sentence as she passed, and more than once, she had seen gestures intended to ward off demons made at her.

She could almost taste the fear, anger and suspicion, hot and acrid on the breeze, when she ventured out into the corridors. Today at least she had an excuse for staying in.

A last fragment:

Bluestocking pinched the bridge of her nose and opened and closed her eyes, as if exercising them.

"I must insist that we close now, Maestress," Copel said. He had been saying it for the last hour, but each time she managed to beg a few more minutes out of him.

The late afternoon was just turning toward evening, and the inner recess of the library was lit by torches around the walls and a balefire lamp which Bluestocking had placed to shine its actinic blue light down onto her notes.

As Copel re-chained the scroll he said, "You seem very happy."

"I am," she said. "Perhaps it's a little premature to say it, but I think I've found the key."

"Really?"

Bluestocking thought, *perhaps it's my imagination, but he looks shocked.* "You look displeased," she said.

"Oh, no," he said quickly. "I'm delighted for you, don't think otherwise. It's a tremendous feat, if you've been able to achieve it. And so quickly."

"Hardly quickly," she said. "It's nearly the end of the year."

He didn't answer but turned away, seeming suddenly deep in thought.

"Good night," Bluestocking called as she left.

Copel didn't answer.

***

Looking back, she had no way of knowing that these would be the last truly happy hours of her life.

Whiterock was a Kingdom in mourning. Shops were shut, bars were closed, and everywhere flags flew at half-mast. Water fell from the heavens. Bluestocking wondered whether the King had made the wizards change the weather to reflect his grief.

On her way home to Kyr, she dashed from doorway to doorway, heart pumping with excitement. Rounding the last corner, water running off the end of her nose, as she reached the covered corridors, she almost bumped into someone. She looked up at a face whose surprised look obliterated memorability. "Beg pardon," he muttered in an accent similar to Daragel's. She guessed that he must Daragel's valet, smiled to show she accepted his apology, and continued.

The lanky boy with the prominent Adams apple and the mop of hair who had shown her to her room on the first day was stumbling toward her, trying futilely to cover a bundle with his tunic before venturing into the open.

"What are you doing?" she said. *Someone else not invited to Evi's memorial.*

"Changing the linen in that room," he pointed at the quarters in the corridor next to hers. "Someone left yesterday." He continued, "I've been put on chambermaid duties." He sounded disgusted. "I have to learn how to work in different parts of the palace, so it's my turn to play at making beds this week."

Bluestocking hid a smile.

He added, "A delegation of nobles from the Southern part of your Empire is here for the funeral. There's so many that we've had to hold their stuff in pantries and cupboards, while they share rooms."

While he had been talking Bluestocking had felt in the pocket where she kept her keys, then quickly scrambled through the others, muttering a very unscholarly curse. At the boy's shocked look she said, "I've left my keys downstairs. At least, I hope so; if not, I must have lost them."

"I've got a master set," he said, dropping the laundry with ill-disguised eagerness, then jangling a huge ring of keys. "I'll open it for you."

"Thank you."

It took several attempts before the young man found the right key, but he threw open the door with a flourish and a shy smile.

As Bluestocking entered her room, he stepped away and nodded in acknowledgement of her 'thank you'. She thought, *what's that noise?* It was less a noise than a pressure on her eardrums.

"What's that?" she said, pointing.

Sitting on the floor in the middle of her room was a large two handled porcelain urn, about three feet high. It was glowing with an unearthly, unhealthy blue glow. Smoke began to pour from its top.

"Balefire!" the youth shouted and pushed her away from the door so violently that she fell. Even falling, Bluestocking's gaze stayed fixed on the urn. A silent explosion rippled outwards from its now vaporised body. The light expanded, growing brighter and brighter; "Look away!" he shouted, diving on top of Bluestocking.

Bluestocking shut her eyes and winced as the youth landed on her. Nonetheless, even from behind closed eyelids the world still brightened.

Chapter 8

Although she had felt nothing from the silent explosion, Bluestocking lay stunned for several moments, the young man lying spread-eagled over her. In the fevered hinterland between consciousness and delirium she heard a voice say, "The third man is not the key." Someone else snorted, then mumbled a reply in a dismissive voice, which became suddenly clear: "cloak and dagger nonsense."

Although she had heard no sound of footsteps, the voices sounded too real, too solid to be phantasms. As she groped her way back to wakefulness, they gave no sign of going away.

Later, she would realize how lucky she had been, and how brave the young man was to throw himself in front of her, but right then, she didn't feel remotely lucky. While the balefire had only caught her clothes in a few places, where it had, it had scorched through the fabric, and in the few uncovered places it had touched, she could feel it start to burn.

Something, some sixth sense perhaps, warned her not to speak. She felt the young man's body rock and rock again, and opening one eye fractionally, saw the thick sole of a man's boot, pushing at the body. "They're dead," he said.

–A bubble of thought tried to force its way up from the depths of her mind, like a bubble of marsh gas rising, but she pushed it back down–

"Damn. Damn. *Damn!*" A woman's voice said. Bluestocking recognized with a jolt that it belonged to Myleetra. "We agreed that she was to be delayed– not killed."

"This was nothing to do with us," the man's voice protested. Bluestocking had heard him before, but at the moment couldn't remember where.

"How in all the God's names are we going to free it now, if we don't have her to finish off the translation?" Myleetra said.

"She'll have left papers," the man said grimly. "If we have time, maybe we can get them, and Copel can finish the job."

"That blind fool?"

"That blind fool is all we have now. Besides, he was the one who said that he would be able to work enough wards to contain it when we release it from its bonds. If you thought so little of him, why did you agree to the plan in the first place?"

"Desperation," Myleetra spat. "Agreeing to that meddling old fart's involvement was a sign of how hopeless I felt. It was no vote of confidence in Copel." After a pause, Myleetra added, "Do you know what it's like to find that every day another so-called true-believer has gone over to the Royal family's personal cult? That every day the church gains more power, absorbs another religion, while they believe in nothing except how to lock us ever more tightly into their regime? You'll say nothing except what they allow, do nothing but what they permit, and believe in nothing except what they condone."

"You agreed to *his* plan, so have some faith in the old man."

"You're right." Myleetra blew out a sigh. "Sorry."

"That's okay. We're all feeling the strain. The boss isn't showing it, but..."

"We should never have relied on that girl," Myleetra said, as Bluestocking felt her nose tickle. She fought the urge to scratch at her burns, which were starting to sting badly. Myleetra continued, "She's good, but finishing the translation so early, would doom us all as well.

Delaying her these last few days has been like holding a runaway horse!" She sighed again. "But this, this isn't what we needed..."

"Yes, I'd like to know who did this!" The man added grimly, "I'll come back later, but meanwhile, we should get away from here. Someone is bound to investigate, and the last thing we want is to be found outside a charnel house."

Myleetra's laugh was a snort, "Especially if we had nothing to do with it."

She no more heard them go than come, and Bluestocking didn't know whether it was safe to move. But her flesh now felt as if it was bubbling away. She bit on her lip until she felt the hot coppery taste of blood and kept biting, anything to distract her from the pain of her burns, and kept counting until she passed a hundred, then two hundred.

–Someone–

The thought tried to surface again, but she pushed it down.

The young man made the decision as to whether or move or not by moaning and rolling off her.

She opened her eyes. The wall facing the doorway was scorched black. A glimpse into her quarters told her of the ruination of the room and its contents.

The youth whimpered. He lay on his side facing her.

"Let me see," Bluestocking said gently. She rolled him gently onto his face, and he shrieked. His clothes had been blasted from his back where he had covered her, and his lobster red skin bubbled and peeled. One of the blisters burst, and pus oozed from it. "I'll get help," Bluestocking said.

"No!" He reached for her. "Stay with me, please!"

–wants– She pushed the thought down.

Instinct told her to run. Bluestocking felt her stomach turn. The boy's wounds smelled terrible already. But he had saved her life; she owed him that much at least. "Help!" she shouted. She doubted very much whether the boy could be saved, but she had to try. She called out to anyone who might hear, "Help us, please! Help, for pity's sake!"

"Will you hold me, mum?" The youth said.

–someone wants–

Bluestocking made herself think of him. Ignoring her revulsion, she put her arms round him. His hair was greasy but she stroked it, ignoring the tear that trickled down her cheek. "You can call me Blue, until the others get here. What's your name, young man?"

"Jalek, mum– I mean Blue. Will you cuddle me?"

So you know you're going to die, she thought. *Else you'd never dare ask such a boon.*

Jalek chuckled. "Papa was so proud when I was appointed to the Royal Household." He coughed, and a little black stream of thick, viscous liquid trickled down the side of his mouth. It smelt foul.

"Hush now," Blue said, worried he would hurt himself.

–you– Dammit all, think of him, not yourself, woman!

Jalek shook his head, needing to talk. "He used to take us fishing in the summer months when we had a holiday. We only got three days in the whole of the season; the rest of it we spent picking strawberries, apples and aubergines for the royal kitchens. You can't imagine how much I hate aubergines," he said with a tired smile. "We used to lie under the canvas, when I lived in Fairhaven, and the rain was trickling in through the gaps, soaking everything, and think of all the horrible things we would do to those aubergines, if we ever got a chance. It rained every night, except perhaps once a month. We have a saying in Fairhaven; 'it'll happen once in a clear night,' meaning something doesn't happen very often. Every night it would rain. Our clothes, such as they were, never ever dried out. We never bothered to wear socks. They would only get wet and rot our feet." He shifted slightly into the crook of Blue's arm and winced at the movement. "When Papa sold himself, he was sent down into the caves to feed the silk spiders."

His voice trailed away. Suddenly he spasmed in Blue's arms. But when she made to ease herself away, he opened his eyes and gripped her. "Please stay!"

"I thought if I went to get help, we could treat your wounds," Blue said.

He shook his head, gasping with the pain as he did so. "No need," he said. "I saw a man barely touched by balefire once. By nightfall, his body had swollen up, and he was dead by morning." He smiled at her. "I knew what I was doing, Blue." He took a deep breath that shook his whole body. "Why would you want to be famous? Why would someone called Blue want to be famous?"

Bluestocking knew that he knew. Something had given her away. Maybe he'd seen through the sudden kindness. *Well, no matter, he's dying. But who else knows?* "Xante's Paradox," she said.

He gave no answer, but frowned.

"About six centuries ago, a heretic called Xante denied the omnipotence of the Gods. He admitted that they were powerful, but not all-seeing and knowing. Nowadays, we take that for granted. Yet then, he fled into exile in the far South, in Khersonesa, and spent his life on an epic poem called The Paradox Sequence, which was published anonymously on his deathbed. When he died, The Gods of Khersonesa attended his funeral en masse, to show that they forgave him his heresy. Xante established that if a scholar commits a crime, the Gods may forgive them if they spend their time on a work glorifying the Gods." She chuckled. "That wasn't why I took the assignment; for me, the translation was what brought me here, Xante's Paradox is the means with which I justify it to myself on the nights when I cannot sleep."

To fill the suddenly endless silence, Bluestocking began to talk about herself. "I was born in Tananarind Province, in the South East of the Empire. My mother died in childbirth, but my father always had female company - I can remember more about the women who raised me, then I can about him. My father was a carpenter; he was very good with his hands. About the only thing I can remember of him is those big, strong hands and the smell of tabac. The trouble was that he drank, and when he was in drink, he gambled. Invariably, he lost. When I was three, he gave me away to the local waif-catcher, who was paid a bounty for each stray child that he collected. Of course, I wasn't a stray, but I didn't really understand what was going on. Years later, when I met the slave-catcher again, he told me that he'd split the bounty with my father."

"You must have been devastated," Jalek said.

–wants you– She shook her head.

"To be honest," Bluestocking said, "I knew so little about him, he might as well have been a stranger." She had said it so often, she almost believed it herself. Then she thought, *This boy is dying; he won't be telling anyone else what you say.* So she took a deep breath. "That's not quite true. Of course it hurt. Like all children who are brought up by people other than their parents, I built this ideal picture of him in my mind. What the waif-catcher told me hurt a lot. Not as much as when I finally found him. He was a self pitying drunk. It took me years to forgive him for not being the man of my dreams. I think that's why I'm so self-possessed. It's a reaction to my father's betrayal."

–someone wants you–

"Who brought you up?" Jalek whispered. He coughed again, and another little trickle of tar-like liquid ran down the side of his mouth, but this time streaked with blood. He clutched at her.

"The Sisters of Beatitude," Bluestocking said, remembering high stone walls around a square courtyard, overlooked by buildings on three sides. 'They raised me as a domestic. But Sister Loyola realized that I could do more, and insisted that the teachers instruct me, together with the novitiates. The other sisters were furious, but they were never going to win that argument. Sister Loyola became Mother Superior a year before I left, but even before that, her word carried weight. In some ways, the cruelty of the other pupils helped me; pushing me harder than kindness would have; my need not to show how much they hurt me only made me more self-controlled than ever."

Jalek took a deep, rasping breath. He gasped, "Keep talking! Keep talking, please!" He added, "How did you end up here?"

"The Sisters knew early on that I learned quickly. I worked hard and could recall what I was taught first time every time. And I had a gift for tongues." She paused. "Before my sixteenth birthday, I was sent to Ravlatt University to study Ancient Languages. I gained my degree at eighteen and my doctorate at twenty. But I have a secret, Jalek. Do you want to know what it is?"

Jalek said nothing, but nodded so imperceptibly that she almost missed it. She said, "I haven't been back to the Sisterhood since I left to go to university. If I do go back, it will be as Blue again. When I went to Ravlatt, I called myself Bluestocking."

"You're a name-changer?"

She took a deep breath. "Yes." Then, "Do you despise me?"

He shook his head, gasping at the effort.

"I'm still a slave," she said, "and a runaway as well. While I studied at the University, The Sisters of Beatitude basked in my reflected glory. I signed my letters 'Blue', and made sure that the letters to my rooms were seen by no one but the messenger that they sent; he waited while I composed a reply, or not– more often not. But should it come out that I masqueraded as a free person, they'll share my disgrace."

He sighed. "You know that I'll tell no one, Mum– Blue," he whispered. "I had *such* a crush on you. When you arrived, I could barely bring myself to speak, I was so awed by you. Freeman or slave, it makes no difference; you're a princess to me." He made a soft sound, like tearing paper and shut his eyes for a moment. When he reopened them, they were wet for the first time. "Do you know what the worst thing is?"

"No."

"That I'll die a virgin." His laugh was bitter, more of a sob. "I've never met the right girl for me, and I couldn't afford a whore."

"I suspect that it's vastly overrated, anyway," Bluestocking said.

"You mean, you've never?" Jalek's eyes widened.

"Of course not!" Bluestocking said.

"Your pardon, Milady," Jalek stammered.

Bluestocking put a finger over his lips. "Don't fret. I'm not offended."

"The comfort women," Jalek said. "The one who died, and her friend, they said that everyone in the Empire, even someone like you, they all..." He laughed to himself, a soft exhalation. 'They were teasing me, weren't they?"

"They mock anyone and everything with any trace of goodness in them. Take no notice of them. No, I've never taken a lover to my bed. But if I had, he would probably have been like you." *A harmless lie,* she thought sadly. She kissed his cheek, and listened to his breathing, which had grown steadily rougher.

She held him until he slipped into a coma. When he grew cold, she felt for a pulse, and finding none, dropped him gently to the floor, as carefully as putting down an egg.

–someone wants you dead.

Now that she no longer had the distraction of keeping Jalek in touch with life, there was no holding that poisonous bubble of fear. It rose up from where she had been trying to keep it locked away in the depths of her mind; rose up and washed over her. She scrambled to her feet and ran for her life.

***

She ran down the corridor and out into the crowds on their evening stroll. She ignored the stares of the people whose shoulders she bounced and buffeted against, gasping, "Sorry!" to those who called out, and "pardon me," to those who snarled. She ran and ran and ran almost the length of Whiterock before she calmed enough to stop.

Fool, she thought. *You had the advantage of surprise. Myleetra and her partner thought you were dead. Anyone who recognizes you will know now that any story of your death isn't true.*

She turned around and walked back the way she had come, fearing that at any moment, someone would call her name.

Her luck held. She made herself walk back down the corridor and pick up her bag and the precious notes it contained, all the time deliberately not looking at the thing that had been Jalek. Then, feeling as if she walked into the lair of a beast, she entered her rooms.

"Kyr?" She feared that at any moment she would find a blackened, unrecognizable corpse, but the rooms that she checked one after the other with hope and fear growing in equal measure, were clear of any bodies. There were, however, poignant reminders of Kyr everywhere that Bluestocking looked. In the days since they had become lovers, Kyr had gradually colonized Bluestocking's room, with potted plants, an embroidered picture, and a few little stones, picked for their odd shapes.

She crammed her few remaining notes into her little carry-sack and drew the strings closed, her mind still whirling. She thought of Myleetra and Copel and an unknown man, none of whom in theory were behind this. *Then who is?*

"No time for that," she panted, finding it hard to breathe, not from the blast, but from sheer raw, naked panic. In the bathroom she grabbed the chamber-pot with trembling fingers, and dry heaved into it, over and over again, until she had torn her throat almost to shreds. She opened up the taps on the bath, as far open as they would go, then slipped out of the tatters of her clothing. She felt cold, too, and wondered whether it was a side-effect of the balefire.

In seconds, clouds of steam from a torrent of hot water filled the bathroom, and she stepped into the bath. She winced where the water touched the balefire burns, but fortunately she seemed to have escaped serious injury– she guessed that only a little of the evil stuff had touched her.

She spent precious seconds washing the stuff off her, but all the time her mind raced. Did Kyr's absence from the carnage mean that she'd had something to do with the blast? *No, she couldn't have. She loves me. Doesn't she?* A treacherous little voice answered, *How do you know? Because she told you so?* She dressed quickly. She needed somewhere to think, somewhere safe. As far as she could tell, that ruled out anywhere on the rock.

She draped an old cloak that she had bought for just this eventuality over her shoulders and up over her face. *There, now you should look like any of the old women who don't want the world to see the ruins of what was once their beauty,* she thought. She left her rooms, and walking deliberately, slowly strolled away.

***

Walking gave her a chance to think, which only rammed home the essential hopelessness of her position. Heart still thumping, she looked westward into the sun, setting over Thamwesh. She sat on a stone seat and wondered where she could go. Whiterock was a huge prison from which the only escape was by air.

She took a deep breath. There was no avoiding it. She strolled along the walkway, ignoring an itching between her shoulder blades and swallowed at the familiar sound of the burner roaring its balefire-fuelled song. The late evening brightened as if lit by distant lightning. She thought of the last time she'd seen balefire, and its effects, and fought the urge to vomit. A huge gasbag swayed in the breeze, and her stomach churned in time to it.

A long queue had formed in the thickening gloom for the last flight of the day, and soldiers of the Royal Guard were checking pieces of scrip. To one side, bystanders huddled by the palace walls, peering over at Thamwesh and the rest of the Western Alliance. Those nearest the air-bags were shoved away by soldiers. One of those soldiers was arguing with a couple of militia-men who grew more and more agitated until one of them laid a hand on the soldier's sleeve. Instantly, the soldier pulled his sword out. Three of his colleagues leaped to join the fray, and the militia-men suddenly found themselves with sword-points at their throats. They backed away, their hands raised.

Bluestocking tugged at the sleeve of the man in front of her who was wearing the tunic of an Alliance merchant. "Where does one buy a ticket?"

He stared at her, clearly abstracted "What?" Then her question registered, and he said, "Oh. One," he emphasised the word sardonically but smiled, "buys the return with the outward ticket. I presume you haven't been off-rock before?"

She shook her head. "My..." she thought furiously, "...uncle in Fairhaven has been taken ill. I was so desperate to get to see him, I never thought about actually buying a ticket." She smiled winningly, and he nodded. "I just assumed that I could turn up." She simpered and loathed herself for needing to play the simpleton.

"You probably can. You may be able to buy passage, if they have space."

She groaned inwardly; the line looked as if it would more than fill the basket on the next descent, and she was uncomfortably aware of militiamen scrutinising passers-by. *They might not be looking for you,* reason insisted, but panic was starting to rise within her.

"Papers?" a man's voice asked someone two or three places ahead of them. Bluestocking took a deep breath and trying not to catch the man's eye, took a step back, aware of the Alliance merchant watching her. He didn't seem to have heard the man ask for papers. "I'll ask if they can squeeze you in, if you like," he said kindly.

"No, no–" She saw him stare at her, clearly surprised. "I've just realised, I've left my purse at home. But thank you, thank you, for the kind offer," she gabbled, backing away.

"Hey!" One of the militiamen called. "You there! Young woman!" Bluestocking turned and ran, and he shouted, "Young lady! Hey, someone stop that woman!"

Bluestocking ran back the way she had come, and again ducked down another narrow alleyway, cursing silently under her breath. She leaned back against a wall and racked her brains without success.

When an old woman glanced at her and seemed to be on the point of speaking, Bluestocking moved on. She dared not risk opening her mouth. Movement was better than conversation.

***

She walked at random through the streets and alleyways, her thoughts whirling around and around, never still, never settling, never giving her time to get behind simple images of death and destruction. At one point, she saw Arial stomping across the street and shrank back. But he looked deep in thought, his short legs moving quickly, his assistant, who was half a head taller, struggling to keep up with him, and after a few moments they vanished down a side-street.

Bluestocking relaxed and resumed her rambling.

She saw a familiar figure slip around the corner and without really being aware that she was doing so, followed the girl. It was only when she took a third turning that she dared to think the unthinkable; *that girl looks just like Kyr.*

Bluestocking rounded a corner to find that the path forked. She swore, then thought, *Why am I worrying? It probably wasn't Kyr, anyway.* But on an impulse she took the right-hand path. It was as if her curiosity was pulling her on a leash. There was no reason for her lover to be up here, unless it was one of those mysterious errands that both the princesses had hinted at and each thought was at the requirement of the other. A small mystery provided a refuge from the reality of her predicament.

It was only when, some ten minutes or so later, that she found herself looking out over the castle walls at the distant mountains of the Southern Spine that she had to face the fact that she'd taken the wrong path.

The urge to find out about the mystery girl had faded with each passing minute. By the time she had twice more taken wrong turnings and finally returned to the fork in the path, she almost didn't go left, down the path that she hadn't taken.

She often wondered afterwards how things would have turned out, if she had simply gone back the way she had come rather than surrendering to curiosity, or if she'd taken the other path straight away before losing those crucial few minutes.

But Kyr might still be down there, she thought.

She wandered down a twisting alleyway with dirty grey walls covered with crudely scrawled graffiti, its uneven, pitted floor strewn with rubbish from which ever more noisome odours rose. She turned a corner and stopped at the sight of a squad of militia men surrounding a shapeless bag. It appeared in the light cast by the torches two of them held to be leaking black liquid across the cobblestones. As she moved, so her perspective altered. The bag was a body, and the black liquid was actually red. It was blood.

"I beg your pardon, mistress." The patrol's leader walked toward her, trying to shoo her away. "This isn't pleasant viewing even for veterans like us, let alone a lady such as you."

"Another victim?" Bluestocking asked. She'd had a lunatic thought about trying to fake an old woman's voice and decided against it, but in any event her voice quavered anyway, although from nerves, rather than age. "I was on my way home." She nodded toward the other end of the passage, blocked now by the little tableau.

"Ah," the patrol's leader said. "Why don't you walk around, past Moneylender's Alley"– he gestured at right angles to where they were standing– "and cut back around, to come to the other end. Do you need an escort?"

Bluestocking shook her head. "No, but thank you. I wouldn't imagine the killer will strike again."

"I wouldn't wager your life-savings on that," another militiaman said. "This old man must have been at least sixty. There was no reason for this, except sheer wickedness."

Whoever did this could only have taken a few minutes, and it couldn't have been anyone but that woman. Could it? But it can't be Kyr, surely? "I'll be safe enough, though, I'm sure," Bluestocking said. "Better your men concentrate on finding the killer." She added, "I hope you catch him soon."

"So do I, mistress," the militia leader said. "I'm glad you're taking it so calm. We could do with a few more people like you."

***

To her astonishment, no one stopped her on her way to her rooms. Even more astonishingly, the guards that seemed to have been posted on an haphazard basis were absent. *Probably called into the search,* she thought. *Perhaps it's never occurred to them that I might come back here.* She almost smiled. *Please, your Majesty,* she silently begged the King, *keep employing dunces.*

She swallowed as she turned off the main corridor into hers. Her mouth was dry, her palms greasy with sweat. Jalek's body still lay where it had fallen, and she silently cursed the people who were too busy rushing around to even seem to notice that the boy was missing.

She opened her door carefully, her heart beating a tattoo. The rooms were empty. "Kyr?" she called, just to make sure.

Silence was her only answer. Shutting the door behind her, she checked each of the other rooms in turn, just in case the militia weren't as stupid as she thought them (Sister Lucretia had once commented, "Don't confuse intelligence and cunning, Bluestocking. Some of the most stupid people I know have more than their fair share of low cunning. It's the Gods' way of making us equal."), but they were all empty as well.

Sighing with relief, she plunked her backside onto the bed and allowed herself a few moments of self-pity. Then, lifting her head, she muttered, "You've been running around like a chicken that's had its head cut off, my girl. It's time to start thinking."

But thinking only seemed to lead her back to the same conclusion. Someone wanted her dead. It wasn't Myleetra, Copel or the man whose voice she recognized, nor his unknown master, though they all wanted her delayed. Why? To get her into trouble with Princess Cavi?

She stiffened. *Could it have been Princess Cavi?* She shook her head. *Maybe she grew impatient waiting for me to be gone in the New Year? Or maybe Myleetra's someone whispered in her ear, seeking to delay me through mischief, and it backfired? No, surely not?* But the idea and all the other possibilities simply would not allow her to sleep.

Her thoughts were still whirligigging perhaps an hour or more time later when a noise dragged her away from them. She sat bolt upright, still fully clothed, as the door slowly crept open.

Chapter 9

Kyr's face edged around the door.

A relieved Bluestocking slumped back on the bed as Kyr yelped "Mistress!" and flung herself onto Bluestocking, raining kisses on her face, lips and neck. "My Blue! I thought you were dead! I saw them carrying a body away!"

"Some other poor soul," Bluestocking said, thinking of Jalek and his family.

"What are you doing?" Kyr asked, looking at Bluestocking's clothes strewn across the bed and the small travel-bag packed with her papers, a few clothes rolled tightly together and a hair-brush. Kyr's face fell.

"What does it look like?" Bluestocking wriggled free of Kyr's grip and stared at her lover. "I'm leaving."

"But, but, you haven't translated the manuscript yet, have you?" Kyr squinted, suddenly suspicious. "Or have you? Did you finish–" She broke off as Bluestocking swallowed her fear, and placing her hand across Kyr's mouth, kissed her.

Where were you earlier this evening? She wanted to ask, but decided against it. *I might not like the answer.* "No, I haven't quite finished the translation," Bluestocking said. "But the situation has changed."

She recounted an edited version of the balefire blast and fleeing to the air-bag station.

Kyr's face grew sombre. "They'll never believe you had nothing to do with the boy's death."

"I know," Bluestocking said. "But someone wants me dead, and I'm more scared of death than arrest." She wondered whether to mention overhearing the plotters, but a vestige of caution made her stay silent. She decided that she definitely wouldn't mention following a woman who looked like Kyr.

"They'll stop you as soon as you try to leave," Kyr said. "They'll be watching all the air-bags and probably even the Pauper's Lift."

"If they recognise me," Bluestocking said, suddenly inspired. "What if I'm disguised?"

"A spell?" Kyr said, thinking. "They'll be looking out for signs of magic."

"They might be looking for signs of magic, but what if the disguise isn't a spell?" Bluestocking said, half to herself. She looked up. "There were actors performing in a play a few nights ago. Would they help?" She shook her head. "Probably not"

"One of them would if I asked him," Kyr said, grinning mischievously.

"If you cut my hair, it might throw them off the scent as well."

"It's worth a try," Kyr agreed. "It'll take me all of tomorrow, though, to get ready."

"That long?" Bluestocking tried to keep the disappointment from her voice.

"I'm afraid so. But it gives us time to arrange things; I may be able to hire a witch to curse someone in the queue– it'll create a diversion. And you'll need to take a sedative of some sort as well, to calm you down. They'll be looking for people who are nervous"

"Not Skrai!"

Kyr's face took on a closed look, but her voice stayed level. "No, not *Skrai*, but a harmless herbal remedy. Unless you think you won't need it?" She bared her teeth, turning the question into a challenge.

"No, no. No, I suppose I had best take something to soothe the nerves."

"Good. Then that's settled. I'll go to the theatre." Kyr blew Bluestocking a kiss. "Don't let anyone in while I'm gone."

"Why should I?" Bluestocking frowned. Then she smiled, "Ah. That was a joke..."

Kyr said. "You're learning."

The next hour seemed to stretch forever, but at last the door opened. Kyr hissed, "It's me! Where are you?" and Bluestocking emerged from beneath the bed where she had dived when she heard the knock. Kyr giggled. "It's like something from a stage-farce– enter lover, while principal player hides under bed."

Bluestocking smiled thinly. *I'm glad you can joke about it.*

Perhaps her face betrayed her thoughts, for Kyr suddenly sobered. "It must be very worrying for you."

"Worrying isn't quite a strong enough word." Bluestocking grimaced. "Try terrifying." She added, "When is the first flight of the day?"

"At seven hours," Kyr said. "Just about first light." Concentrating, she pulled a face as she tried to count. "That is..."

"Thirty-five hours," Bluestocking said.

Kyr nodded. "They'll meet us here the morning after tomorrow," she said. "As you leave, I'll get that witch who owes me a favour to cast a spell." She hugged Bluestocking. "So that gives us two nights." She grinned evilly. "What would you like to do?"

Bluestocking raised an eyebrow, as Kyr kissed her. But all she could think was, *thirty-five hours. Just thirty-five hours, and I'll be free of this nightmare.*

***

The first seven hours dragged. Bluestocking spent a fitful night, waking frequently and drifting into shallow naps, her dreams haunted by nightmares in which Kyr turned into something evil, and Arial offered her sweetmeats that turned into balefire bombs.

Instead, she slid out of bed, careful not to disturb the sleeping Kyr who lay on her back and snored with increasing volume. Bluestocking tenderly wiped a line of spittle where it had drooled out of the corner of Kyr's mouth and with a sad smile, pressed it to her lips. *The Gods, how sad is it when I even love her spit?*

If she couldn't sleep, she decided, she might as well try to lose herself in work.

Looking through her complete text, the vellum where she had assembled all the fragments in order, she counted every third word. "As to *the* beginning, the *third* deity is *man* himself, he *is* fundamental to *the* Buralit Question *key*." She read on, omitting two out of every three words. "If you have read this far, having translated the text, mortal reader, you have achieved more than most." She read on, her heart racing. It seemed to her that the words were pouring into her mind now, as water will burst from a pipe that is holed. But there was also something else trying to hold them back.

When she had finished, she crept back into bed, and sitting upright, leaned back against the headboard, trying to make sense of all that she had read.

Later on, Kyr stirred and rolled against her, and Bluestocking eased down into the bed and cradled her lover. Later still, she slept at last.

When she awoke into daylight, the room was empty. "Kyr?" Bluestocking called, just to make sure. She felt as if she had only slept for a few minutes.

Silence answered her. Slipping out of bed, she checked each of the other rooms in turn, but they were all empty. She threw on her clothes, and putting on a nondescript robe Kyr had left in her room, she slipped out of the door and into the still-chill morning air.

The Silk Palace

She walked as fast as she could without breaking into a run, breathing a sigh of relief when she reached the junction of the two alleyways and saw Kyr ahead of her, walking with the ease of someone who knows every alleyway and dawdling as if she had all day to spare.

Blue followed Kyr down through level after level, becoming increasingly concerned as her guess at Kyr's destination became a certainty. She watched in despair as her lover slipped into Mylectra's den.

Bluestocking wasted no further time on the woman she now thought of as her former lover but instead ambled with elaborate aimlessness back to her rooms, keeping a careful watch out for anyone who might recognize her. She felt so uncertain of being able to tell friend from foe that she felt it best not to trust anyone. When Halarbur strode by she shrank back, and when his gaze flickered over her, time seemed to stop for a moment. He looked away without any sign of recognition.

Enemies seemed everywhere. She held her breath when a man queuing for the daykeeper's oracle looked strangely at her, but she hurried past without speaking to him. The doorways seemed more like places of ambush, and Bluestocking even shrank from the sight of Lexi. The crowds around her seemed tense as well, as if they caught her mood. More likely, she decided, she was imagining it.

She slammed the door to her room closed, and falling onto the bed, instead returned to her translation. It seemed a hollow prize now. Who could she show it to who wouldn't give her up to the Whiterock militia or– worse– her unknown assailants?

She rubbed her forehead to smooth away the headache and stretched out for a few moments. When she felt the tension gradually easing, she turned to the contents of her travel bag, lost herself in the sea of notes and eventually grew calmer.

***

She came out of a near-trance with a start at the sound of voices, both male, and a scraping sound that she realized after much thought was the sound of brushes scraping on the stone of the corridor outside.

"By Brighannon, this is thirsty work," one of the men said. "Maybe us ought to get a drink, heh?"

"Let's finish this cleaning first," the second one said. He sounded older than the first man to Bluestocking. "Get it over and done."

"Well, no one will notice if I take some water from the room," younger voice said.

"Wouldn't go in there– might be bodies in there," older voice said. "I heard there was loads of 'em killed."

"Nah," younger voice said. "Ain't scared of a coupla dead bodies."

Bluestocking scampered across the room and hid behind the door as it creaked open. The young man who stepped through was improbably tall, gangly and red-haired. She shrank back into the corner formed by the door and wall and groped for something to hit him with as he looked around the room.

Kyr's voice cracked through the air like a whip. "What in all the God's names do you think you're doing?"

Red-head spun round and nearly fell against the door in his haste to leave. "I– I was looking for something to drink."

"And what exactly were you doing skulking around here anyway?"

"Hey, hey," older voice said. "Ain't no call for a tone like that."

"What tone?" Kyr snapped. "You've trespassed on unshriven ground, against the King's orders. What tone should I adopt? Who sent you?"

"Arial," older voice said.

"Is Arial running the country against the King's wishes now?"

"Didn't know about the King's orders."

"I heard him speak," Kyr said. "Should I ask him to come down and repeat it?"

"No need to get yer knickers in a twist," older voice said. "We'm going, ain't we?"

"Ar," the red-head said. "Won't stay here."

Bluestocking slumped to the ground and bit her knuckles to stop from laughing out loud. She stiffened again, but it was only Kyr entering and pushing the door shut.

"Are you alright?" Kyr said. "You looked as if you'd found a sov and it turned into a turd in your hand." She frowned. "What?"

"Where did you go this morning?"

"Out," Kyr said. She sat on the bed and reached out to stroke Bluestocking's arm. When Bluestocking stared at the floor, Kyr said, "What's wrong?"

"You visited the witch," Bluestocking said.

Kyr stiffened. "You've been spying on me?"

"Well, deny it then."

Kyr shrugged. "What's the point? You've already decided that I'm guilty. But don't you think it's odd that your room hasn't been occupied, your possessions thrown down the nearest refuse chute?" Kyr snapped. "I had to think of something that would keep them out of your room until the day after next. So I accidentally on purpose let it slip to Myleetra that you'd hidden some notes away and that I'd need time to find them. She bribed some officials and blackmailed others into influencing the King into issuing the orders I just quoted, all– as far as she knows– to buy me time to put a knife into your mattress and cushions and dig up those fancy floorboards that you were so fascinated by."

"He hasn't issued such a proclamation?"

"He will," Kyr said. "With Evi dead, everything's chaotic at the moment, and that gives us a chance, if we're slow and subtle, to do what we couldn't normally and cast some influencing spells." Kyr put a hand on Bluestocking's arm. "In the meantime, be brave. We can survive this, with luck."

Bluestocking looked away. She took a deep breath, summoning a little more courage. *Best to have it out.* "Isn't that *Skrai* I smell on your breath?"

Kyr looked sheepish. "I picked up a packet as my reward for being a good little slave." She shrugged again. "Before you came, I was consuming two, three, four times what I go through now. This I take just to ease the hunger for it." She stared deep into Bluestocking's eyes. "Now is *not* the time for me to stop taking it altogether."

"Where does it come from?"

"Myleetra gets it from the Western Alliance, or from your precious Empire, whoever has it when she needs to buy some. Does it matter?"

Bluestocking sighed. "I suppose not." *Why can't life be simple? The last thing I need now is a slave with a craving. But a slave who's going to help get you out of here,* she thought.

"Come back to bed," Kyr patted the pillow. "Let's catch up on some of that sleep we missed last night."

Bluestocking stared. "You didn't sleep?"

"No more than you did," Kyr said with a tired smile.

Uneasily, Bluestocking lay stiff and unyielding beside Kyr, the slave trying to curl around her back. Bluestocking didn't respond when her lover began to stroke her.

When she did sleep, she was haunted by memories of the blast and Jalek dying in her arms, although in her dreams, the boy wore Arial's face. Several times she awoke, only for Kyr to cradle her in her arms, stroke her hair and croon hushing noises.

She slept until late morning, judging by the angle of the sunlight, and was only awoken by a fully-dressed Kyr shaking her shoulder. Bluestocking reached out for her, but her lover drew away with a small smile to soften the rejection. "You have a visitor," she said, frowning slightly. "I don't know who he is, but I don't like the look of him. I'll go and keep an eye on him, and make sure he doesn't steal anything."

Bluestocking cursed silently. She had intended to check her understanding of the manuscript, to make sure that it wasn't simply the result of an overheated imagination, but first the explosion, then her exhaustion– and now this– seemed to be conspiring against her.

She entered the lounge. "What do you want?" she snapped, and Aton leapt up from the chair he had been sat in. "How did you find me?" she said, her heart suddenly racing wildly. If Aton could find her, so could anyone.

"Would you believe a divination spell?" Aton said. "Using your name?"

Bluestocking swallowed.

"He's lying!" Kyr blurted. "Only royal proclamation will make a Nomenati cast a name-search, and no other wizard would dare."

Bluestocking relaxed, and Aton grinned. He said, "Don't fret yourselves. I saw you the other night, when that fat little toad of a first minister was scuttling round, and I followed you. Since then, I've kept an eye on the place, on and off."

"And I thought no one had seen me," Bluestocking said bitterly.

"Shall I call the guards?" Kyr asked hopefully, but Bluestocking shook her head.

Aton sneered, "No, wouldn't want that, would you?"

"I asked you what you wanted?"

"Not in front of her," Aton nodded at Kyr, who folded her arms across her chest.

"Anything you have to say, you can say in front of Kyr," Bluestocking said. "She knows everything."

"Does she, by Phojeth?" Aton squinted at Kyr and stepped toward her.

She retreated, and Bluestocking snapped, "You stay away from her, or you'll have to go through me!"

Aton grinned at her, but there was a trace of respect in his voice, when he said, "Brave little thing, aren't you? Or is it all bluster? No matter," he added quickly and laughed. "No need to fret, missee."

"For the last time, what do you want? I have work to do, even if you haven't."

Aton breathed through his nose, and Bluestocking belatedly realized that he was laughing. "So have I. I want you to steal some silk spiders from the caves."

There was a long silence, and then Bluestocking burst out laughing. "You must be mad. The fresh mountain air's turned your brains to maggots."

"I don't think so," Aton said. "Didn't you wonder why I didn't turn you in?" He leered. "Any reward money would be chicken feed compared to what's available to people who look the part and can act the part. Someone with your conceit, they'd never think of asking you to empty your pockets. I'll cut you in." He knelt beside the cabinet and picked at the corner. "Looks like wood, doesn't it, at first sight?"

"I know why Whiterock's known as the Silk Palace," Bluestocking said grimly. "I know that there aren't trees to supply their needs, so they use the roughest faux-silk from the spiders."

"Not just as a wood substitute," Aton said, eyes lit with a near evangelical fervour. "Wood, fabric, stone cladding. All of which these proud yokels use rather than import the real thing from outside. As if not buying from their neighbours makes them independent!"

"And?"

"Do you think that Whiterock is the only place where wood, or fabric, or stone, or all of them are scarce. Think, girl!"

"So you'll keep bleeding me, little by little," Bluestocking said.

"Not you, them."

Bluestocking shook her head. "I don't think so."

"Don't be a blasted fool!" Aton snarled.

"Wouldn't I be a fool, to leave myself open to a life of being your slave? Oh, I know you'd call it something else, but that's all it is really."

"One theft then," Aton said. "Then we'll go our separate ways. If we ever meet again, it'll be as strangers."

"Yes?" Bluestocking said scornfully. "And of course, you're a man of your word."

Aton flushed. "Every bit as much as you are *my lady*, but if it'll make you feel better, I'll swear in front of this chit of yours."

"A blood oath?" Bluestocking waved Kyr to be quiet.

"Aye, a blood oath." He nodded grudgingly. "You should be a peddler. You drive a hard bargain."

"Would you have it any other way?" Bluestocking asked.

"Maybe not." He swore the oath she wanted him to utter, agreeing that the gods could damn his soul for eternity and afterwards if he turned them in, or asked them to make more than one theft. "You'll do it?" he asked eagerly.

Ignoring Kyr's objections, Bluestocking nodded. "I'll take a look for you. Once only. I'll make no promises, mind."

He grinned, and she knew that he was just humouring her. As far as he was concerned, he would pressure her into going a second time, to commit the theft, and as many times as needed, Gods or no Gods.

Aton nodded. "I'll be back later to make the arrangements," he said. Just as he was leaving, he turned and stared at her, burning her face upon his memory. "Remember, if you cross me, you'll regret it sooner or later, wherever you go. I'll swear a blood oath to that effect as well, if you wish." Then he was gone, leaving only the echoes of the slammed door.

***

Kyr opened her mouth to say something.

Bluestocking held up a hand. "Not a word," she said and pulled out her notes to work on them but was uncomfortably aware of Kyr's presence. She looked up to find Kyr watching her, as if trying to read something on her face. "What?" Bluestocking asked and ran her fingers through her hair. When Kyr didn't answer, and the silence grew tense, Bluestocking said, "Don't you have things that you should be doing?" She smiled to remove the sting from the words.

"It's sad, I think," Kyr said with a twisted half-smile, "that yesterday you couldn't let me out of your sight, and today you can't wait to get rid of me."

"Not true," Bluestocking said. "But I need to do what I'm here to do, and you need to be attending to your chores, before one or the other of your mistresses talks to the other one, and works out that you're playing games when you should be working."

"Games?"

"Games. Don't play innocent with me, my girl." Bluestocking looked stern for a moment longer before bursting out laughing.

Kyr laughed too, and folding a towel, walked to the door. She sobered and said, "I ought to pay a visit, just to make sure that they know I'm still alive."

Bluestocking nodded and said, "Don't come back until this afternoon. Or else no more games for you, young lady."

"That's twice I've been called a lady today," Kyr said and blew her a kiss as she left.

For a long time afterwards, Bluestocking stared into space, still haunted by after-images of Jalek, blackened skin peeling from his flesh. She wondered if anyone else would mourn his passing or even give it more than a passing thought.

It struck her then that she was translating an epic full of powers and demigods and gods and goddesses, in which mortals were never mentioned except when they perished in their thousands in floods, famines and earthquakes caused by the very deities they revered.

Jalek was just a spear carrier, she thought. *No one will even remember him in a month or two, let alone in a century or more.* She wondered if that was to be her fate, too. Remembered– if she succeeded– merely as one of the scholars so casually mentioned in the texts and forgotten altogether if she failed.

She settled down at last and with a sigh of contentment, gradually lost herself in the world of words. The notes on the last scroll showed it to be even more arcane than the others, but if her theories were right, then it involved some sort of ceremony to create (*Free?* she wondered) a thing, or a person. If she had the sense right, it was called Brighana. *Blasphemy?* she wondered and shivered. *The name sounds suspiciously close to Brighannon.*

The first part of the scroll seemed to be given over to a recitation and the times and locations when it should be uttered. Bluestocking remembered how Myleetra had said that spells were often time and location sensitive. Her tongue sticking out, Bluestocking laboriously copied down what she hoped was the spell itself. It seemed to actually fight her; as she wrote the letters they writhed and danced on the page. But she persevered, squinting to make them hold still, and gradually they made a sort of sense. By the time she'd finished, her head was splitting, and little blue and yellow lights danced in front of her eyes, but she felt an ever greater triumph at having so triumphed over the odds. *A secret spell?*

It had taken such an effort that she felt as if she'd run for miles and miles. Her eyelids drooping, she slept, and this time there were no disturbing dreams to plague her.

***

It seemed like only minutes later that Kyr was shaking her shoulder.

"Huh?" Bluestocking said. "Oh, it's you." She shook her head. "Sorry, I fell asleep."

"How did you get on?" Kyr asked, putting a cloth sack down on a side table..

"It's a puzzle," Bluestocking said.

"I know," Kyr said with a smile. "You've been telling me that ever since you got here."

"No," Bluestocking said. "I mean it's literally a puzzle, like a child's game."

Kyr looked bemused, and Bluestocking explained. "Ever since I mastered the last part of the translation– that is, where the letters are capitals, the word has a completely different meaning from when it's in smaller letters." Seeing Kyr's puzzled look, she tried to make it simpler. "All our languages are different descendants of the old High Tongue. Karnaki evolved one way, Alliance another, and Whiterock a third– a middle– way. But all derive from one language. Yet for all that, the text seemed to have less characters when written than any modern language. But that's because it uses the same characters in at least two different ways." She paused, realizing that she'd been gabbling.

"And where does a puzzle come into this?" Kyr asked.

Bluestocking grinned. "The text seemed to be made up of words that individually made sense, but when put together, came out as nonsense. When I was at Ravlatt University, we spent a term studying Lucius of Coyle, a noted cryptomancer. One of his tricks was to bury the real message in a code. So I tried it. It worked."

"And?" Kyr leaned forward.

Bluestocking wondered if in her excitement she'd given too much away. She sobered. "I don't know. I'm still working on it, but I needed a short break. Now time marches on."

"Even more than you think," Kyr said, producing a small knife with a thin, serrated edge from the sack. She burst out laughing "Your face! Anyone would think I was going to slit your throat."

It had occurred to me, Bluestocking thought, but she managed a smile as Kyr pulled from her sack a small jar and some thin strips of cloth.

"From my actor friend," Kyr said with a grin. "First we cut your hair, then we'll dye it with henna paste. A lot of young men here dye their hair."

"Oh?" Bluestocking raised an eyebrow, and Kyr giggled.

"Now, sit on the bed. First we need to crop these lovely locks."

"Ow!"

"Yes, it'll hurt, sharp though the knife is," Kyr said, sawing through a small handful of hair. "I'll be as gentle as I can, which means cutting less hair at any one time, but we need to be done soon. You need to be at the foot of The Vernal Steps at three hours."

"I don't know if I can do this," Bluestocking admitted. "Going outside this morning frightened me half to death."

"Keep him happy for the day, and you'll be gone tomorrow," Kyr soothed. "And you need to be gone tomorrow. Rumour has it that Daragel's tiff with the King and his message home to his master has caused Alliance soldiers to march on Whiterock."

Bluestocking groaned.

When she had cut Bluestocking's hair, Kyr opened the jar and recoiled from the smell "It's got a root with some unpronounceable name mixed in, which makes it dry quickly. So no time to waste." She took a strip of cloth, and began to paint Bluestocking's hair. When she had finished, she took a couple of strands of the hair that she had cut and began to hack them into tiny pieces. "Now we paint your eyebrows with bits of hair."

It took longer than the hair dyeing process, but at last Kyr said, "Now stand up, and disrobe."

"Is this really the time for this?"

"Quickly!" Kyr snapped, and when Bluestocking had removed her blouse, Kyr said, "That will do." She wrapped the strips of cloth tightly around Bluestocking's breasts. "You can dress again now."

Bluestocking did so and wandered across to the mirror. "Oh," she said. "Oh, my."

Kyr said with a chuckle, "I was hoping that you would say that your own mother wouldn't recognize you." She added with a theatrically heavy sigh, "but then, we artistes are used to being un-appreciated."

"Artistes?" Bluestocking raised one grotesquely shaggy eyebrow. "I look like I have a sheep above each eye, and you talk of artistes."

Kyr giggled. "People will describe you by them, so that if you need to, you can remove them. It'll hurt a little, but if you do it quickly..."

"I understand," Bluestocking said, gazing again at the short, slight young man in the mirror.

"Time you were leaving for the Vernal steps." She added quickly, "Don't worry. I'll give you directions on how to get there. Do this job for that thieving little shit, get back here, and lie low until it's time to head for the airbags tomorrow." Kyr was interrupted by knocking on the door. She flung the door open, and Bluestocking peered over her shoulder at Aton.

"Tour starts in less than an hour," he said without bothering to look at her and added as he turned and walked away, still without looking back, "Follow me, but at a distance. No one must see us together."

"Arrogant–" Bluestocking stepped back, and Kyr wrapped a light shawl around her shoulders. Bluestocking took breaths to calm her wildly beating heart but without success. By the time she'd left the chambers, Aton was at the other end of the passage, striding past the guard who'd been posted there as if the peddler were actually a nobleman incognito. Bluestocking wondered how he got away with such impudence. Then, as Aton passed the guard, the peddler's hand flicked out like a frog's tongue snapping a fly, and Bluestocking caught a glimpse of gold before the guard pocketed the coin with a nod.

"So much for my guardians," Bluestocking breathed. She was unsure whether to be amused at Aton's insolence or outraged at how easily the men guarding her quarters could be made to look the other way. *If Aton had been an assassin instead of my accomplice...*she let the thought trail away and instead concentrated on keeping him in sight. He weaved through the late-afternoon travelers thronging the concourse, before plunging headlong down the steps to the next level and on down toward the caves.

Chapter 10

A party of seven tourists had gathered at the meeting point at three hours after the noon-day gong. They stood separate from the passers-by–mostly heavily rouged young men, who walked hand in hand with their padrones, older lovers whose finances triumphed over love or lust, or single young men out for a stroll. A few pairs of women also walked together.

Bluestocking had noticed fewer such men than in Ravlatt and had simply put it down to an aversion to same-sex couples displaying affection in public. Now she wondered whether there was actually a Queer Quarter in Whiterock, as in some more heterodox cities in the Empire. *It would be typical of King Redoutifalia to want everything neat and tidy and contain them in their own little ghettoes,* she thought.

Several glanced at Bluestocking in her disguise; older men openly appraising her as a replacement for their current boy-toy, a few men of the couples shooting her sidelong glances with little smiles and some of the singles raising an eyebrow in question.

But without exception, every one of the locals stepped away from the group with dark looks toward the tourists, several making warding-off gestures.

Aton had signposted them by stopping for a moment to talk and covertly signalling Bluestocking with a nod toward them, still without looking at her. *He is so sure that I'd follow him,* she thought. *So arrogant, and so right.* He had ambled down so that she had nearly caught him up and had had to hold back.

She bumped into someone and growled a bastard mix of apology and rebuke, as she had noticed the locals often did. *Pitch your voice low,* Kyr had said. *Or they'll realize that you're a woman.*

She sidled across, and when she stood near enough for him to hear, but not so close that anyone would realized they were together, hissed, momentarily lowering her cowl, "Aren't you going in as well?"

He started visibly, and she grinned at the effect of the disguise. "What in all the God's names are you doing? Why are you dressed as a man? The whole idea was that you swan in with your most ladylike airs."

"Meanwhile I have to move around while they're looking for me, you dimwit. I needed a disguise." She repeated, "Aren't you going in?"

He shook his head, and stepped away, but she followed him. "Why not?"

"No need," he muttered. "That's what I've got you for. Just grab a handful of 'em, and shovel them into your pocket. If you're caught, it's on your own fool head. When you come out, pass them to me."

Realization dawned. "You're scared!" she hissed.

He shrugged. "Not scared," he muttered. "Just don't like confined spaces." He waved her away.

Bluestocking grinned at discovering a weakness and sauntered across to join the group, as a pair of soldiers ran past them toward the stairs to the upper levels. "You for the caves?" she asked diffidently, remembering just in time to roughen her voice, and several of them nodded. She stood idly by, trying to calm her nerves– once she no longer had activity as a distraction, she found it increasingly difficult not to run and hide.

When two militia-men rounded a corner and examined everyone they passed, interrogating every second or third person, Bluestocking tried to fight down a rising tide of panic, taking deep breaths. "We're looking for a woman," Bluestocking heard one of them ask a couple of men.

"So am I," quipped the older man. "But it's so I can dodge her– she's my wife." He and his friend roared with laughter.

"Comedian, heh?" growled the militia-man.

His colleague described Bluestocking, although he knocked a couple of years off her age, made her a little taller and ended with, "and no jokes, heh? Have you seen her or not?"

The men shook their heads, and the militia-men then approached Bluestocking.

"Heard ya describe her," she mumbled, in as deep a voice as she could manage. "Ain't seen her. What's she done?"

"Nothing," said the second one, looking her over with a cursory glance. "We need to keep her somewhere safe for a time, but she fled protective custody."

Bluestocking shrugged. "Ain't seen her. Sorry."

The first militia-man gave her a quizzical look but moved on.

Bluestocking fell back against the wall in relief. Her armpits were sweat-soaked, and she struggled for breath against the chest band. She tried to put herself into the meditative state that she had achieved when with Myleetra. She frowned. *Was she trying to help me? Maybe that was all part of their little game.* She had been so preoccupied in her few spare moments that she hadn't really given much thought as to *why* the plotters had had the King invite her. Doubtless he and Arial were innocents manipulated by Myleetra and her cronies, but what was their purpose? Instead, with persistence that verged on obsession, she had kept her gaze firmly on the translation itself.

She gave herself over to reviewing the translation, and the spell within it. As soon as she did, she felt the words writhing within her mind as if they wanted her to utter them. Her contemplation was interrupted by their guide emerging from an alleyway.

"Ladies and Gentlemen, my name is Lurdan," the guide said, as they each handed over a sov into his outstretched palm. His voice was deep and mellifluous, not at all the voice Bluestocking had expected to issue from such a small body. He was short, thin, almost emaciated and even paler than most locals. He wore an ankle-length monk's soutane, belted around the waist with a simple piece of rope. "Welcome. We view this opportunity to brag a little about our spiders as a chance to cultivate an interest in our local industry."

Bluestocking thought, *And gouge a little more money out of the hapless tourists. But who can blame them for wanting to earn every coin that they can?*

Lurdan continued, "We have some way to go before we arrive at the caves, so I'll tell you a little bit about the places we pass. When we're actually down amongst the spiders, please refrain from talking." He added, "Loud noises and voices frighten them."

He led them down a flight of steep steps bordered on all sides by high, sheer walls. Bluestocking grasped the rickety rail to her left then quickly let it go. It felt as if the slightest weight on it would make it collapse.

They moved slowly in the increasing gloom, the group feeling their way carefully with their feet before putting weight on the next step. Lurdan's torch flickered and guttered in the breeze, blowing thick black smoke back into their faces. Several of them coughed.

When they reached the foot of the steep steps, Bluestocking could only see those on the edge as shadowy outlines. Lurdan said, "Gather close." They did so, jostled by the crowds that walked down this side of the steep street. Bluestocking noticed a group of heavy-set toughs come close. "They are with us," Lurdan called out. "Have no fear."

Someone jostled one of the group and muttered, "Move into the middle, damn you!"

"This oaf," Lurdan called, "though rude, has custom on his side. Join me in this centre aisle. Careful, there's a slight rise, so it's clear of the rivers of slop in the gutters."

Blue fought through the tide of people, and stepped up.

"The buildings on either side rise eight floors," Lurdan said. "The top ones are occupied by the rich, while the poorest live down here. But lawlessness is rare, and with the militia present on most streets, you're perfectly safe. Follow me, please. Be careful; the street is steep, and the going underfoot may be treacherous."

They crossed slowly to the other side of the street, working through the river of people. Had their guards not formed a protective ring, Bluestocking and the others would have been knocked over. Instead, their bodyguards took the buffeting and curses of the mob.

Apart from the background muttering of the surrounding throng, the street they were on was remarkably quiet. Bluestocking thought, *I wonder if it's our presence that quietens them so?* They passed a street sign, which said in the local script, *The Street of the Mute*. Minutes later, they reached an archway set into the wall, guarded by two of the biggest men Bluestocking had ever seen.

"We're going to descend still deeper now," Lurdan said sepulchrally. He looked up, caught Bluestocking's eye and winked. She grinned back, temporarily distracted by his theatrics. She stopped grinning though, when two men began to pat down each of the visitors in turn. "A routine precaution," Lurdan said. "There are those who would steal from us. I'm afraid we must impose on each of you, both when you enter and when you leave."

That scuppers your plans, Aton, Bluestocking thought.. Would he accept that it was impossible to steal the spiders? Maybe. She swallowed and held her breath as she was patted down, but apart from a raised eyebrow, the men frisking her didn't seem to notice anything unusual, despite the fact that they must have felt the tight bindings round her chest.

The party followed Lurdan down into a cavern dimly lit by tiny glowing lights embedded in the walls. Bluestocking took several seconds to blink her way back to normal sight and gasped. What she had thought was a small rock moved with a rustling sound. The spider was as big as a dinner plate, and she could clearly see its eyes. It might have been her imagination, but it seemed to be watching her. She swallowed, mouth suddenly dry. "Are," her voice emerged as a quaver, and she stopped, swallowed and tried again, "are they safe?"

"Reasonably safe," the guide said, amusement in his voice. "They're harmless, as long as you stay close to me." He added, "But if you, or any other stranger approached the colony alone, it would be a different story. They'd certainly attack then."

"The colony?"

"The spiders are social animals. They live in colonies extending through several hundred caves around here."

Bluestocking heard the steady drip, drip of water in the background. She reached up to touch the tip of a stalactite. When she rubbed her now-wet fingers dry against one another, it left a chalky residue. The cave was warm, humid and filled with a redolent odour that Bluestocking thought not unpleasant, although the other women held cloths over their faces, and one of the men muttered, "Bit of a stench in here."

Bluestocking had a sudden overwhelming sense of being watched. She felt as if she were in the belly of some great, malevolent beast. Normally she had no qualms about being in enclosed spaces, but now she wondered whether Aton had been right to stay outside and send her in. She jumped as the largest spider yet scuttled across the wall.

"Exactly how dangerous are they?" another man asked, his voice quavering slightly.

"Their bite is toxic. A small child would die, an adult suffer severe muscle pains."

The spider walked toward Bluestocking. She forced herself to stay still. The spider stopped, and she exhaled.

"They're curious," the guide said. "That one is a sentry spider. They're normal sociability has been boosted by low-level spells and breeding programs." He added, "It's supposed to be good luck if they touch you."

I think I'd rather be unlucky, Bluestocking thought wryly. Normally she was unafraid of spiders, but the size of these was overwhelming. She noticed with grim amusement that she wasn't the only one who was concerned. The others had all huddled closer together.

"Follow me," Lurdan said. "We're going to go down much further and see some of them actually spinning spider silk. This is our main export product; both the Empire and the Alliance would buy ten times what we could make and still want more."

They passed another cowled figure emptying a bucket of beetles, grubs and other small clambering creatures onto the ground. They scattered in all directions, scuttling into crevices, and up over microscopic ridges; one small beetle climbed a wall, but found itself stuck on the edge of a small web. Bluestocking and the others left it struggling as a small golden spider crept across the web toward it.

Lurdan led them into the next cavern. "We divide untreated spider-silk into ten strengths. The weakest is one, and the strongest, unsurprisingly, is ten." His audience chuckled dutifully. "Strength one is only marginally stronger than an ordinary spider's web, while ten can hold a man swinging across a ravine."

"What's the point of selling mere cobwebs?" Bluestocking asked.

"The weaker silk is finer and softer," Lurdan said. "An unfortunate side-effect of the breeding process is that strong spider-silk is coarser than worm-silk. Sometimes strength has to be sacrificed for a smoother, softer texture. But unlike worm-silk, even strength one spider-silk can be strengthened by weaving spells into it." He added, "All the strengthening is done in the deepest caverns, and while some of you could endure the greater heat and humidity of the press-caves–"

"Hotter than this?" One of the others, a western alliance merchant by his clothes, wiped his forehead with his cloth.

"Hotter than this," Lurdan said. "Time proscribes us from staying longer than to visit the next couple of caves." They stepped into a colossal, high roofed cavern, again lit by fireflies in the walls. "In here," Lurdan said, "are the more mature spiders." More cowled figures stood round the edges of the cavern, each placing a long bar against a spider's web, one end touching the floor, the other against the wall. "The bars are hollow reeds, picked to be as light as possible so the webs don't collapse under their weight. They form an edge between the web and the nearest wall; once the spider grows used to the new presence and establishes that it's neither prey nor foe, it weaves the web around the reed. It's a slow and laborious process that takes weeks to finish and yields barely a handful of silk. This silk is particularly susceptible to magic; it soaks it up like sponges soak water, and once it's been treated, the silk is as tough as anything in nature. And," he added, "much more versatile."

He turned. "This way please." They followed him into the next cavern, where more people worked. "This cave was set up the same way as the last one, but a full moon ago. Now the silk between reed and wall is ready for harvesting, as you can see," pointing to one of the those carefully scraping it clear, taking care not to rip the silk on the web side of the reed.

After a few minutes, Lurdan bowed to them. "Ladies and gentlemen," he said. "I'm afraid the silk caves are nowhere near as mysterious as the tall-tales make out, but I find it so fascinating that I could probably bore you to sleep. Have you seen enough?"

They burst into spontaneous applause, and as the wardens again felt them over and checked their pockets for stolen spiders, made their way to the exit.

As she left the cave, Bluestocking felt a tug on her sleeve.

Aton grinned at her. "Enjoy that?"

Bluestocking shrugged. "It was educational. It gave me a chance to think."

"Oh?"

Bluestocking nodded. "I need more time to plan this. They search you going in and out." He looked furious, and she added quickly, "There was no possibility of smuggling any out tonight. But give me two days, and I'll have worked out a plan." A lie of course. She had no intention of being on Whiterock in another two days, but he didn't know that.

Aton shook his head. "Tomorrow. Or you go to the Militia."

Bluestocking nodded. "Just give me another day," she pleaded and walked away, leaving him where he stood. She started the long climb back up through the levels to her rooms.

***

It was a long walk, and Bluestocking was tired, almost so much that she didn't have the energy to be scared any longer. She still felt an almost permanent churning in her gut, but there was a limit to how often her heart could beat faster.

The climb up the levels seemed to take forever, but she finally rounded the corner before the last flight of stairs. She noticed more and more militiamen running around with great intent but little obvious purpose. Cresting the last set of stairs, she entered the twisting maze leading toward her rooms.

She stopped, watching Myleetra and a man she had seen before turn the corner ahead of her. The alleyway forked. If they took the right fork, she could relax.

They took the left.

The alleyway led to only one place, the guest wing that Bluestocking shared with the other guests. The last time Myleetra had stepped down this way was to talk about Bluestocking as if she were dead. They might have mistaken Jalek's charred corpse for hers the last time, but they wouldn't be so careless again. And if they knew that she still lived, her life would be measured in minutes rather than years.

As the man turned his face side-on to speak to Myleetra, again Bluestocking felt a sense of recognition. She racked her brains, wondering if it was the fellow plotter, or even the mastermind they had referred to when they thought she was dead.

No, this was no time to go home. She would have to trust that Kyr could look after herself. She felt a momentary qualm at abandoning her lover, but she had herself to look after. She turned and headed back the way she had come.

What could she do? Bluestocking racked her brains and at last came to a decision. Night was falling, and while there were braziers and lamps, there were also shadows beyond them. There was a growing air of tension about the city with each passing minute. The conversations in doorways or as people hurried past looked strained, and several times those talking made the now-familiar warding-off gesture toward Mount Halkyon. Bluestocking almost smiled at the thought that with only days to go before celebrating the Gods walking amongst men, many seemed to be imploring them to stay away.

Bluestocking's smile faded when one old couple scowled at her. She wondered whether her disguise was unravelling, but she managed a glance in a piece of ornate glass mounted by a doorway, and she still looked enough like a man to pass casual scrutiny.

She looked at each dwelling that she passed with a new perspective, with the thieving eyes of the jemmy-girl. She found what looked like a street full of abandoned houses. The first two she tried, the door refused to budge. She heard voices behind her and rattled a third door. It refused to give.

She licked her lips, and glanced around. The voices were getting closer. *One last go,* she thought. She wanted to scream, to release the panic she could feel building within her.

The door opened.

Bluestocking felt around herself. The space inside the doorway was no more than cupboard-sized. Close by was a wall; she felt splinters against her fingertips and drew them back with a curse. The air smelled yeasty, together with a faint tang of timber– proper wood, not the faux-timber of treated silk. *This must be the first real thing I've felt all day,* she thought. *Fake people, fake wood. They should call this Fakeland.*

Kneeling, she felt the floor. It was covered in powder. She lifted her fingers and sniffed it. *Grain,* she thought. She was in a storage area; most likely the rooms overhead were where people lived. But how to get up there? She sneezed. She heard a skittering nearby, and her hackles rose. Rats, if she were lucky. If she were not– there were things that kept some storage areas clear of grain and all other pests. For a price and given the right conditions. *This must be why the frames are wooden.*

Then she saw the eyes. A pair of yellow beacons, absolutely tiny. They moved, quicker than thought. From the darkness, came a whisper; "man."

From behind her, came another. "No. Wo-man. Fe-male."

She spun round, her hand over her mouth, to stop the scream from emerging.

Grain imps. Legend had it that grain imps could talk, but no one had ever verified it. No reputable authority, that is. But all the legends said that if you heard a grain imp, you were already dead. Bluestocking wondered whether they would wait for life to flee her body before they started to gnaw on her flesh. Another story; that when they'd cleared the rats from an area, they'd eat anything else that they could catch. Cats, dogs, babies. To prevent that happening, the store's owner would leave small offerings or face the wrath of his neighbours.

All legends of course, but sometimes legends were based on truth, and Bluestocking had no desire to find out whether it was true that hungry grain-imps would eat anything they could catch.

Such as an adult trapped in a confined space.

"Wo-man, come," came the whisper from ahead. "Foll-ow."

She stood rooted. "Foll-ow," the voice repeated, more urgently. "Foll-ow the lights."

So she followed, and stumbled on what turned out to be a flight of wooden steps and climbed the steps, feeling incredibly weary. Then time seemed to stretch. She might have walked for seconds or for most of the night.

She almost stumbled over the thief-catcher, the step that was raised slightly higher than the others so that the clumsy thief would trip and wake those sleeping in the house. Then she reached the last step, though she didn't realise until her foot came thudding down from a great height, jarring her into half-wakefulness.

As they walked along, she heard the drone of distant voices, and reaching out, felt a wall. People were talking beyond it, but she couldn't make out the words– just a muffled drone.

She stepped back.

"No. Is o-kay," another of the little voices (*or is it the same one?* she wondered) said. "They can-not hear you."

"Why not?" she whispered, taking no chances that anyone might hear.

"Our God," came the reply. She'd assume it was the same one talking now. If it wasn't, it made no difference. "Casts a net of safe ty o ver us. Our god can-not do much, but this much it can do. Keep you safe, while we are here."

"Why?" she said, meaning, *Is the god of grain-imps involved?*

It seemed to understand what she meant. "E-vil walks a-broad," it said. "We need help. You must help. Or we all die. Or worse."

"Me?" She almost laughed out loud, but stopped herself just in time. Divine safety net or not, someone might hear her laughter. As soon as the imp had mentioned something evil, the words of the spell had started pushing and clamouring to be uttered. *Say me! No, me! No, ignore them, say me instead!* To shut them out, she whispered, "You have a god?"

They didn't answer, but it didn't matter– the distraction had worked. She shouldn't have been surprised that creatures themselves semi-mythical should have their own tiny deity. Gods and demigods both took every opportunity to be worshiped. Bluestocking wouldn't have been surprised to learn that even the gods had their own deities. She shook her head to clear it of such fripperies.

Movement in the courtyard below caught her eye. She peered through a dirty window. An old woman tottered across the yard. Bluestocking wondered what she was doing breaking curfew. Then she noticed that the light was wrong. She looked up at the sky and saw the new moon where there should be none, and realized that the grain imps– or their god– were showing her a vision.

The old woman had almost reached a doorway, when a second figure ran across the courtyard and was on the crone before she could turn.

The second figure was hooded. A knife lifted, glinted in the moonlight and plunged into the crone. She turned, and her assailant slashed horizontally. Blood spurted, as the old woman slumped. The assassin's head dipped, as if he or she was kissing the old woman goodbye. Then the hooded figure straightened and threw back the hood to turn and stare up at Bluestocking.

Bluestocking shrank back, even though the assassin couldn't see her, her heart pattering.

The assassin's mouth was ringed with blood, and her eyes blazed with contempt and anger and hatred. How much of that was *Skrai*, Bluestocking couldn't be sure.

Kyr smiled and wiped her mouth.

Bluestocking fell back against the wall and shut her eyes but couldn't shut out the memory of Kyr's gaze. She slumped to the ground. She felt weak, hollowed out of emotions.

"Sleep a little while. Re-fresh your ach-ing limbs. Sleep."

She was tired, but it was the tiredness of near-exhaustion, of receiving body blow after body blow, rather than the honest fatigue of a labourer.

Still she obeyed, at least for a while.

***

When she awoke, it was to a dizzying moment of dislocation. "Where?" She croaked. "What time is it?" For all her fatigue earlier, she felt refreshed, as if she had slept for days, not just hours.

"Look," the little voice said. "Look out-side."

Bluestocking looked.

To the east, she could see the first faint presages of daybreak; the slight light, the yellowing of the sky on the horizon. She realized that she must have slept for most of the night. For a moment, she missed Kyr with a physical longing that was an ache. *Get used to it,* she thought.

"When day comes," a second grain imp said, "it hides. If it grows strong-er, it will be ab-el to face the day-light. Per-haps." Bluestocking couldn't see the imp– legend had it that they would blacken and shrivel in normal light– but she guessed that speech was not easy for it. Every word sounded as if it were only formed with difficulty, but formed the words were, albeit with every syllable stretched. "Every act of cruelty makes it more able to leave the moon behind," it said.

"What is *it*?" she asked. "What are you talking about?"

"It comes," the first voice said.

Bluestocking stumbled away from the window back across the room, the way she had come, with frustrating slowness, but she dared go no quicker. As soon as she was away from the window, the corridor became so dark that she had to feel with outstretched hand and slowly descending foot every single step of the way. The grain imps had vanished as suddenly as they'd appeared, leaving her to grope her way back. She longed for the watch-bell to ring and tell her how many hours she had left to endure, but it stayed maddeningly silent.

She emerged back onto the street, and her heart nearly stopped when she heard voices, but one of them was a woman's laughter. She relaxed slightly, although the laugh was unsettlingly shrill. *There are a lot of curfew-breakers out and about,* she thought. *I wonder if that's why the militia was so active earlier on?* She scuttled to the street corner and saw a mob, locals by the sound of their voices, all headed the same way. There were women and children as well as men. *Perhaps with Last Day so near, it's some kind of festival, and curfew is suspended?*

But there was an undercurrent of tension in the air, and she doubted that this was normal festival behaviour. It didn't matter. Today was the day. If she could just screw up her courage, she could escape this benighted place, go back to the Sisters– go somewhere else and start afresh, if she had the nerve.

The trickle of people had become a stream, and soon it swelled, for with each corner they passed, the numbers grew, as a few more people joined them. With each corner that they passed, Bluestocking relaxed slightly more, for she would be that little less visible. As long as she kept her mouth closed.

Still, something was wrong; there was not only tension in the air, but the light was wrong– far too weak for sunrise.

They rounded a corner, and Bluestocking saw that the weather-cock was lit up, and its golden arrows shone like a miniature cold sun in the reflected light of the lamps.

Then she noticed that the arrow pointing westwards was pointing toward the sunrise.

Except that it was no sunrise.

Chapter 11

What awaited those who entertained any thoughts of flight was a vast army camped on the Alliance side of Whiterock. *That's what all the militia activity was about today,* Bluestocking thought. *And their attempts to keep things quiet weren't only futile, but actually made things worse.* That explained all the anxious looks from the locals at any strangers, the muttered conversations, the air of barely suppressed panic.

The land below was dotted with camp-fires burning as if hundreds, even thousands, of the very stars had been taken down from the heavens and scattered as far as she could see across the plain below, all the way around to the Northern side.

The clouds had clearly built up, and she understood now that what she'd thought was the first hint of dawn was the glow of all the fires bouncing off them; they were a sullen orange, and when she glanced to the North, towards Mount Halkyan, she saw a column of light, all the way from the clouds to the summit of the mountain. In its slowly swirling white light strange shapes moved. *The Gods must be getting ready to leave the mountain to mark the impending year end,* she thought. *As if things aren't already confused enough.*

"What?" She plucked at the sleeve of a dark-skinned youth, barely remembering in time to pitch her voice. "What day is it?"

He shook his head as if she were mad to ask such a question. "Mountain Goat," he muttered and was gone in the swirl of people.

Oh Gods, she thought despairingly. *I slept through a whole day.* She might have escaped in time had she not missed the day. Assuming that she could have faced the descent.

Groups of priests and priestesses stood around, a few of them spouting apocalypse talk. "It's the Last Days of all, not just of the year!" one man cried, but he was shouted down.

One of the girls caught Bluestocking's eye. She was a young girl with caramel coloured-skin, probably barely old enough to bleed, and wore the brown robe of the novitiate that seemed common to all the religions here. Finery was for those nearer their god. Her face was thin with too little food– or too much fasting– but her cheekbones and her eyes hinted at the beauty she might one day possess. *If she lives long enough,* Bluestocking thought. "Do you believe?" the girl asked, in a lilting accent.

"In what?" Voice still gruff.

"That these are the Last Days." The girl was scared, Bluestocking realized with a stab of pity. "That the enemy will attack, put us under siege."

"Dunno," Bluestocking growled. "Where'd they all come from, so quick? Weren't here yesterday."

"The first ones got here the evening before last, according to the rumours, but they were only scouts. They came in the night, all through yesterday and last night. Thousands upon thousands of them. They have scaffolding, and ladders and air-bags, it's said."

"And mirrors," a man passing said. "They use the mirrors to make it look as if there are more of them. And for some damned foreign magery."

"Still, there are enough of them," the girl said.

"It'll be alright," Bluestocking said, but wondering what she could do now. Unless the enemy forces– as she now had to think of them–

hadn't completely surrounded the rock. It was a forlorn hope, but it was all she could cling onto. *They must have been gathering before Daragel argued with the King,* she thought. *A force this size would have taken weeks, months to assemble. They were just waiting for an excuse.*

"Do you really think so?" the girl asked, and Bluestocking nodded. "Maybe the prophecy is true," the girl said.

"What prophecy?" Bluestocking asked, more to give the girl something to think about, but she seized on the question.

She swallowed, but when she spoke, her sing-song voice was strong and clear. "The Prophecy of Shenjoh says that if someone penitent, someone brave, someone honest is prepared to publicly offer herself up to the gods on The Last Day, she will be possessed as the avatar of the chosen god."

The mob surged forward and swept the girl away as easily as flotsam caught in the ebbing tide.

***

Bluestocking managed to squeeze herself out of the rush and onto a side street. Looking back at the mob, she realized that there weren't as many people as she had first thought, probably only several hundred, instead of the thousands that she had thought while she was caught up. It was the tightness and steepness of the street, the pushing of people at the back eager to see what was happening and the panic in the air that had made it so terrifying.

She edged away until she was clear. As she rounded a corner, ahead of her a small group of revellers staggered through the cobbled alleyways in the direction of the air-bag station. Braziers threw their weaving and dancing silhouettes into stark relief. For a moment, she was convinced that the silhouettes had taken on a life of their own. *Get a grip on your nerves, woman,* she thought.

She followed the group until she was almost right behind them, not quite close enough for them to notice, but enough that she could stride forward and hide amongst them if necessary.

They moved at barely a crawl, but it gave her time to try to work out a plan when she reached the station. The only problem was, she couldn't think of anything cleverer than simply walking up to the attendants and asking if it was possible to still take a flight.

That led her to thinking about what she would have to do. To climb into that basket, and sit it in it, while it dropped toward the ground. *And if it breaks, or if the bag leaks, or if the enemy attack while it's in the air...* She flung the thoughts out of her head with the ferocity of a dog shaking water from its coat.

Eventually, she saw at the end of a long, straight street lit by balefire lamps what had to be the air-bag station. "Hey," one of the drunks said. "Who're you?" He slurred until he was barely intelligible.

Bluestocking decided on the same approach. "I bought that last flagon of ale," she mumbled. *Oh, who would ever think acting was so hard!*

"Shit," he said. "Did you?"

"Muh-huh." She nodded vigorously.

"Oh." He looked as if he would be sick and said, "Must've been good stuff. Can't remember drinking it."

"You said." Bluestocking made herself sway. "You said, if I bought a flagon of ale, *you'd* fly out by air-bag."

He reared upright in indignant disbelief. "Never." Then said, owl-like, "Did I?"

"Muh-huh." Bluestocking nodded vigorously again.

"Kay," he said. Then shouted, "Hey, oshiffer!" He waved at the nearest militia-men. One approached, very slowly, his body language radiating disapproval. The drunk said, "Kin I take a flight in o' them there bags?'

"Course not, you drunken fool!" The militiaman slapped the drunk round the head, and the latter protested vigorously. "Come back tomorrow!" He added, "Assuming the parley still holds. It could break at any time."

"They're still flying, then?" Bluestocking growled, sniffing the aroma of tschai that the militiaman was slurping from a mug.

The man nodded. "Alliance men have kept their hands off the air-bags and the station." He grinned. "But 'em ate the foreign horses that was stabled down at the station. Roasted 'em. Seems horse is quite the delicacy where those savages come from."

Thinking sadly of Fourposter, Bluestocking tip-toed away, alert for any shouts.

***

What to do now?

Ahead of her, what seemed to be the main surge of people was pushing through one of the narrow alleyways like a flash-flood. There was a greater edge of panic now to the proceedings. From an alleyway to her left, a militia patrol emerged. "Oi, you!" the officer shouted, and for a horrible moment, Bluestocking thought he was shouting at her.

She stood rooted to the ground for a moment, then dived for cover toward a doorway that was framed by colonnades. Fortunately, as she flattened herself against the wooden door, she was between two equidistant lamps. But if the sliver of moon emerged from cloud at the wrong moment, she'd never escape the men's gazes once they were level with her. She looked around, close to panic. *They're coming nearer. They're bound to see me in a minute*. She tried the door, but it didn't budge, and shaking it hard might alert the militia.

About three feet from the doorway was a boarded up window. Its surround poked out from the wall by a few inches. Looking up above the door, she guessed the lintel was about wide enough for her to stand on it. *If I can find a way up*, she thought.

She grasped the pillars and pulled herself up, feet scrabbling for purchase. Fortunately, the colonnades were highly ornamented with rings bulging out from the central column. She was able to gain purchase. Deliberately not thinking about anything, certainly not about falling and dashing her brains out on the slabs below, she squirmed up the column and hauled herself onto the lintel. When she was in position, she dared not look down.

"Barras!" the officer bawled. "Get those people indoors. The King won't stand for curfew breaking on this sort of scale. You got a whip-man?"

"I can get one," Barras shouted back.

At that moment another militiaman appeared from behind the officer, and he shouted at Barras. "Forget it. Calvos here will do it!" The officer waved Calvos to a junction further up the alleyway and turned back to Barras. "You tell the stragglers, we'll snatch every tenth man and execute 'em under the King's orders. Get one now! That'll sort 'em out!"

The officer motioned Calvos into position, and the whip snaked out with a loud crack, lashing one man in the face. The man screamed and clutched his face. Calvos' whip snaked out again at another man's head. Those at the far end of the alleyway pushed back, creating a whirlpool of panicking people.

"You men!" The officer roared, as if there were no women among the crowd. "You got a half-bell to get to your homes! After that, if we sees you, we arrests you! If we counts ten, the tenth one gets to join the Gods! Like that!"

He waved, and two of his men snatched a muscular man from the crowd. Amid yells and screams he was forced to his knees, while a third militia-man hacked with his sword until their victim's head lolled at an unnatural angle. The crowd fell silent.

"You know the penalties for breaking curfew!" the officer shouted. "At this time, when we needs clear streets to watch for invaders, now is the very time you choose to defy the King! Any one of you we find out on the streets is a traitor." He paused, then bellowed, "Now get to your homes, a-fore we dispenses more justice!"

The crowd filed away sullenly but in an orderly fashion in each direction. The militia watched them, their officer standing impassively with folded arms in the lamplight.

Bluestocking swallowed the bile in her throat. She stared at the body in the now-deserted alleyway, the blood pooling around it.

Getting down was even harder than getting up, and she scraped the skin on both her arms and her legs but managed to scramble down. She sighed, realizing that she was effectively a prisoner. Heart in mouth, she crept from corner to corner, watching for patrols.

***

A crunch of feet on gravel, and she stilled at a junction of three alleys and listened to the voices in the distance. She pressed back against a wall in the shadows. As the five men and their captive passed she felt her spirits sink further.

"Can't we have a bit of fun with her first, Sarge?" one of Kyr's captors asked.

Kyr shuffled along between them, but her head lifted slightly at the militia-man's question.

"No, this one's not to be touched. The boss says she'll bewitch you with just a touch. After she's been interrogated and given up her paymasters, then she'll be hung and quartered." Despite their slow pace, Bluestocking saw that Kyr's ankles were unbound. *Good,* she thought. *There's a faint chance.* For all that Kyr may have been a killer, and Bluestocking had no way of knowing whether the grain-imp's vision was truth or lie, she couldn't simply abandon her lover.

They slowed at a noise to one side, and Bluestocking scooped up a loose piece of rock and tossed it in one easy movement in the same direction as the noise had come from.

As Bluestocking had hoped, the two men on Kyr's left moved to the right, strengthening the barrier between the slave and the noise, but leaving her left side uncovered.

Bluestocking targeted the man at the back who was furthest to the left and ran up behind them, imploring any gods who might be listening not to let her stumble, or step on anything that might give her away, ran as fast as she could…

…nearer…

…nearer…

….and her shoulder slammed into the back of the man at the rear, who was already leaning forward, pitching him diagonally forward into the next man.

"Run!" Bluestocking bellowed in her deepest voice and snatching Kyr's hand, hauled her along. Kyr needed no second invitation and quickly matched Bluestocking's frantic pace, the shouts and a whistle of the militia echoing behind them. "I thought they had you already!" Kyr shrieked.

"The voice didn't fool you, then?" Bluestocking gasped.

"Your soft hands give you away," Kyr cackled.

For a few glorious moments adrenaline and euphoria took over, and they almost *flew* down a long straight thoroughfare. The militia was hampered by their bulky armour, the women helped by their light clothes and mannish leggings, rather than their usual dresses.

It couldn't last. Bluestocking knew that, of course, but it was a last, doomed gesture of defiance at the Gods and rulers of Whiterock.

It ended with them reaching the end of the thoroughfare and skittering to a halt, but still almost ending up in the arms of another squad emerging from one side.

Their leader steeped forward. Arial said, "Kyr, and a brave young man. A fool, of course, but still brave." He frowned. "Who are you?" When she didn't reply, he stepped closer and peered at her. After a moment a smile spread slowly, and he reached for her fake eyebrows.

He ripped one off, and Bluestocking whimpered. "That's very good," he said, the little smile still playing around his mouth. "You almost fooled even me." His smile faded. "I have a warrant for your arrest."

Bluestocking stepped back and looked round, but the passageway was suddenly blocked by two more large militiamen. "On what charge?"

"I think you know," Arial said sadly. "Conspiracy to murder the Princess Evi. Spying for the Karnaki Empire. I'm sure that we can think of some other charges, but that'll do for now. Come with me you foolish girl. You've caused enough trouble." He turned to the sergeant. "This time, manacle them, you bloody fool. If they escape again, you'll replace them in the cells."

***

Arial separated them, and his men marched Bluestocking to the barracks through now-deserted streets. The wind had stiffened, blowing from the west, and it carried a faint smell of soot from the army of camp-fires on the plain below.

"What are you going to do to Kyr?" Bluestocking panted.

Arial didn't answer, which scared her more.

At the entrance to the barracks, a group of figures waited for them in the penumbra cast by a street-lamp. Bluestocking recognized Copel standing beside another man. In front of them stood a uniformed third figure; she guessed it was the local commander. When he moved into the light, she recognized the man who had summoned Arial away the night of the banquet. Half behind him was a fourth figure. When he was led forward, Bluestocking took a breath.

"This is outrageous!" Daragel sputtered, his copper-coloured face even darker than normal. Rage distended his eyes, twisting his mouth into a grimace. "My most trusted servant is murdered, you have no idea how it was done, who did it, why, or when it was done. But you interrogate me like a criminal and refuse to release his body to me!"

Arial called, "You should be grateful that we merely interrogate you about a suspicious death and not intern you as an enemy of the King. That may yet happen."

"Daragel, please be calm," The other man pleaded, and Bluestocking felt her guts clench in fear. His was the voice she had heard talking to Myleetra as she lay stunned outside her rooms. "If we work a spell upon the body, we may be able to divine what happened. We should at least try."

"Absolutely not!" Daragel shouted. "My servant Fadyan was killed five nights ago. His mortal remains should have been burnt already unless you want his shade to roam the earth, seeking vengeance on those who desecrate his body. And before it is burnt, we must prepare it. Will you travel to his village and explain to his family the insults you heap on top of his death?"

"You'll forgive me, Daragel," Arial said, "If in light of the horde of your people that threatens us at the moment, if I have little time to care for what a bunch of peasants huddling in their hut think of me!"

"Five nights ago?" Bluestocking wondered, her mind working through the dates. She thought, *Daragel is either mistaken or a liar; how else could I have seen Fadyan the day after his death?* Her guards pushed her toward the group, and while they all stared at her, as if reading her mind Daragel put his finger to his lip, in a clear gesture for silence. He smiled and winked but said in a chill voice, "Must we bicker in the street, gentlemen?" As Arial's men led him away, Daragel looked back at her, put his finger to his lips again and nodded.

Copel's companion turned and stared at her. "That's her," he said. "That's the woman I saw sneak into Princess Cavi's quarters, and a couple of minutes later, I saw her running away again, just before the Princess Evi called at her sister's rooms."

"He's lying!" Bluestocking shouted.

Arial asked formally, "Do you confess to planting the bomb that killed Princess Evi?" When she shook her head, he said sadly, "Take her below."

The last thing she saw was Copel and the stranger walking away and Copel passing him something that looked suspiciously like a money-bag.

***

They dragged her across a cobbled courtyard and through a heavy door. Somewhere a hound howled a mournful ululation that made the hairs on Bluestocking's neck rise.

When she started to struggle, one of the men yanked her head back by her hair, and addressed a question to the others that was clearly meant for her, "If she don't keep still, lads, then we'll have to teach her, won't we? Maybe we'll take them leggings off her." He added, "Maybe we'll take 'em off, anyway, eh?"

A couple of the men chuckled, but it sounded to Bluestocking more out of duty than because they found it funny. She swallowed her rising panic. "You should be careful about who you say such things to."

The bully dragged her head back further and planted a wet, sloppy kiss on her forehead. "That's all right, dears. You're on our patch, now, see? Whatever fancy friends you may have outside the gates, it's all the same here. See, if I tell the lads to take your trews, off, they'll do it, eh, lads?"

Someone undid the manacles and lifted Bluestocking's kicking legs into the air, while two other men gripped her arms tighter against her struggles. Another pair of hands tore off her leggings. All this happened while Bluestocking's head was pulled back so that she couldn't see what was happening. She took a deep breath to scream, but a heavy, callused hand was planted firmly over her mouth.

Her undergarments were dragged roughly down her legs, and someone's nail scratched her hard enough to make her wince– but she couldn't breathe with the huge paw clamped over her mouth.

"See, dears? You're completely in our power, here. If I decides you wants a bit of Whiterock pork in you, then that's what you'll get, heh?" He said so softly that she had to strain to hear him, "Nod, if you understand." The hand over her mouth eased slightly, and she nodded frantically. "If we takes our hand away, you won't scream, will you?" She nodded again. The hand was removed, and the other man let go of her hair. "See now," he said, "If I tells you to kiss my ring, you will, won't you?" She was unsure exactly what he meant but still nodded. "So you'll walk down them stairs like a good girl, yes?"

She nodded again, and they led her down the dark, twisting stairs. Her foot slipped at one point, but the soldiers held her. She didn't like to think what she might have trodden in. The smell made her want to vomit. It was a combination of stale urine and faeces, the tang of blood and sweat, all merged together in a heady cocktail; the stink of terror. Into a corridor, the only punctuation to their footfalls a couple of distant conversations, a few muted groans and an occasional scream.

"In here," the leader said, and they threw her through an open doorway into a corner filled with straw. Bluestocking shrieked– she could have sworn she saw something move in the straw.

Then the door was slammed closed on the light.

***

She sat in the dark, on a bed of straw and wept a little. In romances, the hero always found a way out, a set of keys hidden in the straw, or worked a spell, but in romances, the hero was never threatened with gang rape. And she had no intention of feeling about in that straw. It was all she could do to even make herself sit on the edge of it.

If the romance featured a heroine, the handsome prince would call upon her and produce the information that would show it all been a ghastly mistake. Bluestocking had no illusions that the Prince would side with her against the sister of her supposed victim.

By the time she toppled over onto the straw, she was already asleep.

It seemed like only minutes later that a crash awoke her. "Come on slut, on yer feet!" a strange man shouted in the dark.

"What?" Bluestocking tried to shake the sleep from her head. She realized that the crash was the opened door slamming against the wall. Someone grabbed her arm and yanked her upright, almost wrenching her arm from its socket. "Ow!" she shrieked as a hand slapped her hard enough to rock her head back.

"You speak only to answer our questions, hoor!" the first voice shouted again.

A second voice hushed him. "No need to be so brutal, Tomar," he said. He added, "We need to ask you some questions, young lady. Tomar is a little anxious. The King fears that you're part of a wider plot and has promised us great rewards if we glean the details from you and terrible reprisals if we don't. So I trust you'll excuse Tomar his roughness."

There was only a faint light coming from out in the corridor, but the door was open enough that a bewildered Bluestocking could make out two shapes. "Do you understand?" The second voice asked again, this time with just the faintest edge beneath the softness.

"Yes," she said, "But–" Before she could speak further, Tomar slapped her again.

"You answer our questions! No ifs, no buts, just answer. Understand?"

"Y– yes."

"Good," Tomar said. "Who sold you the balefire?"

"No one, I–" Tomar slapped her again. "No one!" she shrieked. Before he could hit her again, she shouted, "Hit me as much as you want, no one sold me anything, because I didn't buy any balefire! I had *nothing* to do with it!"

"Come on, Tomar," the second voice said, still gentle but now with a hint of disgust. "We're wasting our time with this one. She's too tough for amateurs like us to crack. We'll have to call in the serious boys. The Gods help her then."

Tomar growled, "We can do it." But his voice was further away, and moments later the door slammed shut.

***

More time passed. Just when Bluestocking thought that they had forgotten about her, she heard voices, fainter at first, but growing stronger until she could hear what was being said.

She recognized the rougher of her interrogators, Tomar. "I don't know about that, worshipful master." While still rough, his voice had taken on a pitiful pleading whine.

A new voice answered him sharply, "Then you should know. Who signed the order?"

"She's in here, worshipful master," Tomar said.

Bluestocking braced herself for the door to crash open again, but just as the key scraped in the lock, another new voice cried "Halt!"

Arial, Bluestocking thought. Despite her tiredness, Bluestocking was thoroughly alert now. *Perhaps the new man, the one with the arrogant voice, is my rescuer. Someone from the fireside songs of romantic fiction, after all.*

"Prime Minister," the arrogant voice– now humbler– said. Bluestocking's hopes plummeted as quickly as they had risen. "I'm surprised to see you here. Are you involved in this unlawful detainment?"

"Not unlawful at all, Torgala," Arial said. "I regret I couldn't involve you before. There wasn't time to apprise you of the situation." He called out, "You men! Leave us now!"

There was silence, and then Torgala said firmly, "There is no need for them to leave us, Prime Minister. Any detainment that does not have the counter-stamp of the Justice Minister is unlawful. These men should hear as much."

"Steady now, Torgala," Arial said sternly. "The King won't appreciate hearing that his instructions are unlawful. Unless you're a secret Republican?"

"Prime Minister!"

Arial chuckled. "No need to get so indignant, young friend. You would not be the first nor last to serve the King while secretly believing that he could do the job just as well." Arial's voice dropped to a murmur, and Bluestocking strained to hear what he said. "Everyone who has held office on behalf of the King– Brighannon bless his soul– has at one time or another wondered if he couldn't do a better job. But thinking it is one thing..."

"I can assure you–" Torgala spluttered, but Arial hushed him, and Bluestocking crossed to the door and gazed out through the little grill at the shadows of the two men, lit in the lamplight at the end of the corridor. Next to Arial's compact frame stood a taller man.

They walked away out of sight, but their voices still drifted faintly down the corridor. "The King signed the order himself," Arial said. "But because a foreign national who was rumoured to be close to the foreign prince was involved, absolute discretion was required. Our neighbour the Empire is far bigger than we, and while we fear no one, we don't want to give unnecessary offence. You understand?"

"Of course," Torgana said. "But without wishing to be accused of speaking sedition, the Justice Ministry has purview over such matters for a reason, Prime Minister. Checks and balances; Arial, checks and balances." The old arrogance was back, but the indignation was fading with each sentence, and Bluestocking's hopes fell. This man was no friend, just another bureaucrat. As it was in the Empire, the ministries were full of men of little ability and much ambition.

"I will not be Prime Minister forever, Torgala," Arial said. "In two years, I'll have served for a generation. The King has granted me leave to step down then, though I'll still be around to offer quiet counsel to my successor, should the King wish it. There are only a handful of candidates for the post. It is now a job for a young man, such as you. When, or rather should, you become Prime Minister, you'll find that temporary exigencies sometimes call for those checks and balances to be stilled momentarily."

"I believe that I'm beginning to see the picture, Prime Minister. Perhaps you could sketch it a little more fully for me later?"

"Of course, my friend. You understand that no one else must know of my likely retirement? It would grievously cripple our governance should our fellow ministers be distracted by irrelevant questions, such as who will succeed me, and when." Their voices were fading, and Bluestocking imagined that she could see Arial slip his arm around Torgala's shoulders.

"What of the girl?" Torgala said.

Bluestocking imagined Arial's shrug, as he said indifferently, "If she has any sense, she'll have been asleep and heard nothing of our non-conversation. And if she hasn't and is foolish enough to repeat it, who'll believe her? She will be confessing soon enough to the murder of the princess, and when she does, who'll believe the desperate lies of a murderer?"

Their voices faded with her last hopes, and Bluestocking sat down again on the edge of the straw. Her head drooped.

***

When she awoke, she had no idea whether it was morning or night. She tried to pass the time by thinking about the scrolls, about the problems with the different tenses, but she couldn't get past her current predicament, and for once her work gave her no sanctuary from reality.

Her bladder was almost bursting, and she had no alternative but to use the far edge of the straw in the corner.

When men came again, they were different– one's voice was slightly higher, the other deeper than the last men, but they followed the same pattern; one kind, the other cruel. When they left her alone, she learned to sleep when and where she could, regardless of what was going on around her. When she couldn't sleep, she retreated into a fantasy world where they'd released her with groveling apologies for their mistake, and she translated the scrolls to enormous acclaim.

The next time they came for her, it was the first pair again. This time the second man tried– or at least pretended– to stop his accomplice from beating her up. Despite knowing it was foolish, she tried to put up her hands to defend herself and succeeded in landing a blow to her assailant's face. It was only a slap, but it enraged him, and with his next punch, he half-spun her around and landed a blow to her kidneys that almost made her pass out. She sank to her knees, retching, as a rain of blows descended upon her. Eventually, the second man pulled the first away, but not before he had landed at least two punches to her face. Blood streamed from her nose, and her eye hurt as well.

They threw her in the cell, and she didn't see them again.

Despite her not knowing how much time was passing, she soon worked out a pattern. Her captors would let her rest for a while, then awake her abruptly, slamming doors and shaking her by the shoulder, occasionally kicking her in the side. The kicks were not hard enough to break ribs, but still left her sore and bruised. Starting with the second pair of men, they would feed her, then take away the watery gruel before she could wolf more than four or five mouthfuls of it.

When her period started, and when she asked for a bandage to staunch the bleeding, they just laughed at her and told her to use some straw. She wiped the blood from her legs as best she could, but most of it dried on her calves. The pain was like being stabbed with a skewer, worse than most moons, and she guessed that she was reacting to her predicament.

When the next pair came– the third– one of the men held her head in a bucket of water until she couldn't hold her breath any longer. Then he lifted her head out, but even as she drew air into her burning lungs, he shoved her back into the water. The second man said, "If you wave your left hand, my friend will stop. But if you do and then don't answer our questions, then we'll kill you. After all, we aren't getting anywhere." He and his colleague seemed to be experts at how long they could hold her head in the water without drowning her, but even so, after a few duckings, she was close to breaking.

"Who are you spying for?" they kept asking her. "Who paid you to kill the Princess? Who sold you the balefire? Or did your spymasters provide it?"

She shook her head.

In the end, she wanted to beg them, I'll tell you anything you want to know, please, please just stop it, and I'll give you what you want to hear. Just as she was about to confess and pick some names at random– she thought she would accuse Arial and Jasmina and Myleetra– anything to make them stop, they left.

The second and third pairs alternated deliberate torture with erratic behaviour often enough that she worked out the routine.

Then they changed it.

Chapter 12

Bluestocking opened one eye.

"My word, what have they done to you?" Cas said. He stood in the doorway, silhouetted by the lamps down the corridor. It was too dark to see his face– and anyway one of her eyes was caked with blood from a cut on her forehead suffered in the last beating, while the other had closed from an earlier one– but she knew it was him from his voice. He couldn't possibly have seen her face in the dark, so he must have referred to the fact that they had left her lying on her bed of soiled straw.

She scratched where her scalp crawled with the tread of insect feet and ran her tongue over teeth coated with fur, but for a moment hope flared. Maybe the romances would come true! Then reality washed over her as she noted that he stood as far away from her as he possibly could.

"They invited me to lunch," she said wearily. Then she began to laugh hysterically, until the laugh became a sob, and then she broke, as they had surely intended. "Please Cas, get me out of here. You can have me if you want. I'll kiss your feet if you want. But please, *please* get me out of here."

As he stepped into the cell, she crawled on her knees, across the hard floor and reaching out gripped the fine linen of his cloak. "Please," she whispered. "What happened to that good man who took care of me on the way here?" Deep inside her, some vestigial dignity whined that what she was doing was emotional blackmail, but she didn't really care. She needed someone to help her.

He lifted her chin with his forefinger and gasped. "What *have* they done?"

She didn't speak. Silence would make her case for her.

Instead, he pulled his finger away. "I'm sorry, I really wish I could help you," he said. She didn't need to be able to see his face blank, as if he'd drawn a shutter down over his emotions. She'd seen it often enough on the journey to Whiterock, how, when he distanced himself from unpleasantness, his voice became brisk. "That good man as you called him realized his priorities."

"Was it because I rejected you?"

"Did you?"

"You might have felt I did," she said. "I realize now I might have given that impression, although I didn't mean to."

"Whatever happened is in the past," he said, and she knew that her moment had passed. "I came to ask you to put an end to this. In Kurla's name," he referred to a god she had barely heard of, "give them what they need. I'm sure they'll show clemency."

When he said that, her last hope died. There was no hero come to rescue her. She was on her own and would have to find her own way out of the situation, or more likely, die.

"Bluestocking," he said. "Why did you do it?"

"I didn't kill her, I swear."

"I'm here to ask you to confess. There was a witness, and you'd quarrelled publicly with the Princess, barely hours before. All they need is your confession. That's why I'm here. Don't drag it out any longer. Let these people heal their wounds. Confess."

"What if I can't?" she said. "Not will not– but cannot?"

His jaw worked. "Then, I cannot help you. Arial says that they've already decided that you are guilty. I'm so very, very sorry."

"I can't confess what I didn't do," she whimpered. *Of course you can. It's the easiest thing in the world.* "Go," she said. "Please."

"I wish I could help you," he said. "But my own position is uncertain at the moment as well. There is growing hostility toward all foreigners, whether those foreigners are from the Empire or those savages in the west. And I sent Halarbur to report back to the Imperial Court. They seem to have mistaken an entirely sensible precaution as another threat."

"Just go," she repeated. "Please."

His footsteps echoed down the corridor, their slowness a metronome, beating out a time to their separate despair.

***

When they next came for her, two soldiers marched in and dragged her out into the corridor.

Another pair of soldiers flanked Arial, who examined her gravely. "Come with us," he said.

As if I have a choice, she thought, but said nothing. Now that Cas had gone, despair was turning to anger. Only a glow, but it was burning.

The soldiers took her into a room with a ceiling window through which weak sunlight shone through diagonally. It was full of metal instruments that were clearly used for torture. She swallowed, her mouth suddenly dry.

To one side was a long bench on which they laid her out on her stomach and stretched her arms and legs as far as they would go. They pulled them until she gasped with pain, then strapped her ankle and wrists. They cut her clothes away with a blade so sharp she only heard a hissing to mark its passage and anointed her back with a cold unguent.

A tall, strapping man wearing a sleeveless serge shirt entered the room. His face was masked behind a simple black fabric visor, but his eyes studied her, as if he were a butcher weighing up a slab of meat to be cut up. His arms were heavily muscled and lined with thick blue veins.

He wore a black leather glove that fitted so snugly it melded into his arm. When he opened the glove, long nails like claws sprang out. It seemed impossible that he would not hurt himself when he clenched his hand into a fist, but they retracted smoothly.

He opened and closed the glove several times, watching her carefully, claws springing, then retracting. She knew it was a game and that he was trying to frighten her. It was working. She felt a great ball of ice in her throat.

"This is the Hand of Brighannon," Arial said, his voice still sad. "It separates the wheat of truth from the chaff of lies."

"Does the name refer to the man or the glove?" Even now, Bluestocking couldn't resist the tug of curiosity. The hand rested on her shoulder, and a nail ran down the length of her spine.

"Both," Arial said, talking into space. "The man **is** the Hand, an extension of the God. How fitting that it should be Evi's God that should be the instrument of her restitution." When he turned to her, Arial seemed almost sad. "Tell me a lie," he said.

"I'm a man," she said.

"No–" Her world dissolved into fire; it was as if every pore on her back was filled with oil and a lit taper thrown on it.

"See how Brighannon will be revenged for the attack on his daughter, the Princess," the Hand said. "Who are you?"

"Who sold you the balefire, Bluestocking?" Arial asked, before she could even draw breath to answer the first question.

She didn't answer, and felt the claws dig into her back as if possessed of an intelligence of their own. She gasped as they dug in fractionally deeper and deeper, second by second. Her world dissolved again, into fire and pain

"If you don't answer, they will dig into your flesh until they reach your heart," Arial said. "Did you kill the princess?"

"I had nothing to do with the princess' death," she gasped, and the pain eased.

Arial said carefully, "Did anyone pay you to kill the princess?"

"No one," she said promptly.

"If no one paid you, why did you kill her?"

She gasped, expecting the pain to return at any moment, "I– didn't– kill– her. I had no involvement with her death. None. You must know that I'm telling you the truth."

She might never have spoken, when Arial continued, "Who are the other conspirators?"

"There are no other conspirators," she said.

"Who are you working for?"

She didn't answer, and again the nails dug in. Her back arched. "If you kill me for not answering the questions, how will you ever learn the truth?"

"Answer, then, dammit!" Arial shouted.

"Very well," she gasped, and the pain ceased. She swallowed quickly, and before the nails could do more than start to dig in again, she continued. "I'm working for no one else. I came here to translate the Scrolls of Brighannon." She said, "I had no other reason for coming here." Emphasizing the last word, she was relieved that the emphasis did enough to spare her the Hand. Of course she had another reason for coming, but not to Whiterock, simply to escape Ravlatt.

"Who are you working with?" Arial persisted.

It's a nightmare, she thought. *Whatever I say, it makes no difference.* Like so many times before, she wanted– ached– to confess, anything to stop the pain and the humiliation and the fear. So she did. "I killed the Princess Evi," she said, and every muscle, every nerve in her body twisted and arced and screamed, "I didn't kill her, I didn't!" The pain stopped, although the memory of it made her skin crawl.

"She tells the truth," The Hand said.

"I can see that, fool!" Arial said. "Who are you working with?"

"With you," she said, thinking of how he'd issued the invitation and had the pleasure of watching his eyes widen at her answer. "And Copel," she continued.

"You dare!" Arial raised his right hand to strike her, and she flinched. She noticed, however, that the Hand was still.

"You issued the invitation to bring me here! Why, if you're so ready to believe that I'm a killer for hire, or a spy, or worse? Because you wanted someone that you could use as a sacrifice! What other answer could there be? You're involved!" She knew no such thing, of course, it had just been a fleeting fancy, but indignation and fury gave the idea momentum.

His hand swiped the side of her head with a ringing slap. She cried out, "So you claim to want the truth? But when you get it, you revert to brutality! Go on, hit me then! The Hand knows that I tell the truth! Don't you?" She turned her head and stared at him.

After what seemed an eternity, he nodded and clearing this throat, said, "If I may speak, Prime Minister?" He removed the Hand from Bluestocking's back.

White-faced and trembling with rage, Arial wiped his mouth with a cloth and nodded. He seemed not to trust himself to answer.

The Hand said, "Either she has divine protection aiding her lies, or she is innocent. You could argue that if she has the first, then she also is the second."

"I'm not interested in your theological speculations, man!" Arial finally spoke, his voice a wheeze. He took a deep breath. "You're right. My apologies. Our augurs all show that she is involved somehow."

"I have a question," Bluestocking said. Before he could object, she added, "Am I the only person your augurs name?"

Arial shook his head and didn't answer her directly but instead said to the Hand, "Of course we could hardly invite the other Princesses and Prince Cas for an interview."

The Hand shook his head with a slight chuckle. "It would have…consequences."

Arial cursed and called to the soldiers outside. "Take her back to her cell. Get her out of my sight."

He stormed out the room, followed by the Hand. The soldiers undid the clasps and helped her to stand up, one of them half-holding her clothes in front of her body. She was so stunned at the change in Arial and so hurt that her knees shook, and she could barely stand without assistance. Her nudity was almost irrelevant.

Perhaps because her survival of the Hand showed that she might after all be innocent, they were gentler with her as they led her back to the cell. A little later one of them brought her a tray of food and a smock and slippers. The unexpected kindness undid her, and she wept soft, gentle sobs that went on and on.

***

The door crashed open without warning. Afterward, Bluestocking realize that they had crept up to the doorway on bare feet then put on their boots, but just then the men seemed to appear from nowhere. One of them held a lamp at head height as if they were avenging spirits come to drag her off to the Hall of Names to answer for her sins.

Neither of them would meet her gaze. Instead, they led her out of the cell, each man clasping one of her wrists.

Arial looked up from his desk. "Release her," he told Bluestocking's captors, and they let go of her arms. "Sit down." He pointed to a low stool.

"I'd– oof!" Rough hands gripped her shoulders and shoved her down onto the stool. She fidgeted, adjusting her posture. She looked at Arial brightly, cocking her head to one side sparrow-like, hoping that he wouldn't be able to sense her fear. *I'd thought I was done with terror,* she thought.

He looked up. "Leave us," he told her captors. She sat still, listening to the door close, while all the time they locked gazes, she as innocently as possible, he silent.

"So," he said, smiling, but it never reached his eyes.

"So," she said, and she noticed him notice her licking her lips.

"You know," he said. "I really thought that you'd murdered the Princess. I was sure of it." He sighed. "What shall we do with you?"

"You could...release me."

His smile grew wider, and he slowly shook his head. "I don't think so. No, I don't think that that would be wise at all."

"Then will you charge me? If so, with what?" Her voice grew shrill. "I've done nothing wrong, nothing at all." *Keep your head,* she thought. *They're talking to you now, not torturing you.* It was easier to think than to do. "You have nothing to charge me with."

Arial put his hands together and steepled his fingers. "What about treason? As a start."

She swallowed, sought moisture for her lips and palate. "You're delusional. I'm not a citizen of Whiterock. Only a Whiterock citizen can commit treason against your King."

"Always the pedant." There was no malice in his voice, only amused contempt. "I don't suggest that you were party to such a plot," he said, and Bluestocking, who had been convinced that he was the head plotter, suddenly felt that certainty waver at the unexpected lurch the direction of the conversation had taken. "You're no more than an innocent dupe, which makes you a threat to the real plotters."

"Daragel's man planted the bomb in my room, I'm sure of that."

"I assumed as much," Arial said. "I also assumed that Daragel was your sponsor in killing the Princess. He and his man have an alibi for her killing, but you don't. My assumption was that they were tidying up the evidence by killing you. Now I don't know their motive, and I still have an unknown killer wandering the streets. So the safest place for you– ironic though it may be– is in captivity."

"You have two killers on the loose," she said. "Not one."

"The slave girl?" He shrugged. "She's a pawn, like you. When the time is right she'll pay for her crimes, but until then we let her take the lives of a worthless peasant or two."

Bluestocking stiffened in fury at this trivializing of the victim's lives. He didn't seem to notice but continued, "Whoever it is behind her, their plan is probably to deaden her soul, to scoop her out emotionally, leaving a hollow woman."

"Skrai?" Bluestocking guessed.

Arial nodded. "It makes the addict pliable, morally and emotionally dependant on their provider." He suddenly changed subject. "How are you doing with the translation?"

"Mostly there," Bluestocking said, for that much was common knowledge once she had blabbed about it in the Library.

"What have you been able to glean from it?"

She had learned caution since the day in the Library, and his sudden interest put her on her guard. *How much has he learned from his informants?* She wondered and decided that the best lie was to stay as close to the truth as possible. "It's not what I expected." She added, "That is, parts of it are exactly what everyone has said they're about– the creation of Whiterock by Presimionari, the origins of man, battles between the gods, and so on..."

She paused, and he said, "I sense a *but*..."

"But," she said, and they both smiled, "there's a scroll toward the end that is at first sight, complete nonsense. I haven't yet been able to work it out."

"Then you shall," he said, clapping his hands. "I will have your notes brought here."

His sudden enthusiasm made Bluestocking even warier than before. "What– what's the rush?"

"The Princess Cavi has the King's agreement that you must complete the translation and be on your way." He frowned. "Surely you don't want to leave it unfinished?"

"But," she spluttered, "There's an army out there! I mean, I have no desire to anger your royal family, but how am I supposed to leave?"

"Measures are being taken," he said airily, "to sort things out. In the meantime, would it not make more sense to continue with your work here, in perfect safety and peace and quiet?"

"How long do I have?" She felt suddenly numb that once again her fate was being decided for her by others who had no interests in her. "That is, before I am to continue on my way?"

"It could be any day now," he said in tones so sincere that her suspicions became certainties. "What would probably help is for us to arrange a recitation as part of the New Year festivities. In the hours between the Last Day and the New Year, we relax curfew, and often have impromptu performances. And after that, when the King hears how the work has gone, I'm sure that you'll receive your just reward." He beamed, and suddenly Bluestocking felt even warier.

As if they were beasts awoken, the words began to whisper in her mind. "When do I, that is, when does the King wish me to leave?"

"Say, the second day of the New Year," Arial said. "The Day of the Ferret."

The date was plucked so breezily from nowhere that she became sure that that was what his real purpose was. The words of the spell were clamouring at the back of her mind to be let out, and it was all she could do to stop her mouth from opening to utter them.

Instead, she nodded, and Arial rubbed his hands together. "I'll have your papers brought to you." He rose from his chair, and from behind a statue of a heroic figure fighting an ice-bear, pulled a decanter and two glasses. He poured a dark dessert wine into each glass and passed one to her. "Let us toast your impending freedom, once this unfortunate situation has been resolved," he said. He lifted the glass to his lips and sipped. Bluestocking did the same, aware of his gaze, and suddenly reluctant to drink more than the barest measure.

Arial reached behind the statue again and pulled up a small bundle of clothes. "I'm aware that you've had no opportunity to clean yourself," he said. "And I'm sorry that we have no civilized bathing facilities. But we took the liberty of bringing your clothes and some of Princess Lexi's garments, which might fit you."

"Lexi?" Bluestocking had almost forgotten the Princess' existence.

"She asks for you every day," Arial said. "She alone seems convinced you are nothing other than what you claim and had no part in her sister's death. I must say that I found her faith in you touching, if a little naïve." He sipped at his drink again, watching her. "You haven't touched your wine."

"I'm worried that it might go to my head," she said, smiling as innocently as she could. "May I change? I'm filthy."

"I'll turn my back," Arial said.

Bluestocking shrugged and stepped out of her smock and slippers, then slowly dressed in her best knee-length black dress, savouring the softness of clean clothes and wondering whether this might be the last occasion she would ever dress up. Almost certainly Arial intended that she be disposed of, together with Kyr, once her purpose was fulfilled.

She became aware of a commotion in the corridor outside. There were shouts, and moments later, even as Arial reached for a sword that had lain unnoticed until then on his desk, the door crashed open.

Chapter 13

"What's this impertinence?" Arial cried, as two masked figures burst through the door.

Before he could say anything else, the smaller of the two held a knife to Arial's throat and hissed, "Silence or you die!" Beneath the croak of a disguise spell the voice of Arial's assailant was strangely familiar. Bluestocking couldn't place it but noted a local accent. As his assailant turned Arial around, a lock of black hair spilled out from beneath the attacker's hat. Arial's eyes widened, but he said nothing.

The second assailant grabbed Bluestocking and backed with her toward the doorway.

Arial licked his lips, but before he could say anything, the first attacker said, still holding the knife to his throat, "We can't leave him to raise the alarm."

"No," the second man said, moving away from Bluestocking and bringing a sand-bag he'd held hidden in his hand thudding down onto Arial's neck. "Now we can."

Bluestocking noted the very slight, imperceptible withering of his left hand and almost blurted "Daragel?" but managed to stay silent.

They ran down the corridor until they reached a junction. "One moment!" Bluestocking called. She reached down the hem of her dress, tore it up to the middle of her thighs and ripped it around from front to back. "Typical of that weasel," she grumbled, "to fetch my best dress and have me put it on just as I'm rescued."

Daragel peeled away and raised his withered hand in farewell. Grabbing Bluestocking's hand, the first man tugged her along behind him.

"The Prince," Bluestocking said.

"Not here," her rescuer said. "Come."

They raced down white walled corridors stained dark with the residue of torture, past sleeping militiamen in doorways whose drugged snores reverberated, up the steps and into the cool night air.

Bluestocking pulled up with a stitch, hand held up in entreaty.

"We'll wait...a...moment," her rescuer agreed, pulling the mask off. Kyr grinned at an astonished Bluestocking. "Surprised?"

She gasped, and the incongruity of the strange croak coming from Kyr's mouth made Bluestocking's gape. Kyr pushed Bluestocking's chin up to close her mouth. She stretched up and kissed Bluestocking, who tasted aniseed and something else, something indefinable.

Bluestocking pulled back, and Kyr grinned. "Don't worry," she said, her voice slowly starting to return to normal. "It was just a potion. Some herbs, some magic, and for an hour or so I have a new voice." Kyr pulled her along an alleyway. "Come along."

They left an almost full Old Man Moon to peer down through ragged hands of drifting clouds, then descended into the bowels of Whiterock. Their run gradually slowed to a trot, then to a slow walk as fatigue took its toll.

Kyr gasped, "If we move too quickly down here, we'll attract attention." She chuckled. "Not that we're exactly inconspicuous."

"How did you and Daragel come together?" Bluestocking said.

"I escaped right after you were arrested," Kyr said. "When they took you away, I offered the guard a little something, and when he took me around the corner, I– no, you don't want to know. Let's just say he won't father any children."

"What about your manacles?"

Kyr grinned. "Well, he couldn't get my legs apart with them on, so he undid them.

Bluestocking stared at this woman who suddenly seemed a complete stranger. *What else are you capable of?* she thought. *Betrayal? Murder? Is this rescue even what it appears?*

Kyr caught the look and shrugged. "I wouldn't have been much use locked away as well, would I, heart?" As they passed a street-lamp, Kyr squeezed Bluestocking's hand.

She was shocked to see the slave blink away tears. Bluestocking asked, choosing a more innocuous question, "Why are there lamps, when they have curfews?"

Kyr's laugh was half-way to a sob. "Trust you to bother with detail like that. It's for when curfew is lifted, or those allowed out with exeats are able to find their way around."

"Oh." Into the silence broken only by their footfalls, Bluestocking said, "How did Daragel come to be involved?"

"Quite the little inquisitor tonight," Kyr said. "I'd have thought that you'd have just been happy to be out of there after three nights–"

*Three nights! It's **that** close to Year End!* "I am, I am! But it's such an odd alliance..."

"Needs must," Kyr said. "After I escaped the militiamen, I headed straight for their headquarters." She chuckled, her laughter bubbling. "I knew it was the very last place those lack wits would look for me. While I was hanging around, I saw Daragel being taken to his rooms in the palace under escort. He misses nothing, so I knew he'd be alert, and I let him glimpse me. He signalled me to follow him."

They stopped at the sound of voices ahead and waited for them to move away. Kyr resumed, quietly, "Thank the Gods that word of my escape hadn't reached the other idiots guarding Daragel. I gave a guard a little present, see? He let me sneak in to see what Daragel wanted– apart from his freedom. Daragel said we had a mutual interest in seeing you released, and so we laid our plans. He always left the door open, so I could hear his jokes with the guards about freeing a prisoner; jokes he knew I would act on." Until then, she had told her tale with relish, but she sobered. "Tonight I waved sleeping salts under the guard's noses, and off we went. She added, "I'm sure he only agreed to help so he could disappear in the chaos."

"Why?"

Kyr sighed. "I don't know. There's so much I don't know."

They walked down through the levels, twisting and turning through the labyrinthine alleyways, shying away from the sound of human voices and trying to shut out the inhuman, the dwellings grew meaner, and to Bluestocking's surprise, started to seem slightly familiar.

"Where are we going?" Bluestocking whispered.

"Anywhere where *they* are not," Kyr said. "Hush now."

They dropped another couple of levels, and Bluestocking muttered, "I know this place." Several of the houses had gargoyles tethered to the frame of the door, and the captive sentinels watched them pass with a scraping of their stony necks. One hissed something, and Bluestocking knew where she'd seen it. The last time she'd been this way, most of the gargoyles would have been hidden, but she knew that long, thin snout, the verdigris-stained copper collar that scraped against stone as it moved– that one had hissed at her before.

"I wouldn't have thought that you've been down here," Kyr said.

"No, I have," Bluestocking said, stopping at a door. "One moment," she said, opening the door and poking her head in. "Mari?"

Kyr gripped her elbow. "What by all the Gods of Whiterock are you doing? Come along, we don't have time to hang around!"

Bluestocking shook her loose. "I owe her this much. We can spare her a few dozen heartbeats, surely? Especially if she's prepared to offer us shelter."

"Do you think that she might?" Kyr whispered.

Bluestocking pushed the door wide open and strode in, trying to stay calm.

In contrast to the neat nest she had seen on her previous visit, the kitchen was a mess. Bowls crusted with food formed a rickety tower. The stone floor was covered with debris and had clearly not been swept for several days. The taint of blood hung heavy in the air. "Mari?" Bluestocking called. She noticed a dark stain on one side of the floor.

"She's not here," Kyr said. "But we need to find somewhere safe to hide."

Bluestocking stepped toward it, then stopped and looked down at the discolouration. She reached down and touched it. "Blood. And something else."

Kyr sniffed at Bluestocking's fingers. "Someone's water broke."

A groan issued through a narrow doorway at the back, and Bluestocking pushed her way through the piles of rubbish. "Mari?"

The young woman lay in a corner, clutching a small baby. Mari opened her eyes. "So tired," she whispered. Her forehead was beaded with sweat, and her dark skin was unhealthily pale. Bluestocking noticed her hands were covered with the dark red of dried blood. Mari met Bluestocking's gaze. "Couldn't stop the blood," she whispered.

Bluestocking asked Mari, "Have you named the baby?"

Mari shook her head weakly. "Get a Nomenati, please," she whispered.

"We don't have time. Besides–" Kyr caught Bluestocking's glare and added hastily, "I'll see what I can find." She fled, leaving Bluestocking alone with the young mother.

The baby grumbled in its sleep. "Is it a boy or a girl?" Bluestocking asked.

"A boy," Mari whispered. "I managed to tie off the cord, but I kept bleeding and bleeding." She crooned something unintelligible at the baby, but her voice was growing weaker by the second it seemed.

The boy made a sighing, gurgling noise but was unusually quiet, even to Bluestocking's inexperienced eye. "Have you fed him?"

Mari nodded, her eyes closing. She jerked herself awake.

"Why were you alone? Have you no husband?" Bluestocking asked, moistening a cloth with some water from a metal jug.

"He hasn't been home since the night the Alliance arrived," Mari whispered. "I'm scared."

Bluestocking squeezed her hand. Mari jerked herself upright, but her breathing was growing increasingly laboured. *Where are you, Kyr?* Bluestocking thought. *Hurry up, or it'll be too late.*

"My family are mostly dead, as well," Mari whispered. "Those that weren't– I thought they would be here. I don't know why they didn't come..."

Bluestocking wiped the woman's mouth with the moistened cloth. "Save your strength," she said. She wondered if any of the wizards would help them. Nothing but magic could save Mari now.

Mari shook her head. "Have no strength," she whispered.

Bluestocking heard voices outside and stiffened. She looked around for something to defend herself with and had to make do with a heavy clay skillet. She relaxed when she heard Kyr's voice say, "In here, Your Worship."

Kyr urged a scared-looking young man into the room. "Landor is a Nomenati," she explained and added. "He qualified a month or so ago."

The young man nodded eagerly and fumbled in his pockets. "My first Naming. I wish that the circumstances were better."

"My first, too," Bluestocking said. "I stand in place of the father, who is absent."

Landor tsked, probably in condemnation of feckless fathers, Bluestocking decided. He produced a dark-green crystal shaped like two pyramids whose bases lay against one another. "All the way from the mines of Tain. The Alliance quarry good stones, better than anything you're used to, I suspect."

"We tried to find a medicine man," Kyr explained, but they're all above or hiding." She grinned and whispered, "I had to press a piece of glass to his throat to get even this miserable specimen to come."

Bluestocking raised an eyebrow. "Threatening a Nomenati? Where I come from, that carries heavy penalties. Imprisonment. Mutilation."

"I think upsetting the priesthood is the least of our worries at the moment," Kyr said.

Landor kissed the stone. Bluestocking had heard so many different stories, that the stones were semi-intelligent; that they were the footprint of the passing gods; that they held the spirits of the recently departed in a sort of halfway house to the heavens; each depended on the religion of those offering their theory. Landor recited the spells that would awaken the sleeping spirit within and render it receptive to the baby's breath.

Landor placed the stone under the baby's nose, then shook his head and removed it. He leaned close to the baby. "He's hardly breathing." He pushed the stone into its mouth.

"Don't choke him!" Mari cried.

"We must get him named," Landor said. "Else he be condemned to wander the Fields of Llyrain for eternity." He pushed the stone again, and licking it, the baby let out a plaintive little mew, pulling his mouth away. "Good boy," Landor crooned. "Again, just to be sure it has your essence." He pushed again, and the baby cried. "Good little man!" He took the sacrificial knife from its gold-leaved scabbard and searched for the flaw in the stone that every gem had. "It's almost half-way," he mused aloud. "It'll look like a pyramid."

He pressed the knife to the flaw and whispered the spell of relief to free the spirit, which would cry the baby's name on its way to freedom.

"Har-gett," came the thin little voice of the namestone's spirit. "Hargett."

"I name this boy Hargett," Landor intoned. "May he have a long and healthy life and serve the gods well." He stood and bowed.

"Will you take a glass of wine, Brother?" Bluestocking chewed her lip to control the rush of emotions. "I don't think that I can offer you food. I mean, I'm sure Mari has some–"

Landor held up a hand. "Thank you, no. This poor lady can probably ill-afford it, and I must be on my way. I think that the forces around Whiterock will still hold to the vow of not interfering with us Nomenati on our business, but I wouldn't want to wager on it. So I must find a mage and have him direct a gem-bird to carry the stone to the Hall of Names. I may even have to do it myself." He shuddered. "I've never had to catch one of the cranes before. Their beaks are fearfully sharp." He gathered his knife and his vials, and smiled. "I will bid you a safe day, ladies."

When he had left, Bluestocking knelt by Mari. Her breathing was shallow and ragged, but she opened her eyes and smiled, though it was twisted with pain. "He's gone," she said, and Bluestocking thought she was referring to Landor. "But Hargett has his name. He will walk with the Gods." She lifted the baby, which had turned blue and was no longer breathing. "I am so glad," Mari said with a suddenly radiant smile, "that you came to Whiterock. That we met, and I helped you that day. You have repaid me twenty times over."

Bluestocking dug her nails into her palm to ease her own ache and made herself smile back. "No, the debt is still mine," she said. "You've taught me something I can't repay you for: to have the strength to fight on, whatever the odds."

Mari spasmed, fighting for breath. "I'll be with him soon–"

"Hush," Bluestocking said, wondering what she could do, knowing there was nothing.

"I–" Mari spasmed again, and her eyes rolled up into her head.

Bluestocking felt the base of her neck and then closed the woman's eyes.

She threw her arms around the dead woman and her baby and wept.

***

She had barely begun to weep, it seemed, when Kyr touched her shoulder. "This may seem callous, but there are still the living to think about."

"You're right." Bluestocking wiped her nose and eyes on her sleeve. She froze. "What was that noise?"

Kyr listened, then after a few seconds, shook her head. "I can't hear anything." She dropped her voice still further. "Probably the people next door. We can't stay here. These walls are parchment-thin, and if we haven't already been overheard, we'll be marked as strangers the moment they knock on the door to offer congratulations or commiserations on Mari's birth." She added, "They'll have heard us tonight."

"But she'd been left alone for days!" Bluestocking said. "How can they have done that, if they can hear everything?"

Kyr shrugged. "Maybe they had a falling-out. Maybe you're right, and there's no one there. But if they've gone somewhere else, they could just as easily return. You want to take a chance and stay here over New Year?" She smiled. "I thought not. Still, they haven't come around yet. Maybe they're up on the walls, part of that mob gawping at the Alliance forces."

Cupping water from the jug in her palms, Bluestocking splashed her face. "We'll take food and water. Mari won't need it, and I think her man won't be coming home, so we may as well strip the place." She added, "Though it seems like grave robbing."

"We'll make things right with any of her family that live later," Kyr said.

"Kyr," Bluestocking said.

Kyr turned to face her. "Yes?"

"I know," Bluestocking said. "About the murders."

Kyr staggered. "How?" She leaned against a wall for support and licked her lips. Her eyes widened, and her pupils shrank to pinpoints.

"Are you going to kill me?" Bluestocking said.

Kyr shook her head. "No, never. I'd rather, I mean, I would never, ever do anything to harm you, I..." She covered her hand with her mouth, and Bluestocking reached for her. Kyr fell into her arms and clawed at her through their clothes. "I'd sooner rip out my own heart than hurt you," Kyr whispered into Bluestocking's hair. Kyr pulled away and gripping each side of Bluestocking's head, stared into her eyes. "You must believe that."

"I do," Bluestocking whispered. "But while I trust you now, how can I rely on the you that comes out when you've taken *Skrai?*"

"There's no me to come out," Kyr said. "When I take *Skrai,* I do whatever you want." She laughed bitterly. "Myleetra gave it to me to ease the cramps each moon. By the time I found out what it was really like, it was too late. The only thing that comes out under *Skrai* is–"

"–what Myleetra wants." Bluestocking finished for her. "We should tell someone. The King, the Prime Minister."

Kyr shook her head. "Even if they believed a foreigner and a slave who's a known trouble-maker, what makes you think we'd live long enough to testify? Myleetra has friends in the Ministries."

"Who?"

"Don't know." Kyr chewed her lip. "I'm sorry," she said, "for bringing you into this."

She looked so wretched that for a moment her shame highlighted Bluestocking's own hypocrisy. She had almost told Kyr of her own secret so many times, but each time the desire to protect Kyr, so that she could not be an accomplice to what she didn't know (*like Visohn's family,* the treacherous thought whispered. *Their innocence really protected them, didn't it?*) helped her hold her tongue.

The spell started its insidious clamour for release again. She opened her mouth.

Kyr saved her. "Our best plan is to keep moving and hide until the siege lifts."

"But that could be weeks! Months even!"

Kyr covered Bluestocking's mouth, and she realized that she'd been almost shouting.

"Not so loud," Kyr whispered, pointing at the wall.

Bluestocking nodded. The adrenaline that had helped her so far was fading, and her arms and legs were hurting. When she changed position, a muscle protested, and she winced.

"I can give you something for your aches and pains," Kyr said, "but the after-effects will be even worse when it wears off." She held up a hand, "Not *Skrai*. This is more a muscle relaxant. But take more than a few doses, and it is highly addictive."

Bluestocking nodded. "I need something. You'll need something, if we're going to keep going long enough to get away."

"Me?" Kyr asked. "I came to get you. Once you've left, my darling, I'll go back to being the tabby-cat slave they all know and love."

"But you can't stay here!" Bluestocking said. "They'll be tearing the place apart– and Arial recognized you."

"Oh I doubt that," Kyr said, laughing, but Bluestocking saw the fear in her eyes.

Is she really so stupid that she thinks she can just smile her way out of this?

Kyr continued, "I've had a little time to think, and I'm good at listening at keyholes, see, or hiding behind drapes." She stared into space. "I think the siege will lift fairly soon." She smiled at Bluestocking, whose heart felt as if it would turn over. "The Princess Lexi thinks that the troops are here to force an early marriage between her and the Emir and that her father will agree. I think Daragel will make him give up the throne, myself, but she doesn't. She won't believe that they'd have her Pa abdicate and leave her, the eldest daughter, on the throne with a puppeteer husband. Her desperation makes her ignore what she doesn't like."

"Yes," Bluestocking said. "Funny how people do that, isn't it?"

Kyr refused to meet her gaze. "And I heard your Prince tell Cavi that he'd sent that stuffed-shirt servant of his for help from the Empire," she finished defiantly, " So you see, you'll be gone soon, and I'll go back to how things were before, before...." She pressed Bluestocking's hand. "Don't fret yourself, my love. I'll be alright."

Bluestocking kissed Kyr, taking her lover's lower lip between her teeth, hands framing Kyr's face. She let Kyr's lip go and panted, "Come away with me."

"I can't." Kyr said. "Any more than you can stay here for good. You know what they do to renegade slaves! Don't do this to me. I like it here. I know my place in the world."

"You like it?" Bluestocking said. "You like being tortured? Used as a whore? Killing? Stealing?"

Kyr looked abashed. "Maybe like is too strong a word," she said. "But I know this place. It's–" She stiffened, then stilled at faint voices coming down the street. "If we can get away..." she whispered, her breath tickling the inside of Bluestocking's ear, "...we'll go back to my quarters."

"You have quarters?" Bluestocking whispered into Kyr's ear in turn. "I thought slaves shared a dorm."

"Not royal slaves," Kyr breathed. She stopped as the voices drew near, then relaxed as they went away. "It's a cupboard. It's tiny even compared to the one I use in your rooms."

"Could we go back to my chambers?" *Come on, think Bluestocking!*

Kyr shook her head. "They've already moved other people into the rooms."

"What about the caves where the silk spiders are?"

Kyr stared at her and shuddered. "Are you mad?"

Bluestocking said, "I know they're caves, but–"

"But nothing. Bad things happen to people who go there."

"Tourists visit all the time."

"Aye," Kyr spat. "They know no better. Stay away from them, for Brighannon's sake."

Bluestocking stared at her. "So I suppose that the caves are out of the question, then."

Kyr ignored the sarcasm. "It's my quarters or nowhere."

"Very well."

Kyr went first, poking her head out of the doorway and beckoning Bluestocking.

The spell whispered in Bluestocking's head, forcing her mouth open, but she clamped it shut. *This is folly,* she thought. *Does she seriously expect that we'll be able to hide behind the curtains until we find a way off this blasted rock?*

They crept through the streets, and Bluestocking grew even more anxious at movements in the shadows. Tonight Whiterock seemed haunted by them moving with the intermittent covering of the moon by the raggedy clouds. Her caution opened up a gap between her and Kyr, who seemed much bolder now that she had somewhere to go.

From somewhere behind them came the same mournful howl that Bluestocking had heard the night that she was arrested.

"Bloodhounds!" Kyr gasped and moaned. "Could they have given them something of yours to smell?"

"The straw I lay on?" Bluestocking asked, and Kyr nodded, her face pinched. "There's worse," Bluestocking continued. "I menstruated and couldn't clean it off." She lifted her leg, and the tiniest petty part of her exulted in the look of fury that crossed Kyr's face.

"The bastards," Kyr spat. "The verminous pigs. They didn't even have the decency to wash you down–"

"No time for that," Bluestocking pressed her fingers to Kyr's lips.

The moon vanished behind another bank of clouds. They ran, Kyr slightly behind her, the slave's shorter legs struggling to keep pace.

Bluestocking heard noises from ahead but couldn't stop in time. She cursed under her breath as she skidded round a corner and nearly ran into a group of six or seven men.

The noise was from them larking about, laughing and joking amongst themselves. She looked around the courtyard before ducking back, realizing just how lucky she'd been. No more than ten yards away from where she'd skidded, a pair of soldiers stood watching in the opposite direction. If they'd turned around at the time, there would have been no way of them not seeing her, but fortunately their own racket had drowned out her skidding feet. On the far side of the courtyard, another pair of soldiers marched at right angles to the first pair.

Desperately, she racked her brains for some way out of this living nightmare. She hissed at Kyr, "Surely you don't believe that we can carry on living here? There are soldiers and militiamen everywhere!" *If only I could have just a few minutes to think something up, rather than skittering around like rats in a maze.* But the pursuit had been unrelenting, and they seemed destined to lurch from one crisis to another.

Again, the spell started its ominous whispering in her mind, and she felt her jaws working. She clamped her teeth shut so hard that she nicked her tongue and had to swallow the blood. Its taste was foul enough to distract her.

The slap of the men's boots on the flagstones came nearer and nearer, and Bluestocking tried to shrink back so far, she almost pushed back into the very stone of the wall. The moon chose that moment to duck behind the clouds.

"Shouldn't we wait, Sarge," one of the men asked, "'til the moon comes out again?"

"Nah," Sarge replied. "We'd a seen them if they was here. Keep going. I can hear a hot toddy calling my name and a chair waiting for my arse."

That brought some ribald comments as the men passed. Bluestocking was sure that they would hear her heart beating. She could smell them; a combination of stale beer and sweat and– accompanied by a long ripping sound, and groans and shouted laughter– a sulphurous waft of flatulence. "Better out than in," the perpetrator said with evident satisfaction.

When the moon appeared again, they had passed and were walking with their backs to her. She had just allowed herself to breathe again, when she heard voices coming nearer.

If she'd been able to curse out loud she would have done so, but fearing the noise might attract their attention, she contented herself with a grimace of distaste. She felt for and took Kyr's hand.

"Found this lady roaming round, sir," a man's voice said.

"What are you doing here?" Arial's voice was filled to bursting with exasperation. "The messenger sent down to me said simply that they'd found a woman. I assumed that it was Bluestocking!" He added– Bluestocking assumed to someone else– "Leave us now."

"Well," Myleetra replied after a pause, "I assume they'd recognize the head witch. Why didn't the moron who took you the message specify it was me?"

"Who knows?" Arial sighed. "So what brings you out and about?"

"What you mean is, what am I doing getting under your men's feet–"

"Exactly."

"I came to help," Myleetra said. "I don't like the omens I've been reading. There's a storm building, and this girl is at the centre of it. I can't see beyond the end of tonight. It's like the gods have built a big black wall, hiding what may be from my eyes. I've never known anything like it."

"Leave it to us," Arial said. They were starting to walk away now, and Bluestocking had to strain to hear them, until—

"What?" Myleetra's voice cracked the word like a whip lashing.

"The less that you're seen to have to do with this, the better. Your part will come in the New Year, once she's recited the incantation."

Maddeningly, their voices faded into the night despite all Bluestocking's efforts.

They scuttled forward from doorway to doorway, keeping a wary eye out for patrols. "They'll kill me for sure, if they catch us," Kyr moaned. 'They'll keep you alive, at least until you're no more use to them. But a slow, lingering death awaits me."

"Keep your head," Bluestocking urged, although she was finding it hard to follow her own advice. Her chest felt as if a broad band was being tightened moment by moment, every breath costing a greater effort. Her legs were leaden, and she desperately wanted to sleep.

In the distance, the dogs howled again, and Kyr's teeth began to chatter.

The spell began its insidious whispering again. "Why the New Year?' Bluestocking asked to distract her thoughts from it.

"All things are malleable in the New Year," Kyr whispered. "The very stuff of life is like wet clay." She added, "So I've heard them say. Believe it or not, they don't confide much in slaves as a rule."

Her sarcasm made Bluestocking smile, and on an impulse, she turned and kissed her hard. "That's my girl!" she hissed. "Sarky to the end! Let's give their bloody dogs a run!"

They fled through the night, ducking and weaving and skidding in an irregular zig-zag toward Kyr's room, bobbing and sliding their way toward safety, alleyway by alleyway. "Promise me," Kyr panted. 'That you'll kill me if they take us."

"Never," Bluestocking panted, the spell whispering, clamouring to be released. "But they'll not hurt you. I promise you that. I'll find some way of protecting you."

She thought, *It can't get any bloody worse than this, surely?* Then she almost burst out laughing, despite the stitch that was setting into her side. *For all that you're fleeing for your life from conspirators and cut-throats, don't make that mistake, woman. Things can always be worse–I'm just not sure how at the moment.*

They raced across an alleyway, into a courtyard, when she heard shouts; "Hey you there! Stop!" She looked around and saw the militia behind, running toward them.

They ran down a side alley, straight into the arms of another patrol.

"We have them, Prime Minister!" One of the men shouted, his sword-tip pressed against Bluestocking's throat. The spell started its tiny, tinny clamour in her head.

Arial strode toward them smiling.

What to do? I'm just a linguist, here to translate some bloody scrolls, she thought. And that was all she could do.

"Well, well," Arial said, as Bluestocking gave way to the pressure inside her head and so quietly that he could not hear her, began to mutter the spell.

Chapter 14

"Ladies," Arial said. "This *is* a pleasure, although rather like the deflowering of a tiresomely reluctant virgin, it's been too long delayed and required far too much effort."

His smile slipped for a moment, and his hand lashed Kyr across the face. "I'll deal with you later," he said, and turned toward Bluestocking. "A shame that you had to rip that nice dress to pieces, for no good purpose. Never mind. You have some work to finish for us, and if necessary, you'll do it in rags." He looked quizzical. "What are you doing?"

The conversation had taken less than a minute, and Bluestocking was no more than part way through the spell. She had felt the slow turning of the earth, the movement of the magma, and also felt the presence of something else straining at the confines of its prison. It howled its frustration silently, and she urged, *be patient,* though she had no way of knowing whether it could hear her thoughts. She stopped the recitation.

"Just getting my breath back." she added as plaintively as if she had no idea of what the slippery little turd had in mind, "Why are you doing this?" He opened his mouth, and she blurted, "And no more lies!"

"You want me to play the gloating master-villain?" Arial shrugged. "So be it." He leaned across and licked thick lips as red as tomatoes. "Do you know what it's like to know you've gone as far as you can? That at best, as clearly as you can see half the world from up here that you know the path of your life for the rest of your days? To know that you've climbed as high as you ever will? And that's the *best* the gods have in store for you; any surprises will be bad ones. In your case, little girl, no mighty-thewed warrior is going to throw you across the pommel of their horse and carry you off to Outer Valkyr or wherever, to make you their queen. Instead, if you're wrong about your life, it'll be because a rock falls on your head, you die in an uprising, or you cough your lungs up from the plague."

He laughed bitterly. "No? Don't look so shocked. If you don't know, it's because you're young, my dear, and you have the whole of your blissful little life stretching out ahead of you." He held his hands out and opened his arms.

She'd been able to buy another forty seconds to mumble the spell. The hinges of the world turned slowly, creakingly a little more, allowing the prisoner elsewhere the chance to ease out of its prison a fraction more.

Not knowing what else to do, shocked by his bitterness, Bluestocking swayed onto the tip of the sword that the soldier still held to her throat and felt a trickle of blood down her throat.

"Careful fools!" Arial lunged and caught her as she slumped.

"So tired," she gasped. Momentarily inspired, she smiled at Arial. "Cas, darling."

"She's delirious!" someone cried, and she clutched at the voice.

"Don't let them take me, Uncle!" she cried.

"Get her indoors, and send for a physic!" Arial barked. "We *must* cure her tonight!"

Bluestocking caught Kyr's anxious face staring at her and longed to give her a wink, but dared not. Instead, she gave way to the insistent clamour in her brain and resumed the mumbled release of the captive, urgency growing by the moment.

The Silk Palace

But even as she felt the urgency, she felt a slight, almost imperceptible counter-force working against it. It was hard to pin down what or where it was, but it was definitely there.

Arial's men carried her and marched the others through the maze of side-streets. It seemed to have been the longest night of Bluestocking's life. When she reached what she thought was the penultimate stage of the spell, she broke off and asked, "What's the time?"

Somewhere in the bowels of the earth, Bluestocking felt a shifting of the continents and heard a distant howl of frustration. She wondered if anyone else had even heard it.

The militiaman she asked ignored her, so she shook his arm, wondering whether she would get a sword in the gut for her trouble. "What's the time, Uncle Wolf?"

"Five bells after midnight," he muttered, shaking her off and making the warding gesture. "Possessed," he muttered to his comrade.

Without warning the party swung right. Bluestocking felt a wondrous power and a murderous rage growing within her, and she wanted more than anything to slash and maim her captors with whatever came to hand. She reached the last verse just as they were led down the steps again, back to her previous quarters, and as she and Kyr were separated she felt the power surging through the earth.

Bluestocking looked back as Kyr gazed back at her, just as Bluestocking reached the end of the spell. She felt again that vast, old consciousness, but now it moved up through the rocks toward the surface, upwards and again, she felt the tramp of feet on the lowest floor, as the militias returned to quarters, summoned to stand down. Again, upwards, and it was in the library walls, swimming upwards and through them. It raced through the walls of the silk palace as if they were no more substantial than air, and then it was racing toward her–

–And she shouted, "I love you, Kyr!" as they led her lover away around the corner.

***

They put Bluestocking in Arial's office and laid the scrolls in front of her. "Best get on with it," a guard said, but before she could begin, Myleetra stood in the doorway, studying her.

"Are you recovered?" Myleetra said, and Bluestocking wondered what the witch knew, or what she suspected. "They said that you were rambling, delusional even."

"I took a knock to the head earlier this evening," Bluestocking said, and thought, *what does it matter, anyway? You've said their precious spell, and much good it's done. You might as well have not bothered.* Deep down in her heart she knew that it wasn't true. Something, somewhere had changed– she just didn't know what it was yet. "It just shook me up for a little while. I'm better now."

"Let me look," Myleetra said, and Bluestocking pointed to a lump on her head. She had been so knocked about that there might have been something there. "Hmm, can't feel anything," Myleetra said, and again Bluestocking wondered how much she suspected. "I'll leave you to your work," she said, with a smile.

***

She lost herself in the scrolls, but now they seemed futile. She felt spent and wondered where Kyr was, what they were doing to her, if she could somehow trick the guard–

–the door crashed open.

"Kyr!" Bluestocking hissed excitedly.

Kyr stood silhouetted, a burning brand in one hand, a sword in the other. "Come on! Let's go!" Kyr threw her the sword. Bluestocking caught it clumsily, nearly cutting her hand. Kyr turned around, and Bluestocking saw cowering in the corner two frail old men on whom the Whiterock militia uniforms hung like shrouds on skeletons.

Bluestocking saw Kyr make a gesture, finger to lips and grab another sword. She grinned wolfishly. "Show 'em a blade, and they go all of a quiver."

"How did you escape?" Bluestocking asked.

"They," Kyr jerked her thumb at the pair, "were detailed to guard me. Even if they hadn't been so addled as to leave the door open as they turned their backs on me and let me steal a sword, I could probably still have wrestled them into submission."

She pushed past Bluestocking who said, "Arial's people must be desperately short of men if they detail an old pair like that to guard you."

"They're all out manning the walls," Kyr said, "a second army has started to arrive, and there are clashes down on the plain below."

"The Empire?" Bluestocking felt a sudden surge of hope and wondered why. There would be no safety for her, even if the Imperium prevailed. Still, there was a raw burst of joy within her that her own countrymen had arrived, illogical or not.

"Doubtless," Kyr said, and turned and kissed Bluestocking on the lips. "That's just in case you thought I wasn't pleased to see you." They stopped at the sound of voices ahead.

The voices faded.

"We need to get off this rock," Bluestocking said, adding, "You can't go back now."

"It'll be Arial's word that I was involved against mine as a trusted royal slave that I wasn't," Kyr said. "But whether I come with you or not, my love, I agree: we need to get you away, one way or another."

Bluestocking wanted to protest that Kyr couldn't possibly stay in Whiterock any longer but realized that it wasn't the best moment to bring it up.

Kyr hissed, "Come on!" She ran down the passage, skidding to a stop where it crossed another and scuttling across the open space. Bluestocking was taller and fitter than Kyr, and laden down with only a sword, rather than Kyr's sword and torch, and she soon eased past her lover. The moon re-emerged, and Bluestocking felt a sense of growing unease at their being visible.

The moon went in, and Bluestocking slowed. "Where now?" she panted.

"That way," Kyr said. She seemed barely to be breathing hard, to Bluestocking's surprise.

***

They detoured down a side alley and emerged by the palace walls. For the first time, Bluestocking felt the chill of the night as the wind plucked at her sleeves. They ran along the walls but had to stop at each section. Several times they had to wait as soldiers crisscrossing the palace's labyrinthine alleyways passed them by, but each time they were lucky.

Although Bluestocking didn't feel lucky. *Still,* she thought, *where are these soldiers guarding the walls, that left Kyr's captors so short-handed that they had to guard her with old men? If anything, now that they think they have us, the place is quieter than ever.*

Something wasn't quite right. She tried to work out what it could be, but this constant running around was wearing her down. Instead, the vague, formless feeling of dread grew all the time. Bluestocking couldn't quite put her finger on what was causing it. Oddly enough, it seemed to grow worse whenever the moon came out, rather than when it was dark. Like many others, she'd always been more comfortable in moonlight than in the dark, although it wasn't something as concrete as a fear of it– more like a vague disquiet. So it was that she thought that she was just fearful of being spotted by the guards that made her so edgy.

Something caught her eye on the edge of her vision– movement. *Don't let them have allowed an afreet to slip through the defenses while they're looking for us,* she thought. Her anxiety soared when she saw a shadow ahead of them, static and immobile. Like a scarecrow stood in a field.

Kyr nudged her. "We may need to cut inside, then duck around it," she hissed.

"What is it?"

"One of the king's pet wizards," Kyr said, in a scornful tone Bluestocking hadn't heard before. "Keeping an eye out for us. There are normally a couple of them out anyway, but they're usually gathered at the southern end of the wall. There are a lot more of them out and about tonight. Not that they'll have any chance of stopping us!"

Watching it as they ducked around, Bluestocking heard a sudden cry and saw the figure topple forward, clutching at his chest. She looked around and saw Kyr crouching, gasping as if she had run half around the world.

"Was that you?" Bluestocking said.

After a long silence, Kyr said, "Was what me?"

If it was, then you're not going to admit it, are you, my love? "Never mind," Bluestocking said.

They ran, Bluestocking stumbling at one point, but before she could fall on the cobbles, Kyr hauled her upright. They ran on, Bluestocking too winded even to gasp thanks. She panted, "How much further?" At what must have been their third such diversion, she gulped air into her burning lungs and tried not to cough as cold collided with warm.

For a moment, Kyr didn't answer, and Bluestocking felt the sense of dread grow. She thought she heard something chitinous scrape, like a great hoof on stone, and she was torn between turning her head to see where Kyr was, and not wanting to for fear that she'd see something unspeakable lurking just behind her.

The moon went in, and her panic subsided. Kyr said, breathing into her ear, "Almost there. Just around this next corner."

The wall was low on this last part, and as they ran, almost crouched double to avoid being seen in the lamplight, Bluestocking looked up at a vast, almost formless, shadow that seemed to come from behind her. She glanced over her shoulder, but Kyr was alone.

"Nearly there!" Kyr panted exultantly. It started to drizzle, whipped by the gusting breeze so that it stung the skin, adding to Bluestocking's growing unease.

"Where? Oh no!" Bluestocking whimpered. Ahead was the bumping, jostling shape of a partly deflated airbag, nuzzling another in the breeze. The bays were full of them, she realized. They had come upon them from another angle. Vast, bumping bags, that would carry her out into the night on nothing more substantial than a wicker floor, that if it snapped, she would fall screaming hundreds of chains to her death…"I can't go in that again," she whispered. She'd heard of being sick with fear, but had always thought it a cliché of the tale-teller's, until now. She wasn't sure which was worse, the prospect of flying it in daylight, when she could actually see the land laid out below, or in the dark, with her imagination adding to her terror.

"You have to!" Kyr snapped. Then, more gently, "I'll come with you this time."

"You mean it?" Bluestocking whispered, a huge smile spreading across her face. For a moment, her joy was almost enough to obliterate her fear.

"I mean it," Kyr whispered back. "I could do with getting away from Whiterock. Somehow, the place has suddenly begun to feel like a prison tonight." She looked worried.

"It'll be alright," Bluestocking said. She guessed that part of Kyr's worry was at the thought of having to leave the familiar for the unknown. Bluestocking kissed and hugged her. "I won't leave you. Where I go– you'll go too. And we'll go as equals." *A pair of runaway slaves*, she thought. *Yes, a fine couple we'll make.*

Kyr nodded. "Emotional moment over," she said. "Time to get on with escaping."

They ran headlong, Bluestocking pulling away, but slowing whenever she thought Kyr was too far behind. The gods must have been smiling on them, for they managed to run for several minutes, until the stitch in Bluestocking's side made her slow up, and Kyr closed the gap. Several times Bluestocking felt uneasy, but there was no obvious reason for it, and she forced herself to concentrate on the path ahead and not stumble over an uneven surface.

***

Then they reached the balloons, and Bluestocking's heart sank. She stopped dead, and Kyr ran into her back "What's the matter?" Kyr said.

"Look," Bluestocking said, tugging at the fabric, which, now they were up close to it, they could see wasn't fully inflated. "We'll need to light the burners," she panted. "Even if I knew how to, they would make so much noise, someone would hear us." She stood still, and bowing her head, rested her hands on her knees. Her mind would simply not work.

"We'll think of something else." Kyr stroked Bluestocking's back to comfort her. Then Kyr put down the burning torch and ground it out beneath her heel. "It's no use to us now," she said. "We'll just have to trust to luck to see where we're going."

In the distance, shouts; one of the guards banged a gong. The hounds howled again.

"Is that for us?" Bluestocking said.

"I think so." Kyr started down a passageway that was open to the sky. "This way!" As they ran, Bluestocking heard a heavy scraping and looked up at the moon peeking through the clouds. By the time she turned the corner, it was covered again. *Just for a second, Kyr's shadow looked distorted,* she thought. *Get a grip on your nerves, girl.*

"If we can get to the winch, I know one of the guards," Kyr called over her shoulder. "He starts work in the early mornings. I'm sure that I can persuade him to lower us down."

"How far down does this lowering go?" Bluestocking gasped. She had a stitch in her side, and her lungs burned. "And what exactly will we be in? Not an air-bag, I suppose?"

"Down to the ground, of course," Kyr said, and a trace of impatience crept into her voice. "They lower a sack that's open at the corners to allow you to poke your legs through."

"Um, I'm not really sure that I can do that," Bluestocking said, aware of how pathetic she sounded, but unable to get the thought out of her head, *What happens if I fall through?*

Kyr rounded on her. "Are you mad? They won't simply kill us, they will kill us very, very slowly. You and I will wish we were dead long before we are!"

Kyr set off again, clearly considering the subject closed. Bluestocking took a deep breath, filling her lungs, and followed her. They rounded a corner at headlong pace. Then Kyr skidded to a stop and pushed her back around the corner, looking back over her shoulder. "It's not Rafi guarding the winch tonight," Kyr whispered. "Come on, we'll have to try another way down."

They ran back part of the way they had come, then turned the opposite way, running toward what Bluestocking eventually realised was the courtyard at the front of the Palace.

"They've only left one man guarding the gliders," Kyr whispered, crawling forward.

Bluestocking pulled her back. "I can't do it," Bluestocking whispered. "I'm sorry, but there's no way I can fly one of those things. I feel giddy standing at the top of a flight of stairs."

"You damned fool," Kyr gripped either side of Bluestocking's mouth between thumb and forefinger. "There *is* no other way down! Be brave, my love!" She kissed Bluestocking, pushing her tongue between her lover's teeth. They ended the kiss and broke apart, Kyr still pushing Bluestocking toward the gliders, as if she were pushing a recalcitrant dog out into the rain.

They reached the gliders, by some miracle still unseen. Kyr manhandled the glider next to the wall. Each wing was probably wider than Bluestocking was tall. A frame shaped like the letter 'A' with a padded horizontal bar about as wide as Bluestocking's arm span joined the wings.

"You lie on this," Kyr patted the padding. "As long as you lie still and in the middle of the padding, you're quite safe." Kyr avoided looking at her.

As she climbed the steps to the launching platform, it felt as if her weight increased with each passing step, until she could barely lift an arm or a leg. Her feet seemed to sink into the stone steps, which to her wobbly legs had taken on a spongy feel. Her body began to sway. She could feel the distant ground below pulling at her, and no surface had ever seemed as narrow as the platform that she stood upon.

"It's *worse* than an airbag!" She swayed and stepped back from the wall, dropping the glider. She leaned against the stone and vomited.

"There's no other way," Kyr repeated.

Bluestocking fought down the urge to slap her. "Then we need to think of something else," she panted. "Do you *really* believe that you can fly one of them in the dark?"

"What if we wait until daybreak?" Kyr said. She saw the look on Blue's face, and sighed. "Okay, what now?"

"What about the air-bags?" Bluestocking wasn't sure that she could even face that prospect, but at least she could cower down in the basket, and shut her eyes. *Gods, you're pathetic,* she told herself sternly. Knowing that didn't obliterate the fear.

"Do you want to try?" Kyr said. "I don't know whether we can get near enough to them to steal one. But if you're willing to..."

"I am."

They raced down through the alleyways like the rats dressed as people that Bluestocking had seen at a country fair on the way to Whiterock where they had only stopped to check directions. It had only been long enough for the women to stroll around, and for Bluestocking to see a giant doll's house, in the shape of a walled town. Within it, brown furry bodies dressed in blue and pink cotton had skittered in blind panic from corner to corner. The fugitives' own progress seemed an eerie parallel.

They seemed suddenly possessed of divine protection, for though they weaved from street to alleyway and back again, and nearly bumped into one of the many patrols that were still moving around in the darkness, they somehow managed not to actually collide with any of them. *As if,* Bluestocking thought, *our bodies are moved slightly out of sequence with the mortal world.*

Finally they rounded the corner to see, laid out in a long line, the limp skins of other air-bags hanging over the edge. Kyr turned and moved toward the lone guard. She seemed to ripple across the ground in the moonlight.

The guard stood, fidgeting, looking eastward, toward the army camped below the Silk Palace. He seemed completely unaware of Kyr's presence. Only when her hand reached toward him, did he turn at the last minute, but too late. Her hand touched the back of his head, and he slumped to the ground as if pole-axed.

She beckoned Bluestocking and when Blue didn't move, beckoned her again with frantic waves, hissing, "Come on! We'll only have a few minutes, if we're lucky!"

Slowly, Bluestocking walked toward the waiting air-bags. Her feet seemed to be under some outside power's control, and she couldn't stop walking, even though it was the last place she wanted to go to. There seemed suddenly something very, very inhuman about Kyr's movements, and the closer she got, the more her feelings of dread grew.

Kyr began to manhandle the fabric of the air-bag. "Help me with this," she called, and for a moment, her voice seemed to take on alien quality. She looked at Bluestocking, and more and more Bluestocking began to get the feeling that the something wrong was with Kyr. It was nothing she could put her finger on, just a feeling like the things that Kyr said and did that were so inconsistent that it was almost like she were more than one person.

Bluestocking heard voices and hissed, "Hold still!"

The wind whipped at her hair. She heard a moan behind her and looked around as the moon came out. Instead of Kyr, something else stood where Bluestocking's lover should have been.

Colin Harvey

Chapter 15

The creature was as big as a house, blocking out the moon and clouds, which back-lit it. Bluestocking counted at least six arms, but there could have been more. Some of its limbs seemed to flicker in and out of existence. Its features were blurred and gave the impression they were made up of a myriad of human faces, all pulsing in and out of sight.

"Who-" Bluestocking said. "What are you?"

It turned its vast, slow gaze on her, and it was as if it turned over every rock that hid a lie; every act of her life, every word she had ever spoken was scrutinised in a moment.

When it spoke, a thousand flies buzzed in Bluestocking's ears. "I am Brighana. Thank you for what you did and for your kindness to my mortal form."

"It was nothing," Bluestocking answered, her voice shaking with fear. She felt an overwhelming urge to surrender herself to the militia, but a quick survey revealed that none were around. *What were you thinking, to unleash this...thing?*

"I will decide whether it was nothing, little one," Brighana said. "What you did was not nothing. Had you waited, as was possible, things would have been much harder to have arranged. That debt of gratitude means that you shall live."

"What have you done with Kyr?" Desperation gave her the illusion of courage.

"She is here. Within me, as I am within her."

"Can you not let her go? If you would be merciful–"

"Merciful?" The strength of its scorn almost knocked Bluestocking backwards. "These upstarts have corrupted my name, turned my image into a milk-and-water travesty, used it to control their sheep, and you ask for mercy?"

"She helped free you, almost as much as I did. How about showing her gratitude?"

"As well ask the moon to show you gratitude, mortal child. Besides, I cannot." Its buzzing chuckle set her nerves on edge. "Even demigods have their limits."

"Take me instead then," Bluestocking said. "Leave her, and come to me."

Brighana never moved, but something in its posture made Bluestocking think that it was performing the equivalent of peering at her. "You would do this much for her?"

Bluestocking shrugged.

"Don't worry," Brighana said. "I mistrust altruism. And she's fortunate to be useful to a god."

"Not a God, surely? At best, a demigod?" Even as she said it, she winced. *Pedantic to the end, Bluestocking,* she thought.

"Be careful, mortal scholar. You dare quibble?" The buzzing flies took on a deeper, threatening tone.

Bluestocking shrugged, feigning bravery, but she didn't feel at all brave inside, and for all she knew, it could read her as easily as she could read a scroll, and would know she was faking. *Probably best to assume you have no secrets from it,* she thought.

"All I wish is to understand who or what I've brought into the world. Knowledge is important to me. It's what brought us together, after all."

Its laughter was like a billion bees buzzing. "You'll never know what brought us together! It was written at the very beginning of time that you would release me."

The clouds scurried across the moon again, and suddenly Kyr stood there once more, her alabaster face pinched with fatigue and fear. "What have you done?" she gasped.

"I thought–" Bluestocking started, but tears welled up. "I thought I was helping!"

Kyr closed her eyes and swayed, and Bluestocking clutched her. When Kyr opened her eyes again, Bluestocking thought it was as if a wild animal caught in a trap stared out at her, but then she closed them again and leaned on Bluestocking for support. "I suppose you did," she said quietly. "It could have been far worse. If you'd incited it in the New Year, Arial and Myleetra could have controlled it, but now…" she trailed off and stood upright, pulling free of Bluestocking. "You must get away from here," she said.

Bluestocking shook her head. "Not without you," she said. "Come with me, and we'll find some way of undoing this."

Kyr shook her head sadly. "Unleash this on the wider world?' she said. "Though it won't be happy to stay here much longer, anyway. Just as it knows everything I know, I can sense its desire."

"Can it read my thoughts?" Bluestocking asked.

Kyr shook her head. "No, more like the language of your body, your emotions, and from there it can make guesses. Don't believe everything it tells you. It's well disposed to you at the moment, but it could change in an instant. Its promises are worthless. Human morality means little or nothing to it. Get away before the moon emerges again!" She grabbed Bluestocking and kissed her fiercely, then, "Run now, while the moon's still hidden! Hide amongst other people! At the moment its power is still limited, and it needs the moon to be visible to manifest. But as it feeds and grows, it will gain in strength." The moon peeked out again, and for a half-second it became Brighana, then a screaming Kyr, "I'm sorry! I'll not tell her any more!" Brighana reappeared, and then Kyr once again.

"I'll not leave you," Bluestocking said, her voice shaking with emotion. "The gods, I did this to you. Whatever I've done, I should stay to try and undo it."

"You did what you thought you had to," Kyr said. "I should curse you," she added, then laughed. "You can't imagine what it's like to be part of something so–"

The moon emerged from behind the clouds, and without any sense of movement or change, it was there again, just as it had been not there a moment earlier.

"—powerful," it said. "You can't know how it feels to be free after millennia of confinement, my essence straitened by the stones and rocks. The mortal who is part of me loves you deeply, so I'm inclined to be kindly disposed to you, little mortal. I'll overlook your impudence, but do not strain my tolerance–"

Clouds covered the moon again, and Kyr gabbled, "Get away while you can. It's weak at the moment, so if you shelter among other people for the time being, well, it can't yet distinguish you from a crowd of others. If you can survive 'til morning," she said, "you can leave then. It'll be weak in daylight. The moon is its sigil; it needs moonlight. But that will change," she added. "As it feeds, it'll grow stronger, night by night, day by day, until it will be present all the time." She shooed Bluestocking away. "Now, go!"

Bluestocking turned and ran, but when the moon shone it stood in front of her. Bluestocking found herself cupped in a huge palm. Its hand seemed to defy nature, as she understood what was natural. It was big enough to wrap comfortably around her from feet to shoulder. Hand and arm seemed to be perfectly in proportion to the rest of Brighana's body, although there were four arms, two growing from each shoulder, one above the other. And Brighana seemed to be normal sized. *Could I have somehow shrunk?* Bluestocking wondered, but the rest of the courtyard seemed to be perfectly normal sized. Nor could she tell at which point illusion ended and mortal perspective began.

A familiar voice said hesitantly, "My god, you have returned!" Arial stood head stretched back, gazing up at Brighana watching them.

Another of Brighana's hands reached out and scooped him up. "I am your god?" It asked, and Bluestocking thought she caught mockery in the question. Someone ran across the edge of the yard, but apart from that, the whole city seemed eerily still, as if everyone in it were holding their breath, or as if they were cocooned inside a bubble of silence. A still lucid part of Bluestocking's mind wondered how long it was to daybreak and respite.

"Always," Arial barely breathed, but it was so preternaturally quiet that he might have shouted the word.

"You will worship me? Whatever form that worship takes?"

"I am yours," Arial breathed.

A third hand stretched right across the courtyard and snared a figure running from shadow to shadow; Myleetra. An extrusion shaped like a giant snake but ridged with spines grew from the god's waist. "Then you won't mind if I refresh myself?"

The next two hours were a kaleidoscope of sex and pain, and to someone taught that sex was linked with spiritual love, what happened would have been laughable had it not been so deeply shocking. Myleetra seemed to actually enjoy the pain and sex. Bluestocking looked away, still clutched in Brighana's huge hand, but couldn't cover her ears against Myleetra's shrieks, screams and even occasional laughter.

"It's choking her," Arial groaned, rolling toward her, then half-climbing to his knees.

Then the moment came that Bluestocking had been dreading. "I think it unfair," Brighana said, its buzzing voice slightly louder, stronger and clearer now. "That you should miss out on so much pleasure– little one whom a part of me adores."

Bluestocking suddenly felt her hands move of their own volition, unbuttoning her clothing and sliding it off herself. Brighana moved its hands together, and she and Arial lay in the same cupped palm. He too was tearing off his clothes with frenzied haste, but he wore a beatific expression.

Then she was lying beneath him and opening her legs, while all the time a silent scream echoed in her mind, but never made its way to her opened mouth that howled her rage at the glowing moon. Moments later, Arial's wet slobbery mouth was planting kisses on her, and he was crooning and drooling–

–there was a sharp tearing pain, and he was inside her, but she was dry, and she finally found words, "It hurts! Please stop! You're hurting me!"

"Serves you right," Arial sobbed. "You nearly wrecked the whole thing. Even the spells to make the text incomprehensible didn't stop you."

When Brighana had first Arial, then Myleetra, then both together couple with Bluestocking, she thought she might go mad but instead made herself remember, one after the other, all the scrolls and manuscripts in the Imperial Library that she had looked at. Then she pictured in her mind's eye the shape, the look, the slightly pitted feel of the vellum, rather than look at Myleetra's bleeding mouth that planted a kiss on hers. In their agony, or in Myleetra's case, ecstasy, they gradually rolled and writhed away from the middle of the square.

"Tell my mortal's little friend what you planned for her," Brighana's voice said. "Tell her how you thought that you control me, upstarts. It amuses me to hear you try to engage in discourse, even as your tiny little minds try to reconcile agony and ecstasy."

"I never thought it would be like this," Arial sobbed between thrusts into Myleetra from behind. Bluestocking pushed a hand over his mouth– *just think about the smell of papyrus–* but pulling it free, he said, "If it can truly read me, then it knows how I feel." He clutched at his left arm;

"There is such a pain in my chest!" He slumped then as if he had been released from some other's control and rolled back, leaving Myleetra lying on top of Bluestocking and both of them half-lying in Brighana's vast lap.

"We thought," Myleetra cried, "that if we released it, we could at least partly control it, enough to bring down the King's petty little tyranny, where his own daughter controls the main church." She was about to say something else then but instead broke off into a half-groan, half-scream. "I..." she gasped, "can't take any more..."

"I thought you liked pain," Bluestocking said implacably. "Especially with sex."

"Even gluttons can be sated," Myleetra whimpered. "When you're full to bursting, and your belly will explode, you try forcing a whole half-hog down your throat." She broke off as Brighana ceased what it was doing and moved so that it stood in front of her.

"You will worship me," it said.

"I thought I had– aagh!" Myleetra's screech echoed for several seconds. She clapped her hands to her temples and held her head. Brighana waited silently– for a moment the clouds obscured the moon, and Kyr stood there once more. But before she could say anything, the moment passed and Brighana stood there again. It seemed somehow more there; not more solid– if anything quite the opposite, for it swirled and flickered and changed shapes faster than Bluestocking could see but always keeping the same outline. Rather, it was that its voice seemed louder and stronger. *It's feeding on us, on our pain,* she thought, and trying to act without conscious thought, pushed her body a half-step away, so that she was at the edge of the square, propped up against the wall. She noticed it flicker into insubstantiality, as had happened maybe a dozen times or so in the time that Brighana had been indulging itself.

"You will swear fealty," Brighana said.

Lines sprung out on Myleetra's skin as if someone were drawing on her. The lines raised into ridges and turned pinker and pinker. Then they blackened and turned into wires. They tautened, and Myleetra screamed as they cut into her flesh. "See what I could do, if I chose," Brighana thundered.

Myleetra screamed again and clutched at her head, "Please," she whimpered, "The voices, they're like knives cutting at my eardrums. Please stop them."

"Swear."

"It wouldn't do any good," Myleetra said. "I am their representative, not their queen. If enough disagree with me, they can always choose a new coven-leader."

Even before Brighana spoke again, Bluestocking knew that the moment had taken on a far greater significance than whether Myleetra simply gave into the divine bully. This was important to the power, for some reason. *Why?* she wondered. *Simple numbers? If say, three worship it, that's much more important than, for example two devotees? Or is there some significance in the witch, more so than Arial? Because she's of the spiritual world, rather than the temporal?*

"Name them, in order," Brighana said.

Myleetra said a name, where they lived and how old they were. Then another, and a third, and yet another, until Bluestocking had lost count of how many names she had recited, with where they were likely to be.

"That necklace you wear contains a locket, does it not?" Myleetra nodded. "Containing a fingernail from each, just the thinnest little sliver, binding you all together, body to body."

"How did you know?" Myleetra said, then shrugged. "Yes."

"I know everything," Brighana said smugly. "Take them out and hold them in your hand." Whatever the reason, Brighana repeated, louder, angrier now, "Swear fealty. Or..."

Myleetra nodded, clutching the fingernails in both cupped hands and knelt in front of the power. She bowed right over, until her head was so close to Brighana's feet that no gap, no separation was visible. She said, "Almighty Brighana, divine one, I swear by my body and soul and all that I have and will have, that I shall worship no other, and forsake all others. I swear that all the witches of Whiterock, each of the massed covens, will serve and obey, recognizing only one true god." Myleetra's voice was a ragged gasp.

"Do you swear this only for yourself?" Brighana asked.

Myleetra shook her head. "I swear by each and every member of the coven, that we shall follow you, obey you, suffer for you, live and die for you, until the world ends."

Brighana threw its arms out wide, as if it would wrap all of them around the moon, which half-vanished behind clouds; this time Kyr only flickered in and out of existence. "I cast our images into the mind of every member of your coven!" Its triumphant shout echoed off the walls. "There are, as you say, many who will reject me, but there are many others who do not, now that they have been awoken from sleep, to see my power!"

Bluestocking realized that Brighana was growing stronger. She slid along the wall, and waiting while Brighana gloated, she tried to blank her mind– not difficult, given how truly exhausted she felt. In the distance, the watch-bell chimed again and again. She made her mind go blank. *Count the chimes*, she thought. *Five, six, seven.*

The moon slid behind the wall of clouds that were building from the South. *The Rainwall,* Bluestocking thought. *It's late today and nowhere near as solid as most mornings. Of course! That was why she killed that wizard. I wonder if she's been picking them off.* She looked up, back at Kyr, who was suddenly standing in the square, looking around anxiously.

Bluestocking turned and ran into an alleyway and pushed open the first door that she came to.

***

She was back where she had stood days before and what had been cryptic then now made perfect sense. "Grain imps," she called. "Please, come, talk to me."

There was silence for a score of heartbeats, then, "Wo-man," came the familiar voice.

"What can I do?" she said. When it didn't answer, she asked, "It needs the moon?"

"For now. The moon is its source of strength. But not for ever. Blood and pain are its food, as flesh is ours."

"What can I do?"

"Learn. Wait your mo-ment. For now, on-ly watch."

So she did.

Down in the courtyard, Brighana still stood, but now others gathered around, though they moved with no more animation than sleepwalkers and were no noisier. It shifted and flickered, as it had all night, but there was no doubt in Bluestocking's mind that Brighana had grown stronger feeding on its banquet of pain and humiliation.

She felt for the frame of the window, and groping around, undid the catch and slid the window open. She had no idea whether she risked exposing herself to it by doing so, but her instinct told her that she didn't, and she had been working on instinct for hours now– as if her head, tired of constant thinking, had given over the reins of her body to her heart.

She strained to hear what was being said.

"I want her found," the thousand flies buzzing voice said. "She had no right to leave. I will not have my favour so abused."

Arial picked up a length of rope, knotted in several places, from the side of the square.

"Arial!" What are you doing?" a woman's shout reverberated the quiet. Even a few of the sleepwalkers turned their heads.

"Oh, my love," Arial crooned. "Come and join us!"

"What," Jasmina's cry contained a world of loathing in one word, "are you doing with that hag?"

"We feed our God with our senses, with our pleasure," Myleetra sobbed, as the knotted rope slapped into her back, forcing the last word out in an explosive groan, before adding, "and our pain. Come join us."

"That," Jasmina spat the word, "is not Brighannon. *That* is not our God. It is a mockery, a fake, a counterfeit."

Bluestocking watched as the snake extruding from Brighana's waist reared up and swayed, like one Bluestocking had seen in the weekly market in Ravlatt. Then it thickened, and became instead a marrow, but still with the deadly spines along its crest. "What you worship, you raddled hag, was the mockery. I could kill you in a moment, but that would be too quick. So instead I will let you live while taking what you value most in the whole world."

Her jewelry? Bluestocking wondered.

Instead Arial knelt in front of the God, and it crouched. Bluestocking watched, horrified, as it lifted Arial's backside, and it raped the man with the deadly marrow. She wasn't sure where the screams came from as it, whether it was Arial or Jasmina screaming, or even Bluestocking herself.

"No, please." Arial's whimper drifted up on the breeze, and Bluestocking saw that he had pulled a knife from somewhere. She peered and could have sworn that she saw his hands shaking, but that might have been her imagination.

Slowly, carefully, Arial drew a diagram with the knife on his own stomach. Then he pulled down the flap of skin, and began to pull out his own intestines, his face twisted with pain and a smile that Bluestocking guessed had been frozen on his face by Brighana.

"Thus, mortal," Brighana said, "Do we punish insolence."

For a moment, the power looked up, and Bluestocking was sure that it must see her, but she kept absolutely still, for fear that movement would catch its eye. Then it was gone, leaving its followers standing, bemused.

She saw Jasmina kneel on the edge of the courtyard, cradling Arial's head in her lap.

Bluestocking lay down and curled into a foetal ball for what seemed like hours, but which, unless that night was divinely (or infernally) long, which she wouldn't have ruled out, was probably only minutes. At last she rolled onto all fours, and was violently, brutally sick, retching until there was nothing else to come up, and her throat felt raw and scraped from the effort. She crawled on her belly and stared through the window of the attic, out onto the courtyard.

It was empty. There was no sign of Brighana or its acolytes.

Jasmina had climbed to her feet and was trying to move the ruin of Arial's body. Bluestocking saw no movement and guessed the prime minister had died or was dying.

With each passing minute she became both safer and more in danger. Once daybreak came, Brighana would probably go to somewhere where it could rest until nightfall, then return to wreak fresh havoc. But for all she knew, there might still a price on her own head, and she was much more conspicuous in daylight.

Nonetheless, she stumbled to the door, found the catch and slipped out onto the street. No one screamed or hollered, and after a few paces, she began to relax. She skirted past the edge of the square, where there was now no sign of Jasmina. Bluestocking wondered how long it would be before someone noticed– or indeed, how long before someone asked where Arial was. *What happens when the King finds out what's been going on?* She wondered with a little dread what would become of her should her part in releasing the trapped power become apparent. *If it is still a power,* she thought. She wished she'd paid more attention in scripture to the differences and the relationships between the celestial hosts. When did a power become a demigod, and when did a demigod ascend to full godhood?

She guessed the royals were in hiding somewhere. How else to explain how quiet the citadel was? More than ever, she had to find some way of screwing her courage together enough to be able to descend from the rock.

She heard screams in the distance, and then someone was running past the end of the alley. *Soldiers, from the sound of their boots,* she thought.

All the time she'd been thinking, she'd also been keeping an eye out, as she made her way toward the very last place she wanted to be, but where she needed to go if she were to escape. Even at this early hour, the air-bags station was starting to fill up with bustling servitors, balefire burners roaring in the first pair of air-bags, lighting up the darkness like a flash of summer lightning. Other balloons were being unfolded in preparation for the next flight. She wondered at her chances of boarding one undetected. Nil, her common sense asserted. Although there were nowhere near as many as the last time she'd been here in daylight, already a small mob of foreign travellers and merchants was starting to congregate around the gates, jockeying for position in the light cast by small balefire burners. A couple of men turned to look at her. Unsure whether they were simply eyeing up a lone woman, or whether they were trying to work out if she were the fugitive for whom the hue and cry had gone up, she sank back into the shadows. All of them clutched pieces of paper, which they waved under the noses of passing militiamen on request. Bluestocking guessed that these were the precious exeats, which would allow passage around Whiterock during curfew.

Nearby, a horse was led to a separate gate, and a hood placed over its head. A man chanted and waved a pattern over the bag, and the horse seemed to slump slightly. As it did, so did Bluestocking's spirits. Both the horse's handler and the wizard wore uniforms. *So did everyone else around,* she noticed.

She leaned into the lee of the wall, allowing the chill to seep into her bones, and slid down the wall, until she crouched in the shadows. How long she crouched there, she had no idea. She may have slept, cat-napping for periods, but her mind refused to work.

The increasing hubbub, voices from ever-more frequent passers-by finally penetrated the fog of her stupor.

It was half-light now, the hour before sunrise. Soon, she would have to take her last chance of escape. If she could manage an Alliance accent, it might be that they would let her through. She simply didn't know and would have to risk it.

Some perverse inner imp made her inch toward the edge. *Maybe it's not so very bad,* she thought. She made herself creep to the very edge, almost forgetting to breathe, and look out.

It *was* so very bad.

Chapter 16

The fields were laid out in their now-familiar checkerboard pattern, but there were more brown patches now where the King had allowed his wizards to slacken the tightness of their control.

She felt the bile rising in her throat, and the ground seemed to sway beneath her feet. Even as it repelled her, the outside air tugged at her, crooning a silent lullaby of death to entice her outwards, and she leaned out onto the parapet, the wind tugging at her hair.

She pulled back with a gasp and saw the shapeless maw of an elemental, flying past. She crouched, shaking, arms wrapped around her knees for support. The very idea that she could climb into the basket seemed a hollow joke now.

She wandered back toward the palace with leaden feet and almost walked into a woman. "You!" Jasmina croaked. "Are you happy, now that he's dead?"

Bluestocking stared at the older woman and slowly shook her head. "If I could undo this..." She ran her hand over her face. "...but I can't. I'm sorry, so, so very sorry."

Jasmina shrugged. "You'd better slither off the rock."

"I can't."

Jasmina stared at her but said nothing.

"Have you slept at all?" Bluestocking said.

"I don't want to sleep. I want that thing dead."

"I want it stopped as well, but I have no idea how."

Jasmina said, "Well we won't do it standing here, will we?" She looked at the royal citadel, raised slightly above the rest of the rock. "I'd rather sleep with snakes than consort with them, but they're our only hope of stopping that thing..." Her voice trailed off, and her jaw worked. They set off, Bluestocking drifting in the older woman's wake.

***

They had travelled only a few of the maze of streets when they heard screams ahead of them. Bluestocking stopped and tugged at Jasmina's arm, but the older woman seemed propelled by momentum and crossed the thoroughfare that ran at right angles to the one they were on.

Bluestocking darted forward and seizing Jasmina's arm, pulled her back toward the edge. "I learnt last night to avoid screams and yells," she growled.

Further down the thoroughfare, which ran long and straight for at least a furlong, Brighana stood, ringed by militiamen, soldiers and snapping snarling gargoyles. Dead soldier's bodies ringed the power, but the local forces stood their ground with suicidal bravery. Bluestocking could not help admiring their courage.

Brighana had grown at least six arms– how many exactly was unclear because they whirled and flickered and snapped at the defenders with such speed that it was hard to keep track of them.

"I thought," Bluestocking said, trying to swallow the fear that had spilled up out of her gut, "I thought that it could only appear at night, when the moon was visible."

"Look." Jasmina pointed upward, and Bluestocking peered up at the early morning blue sky, in which a waxing moon as near full as made no difference hung.

"I suppose that the hope that it might crawl into a dark hole until nightfall was a little optimistic," Bluestocking said.

"I think that it was *very* optimistic," Jasmina said. "What's it doing now?"

Two of its many arms waved behind it, on the side of it away from its attackers and did something to the dead bodies behind it. After perhaps a dozen heartbeats, some of the bodies began to move, climbing clumsily to their feet and picking up their weapons.

The soldiers and militia were already being driven back, and at the sight of their late comrades picking up swords and pikes and slowly advancing toward them with obvious menace, their heads dropped. Only the gargoyles seemed unmoved– if anything, they fought even more fiercely than before, one of them decapitating a corpse with a slash of its claws.

Despite more and more reinforcements arriving, Brighana advanced steadily on the palace, scything through the defenders, calling up ever more of the dead as its own reinforcements. Few of the dead fought for more than a few minutes before falling back to the ground, their clumsy remorselessness no match for the ferocity of the defenders, but even so it gave Brighana the impetus it needed.

"It can't be very powerful if it can only revive the dead for a few minutes," Jasmina said. "Why does it not animate them for longer?"

Bluestocking remembered a passage from the scrolls. "It can only delay their spirit's journey to the world beyond for a few moments. There is a period of transition. Brighana can only hold them up for as long as it takes sand to travel to the other chamber of a timer, but that is enough for the moment. Later, as its power grows stronger, it may be able to do more than delay some of the weaker ones and then even the strong."

Jasmina's head drooped, and Bluestocking squeezed her shoulder. "We might as well bend our knee to it now," the older woman said. "Or throw ourselves off the cliff."

"Don't say such things! Don't *ever* talk– of throwing yourself off! If you only knew..."

Jasmina stared at her. "So that's why you're still here." Her face softened for an instant. "You could probably have got away if you could have faced the journey down. I would have thought being taken prisoner by the Western Alliance would be preferable to whatever that thing has in mind?"

"Maybe this was meant to be," Bluestocking said. "I must stay and see the end of what I started." She was talking to Jasmina's back as the older woman wandered away.

***

Soldiers and militiamen ran past them with no interest in two grubby, battered-looking women, one of them old enough to be the other one's mother, drifting away from the palace. Behind them the sounds of battle faded with distance.

They reached the entrance to one of the flights of steps down into Whiterock. Jasmina stopped and looked around, as if seeing her surroundings for the first time. "I don't know where to go," she said. "If I go home, everything I see will remind me of him. We've been– we were married for nineteen years." She broke off and covered her hand with her mouth, her eyes watering.

Jasmina's face had almost fallen in on itself. She looked a generation older than at the banquet. *Don't be so heartless,* Bluestocking thought. *The poor soul's grieving for her husband. She's probably had no sleep and is living on her nerves.* Hesitantly, she touched Jasmina's shoulder, and the woman spun away to face a wall. Her shoulders shook.

By contrast, Bluestocking felt numb. Now that she had uttered the spell, she had absolutely no idea of how to reverse it– or whether it *could* be reversed...

"Where are the mages quartered?" Bluestocking said.

Jasmina snapped out of her reverie. "In their own village in the East Wing. Why?"

"The three arms of the state," Bluestocking said. "Government. Church. What's the third? The military are fighting it, but has anyone roused all the mages?"

Jasmina looked pensive. "Of course," she said slowly. "Most mages on station will be looking outwards, and while some may have been alerted by what's happening here, most will be going about their business, unless instructed otherwise by the King or my hus–" Her face almost crumpled as the implications struck home, "—the prime minister." She thought for a moment and reached a decision. "Let me think." She chewed on a nail. "I'll rouse the mages. You stir the churches of the lesser Gods. They're threatened by this as well. Where shall we meet?"

Bluestocking stared at the steps. "Brighana's been held in the rocks for millennia. I believe that the last place it will want to venture is back into the bowels of its prison."

Jasmina could barely control her obvious revulsion. "You mean the spider caves?"

"How much of that dislike is due to the teachings of the church of Brighannon? Or Brighana, as it prefers to be known now?"

"Some," Jasmina said. "But I don't like things with more than two legs."

Bluestocking asked, "Can you think of anywhere safer?" and Jasmina shook her head. Bluestocking added, "I could be wrong, of course and be condemning us to a slow death."

Jasmina stared at her. "You can joke at a time like this?"

Bluestocking shrugged. "Why not? If we're going to die, should we go out sobbing, wailing and rending our clothes?"

Jasmina sighed. "You're right." She gave a feeble smile. "I'll meet you at the caves."

***

Bluestocking descended through the levels.

As she neared the Street of Temples, the number of people grew. So did the tension in the air. There was a nervous excitement in many people's eyes, and imps and other strange beasts scuttled from shadow to shadow. Incense hung heavy on the air.

Bluestocking sneezed. "Blessings upon your breath, child," a sepulchral voice said from behind her. A priest stood in a doorway, bending down to put out a mangy grey cat. His face was ruddy and as cheerful as his voice mordant, and his body strained at a simple brown robe a size too small. Wisps of greying hair peeked out from beneath a toffee-coloured cap.

"Can you help me..." *What to call him? Father? Brother?* She let the sentence hang.

"Spiritual help I can provide," he said in that unlikely voice. "What do you need?"

"It's what the King and the people need. Whiterock is under attack." She saw his eyes widen and pressed on. "A rogue demigod is loose in the palace, and it looks as if your– our soldiers are no match for it."

"Interfere in...*earthly* matters? Oh no, no, we can't do that."

"But its presence threatens every other church here," she implored.

"Only the unbelievers," he said. "It will not threaten the adherents of other Gods. It has only attacked unbelievers, surely?" He chuckled. "I am sure that even the adherents of the mysteriously invisible but omnipotent Brighannon are safe." He shut the door quickly.

When she tried the next temple, a battered little place, she got the same response. When at the third attempt she claimed that the rogue demigod was the original version of Brighannon, disbelief turned to outrage, and they threw her into the street. At the next three her story was met with similar disbelief, fury at her supposed heresy of a brother God and a smug satisfaction that the majority were suddenly themselves in the spiritual wrong. "Serves 'em right," a thin-faced priestess muttered. "Teach 'em to worship false gods."

Head hanging, she trudged away, not even noticing that the air of fear had coalesced into anger until she turned a corner. "Oh, bugger," she muttered.

***

The mob stretched right across the street. They were slowly but methodically ripping the houses to shreds and pulling the owners shrieking and struggling from their homes.

One of the men at the front of the mob pointed at her. "A spy!"

The mob surged toward her with a single fluid movement. Bluestocking hesitated for only a moment and fled down a side turning, pursued by the shouting, screaming mob. She turned at the next junction and turned again, the still chill morning air burning in her lungs, cramp digging its fingers into her flank. Still the mob came.

Bluestocking felt a tug at her sleeve, but she managed to shrug it off.

"It's me, you silly girl," panted a now familiar voice.

"Jas–" Bluestocking gasped in relief but couldn't even say the name as they fled. She tried to smile, but the effort of pulling her face out of its rictus was too much, and she gave up, instead fluttering her fingers in acknowledgment, even as her arms pumped harder.

They ran, tumbling, barely in control of their bodies, down flight after flight of steps, several times nearly stumbling and falling. Once Bluestocking caught Jasmina, and once the older woman steadied her as Bluestocking stumbled. The corridors grew gloomier and gloomier, narrower and narrower. If they were caught now, there was not a single way out. The yells and screams and shouts of the crowd formed a bestial cacophony behind them. Then they were joined by the familiar howl of the bloodhounds.

"Look out!" Jasmina said as a young man, whose eyes widened as he saw the women and the mob behind them, stepped in front of them both. He just managed to leap out of the way. The incident slowed them fractionally, and Bluestocking felt a hand grab her arm. They rounded the corner and saw the entrance to the caves ahead of them.

Bluestocking threw herself into the mouth of the cave and ran to the first corner. "They," she panted, doubled over with hands resting on her knees, "haven't followed us in."

She and Jasmina stood just around the corner, the shouting, yelling mob out of sight for the moment. They seemed reluctant to enter the cave.

"I... guess," Bluestocking panted. She took a deep lungful of air, then coughed. "You had no joy rousing the wizards?"

"Most of them," Jasmina said when she had regained her breath, "were already up and at the thing. They slowed it down fractionally, but when Brighana killed one, it revived the poor man, and the corpse attacked its former colleagues. Once they saw how things were, many of the remainder fell back quickly. Redoutifalia hired mercenary mages, and their loyalty doesn't extend to dying for a few sovs." She slumped to the ground. "I assume you had no better luck?"

Bluestocking shook her head. "I think we should hide down here for as long as we can, and hope that they don't come in after us." Ignoring Jasmina's shudder, she thought, *I can think of better ways to wait for dying than cooped up like rats in a cage.*

"Okay." Jasmina's agreement was a rasping sob; she was clearly struggling for breath. Bluestocking thought, *As well we got here when we did. How much further could she have run?*

"We mustn't assume that they won't pluck up courage, though," Bluestocking added. "At least enough to mount a quick dash and withdrawal. We should move further in."

"Yes," Jasmina said, but leaning against her, Bluestocking felt the older woman shudder.

They stumbled further away from the mouth of the tunnel and walked deeper into the cave. Bluestocking saw a shape in the pink-tinged gloom cast by fireflies embedded in the walls and reaching for it, felt her hand close around a lump of wood. She wondered whose hands had carried it here, why it should have been dropped where it was. *Stop wool-gathering*, she thought.

They walked down a path that twisted and turned deep into the caves. "We might be secure here," Bluestocking said.

Jasmina didn't answer. She rocked backwards and forwards and sobbed. Then her sobs became keening cries, like a wounded animal's. She stood, leaning against the wall and gave way to the grief that she had carried since Arial's death. After a few awkward moments, Bluestocking gingerly put her arms around the widow and held her as she broke down.

When Jasmina had sobbed herself out, they pressed ever deeper into the caves.

"How long do we hide for?" Jasmina said, her voice harsh. "We can't stay here forever."

"Maybe we can sneak out while the Year End festivities are going on?"

"Good idea," Jasmina said. "On the Last Day, it is written that no god, demigod or power may harm a mortal, for fear of judgement by its peers."

"We have that on The First Day in the Empire," Bluestocking said.

"You lot do everything back to front," Jasmina said, but her mouth twitched.

At some point, Bluestocking and Jasmina were separated, and even though she doubled back and called Jasmina until her voice was ragged, Bluestocking couldn't find her.

Instead, she stumbled through the caves like an automaton, until she couldn't go any further. She was grateful for the gentleness of the soft pink luminescence, for her eyes felt as if they were full of grit. She had had little sleep for as many nights as she could remember; night after night in captivity, her jailers had awoken her whenever the mood took them. When she had dozed, fear of their brutality had kept her from the deep sleep that she needed. All the time that she and the others had been careering around the Silk Palace, adrenaline had kept the worst of her fatigue at bay. But even adrenaline cannot last forever, and now she simply wanted to sleep. The caves were warm and cosy. Above all, they were quiet. She hadn't realized how tired she was or how much the constant noise had hurt her ears, but the feeling of safety and the all-enveloping quiet was soothing.

She sat and dozed.

The same indefinable smell she'd noticed on her last visit drifted on a gentle breeze. To her right, something clicked and skittered in the darkness. She awoke instantly but froze in place. Voices drifted on the breeze from deep within the caverns. She strained to hear.

"Vigo should have been here by now. The hour-glass is already a quarter empty from the setting when he was due to be here."

"Vigo never could get out of bed," a second voice said sourly. "No point in us both waiting, but we can't leave the caves unattended. Will you wait while I call at his rooms?"

"Just as long as you go straight there," the first voice answered with a slight chuckle. "I know your appetite, old man. You'll get distracted and be in Mistress Criddle's pie-house before I can say knife."

The men approached, and Bluestocking was torn. If she announced her presence, it might be a futile gesture; if they did not believe her, as the churchmen had refused to accept the new situation, they would simply blunder off to their deaths. Or, they might give her up.

But Brighana knows you're here anyway, her conscience argued. *The mob is camped outside the cave mouth even if they can't or won't come in. What difference can it make, these men knowing you're here?*

Because, caution said, ***they*** *can return, even if the mob won't enter. Their knowing that you're here is one thing. Revealing yourself to people who might* *be used as a tool if they're captured, who know what and who to look for and exactly where you are is something else entirely.*

The spiders made the decision for her. Two tall men in the loose brown robes that seemed to be a uniform for those who worked in the caves stepped around the corner. One was thin and held up a lamp to reveal a pock-marked face. The other was fatter, his face covered with a livid purple birth-mark in the shape of a spider. She felt a little tickle on her hand and gasped, more in shock than fear, but loud enough for them to hear her.

"Who's there?" the pock-marked man called with the sour voice of the first speaker.

"A refugee," Bluestocking said, putting down her lump of wood and emerging from the shadows with her empty hands held in front of her. "One seeking sanctuary."

"Sanctuary?" the sharp-voiced one said. "From what?"

Bluestocking swayed, and the fatter man said, "She's exhausted, Glamis. Let her sit."

Glamis helped her to sit down. He said, more gently, "I have a bit of honey-comb here." He glared at the second man and said, "I keep it in case Deldrow runs amok with hunger."

Deldrow chuckled. "He's worried that I might gnaw on his bones. As if there is enough meat on his carcass, even for a snack."

Bluestocking realized that they were joking to set her at ease. She sat on the dusty floor and shifted her bottom where a sharp stone poked into it. "Whiterock was attacked last night," she said, chewing on the honeycomb. "A power, or demigod was unleashed." *Best not telling them what part you played in that,* she thought. "It went on the rampage, and collected a mob that has attacked many of the churches—"

"The gods allowed this?" Deldrow interrupted, and Glamis touched his arm.

Bluestocking continued, "They were like animals, attacking anyone who wouldn't swear allegiance to their god. It accompanies them, feeding off the pain they cause. They chased us, my friend and I, in here." She added, "We were separated here in the caves."

"What of the King?" Glamis asked. "His family? The Prime Minister? Who leads the kingdom?"

"I don't know," Bluestocking admitted miserably. "It killed Arial, the Prime Minister, and coerced the witches into swearing allegiance. I've heard nothing of the royal family."

"If the rebels had captured or killed them," Deldrow said grimly, "you can be sure that they would be shouting it from the roof-tops."

"The rebels chased the Prime Minister's widow," Bluestocking said, to shocked looks from both the men. "It was she that I accompanied here. I'm sorry," she said tearfully. "I seem to have been running all night, and it was so confusing, and, and-"

"Hush, now," Deldrow soothed. "You say they chased you here?"

Bluestocking nodded, wiping her nose. "They stopped when we entered the caves."

"Ah," Deldrow said.

Glamis nodded, a grim smile on his face. "Ah, indeed. Not that powerful a god, if it does not want to take on Our Lady of the Spiders."

"Its strength is growing," Bluestocking said. "It may not yet be strong enough to attack." They glanced at one another sharply, and she added, in case they grew suspicious of her knowledge, "My friend said that was why it was making people swear allegiance."

"Whether she's right about that or not," Glamis said. "We should gather the other attendants with the acolytes down here in the caves. If they become bold enough to attack at least we will be together in a defensible position."

"Wait here, my dear," Deldrow said. "I'll go and scout out the situation. Glamis will gather the others of our order who are still here in the caves. Sadly, most of them are above in their homes where they are as vulnerable as anyone else." He patted her knee kindly. "Fear not, we'll not be long, and we'll return with friends and allies."

Bluestocking nodded.

***

When they were gone, she felt suddenly lonelier than she had since she'd escaped from the prison. She tried to rest, but although she was exhausted, she was so keyed up that it was all she could do to sit still. To pass the time, she wandered around and around, until she came upon a small cave, barely bigger than Kyr's little room in Bluestocking's palace suite.

Hearing footsteps in the darkness, Bluestocking tensed. She dared not venture in there; with the light from the fireflies back-lighting her she'd be an easy target. But there was no other way out.

A shadowy figure staggered into the cave-mouth, and she tensed and gripped her lump of wood, splinters stabbing her fingers. The figure took two, then three more paces in, and she relaxed slightly.

Aton swayed in the wan light cast by the fire-bugs. His tunic was torn in several places, and he seemed to have lost the carry-bag that he usually had slung over one shoulder. Blood had run down one side of his face from a gash just below his hair-line. He clutched a knife and waved it about theatrically but with little practical effect. "Who's there?" His voice had a rasp to it not there before. "I can hear you," he said, but the certainty wasn't there, and Bluestocking knew he was bluffing. *If you keep absolutely still,* she thought, *he might go away again.*

He didn't. Instead, he leaned against the same wall as her and closed his eyes for a moment. He looked gaunt and exhausted, the lines of middle-age now etched so deeply into his face they were almost cuts. He turned slowly toward the cave mouth, and Bluestocking crept toward him, silently, every footstep accompanied by held breath in case her foot crunched on gravel.

She brought the lump of wood down hard onto the back of his head, and he crumpled in an untidy heap against the wall but shook his head. Before he could pull himself upright, she hit him again, and this time he toppled forward.

She grabbed the knife from where it lay and pocketed it. Rolled him over, pausing when he grunted, but he didn't stir, so she resumed. *No other weapons*, she thought. *A few trinkets*. She left those where they were. *Nothing with which to bind him.* She almost laughed out loud at the absurdity of it– here she was in the middle of countless silk spiders, but she'd never persuade or encourage them to spin silk on command, so she was left hunting for materials.

Instead, she sat back on her heels and decided the fate of the helpless man.

He'd been a thorn in her flesh ever since he'd seen her. If she killed him, she'd be safe forever. *No, not forever*, a small voice said, *until the next person you know from the old days recognizes you.*

She crouched, watching him, waiting.

Chapter 17

Aton was unconscious for several minutes. Bluestocking tried not to fidget, to remain calm, but all the time her nerves were urging her to flee. She saw his body tense almost imperceptibly. "I know you're awake," she said. "You needn't play dead for my benefit."

"Blue?" Aton whispered. In the half-light his face, as seamed as an aerial view of an open-cast mine lit up, transforming his normally surly expression. "I thought that the mob had killed you." He let out a long sigh. "I'm glad." The words dropped into a pool of silence, ripples of meaning spreading out from the two simple syllables.

"Why?" She retreated from the implications of his comment and of the look on his face. Life was messy enough without making it worse. "So you can blackmail me again?"

"You like to think the worst of people, don't you?" he said.

"Not people–just you. The Gods know I have reason enough."

"I suppose you do," he said. "But I'm a thief and a cheat, not a man who kills, except in self-defence. I wouldn't have wished on my worst enemy some of the fates that I saw befall people in the last few hours. There are mobs roaming the rock, looting, burning and killing. The air stinks with the smell of burning pork."

"Pork? Oh," she said. "Human flesh smells like–"

"Yes, it does."

"What about the Royal family? Cas? Is no one leading any kind of fight back?"

"No. Everyone seems to have been caught unawares. For all their supposed vigilance, the locals seem incredibly complacent. They spent the night chasing a fugitive round the rock–"

"That was me," she said.

He blinked, once. "Well, well. Who would have thought it?" He gazed at her intently. "But I *am* glad that you're okay. Their Prime Minister is missing, and Brighana's followers have surprise on their side, but I'm amazed that the militia haven't fought back."

"I'm not," she said, and recounted the night's events. She decided she might as well. *The others might not come back, and he might, just might, know a way off this blasted rock.*

So she was disappointed when he said, "I think we both know that we need to get away, but I don't have a clue how. Do you?"

She shook her head. "There's something else that I have to do, first." If he'd had a plan, she might have managed to ignore her conscience.

"What's more important than saving your neck– and mine, if it comes to that?"

So she told him.

***

They were on the way out when Bluestocking heard voices. They were talking too quietly for Bluestocking to hear what they said, or to work out who they were. "Hush." She gripped Aton's arm. She brandished her piece of wood, knowing it would be little use against an enemy with a sword or crossbow. They flattened themselves against the wall, Bluestocking yet again steeling herself to die at any moment.

Then the last person Bluestocking expected to see crept through the entrance to their cave. "Majesty?" Bluestocking whispered, incredulous.

Queen Ana stifled a shriek and spun round. Too late, Bluestocking realized that the Queen might have been taken hostage, even be press-ganged into serving the enemy. The half-relief and anxiety on her face did nothing to allay Bluestocking's fears.

"Are you alone?" Bluestocking stood on the balls of her feet, ready to spring. "Who is that with you?" Her heart sank as she belatedly noticed silhouettes at the cave mouth.

Queen Ana said, "My children." On cue the others crept into the cave, their body language even in the half-light clearly that of whipped dogs. Several of the accompanying courtiers nursed injuries; one almost mummified in bandages. "The Prince. Daragel. Some courtiers." She seemed unable to string sentences together. Instead she fired single words as conversational crossbow bolts. "You?"

Bluestocking made a little motion to Aton to stay back. "What of the King?"

"A prisoner. That–" Queen Ana stopped, composed herself. "The enemy has taken him. Many of those we thought friends have thrown themselves behind that creature."

"That creature is the *real* Brighannon," Bluestocking said. "Not the neutered travesty your daughter's church foisted on your people. Not the lie," she spat the word.

"Bluestocking!" Cas cried.

Even now he lectures me, Bluestocking thought but ignored him, something she'd never dared do before. It was the safest thing she could do. She was a boiling cauldron of emotions that felt too big for her body and combined in such a complex mix that she couldn't put a name to them all. Anger, which was the largest part, was almost boiling her blood; her whole body might explode if she didn't release it in small doses against this woman and her brood.

"I don't think your people exactly *hate* you," she said, her anger showing in the precision of her words. "But they do fear you; you represent the gods, and your power over them is almost as great as the gods over you. But if some do hate you, who could blame them, given the lies they've lived under? They look to you for security. They tolerate your impositions in return for your protection. In that one, solitary, thing, you failed them."

Before the Queen could speak, Cavi snapped from the shadows, "Is that why you killed Evi? Because of her collusion in our supposed fraud?"

Bluestocking looked at the people filing into the cave and wondered if she'd made another mistake. There were more than twenty of them, including several guards, who stared uneasily round the caves and started at every slight sound. *If they attack me, I won't last a second.* There were also courtiers and a few priests and priestesses. So she ignored Cavi and Cas and looked only at Queen Ana, though her words were for all of them. "I did not kill her. Your thugs have tortured me to near death, but if I had confessed to something I didn't do, I would have only shielded the real killer. Whoever it was, it wasn't me. Like the reign of your whole dynasty, my supposed guilt was a lie."

"I didn't know." The Queen spoke quietly, but firmly: "I swear to you by whatever gods that you worship that I had no idea of any of this."

"Majesty," Daragel stepped forward, his hand on the pommel of his sword. "Why even bother explaining yourself to this villain?"

For a moment, Bluestocking almost blurted out what she knew about his duplicity but some impulse stopped her, even as the Queen said, "No, Daragel!"

He smiled evilly at Bluestocking, who glared back, but thought, *No, let's give you enough rope to tie a noose round your neck.* She made herself relax.

Queen Ana said, "There's been enough killing, Daragel."

Daragel bowed and murmured something inaudible.

Bluestocking stepped forward. The guards reached for their swords but stopped when Ana held up her hand. "I think that for all your fierce words, you mean me no harm," she said with a ghost of a smile.

"Majesty, I don't," Bluestocking said. For a moment she considered curtseying, but decided against it. She had had enough of pleading. While she needed an ally, and the Queen seemed sympathetic, she would not grovel. Instead, she said, "I may have spoken harshly– more than was appropriate, but I don't have the tact to dress my speech up in flowers– and I beg your forgiveness."

Queen Ana giggled. "That was almost flowery in itself." So quick that no one else would see it, she winked, as if to say, *ignore them.* Bluestocking returned her a smile. But before anyone could speak, they stiffened at shouts in the distance.

Bluestocking tensed to flee again. Instead, Jasmina's voice called out of the darkness from the side of the cave opposite the Royal Family, "Bluestocking! Look what I've found!" She entered, her arm wrapped around a priestess' throat, pushing her into the light. Behind them, several younger versions of her captive squawked protests, their robes flapping like squabbling birds. Behind them all, Aton pushed the last of their number. From the way the girl arched away from him, Bluestocking guessed that he either had a blade pressed against her spine or that he had convinced the girl that he had. He shot Bluestocking a broad grin. Bluestocking knew that she would have to wait to piece together the events that had brought the wife of the late Prime Minister into an alliance with a thief and blackmailer and wondered when he had slipped away. *So much for your powers of observation, my girl.*

"We were hiding from the mob!" the priestess choked out. "Please! They would tear us to pieces!"

"Aye, but you were one of the sects whose doors we knocked upon," Jasmina said grimly. "Where were you when we were looking for succour?"

"It doesn't matter," Bluestocking said wearily. "That was then, and now we have to decide what we're going to do. How long can this many of us shelter in here?"

Queen Ana shook her head. "Our first job is survival. Then we decide how to free the King."

"You'll need allies for that," Prince Cas said. "Given that I'm almost your son-in-law, I hope that it's not too presumptuous to commit Imperial troops to your safety, Mama."

"That's well said," Daragel interrupted. "But it's ten days hard ride to the nearest sizeable garrison."

Bluestocking was staggered at the level of Daragel's knowledge. *That proves beyond doubt that they have spies in the Empire. Maybe we have spies too, men who can cross borders with few questions asked.* She stared at Aton, who raised an eyebrow.

Daragel continued, "Think on it Majesty, by the time your messenger has ridden to the borders of the prince's precious Empire, the invader will have established a foothold that it will be difficult to dislodge it from. My countrymen are that much closer."

"Aye, that they are," Aton growled from beyond the group. "Just how close are they, Excellency?"

"Close enough," Daragel said smoothly.

Aton said, "I know. One of your countrymen tried to slit my throat last night. I discovered him clambering over the wall. Only the presence of the militia saved my life."

Bluestocking stared at him. He sounded entirely convincing, and for a moment she almost believed him. Then he winked at her.

"You lie!" Daragel stepped forward, hand on sword, and Cas drew his own.

I've had enough of this bickering, Bluestocking thought and taking a deep breath, bellowed, "WILL you all be quiet?"

"She's right," Jasmina said into the stunned hush, "while we squabble amongst ourselves, we achieve nothing."

Bluestocking looked at her. Maybe she saw the widow from a fresh angle, maybe it was some trick of the light catching her eye, but whatever made her do so, Bluestocking stared at Jasmina, noticing a change beyond the obvious. Jasmina's make-up had smeared into a hag's death mask, and her finery hung in tatters, trailing along the ground and ripped sleeveless where she had used strips to tie her hair back from her forehead. In many places the billowing satin was stained by Arial's blood from when he lay dying in her arms, and only the rings remained on her fingers, glinting in the half-light as a reminder of her former status. But there was a greater, inner change as well.

Perhaps because Arial's death had forced her to act alone– rather than rely on him– or because what she had seen had brought her face to face with the harsh reality of her people's daily life, she seemed to have been scoured clean in some way. Only one thing remained. The need to remove Brighana. She caught Bluestocking watching her. "What?"

"I think you're right," Bluestocking said. "You said something else, earlier on. How I could go without worrying about anyone else. But there is someone. If I leave here, Kyr will still be in that thing's thrall."

"If you do that," Jasmina said. "You damn her to everlasting torment."

"What's this?" the Queen asked sharply, all hint of the friendly matron gone.

Bluestocking swallowed nervously. "I know a little of what happened last night." She licked her lips. "A slave girl, Kyr. She—" Cavi made a little choking noise, but Bluestocking ignored it, "—was given into my charge to ensure my comfort, and I suspect," she said with a grim chuckle, "to report about where I went, what I did, and who I associated with..."

"And what *did* you do?" Cavi asked.

Bluestocking ignored her. "I discovered last night that Kyr served others. Myleetra, who was in jeopardy as the Church of Brighannon squeezed out other forms of worship." She paused, licking her lips and taking gratefully a small flask of water proffered by Cas, swigged from it. "I discovered too late what Myleetra was about," she said. "It was

Myleetra who was mostly responsible for unleashing the power upon you."

"Mostly?" Daragel pounced.

"There were others," Bluestocking said and gripped Jasmina's arm, mentally pleading with the other woman to trust her and keep silent. "I didn't recognise the others who served her, but if you go to the demigod's court, I'm sure *you'll* know their names." She stared at him as she emphasised the 'you,' hoping to throw suspicion on the courtier. "Arial died bravely, fighting the demigod."

"That he did," Jasmina said.

"Why should Daragel know them?" Cavi asked.

"Ask him," Aton said, "just how close his countrymen are."

Bluestocking thought, *Good man, keep feeding their fear of Alliance spies.*

Daragel shrugged angrily. "I had a feeling that something like this would happen, that something would befall my charge."

"Who is where exactly?" Bluestocking said, asking the question she'd wanted an answer to ever since she'd realized that Lexi wasn't with the others.

Daragel stared at the ground. "I don't know," he said. "We were separated when that parody of a deity attacked us." He lifted his head and stared defiantly at them all. "And when I asked my master, the Emir, for guidance, when I realized that the King had no control over the events," he raised his voice to drown out the shouts of protest from all around him. "I wanted only to protect the Princess Lexi, not to threaten Whiterock."

The Queen and Princess complained that he had no right to interfere in the internal affairs of another sovereign state, while Prince Cas bellowed that Daragel was creating a diplomatic incident between the Empire and the Alliance.

Daragel smiled superciliously. "This has nothing to do with the Alliance, merely the Emir and I acting on our own."

"How convenient!" Cas said. "So if the Empire launched a raid on your precious Emirate, the other Alliance states would stand by and do nothing?"

Daragel said nothing but merely made a dismissive gesture

"What was your master's response?" Bluestocking asked as the others' indignation petered out.

Daragel did not answer, and the silence grew awkward.

"What now?" one of the courtiers asked.

There was a long silence, that stretched on and on, only finally ended when someone cleared their throat. Cas turned to the source of the noise. "Yes?"

It was a young girl, dressed in the tattered remnants of a priestesses' robe, which was torn half-off at the back. The girl's caramel-coloured face was smudged and cut above one cheek, but Bluestocking still recognized her from when they had gazed out over the Alliance's forces.

The girl swallowed and said in a high, thin voice, "Our church has a prophecy that on the Last Day, if a penitent sinner confesses all, the Gods will grant them a boon. Perhaps if someone were to ask the Gods to set us free–"

"That's your master plan?" Cavi snarled. "We go to Gallows Square and say, 'I'm sorry, I've been bad, now throw this demigod out?' *That's* your great idea?"

The poor girl looks like they've just whipped her, Bluestocking thought, and more to distract the girl than from any genuine interest, asked, "Does it need to be someone from Whiterock?" She saw Aton watching her.

"I don't know," the young priestess said, looking dazed. "It's possible."

"Why?" an older priestess asked, her seamed face crinkled with suspicion.

Bluestocking shrugged. "Just curious."

"It's a damned silly idea," Cavi snapped, closing the subject.

The Silk Palace

In the strained silence that followed, they settled down to rest. Bluestocking must have dozed for when she opened her eyes, it was with the gut-wrenching feeling of dislocation that accompanies a sudden awakening.

The others were milling around. "What's happening?" Bluestocking asked.

"Voices," Aton said, "we're not sure if they're friend or foe. Hush, now!"

They moved off in silence in single file, Prince Cas and the guards leading the way, Bluestocking bringing up the rear. They clutched whatever weapons they could lay their hands on, Cas holding his sword at the ready, the courtiers and others a miscellany of knives, axes and Bluestocking her lump of wood.

They wended their way through the maze of tunnels in silence, straining to hear the other voices, but they too seemed to have fallen silent.

Without warning they ran head-first into the other group at a junction between theirs and another tunnel. Just as the Prince raised his arm to bring his sword down on the last man, the sight of a thin lanky body in brown robes forced its way past Bluestocking's panic, and she recognised a familiar face, the sour expression set in thought.

"Glamis!" she called, and he spun round. Bluestocking called to Prince Cas, "Hold your hand, Majesty! He's friend, not enemy!"

The Prince couldn't stop his sword but instead twisted so that it clanged on bare rock. Glamis threw himself back and called, "Be still! Be still, all of you!"

Then Bluestocking had pushed herself between the two men and more to defuse the situation than because she was really so pleased, threw her arms around Glamis. "Be calm!" she hissed, then called in a loud voice, "it seems as if you've been gone for days, old friend. What news?"

"As you can see," he said dryly, pointing to the crowd of men who milled around in the tunnel behind him, "I have managed to gather the others together, young lady. About a dozen of them, as many as we could find. Oh, and I have found a few pieces of food, nothing very much, but they can be shared out for those who need them."

"I'm sorry- Glamis, is it not?" Prince Cas offered his hand, now empty.

"It is, Highness," Glamis bowed, a fractional inclination of head and shoulders.

"We are all a little tense," Cas explained sheepishly.

"Quiet!" Jasmina cried, and the babble of voices died away. "Listen," she said.

In the silence, a long, metallic bong echoed through the gloom of the corridors.

Chapter 18

"The Sunrise Gong," one of the guards said, and added for Bluestocking's benefit, "It's sounded on holy days, and marks the start of The Last Day."

"This time tomorrow," Cavi added, "it will be a new year."

"If we're alive to hear it," Jasmina added.

"I may be suspicious," Aton said, "but how do we know it's The Last Day?"

Bluestocking saw doubt cross the others' faces.

Jasmina said, "He's right. The clock tower is manned by bell ringers, who are advised by The Sage of the Days. What if Brighana has taken control of the tower through them?"

"They wouldn't dare!" the young priestess cried. "The Gods would sit in judgement, and their punishment would be truly awful."

"And when would they sit in judgement?" Bluestocking asked. "This instant?"

The priestess shrugged. "When they decide is most fitting. It's not for us to question their wisdom."

Aton chuckled. "Meanwhile, Brighana lures us out and while standing on our corpses cries, 'I'm sorry, Divine Pantheon, I didn't know that they hadn't realized that it wasn't The Last Day. I thought that they understood that we made a mistake.' For pity's sake girl! You think

Brighana will worry about a little thing like the protocol of when the last day starts?"

The priestess fell silent. "Does anyone have any kind of plan?" Bluestocking said.

In the silence that followed, Cavi said, "It's a shame we couldn't get the forces below to attack today, if it is the last day. Surely Brighana would have to be circumspect about defending itself."

Those around her nodded without any great display of enthusiasm.

In the now strained silence, Daragel said, "It seems to me that you need someone to go up and check that it's safe. Someone able to go there and back without being discovered."

"And no doubt, you are the one best able to go?" Jasmina snapped. "The man we can trust implicitly? Not the man who seeks his Emir's favour, accompanied by an army?"

Daragel splayed his hands and shrugged, a slow smile staining his face.

No doubt it's meant to look apologetic, but he just looks smug, Bluestocking thought.

"Who would you like to lose the least, Milady?" he asked, pointing at Cavi. "Your daughter? Or will you go?"

"Daragel," Queen Ana interrupted. "How can we trust you?"

"If you can't, Majesty," Daragel said, "then you must choose who you want to lose."

The Queen nodded. "So: It seems we have few options. Come back safe and well."

Daragel left the cave without reply. Bluestocking followed him to the corner, waiting for sounds of a struggle, but the only noise from the corridor was the low moan of the wind.

***

They slept again. *It's like being in one of the colonies of small bears at the foot of the White Ridge Hills,* Bluestocking thought. *As the winter closes in, they retreat to caves to sleep until the weather warms up. Some of the younger bears came out early in a thaw, fooled by the warmth, to be killed by the onset of a sudden cold snap.* As she climbed to her feet and still half-awake looked around the others, she shied away from that analogy.

She took the young black priestess to one side. "This prophecy," she said. "Does it apply only to local people?"

"I don't know." The priestess stared at Bluestocking as if she were a ripe dish of fruit. "Traditionally this usually works better with women. But whether it must be someone local, who can say?" Bluestocking was saved from answering by the presence of the Queen and Cavi.

"He's taken too long," Cavi said, "I knew we shouldn't trust that shifty little toad."

"I have an idea," Bluestocking said. "It's a long shot, but we can't rely on Brighana's people staying out of the cave for much longer." She smiled grimly. "And with Daragel out of the way, if he is planning something evil, he won't know what we're about."

Outside, there was a scraping noise, and Bluestocking stiffened. She crept to the cave mouth and cautiously stuck her head into the passageway. She sprang back, muffling a cry.

"What is it?" The Queen asked.

"Something with too many arms and an eagle's head, walking along the corridor," Bluestocking said.

"Horakh," the priestess said. "A demigod, such has Brighana may become, rather than a mere power." She ventured to the cave-mouth and stood in the corridor. Bluestocking joined her, and they watched the striding demigod round a corner in the gloom and disappear. "The Gods walk among us. It is indeed The Last Day." She made a little motion, and it took Bluestocking a moment to realise that she was genuflecting.

"I'm going outside," Bluestocking said, trying not to think of young bears.

"I'll come with you," Aton said, and they spent several minutes bickering, until the Queen ruled that Aton and Jasmina would accompany Bluestocking on a short scouting expedition while the others remained behind.

Bluestocking cautiously led the little group out into the corridor. They spent several minutes checking down the nearby corridors, which seemed mostly deserted.

"It's as if they all over-indulged last night and are sleeping off the after effects," Aton said.

"That would be one mighty hangover, if your idea is right," Jasmina said sourly.

Bluestocking sighed. "Do you know, this is the first morning when I have walked abroad and there hasn't been that fine curtain of rain that Whiterock specialises in?"

"It's Last Day," Jasmina said. "The King always decreed that holy days should also be observed by the hedge-wizards. Still," she added with a short, humourless chuckle, "I think it possible it may not rain tomorrow morning, either."

"That's maybe not such a bad thing," Aton said. "I'm deeply suspicious of any country that's so regimented that it even wants to rule the weather."

"We like our weather," Jasmina said sharply. "It brings us comfort to know what it will be like each morning, to know that the sun will shine in the afternoon. We couldn't support so many people without needing to buy crops from our neighbours, and when you are a little kingdom surrounded by bigger countries, you do not want to be any more beholden to them than you have to be."

"I did not mean to criticise," Aton said, with a little wink at Bluestocking to show that that was exactly what he'd meant to do.

"You have no idea what it was like before the King came to the throne," Jasmina continued as if she hadn't heard him. "Yuri the Mad, we called his father. Yuripatalia was as capricious as a mountain breeze so that it could hail stones as big as a man's fist in mid-summer or blow sand-storms in winter if he wished." She said squeezing Bluestocking's hand. "I'm babbling about the old days like a crone with nothing to think of but the past."

"I understand," Bluestocking said. "You were just explaining why the King is the way he is. Orderly. Regulated."

"Exactly," Jasmina said. "We needed order when he came to the throne. We need order now, for reassurance against our covetous neighbours."

But how easily, Bluestocking thought, *order can turn to stagnation.*

They returned to the caves after a few minutes. "Majesty, I have the glimmerings of a plan," Bluestocking said. "It's not much of one, but it's all I can think of. If Daragel does as I think he will, good, and if he does what I fears– well, this will be a surprise for him."

So she told them of the plan that had been bubbling away in her mind and watched their jaws drop with a great deal of satisfaction. After another lengthy debate, which had Bluestocking on the verge of screaming at them in frustration, the group finally moved out at a snail's pace

"Bluestocking's right," Queen Ana said. "We need to gather our people. We can hardly expect them to rally around us if they can't even see us."

In a column of twos, they headed toward the palace in the early morning light, some of the courtiers peeling away to talk to the crowd, hands waving, heads bobbing intensely in time to their speech.

***

They crawled cautiously through the almost empty streets, ready for flight at any moment should they run into Brighana's forces, but desperate for commoners to see the royal family alive. They passed a pair of dead bodies, the men's hands locked around each others' throats.

On an impulse Bluestocking searched the men's bodies and pulled out a knife and a short sword. She shoved the knife in her pocket and tucked the sword into her belt, and they resumed their stately crawl.

"There aren't many people about," Bluestocking said.

Jasmina shrugged. "More may appear as the morning matures," she said. "Would you blame them if they stayed indoors after what happened in the night?"

Occasionally parties of devotees gathered in the squares, praying to the same gods who strode round them as if they were not there. One ant-headed, four-armed deity brushed against a celebrant who fell back as if he was suffering a fit.

Most of the deities were curious amalgams of humans and animals, but some seemed comparatively ordinary– if any man or woman standing at least twice normal height could be ordinary. Even these, Bluestocking noticed, seemed to be more vivid, more *real* than mere mortals. There were a few who had no human traits, and a couple who barely held any shape for long periods of time, but there seemed no rhyme or reason to the groups.

"Some of the Gods are said to pass on to another plane of existence," the caramel-coloured priestess said, catching Bluestocking's gaze.

Eventually, they reached the palace and cautiously entered, moving through the empty corridors until they reached the King and Queen's personal chambers.

Cas stepped over the remains of a drape torn from the wall. "Looks like there's been a pitched battle here," he said, pointing to a pool of blood in the corner. There was no body, but it looked enough to have been a man's body full.

Masonry from one wall lay in a pile, and they could see through the hole where it had torn through into the next room and the room beyond that. *It looks as if something huge has dashed straight through the walls of the rooms on some madcap sprint through the palace.* Dust hung everywhere, along with the smell of stale body odours, blood and excrement. Flies buzzed around the mangled corpse of a soldier in one of the doorways.

They continued their trudge through the now deserted state rooms. Bodies, swords– which some of the party picked up– and armour littered the rooms.

"They died fighting to defend the King, or to mount a rescue mission," Queen Ana said, "But they died bravely."

Only when they reached the banquet hall where Bluestocking had dined on her first night did they hear the sounds of voices. They tensed, and Cas held up a finger to signal them to stay where they were. He stepped cautiously toward the doorway but had not quite reached it when Kyr's voice called, "Why don't you bring your friends in, dear Prince Cas?"

Bluestocking backed away but on looking around saw armed men step one after another into the corridor behind them, grinning as they cut off their retreat. She looked at Cavi and then at Cas. He shrugged and stepped into the banqueting hall.

***

Kyr sat, Mylcetra at her feet on one side, the King on the other. Bluestocking saw how his arms hung at an unnatural angle and guessed that his obedience had been bought with torture.

"Husband?" Ana called. "Are you alright?"

The King didn't answer, didn't look at her.

Copel stood to one side of the room, his head bowed. Princess Lexi stood behind, head bowed, flanked by armed men who were clearly the demigod's henchmen. She looked up and gave Bluestocking a wan smile. She looked tired and ready to burst into tears at any moment but seemed unharmed. Without warning, one of the Queen's courtiers drew his sword and lunged toward Kyr. She merely raised an eyebrow, and the courtier gasped. Moments later he dropped his sword and began to scream, a thin, high keening that scraped their nerves. He clutched at his hand, which looked as if it had been boiled. Kyr waved her hand, and the courtier ran headlong into the wall, again and again until the blood flowed from his head and then kept butting the wall until his skull was a bloodied, battered mess.

Kyr ignored their shouted protests and gazed dispassionately at the man, who kept pounding his head against the wall, until she waved a hand, and he dropped to the floor. "He is dead," Kyr said. She added, staring at the Queen and the others in turn, "The next man who is foolish enough to draw his sword will skin himself with it."

She turned. "Bluestocking," she said, her voice no longer Kyr's. Something had been added to it, almost– but not quite– an echo, an added timbre that resonated with the demigod's presence. "Welcome."

"I didn't expect to see you like this," Bluestocking said.

"What? You don't like this form?" Kyr pouted and played with her hair with one finger, wrapping a strand around her fingertip. "Do you prefer this?" The figure suddenly overflowing from the chair was Brighana's, though again there was no moment of change– it simply happened.

"I do, surprisingly enough," Bluestocking said as Brighana returned its form to that of Kyr. "I know what I'm dealing with. I have to keep reminding myself that you're not the woman I loved."

"Oh, but I am," Kyr said.

The voice was again hers, but Bluestocking caught a look of entreaty. *Get me out of here.* It passed quicker than a shaft of sunlight in the midst of showers.

"Prince Cas," Kyr said. "Your countrymen are camped all around our Kingdom, yet even now you have the impudence to approach us."

"*Your* Kingdom?" Queen Ana called, but Brighana ignored her.

"I could, if I so wished, count this as a declaration of war." Kyr stared at her nails. "When did you summon them?" she asked, and waved a hand. "The truth, now!"

Cas stood on tiptoe, and his face went purple, but he coughed his answer out. "Didn't summon them," he coughed. "If they didn't hear from me after a ten-day, they were to send a rescue mission. I was sending home messages via traders. My servant arranged it."

"Ah, that one. He ate his own sword this morning. Slowly," Kyr added with glee. She patted one arm of the throne. "Come sit here, my love." When Bluestocking didn't move, she arched an eyebrow. "Sit with me. I won't hurt you."

"Why not?" Bluestocking asked. "You've hurt everyone else. Does it give you pleasure?"

"Curious as ever," Kyr said, still studying her nails. "Not pleasure; sustenance. All emotions are food, but some are stronger meat than others. As to why, I'm still Kyr, but more so, rather than less. I said when I first appeared that I'm grateful, and I am, so you're safe."

Bluestocking said nothing, but thought furiously, *And you know that it hurts me to see Kyr but not-Kyr sitting there, and you're even feeding on that. Can you read my mind?* "Safe for how long?" she asked. "Gods are notoriously capricious, aren't they?" She tried not to shake with fear as she said it, especially as the memories of the slaughter were still fresh in her mind. *Not that you're a god, you shitty abomination.* "How long before the cat decides to cut this particular mouse's head off?" *Read my thoughts on this, you pain-eating travesty; I'll see you scattered to the four winds even if it costs me my life and soul.* Her cheeks ached from smiling, but she wanted, needed to see if Brighana would read her thoughts.

"For as long as I decide, little one." Kyr turned to the side. "What's this? Another old friend?" She looked up at a pair of heavily muscled but slack-faced peasant-guards who pushed their now-struggling captive before them. "Why, Daragel, how good to see you. I'll enjoy getting to know you now that the balance of power has shifted slightly." She smiled to Bluestocking, and said, "Do excuse me. I'm sure Daragel has lots of things he wants to tell me. Like who killed the Princess Evi to create the pretext for his invasion of *my* realm."

"Majesty," Daragel stammered, licking his lips. "Almighty worshipful one-"

"Be quiet, unless I ask you a question," Kyr said. She waved a hand, and Daragel's face contorted. His hands flapped at his throat, and his face turned puce. "Oh, very well," Kyr said, sighing, and waved her hand again. Daragel gasped for air, but even so, had the presence of mind to reach for a piece of chalk lying nearby and scrawl, *no need for that.*

"Speak," Kyr said.

"I'll happily tell you all I know," Daragel croaked.

"Then come," Kyr said. They walked away, Kyr's arm round the vizier's shoulder.

"What do you think?" Cas growled. "Will he turn traitor and snitch on us?"

"He'll sing his little heart out," Aton said, equally grimly.

"And tell her what?" Bluestocking said. "That his forces are going to attack, while Brighana is hampered?"

"You assume that his people are going to attack," Aton said. Maybe he's making an alliance with that thing..."

Jasmina said. "The last thing we need is to be fighting amongst ourselves and doing Brighana's work for it. Let's trust Daragel. For the moment."

Cas nodded, and they subsided into a tense, watchful silence. The room was quiet, apart from the sobs of a wounded man and an occasional cough.

"What are they doing in there," Cas grumbled, "getting married?"

"I wouldn't joke about that," Queen Ana said. "I'd put nothing past that *thing*." She stepped toward Lexi, but two of Brighana's men guarding the princess raised their swords. "You would dare?" The Queen straightened and looked down her pointed nose at the guards.

One of them grinned sheepishly and scratched his crotch with his free hand, but his sword point never wavered. "We'd rather not, Majesty, but if you force our hand...better we displease a mortal queen than a demigod."

"It's alright, mother," Lexi said wearily. "They've not hurt me."

The gods only know what they've made you watch, girl, Bluestocking thought, then smiled wryly. *For an apostate, you invoke the gods far too readily.*

They fell silent again, and waited. Bluestocking heard a clock chime the three quarters of an hour. Daragel and Kyr– Bluestocking still had difficulty knowing when to think of it as Brighana and when as Kyr– had left the room as the half-hour had chimed.

As silently as sneak-thieves, Kyr and Daragel re-entered the room, Kyr with her arm still draped around his shoulder. Daragel looked relieved– which immediately made Bluestocking suspicious– but also worried, as if he were too close to a man-eating leopard. *He'd probably prefer that he was,* Bluestocking thought. *What deal have you done, reptile?*

Kyr released Daragel, and he moved away from her to stand midway between the factions. He licked his lips. "I believe, your Divinity," he inclined his head toward Kyr, who smiled knowingly, "that we have been able to put right any initial misunderstandings?"

Kyr smiled again, "I think that what you are trying to say, Daragel, is that your interest is only in your princess?" Daragel inclined his head in assent. "Then by all means, take her and leave under passage of safe conduct. My felicitations to your master, the Emir."

"I want no part of this!" Lexi cried. "Don't you dare to try to drag me into your little schemes!"

"My princess!" the vizier protested, "I seek only to protect a citizen of the Alliance and my future ruler."

"Daragel," Lexi said fake sweetly, "the only person you want to protect is yourself." At a noise she turned, and Bluestocking followed her gaze, to where a goat-headed man stood idly in the doorway, chewing on a drape.

Lexi turned to the watching Kyr with a huge grin splitting her face. "Call your thugs off. You can't touch any of us today without repercussions from the gods. If Raikavyi is watching, you can be sure that it's no accident."

She looked away from the apparition and round at Bluestocking, as if unsure whether Bluestocking was real or illusion. Lexi edged forward and clutched Bluestocking fiercely. "You're safe," Lexi said. "I'm so glad."

"Me too," Bluestocking said, hugging the princess back, ignoring the glares or sniggers of some of the courtiers. Lexi seemed to have shrunk in on herself since Bluestocking last saw her; she looked gaunt and hollow-eyed. "Are you alright?" Bluestocking asked, and when Lexi nodded a couple of little dips of the head, Bluestocking turned her attention back to Kyr.

"I have no intention of touching anyone," Kyr said, but her voice held more of Brighana's ever threatening tones now, and the rumbling undertones sounded distinctly unhappy. "Whether or not goat-boy is here spying on us. Nor am I sure why you refer to them as my thugs. They are their own people."

"Shall we see about that?" Queen Ana interrupted, and Kyr momentarily adopted Brighana's form, before flickering back as the slave. "Shall we ask the priestess to run a little spell? Perhaps something that blocks your possession of them?"

"No need," Kyr said, but the fury was clear now in the icy tones. "Most have sworn fealty; they are not possessed at all. They're the clever ones who know what will happen to them tomorrow when the Gods are gone. Is that not right, Highness?" Kyr turned to the King, who knelt, head bowed, not meeting their eyes. "Show them the new order, Redoutifalia," Kyr purred. "Show them who rules the roost." Her voice hardened as the King did not move. "Show them, or I will remember this act tomorrow. My patience is limited."

The King leaned forward until he was prostrate and kissed Kyr's bare feet.

The Silk Palace

Chapter 19

Bluestocking felt sick at the King's humiliation, and from the hiss of in-drawn breath from the Queen, guessed that Ana felt the same way.

Kyr looked up and shot Ana a gloating smile. "The reality of power, little Queenie, is that most of your people, even your big, brave, handsome husband, have enough sense to know you are creatures of the past, your power extinct." She smiled, and the hate that showed in her eyes chilled Bluestocking to the marrow. "Your kind spent generations as parasites, feeding off my power, basking in the heresy that you perpetuated on your own people. For that you have forfeited the right to rule. You," she spat the word, "wretch!"

"I knew nothing of that," Queen Ana said calmly, but Bluestocking's sharp eyes saw her tremble, and she guessed that the Queen was drawing on generations of power to ensure that she showed no weakness. She wondered whether Brighana had seen the tremor as Queen Ana continued, "I married into the family, and I'm sure that none of my children or my husband knew what was going on. And," she added, "it is irrelevant. The issue is that you have taken power by force, with no legitimacy. Worse is the deal that you have done with this termite over my daughter's fate." Queen Ana glared at Daragel. "You have connived at civil war. Whatever your master's instructions, for that I could have your head parted from your shoulders. Don't tempt me."

She added. "Get out of my sight." She called to Lexi, "Come here. We'll run a spell to see if we can dispossess our people. One of the priestesses will know one, I'm sure."

"Can they do that?" Bluestocking asked the priestess. "Run a spell that would free Kyr of possession?"

The priestess shook her head, her eyes wide with warning.

Bluestocking had hissed the question, but Kyr still appeared abruptly beside her; Bluestocking couldn't help jumping.

"I'm not possessed, lover," Kyr said. "Brighana and I, we are one person now, so there's no need for talk of nonsense like possession." She fastened her gaze on Bluestocking, who felt the tug of her power threatening to pull her spirit from her body.

Kyr continued, "As you and I could be if you gave yourself willingly to me, worshipped me instead of one of the other Gods." She added, "Think of it. When we make love we try with all our might to become one with them. This way, you and I can be joined forever."

Bluestocking felt her face burn, felt desire throbbing within her with a physical ache. She licked her lips and tried to remember to breathe.

Kyr gazed into Bluestocking's eyes. "There is still love for you in here." Kyr touched her chest. "Don't let these charlatans fool you. They're using you, as they've always used you. You and I could be everything we dreamed of when I was your slave." She leaned forward, so close that Bluestocking could smell her fragrance, the same musky combination of dirt, talc and sex as always. "I would wash your feet, now," Kyr breathed, "even in front of all these people, such is my love for you, little darling."

Whether it was the 'little' or whether there was something else, Bluestocking was unsure ever afterward. She thought later that Kyr's odour included a hint of carrion, and it was enough to shake her loose from the web spun by Kyr's words. Then she thought, *You don't know!* When Brighana had said "instead of one of the other gods," she hadn't initially caught it. *Brighana doesn't know, because I never told Kyr I was an apostate.*

Bluestocking said nothing but instead shook her head. "I saw the look Kyr gave me before you took her over. That wasn't the look of someone making love; that was the look of someone being raped."

Kyr's eyes narrowed. "Don't presume too much on our friendship, mortal."

Bluestocking smiled coldly. "Ah, the real Brighana shows itself?" She suddenly noticed the shouting around them as Lexi stormed out of the throne-room with a pleading Daragel behind her. Ignoring Kyr's shouts of protests, and half-expecting to be blasted into the next world for her insolence, Bluestocking followed.

"Good idea," Ana whispered from just behind her.

Lexi was shouting, "I want nothing more to do with you!" Daragel's reply was inaudible, and Lexi railed, "You can tell that fat hog when you next see him that he can marry one of his hundred whores!"

Looking around, Bluestocking caught a distinct gleam in Queen Ana's eye, and her mouth twitched.

Another murmur from Daragel and Lexi shouted, "No, I won't change my mind when I've calmed down! I've seen you play your little games too often!"

Daragel murmured, and this time Lexi's reply was quieter, but the menace in her voice sent a little icy-footed centipede galloping down Bluestocking's spine; "You dare to threaten me? You have an hour to leave this land before I issue a warrant for your arrest for treason."

Another murmur and Lexi said coolly, "I'm sure that my mother would reconsider her former attitude if I told her what you just said to me. Now get out!"

While they'd been arguing Kyr had followed them in. Now she clapped her hands and leaned forward. "Why don't you all gather round and watch the fun?" She instructed one of her men then, a sallow, mournful looking youth whose eyes were glazed with the sight of too much death and agony, "Guard them as if their lives were yours, while I go and greet our new visitors down on the plain."

She smiled at them all. "I'll allow you to look through the eyes of one of them." She wiggled her fingers, and a window seemed to open in mid-air. Through it they saw the White Rock in front of them, rearing toward the sky as it had when Bluestocking first saw it. The view altered as the soldier whose eyes they gazed through turned to look his comrades. Suddenly there were the sounds of horse's harnesses clinking in the air, the tramp of marching feet and the soldier's comrade saying, "...I heard them eats off gold plates."

"Garn!" someone replied.

Back in Whiterock, Kyr leapt from the throne and with two strides crossed the room. Standing beside Prince Cas, she stood taller than he now. "Let's greet your countrymen," she whispered, loudly enough for the whole room to hear. She put her arm around him; they each lifted a foot in unison and stepped through the invisible window into the scene.

To Bluestocking, watching through the unknown soldier's eyes, Kyr and the Prince seemed to step out of nowhere to stand in front of the leader of the Imperial force. "Highness!" he cried. "You're safe?"

"Duke Dorealis," the Prince said. "My servant was killed, and it was impossible to get a message to you in time. Regrettably, you've had a wasted journey."

"But Highness!" Dorealis said, "no word in a ten-day, and then you just appear, with," he pointed at Kyr, who seemed to have grown even taller than before, "this–"

"Demigod," Kyr's voice boomed, and then Brighana stood in front of them, and as one the soldiers drew their weapons, Brighana waved one of its arms. One after another Whiterock soldier stepped into view. "You dare?" Brighana thundered, voice crescendoing to avalanche loudness. "You invade MY realm, question your prince, then draw weapons ON ME?" Several Imperial troops covered their ears. Clashing swords, screaming men and blood everywhere blurred the next few minutes.

"I thought that the gods couldn't harm mortals today?" Bluestocking cried.

"Do you celebrate the Last Day in exactly the same fashion as here?" the younger priestess asked. Bluestocking shook her head, and the other woman continued, "There you are. Brighana will doubtless claim you are infidels, with no right to adopt our beliefs when it suits you to claim safety." She squinted upwards into the scene. "Something flies above, so the gods know what is going on. It suits their purposes not to intervene at the moment."

Then, without warning, Bluestocking found herself looking down through his own eyes at the soldier's thigh, over which his fingers clutched, in a desperate but futile attempt to stop the blood that spurted everywhere. The scene faded, as Bluestocking buried her head in her hands.

"This cannot go on," the Queen whispered, squeezing Bluestocking's shoulder. She seemed to be thinking aloud. "This monstrosity, this abomination, a travesty of everything we have worshipped, will not rest until it has set us at each other's throats for its amusement. Somehow, we must find a way of stopping it."

The scene reappeared. This time a small knot of men, perhaps a half-dozen in number, stood staring at the group in obvious defeat. Horses stood by, cropping the grass, while bodies lay scattered around, many of them decapitated or disembowelled– or even both.

"You survivors," Prince Cas said, "go home and warn our countrymen of the folly of trespassing onto Whiterock lands and the hospitality that awaits those who do."

The Prince stepped through out of the soldier's view and back into the room. He shook his head and cried, "Oh by Marn's arms! I stood and did nothing!" He leaned against the wall and took heaving lungfuls of air. "That thing took over my hands and mouth as if I was a puppet, and it had its hand up my arse working me!" He spat on the ground.

***

Through another soldier's eyes, they watched the Imperial soldiers withdraw, leaving their dead. Brighana flicked a finger, and corpses flew end over end to land on a pile. Then the scene vanished, and Kyr reappeared. "I do so hate mess and untidiness," she said, smiling.

The others stood around looking stunned, while Prince Cas slumped as if ready to throw himself out of the nearest window. Bluestocking's heart turned over for him.

She turned to find Kyr watching her. Her lover reached out a languid hand and ran her fingernail down Bluestocking's bare arm. "We could have been lying in bed together now, wrapped in each other, listening to the assorted gods and demigods from within the comfort of your rooms. Arial, Copel, Myleetra, they told me all I had to do was occupy you; Kyr was supposed to be your distraction. Little Kyr was good at what she did." She leaned closer. "Give yourself to me. We can lie together again." She breathed into Bluestocking's ear, "We could slip between the sheets now, if you wanted, our bodies slick with sweat and love in barely moments. Come with me, my love,"

Except that it's not Kyr, Bluestocking reminded herself. She'd seen the look of anguish on the slave's face the last time she'd been subsumed by that colossal presence.

Bluestocking shook her head. While the last few hours had been demoralising, she felt a strange kind of exhilaration. *There are obviously constraints on you, monster. I don't know what they are yet, but you clearly have them. I'm going to work out what they are.*

She turned away, and Kyr grabbed her arm. "Don't walk away from me!" she hissed and flickered back and forth between hers and Brighana's form.

"Now we see the real Brighana," Bluestocking said, putting as much mockery into her voice as possible. "The shit-eating travesty of a real god."

"Do not presume too much on my mortal part's love for you," Brighana growled– now it was Brighana starting to show through. She reappeared as Kyr. "Bluestocking–"

"I'm not a frightened little girl anymore," Bluestocking said, suddenly drawing on reserves of strength that she hadn't realized that she possessed. What she'd said was true. The last few days and nights had been a crucible, burning the old Bluestocking away, leaving something smaller, fiercer, tougher and harder in the frightened scholar's place.

She looked round, caught Ana's eye and winked. The Queen smiled, and Bluestocking thought, *I wonder if you, or that beast can see me shaking inside, for all my brave words?*

Bluestocking motioned with her head toward the doorway.

"Don't do this..." Kyr /Brighana's, voice oscillated between one and the other, human plaintiveness giving way to the angry buzz of the demigod and back, all in three words.

"I've seen enough pain and death for a lifetime," Bluestocking said. "Maybe I wasn't destined to live long."

The Queen had joined them. "Shall we?" Bluestocking asked, tilting her head toward the door.

Queen Ana smiled. "I think that it should be you who calls the others." She leaned close and whispered, "I don't know quite why, but I think that we're in your hands, now."

"Aton! Jasmina! Your Highnesses and assorted hangers on!" Maybe it was tiredness, or simply relief that they had earned a few hours grace, but for whatever reason Bluestocking felt a wild exhilaration. "We have a few hours before this–" she jerked her thumb at Brighana, "–comes a-huntin'. Shall we go somewhere a little more salubrious?"

Brighana never moved, but suddenly Bluestocking found her path blocked, and her heart beat faster. "I've forgiven you much, mortal," Brighana said, its words echoing round the room. "But with that comment, you condemn them all. You will watch as they die, slowly, and in agony, one after the other."

"Come on!" Jasmina snapped, only her eyes showing her fear. "Let's leave!"

"Did you hear her, Redouti?" Ana called out to her husband. "The mask has dropped. I know why you pretended to pay fealty, but there's no need now. Come with us, husband." The King still crouched on his haunches. He began to rock, backwards and forwards, shaking his head. "Redouti? Dear?" the Queen called. "Will you not join us for one last day?"

The King muttered something, and his rocking increased in tempo. At last he looked up at them, and Bluestocking had to look away from the despair in his eyes. *No one should have to look like that,* she thought.

Queen Ana crossed to where he knelt, took his face in her hands and kissed him once, fully on the lips. Slowly, with obvious reluctance for some, they gathered their belongings, and left him kneeling there.

***

"Where now?" Bluestocking asked when they had left the palace.

The Queen shrugged. "I've no great preference. I simply wanted my children away from the presence of that thing. It's enough that we can walk free and let our people know that we are alive and still here to rally around." She smeared a tear angrily away from her eye and said, "I will never forgive it for humiliating my husband."

Bluestocking wondered whether even if the royal family regained power, the King would be able to rule again. His humiliation would become public knowledge. She decided not to say anything. *It will do no good.*

Instead, they drifted through the streets as if taking the air. The morning passed with glacial slowness. Bluestocking kept hoping that by some miracle, the Gods might intervene and spare her from what she would have to do. But although she heard the occasional shout and clash of swords, no *deus ex machina* appeared.

"Amazing," Bluestocking breathed, pointing at what lay ahead of them. Away from the fighting, some of the streets had slowly started to fill while they were inside the Palace. Impromptu markets sprung up on street corners, selling roasted nuts, cooked and cold meats and freshly baked bread, their gaudy banners incongruous between bloodstains half-hidden beneath badly-placed piles of sawdust and cracked masonry above the stall-holder's heads.

"The triumph of greed over fear," Jasmina said with a grin. "Never underestimate how appealing a coin is to a Whiterock stallholder." She added, "It's nowhere near as busy as previous years, though."

Bluestocking's stomach rumbled, and she grimaced, hoping that no one would notice.

The Queen turned to her with a smile, but also a frown. "When was the last time you ate, child?"

Bluestocking shook her head. "This morning? Last night? The days have become a blur of late." She shrugged. "No matter, Majesty." She thought, *After today, it probably won't matter, anyway, I'll be dead, or worse.*

The queen murmured to Cas, and he nodded vigorously. Shooting a huge grin at Bluestocking, he strolled over to a couple of stall-holders, and they all shouted and gesticulated, then shrugging, waved their hands again. The prince turned away, and one of the men tugged on his sleeve. The prince whirled, and the man snatched his hand away as though he'd grabbed a red-hot poker and bowed again and again, his head bobbing up and down.

The men cut slices of meat from their roasts and wrapped them in bread, then brought two each, one in each hand, across to the Queen and the others. "Majesty, we would count it an honour if you would sample our poor fare and give us your opinion."

The Queen inclined her head and said graciously, "Kind sir, what is your name?"

"Arvi, Majesty." Arvi grinned and waved his hand at his colleague, who Bluestocking belatedly recognised as the stall-holder who had offered her food at the Retribution. Arvi introduced him. "This rascal is Claybar, Majesty."

Claybar grinned. "It's good to see that you've survived all the goings-on, Majesty, and," he bowed to Bluestocking, "noble guest."

"It's a pleasure to see you again," Bluestocking said, surprised that she really meant it. Claybar seemed a link to a time, now long-gone, when however unpleasant things had seemed, at least her world had not been turned upside-down. He proffered her a roll, which she took, suddenly shy with gratitude. "I seem never to have any money with me."

Claybar shook his head. "No matter," he said. "I'll get you another in a minute. Your countryman said that you hadn't eaten for days. I thought he was some mercenary free-loader 'Twas only when I saw you that I realised where he came from." He added with a rueful shake of the head, "Things is bad. It's fearsome enough at Year End anyway, never knowing whether some demigod is going to turn you into a radish next day 'cause you ain't polite enough, without all these goings on." He leaned into her, and his breath was so sour that she had to blink but managed to keep a diplomatic silence. "Normally we'd be busier, but they've all but stopped flying the air-bags, with the foreigners laying siege below. They're from the other people, heh? The Westerners?" Realising that he was referring to the Alliance troops, Bluestocking nodded. He continued, his voice dropping another level, so that she could barely hear him, "They say that the King's a prisoner and that the rebels have broken him. Is it true?"

"For the moment," Bluestocking said and added fiercely, "But things change."

He stood straighter, and he looked happier than at any time since they'd first seen him. "I'll get you that second roll," he said, "and one for the others."

Bluestocking thought, *strange, how just a few words, only half-truths, can lift a man, and make him happy.*

As they stopped and ate and stood in full view, gradually more people approached them, most holding back at first, and then seeing that the Queen and the two princesses were real, not some imago cast by a capricious god and that they appeared to be free to roam the streets, many sidled up to them and hesitantly reached to touch their sleeves or arms. Some broke down into tears; a few cursed them for abandoning them, or for not making more of a fight of it. To all of them, the Queen answered simply, in a serene voice, and Bluestocking saw their spirits lift. Almost all of them wanted to know if the rumours were true, that the King was held prisoner. The Queen simply deflected their questions, with those of her own, mostly about the other person, their circumstances and family.

Only when they were approached by a man who held his hand conspicuously on his sword hilt and who gave them a patently false smile did Bluestocking reach out and touch the Queen's sleeve. "I think these are Brighana's men," Bluestocking hissed.

Chapter 20

"You should move along from here," the swordsman said. A dozen other street toughs stood behind him, leaning against the walls. One of them spat on the street.

"I will go where I like in my streets," Queen Ana answered calmly. "I see no reason why I should not."

"By order of the King," the swordsman said, his smile becoming a leer, so clearly enjoying himself that Bluestocking wanted to punch him.

"Then the King must come and order me in person," the Queen said. "My husband wouldn't send a common ruffian to carry out his orders."

The swordsman swore and drew his sword, but before it was more than half-out of its scabbard, he stopped. Prince Cas' sword tip pressed against his throat.

"I wouldn't do anything too hasty, lads!" the Prince called to the others, who were peeling themselves away from the walls. He said to the ruffian's leader, "I suggest, sir-rah, that you take yourself away from this vicinity, and that if you see us again, you walk the other way. You may be good for frightening yokels or leaping out of dark alleyways onto unsuspecting victims, but I would be a different, tougher opponent for the likes of you. And no matter how many foes I'm faced with, I know how to spot the leader of a group and attack him even if I have to ignore all the others." Cas bared his teeth in a wolfish grin. "Are we in agreement, *friend?* Shall we leave each other alone?"

"Ack!" his opponent squawked, his bulging eyes trying to find the prince's sword tip.

"Good!" Cas sheathed his sword, clicked his heels and bowed, all in the second that the ruffian gathered his breath and wits. "Delighted to make your acquaintance," Cas said, offering Princess Cavi his arm, and with a broad wink to Bluestocking, giving his other arm to the Queen. "Ladies, shall we stretch our legs?"

In a parody of the Prince, Bluestocking took an elaborate farewell of the stall holders, and the party moved on leisurely in the opposite direction to their would-be attackers.

So they continued throughout the day of the spring equinox. As the day ripened the streets filled as people, reassured by the truce, and the customary presence of the local pantheon, gradually emerged from their homes, churches or wherever else they had taken shelter.

With the continual buffeting from the crowd and her still unpaid debt to the gods of sleep, Bluestocking was fit to drop by the time the sun was at its zenith.

And everywhere she went, it seemed to her, she saw Brighana's face. Men, women children– all seemed to momentarily take on her enemy's features. *It's probably put a haunting spell on me,* she thought.

The Queen said, "I wish we could find somewhere to rest, but I'm reluctant to make more people than necessary the target for Brighana's spite should we fail."

Bluestocking thought the comment odd, given that the Queen had had few qualms about risking the stallholder's necks. She said, "I feel as if I could sleep for a week. And that's probably unwise."

Lexi chuckled. "We need to be somewhere from where we can act quickly, once the day of truce ends."

Cavi called from the middle of the line to the Queen, who led them, "Would we not be safer back down in the caves, Mama?"

The Queen halted, and they conferred. Bluestocking caught the Queen's murmur, "I resent being harried into sanctuary in my own realm."

How soon we return to our old arrogance, Bluestocking thought.

They moved on, still seeming to drift aimlessly, while the courtiers and priest held whispered conversations at every street corner. Several times, Bluestocking caught bystanders eying her speculatively and wondered how much the enemy had learned of their plan, whether either the Alliance or Empire would attack as she half-prayed that they would. *Daragel, did we give you enough time to play into our hands? Will the Empire mount an attack anyway to stop Whiterock from falling into hostile hands?*

They had just cleared the entrance to a square when Bluestocking heard a crack, a crunch and a dull roar. Someone screamed. A voice shouted, "Look out!" They looked around in panic, then Bluestocking was lifted off her feet, and the Prince threw himself- with her in his arms– across the street.

Where they had stood a wall had crashed down, missing them by only a few feet and one of the priestesses by a whisker. Bricks and bits of plaster had flown in every direction, scratching faces, hands and arms. Bluestocking turned away, shielding her eyes.

"Sorry!" A cheery voice called from above. Bluestocking looked up. A half-dozen workmen stood around the stump of a chimney. Their leader leaned down. "Are you hurt?" He rested his hands on his knees.

"We're not!" Aton shouted. "No thanks to you!"

"Hoi!" one of the workmen called back. "No need for that! It was an accident!"

"What in the God's Eyes are you doing working today?"

"Is it a crime?" the leader bellowed back. "For honest men to toil today to make up for lost time? Not that it's any bloody concern of yours!" He turned away and shouted at one of his men, "Be more careful, next time, heh?"

"Was it an accident?" Bluestocking murmured when they walked on.

"Who knows?" Jasmina muttered back. "It only needs some bad luck, and Brighana's work will be done."

At some point Bluestocking, Aton and Jasmina were separated from the others and wandered into an area that was unfamiliar to Bluestocking. She had thought that she had roamed every single street and alleyway the last few nights. But now they walked through crowded, twisting alleys filled with noisome rubbish and that seemed to ooze menace. Men watched them with eyes half-closed but that she guessed missed nothing. Tatty silk-lace curtains twitched in windows.

"Come on," Jasmina said. "These alleyways are a touch too deserted for my liking. Any one of a number of different accidents could befall us; back to the main concourse."

At a junction they paused, unsure of which way to go. Then, as they took a cautious step down one alleyway, a light like a miniature sun flashed across their path and hurtled down the other path. "What was that?" Aton whispered.

"I've absolutely no idea," Jasmina replied. "Do we follow it, or go the other way?"

"Follow it," Bluestocking said. "And pray that it doesn't lead us into a trap."

They hurried back without further mishaps, though Bluestocking noticed that several pairs of young toughs appeared during their walk.

"Don't look backwards." Aton hissed at Jasmina, "I *said* don't look backwards!"

"How many are there?" Bluestocking asked, risking a sneaked peek behind her. The toughs were following them, one slapping a small sack into his palm with the other hand. *Probably filled with sand, Bluestocking thought.*

"About a dozen," Aton said. "If we stay in the busy places, we'll be safe enough," he added. "But if we wander off into somewhere with no witnesses..." He drew his finger across his throat then grinned and rolled his eyes.

"Stop it!" Bluestocking snapped.

"Sorry," Aton said, instantly contrite. "I really think that we're safe enough as long as there are other people around."

"Then we need to stay where there are lots of people," Bluestocking said.

They followed clumps of revellers. The thugs kept an even distance, slowing down when they slowed down, hurrying when Bluestocking's group hurried.

"Oh, no!" Aton groaned. "This turning goes nowhere!"

"And our 'friends' are behind us," Jasmina said.

"Well, well," the gang leader said. "There's nowhere to go, heretics."

"Who says we're heretics?" Bluestocking asked. *Keep them talking while we look for a way out.*

The leader shook his head and smiled mockingly. Bluestocking realized his eyes were slightly unfocussed and wondered whether he was possessed. She had her answer when he said, "You won't get away, Bluestocking. Don't waste time looking."

He stepped forward, and there was the flash of a concealed blade taken from up his sleeve. Then he stopped, gazing beyond Bluestocking at something. He muttered to a second man, who stepped back.

Bluestocking darted a glance over her shoulder; the biggest dragonfly she had ever seen, as big as a large dog, hovered just above the top of a wall, its huge blue-green wings glinting. It darted toward the thugs, who backed away, creating enough space for Bluestocking's group to edge through.

"We're not done with you yet, girl!" the tough's leader spat.

"I rather think you are," Jasmina said with a huge smile. "Good morning, Highness!"

Princess Lexi, accompanied by soldiers in Whiterock regalia, beckoned Bluestocking. "Their vermin are blocking off the way to the caves. But we've found a bolt-hole for a couple of hours. Until then," she added, her eyes darting to the toughs. "Don't say anything."

She led Bluestocking's group away. When Brighana's toughs tried to follow them, several courtiers stepped between Bluestocking and her would-be pursuers. Bluestocking looked back. The leader shrugged, as if to say, *it doesn't matter,* then looked up, smiled the smile of a shark, and drew his finger across his throat.

Bluestocking shuddered, but as Lexi led them away, she tried to put him out of her mind. By the time they had reached the safe house that Ana's family was staying in, she had almost succeeded.

Almost.

***

She arose a few hours later, the afternoon shadows lengthening. Bluestocking had slept fitfully, but she still felt a deep, aching tiredness that had seeped through to the very marrow of her bones. She made a careful toilet, running a comb through her hair and hissing as it caught on snags. Then she washed her face, and wiped her clothes as clean as she could with a damp cloth. She wished that she could sneak back to her rooms to collect a change, but had the feeling that if she did, there would be a reception committee waiting for her, courtesy of Brighana.

"Are you ready?" Jasmina asked, interrupting her reverie.

"Not really," Bluestocking said, her voice a squeak. Jasmina led her to face the others, whose sympathetic looks and offers of, "good luck," worried her more than anything else.

Outside, the people of Whiterock now thronged the streets, spilling over into areas that they were not normally allowed into, but many of them looked anxious and white-faced, and Bluestocking suspected that they wondered what price the privilege carried. Many were armed, and she realized that these were their guards.

She felt the same familiar jostling as on her first day in Whiterock and for the first time since that day, felt at ease. Then she thought of what might happen to her over the next few hours, and any feelings of ease evaporated. They pushed through the throng, through which whispers were running like the hiss of waves on a shingle beach. Several times people looked at Bluestocking, and she was sure, with a wild surge of paranoia, that the whispers were about her. They pushed and shoved with as little result as if they were running up the side of Whiterock itself, with Jasmina leading Bluestocking, and the others trailing in their wake.

"Keep close!" Aton called and grabbed her hand.

Normally she would have snatched it away from the peddler's greasy grasp, but she was so nervous that the contact was actually a relief. She looked back, and he gave her a ferocious grin and a wink.

"Head up, girl," he growled and squeezed her hand.

She could have kissed him out of gratitude, but the crowd was pulling and pushing and tugging as they surged in all directions. She looked down at his other hand and saw that Lexi held it, forming the next link in the chain. *Well, well,* she thought. *Who would have thought it? A princess and a peddler, holding hands.*

"Something is definitely afoot," Lexi said. "They know there's sport coming today."

"Well, there is, isn't there, as far as they're concerned?" Aton said. "Whatever happens, if Brighana triumphs or we prevail, they're assured of entertainment."

We prevail? Bluestocking almost boggled at the sentiments but decided that Aton was displaying a dry sense of humour. *Still,* she thought, *I suppose if I go into this thinking I have a chance, then maybe something will turn up.* It was easier to think it than to believe it.

When they neared Gallows Square, Jasmina tapped her on the shoulder. "A word, if you please, before we enter."

She drew Bluestocking to one side, while the others pushed on. "This will not be easy, I warn you now," the other woman said. "You must be absolutely clear in your own mind and sincere about this. Otherwise, everything that you have been faced with until now will be preferable to the God's retribution. Are you sure, deep down, with every part of your being, of what you are doing?"

"I'm not sure of anything, at the moment," Bluestocking said, heart beating wildly. "But I don't really have too many choices, do I?" Seeing Jasmina's horrified look, she added quickly, "I'm sorry, that was an attempt at humour. Yes, I'm sure." She thought, *What I regret more than anything is all the people that I've lied to, how hurt they will be when they find out.* She added, in a trembling voice, "I'm scared witless, to be truthful."

Jasmina made a little gesture of sympathy. "Even to the truly penitent, this will also involve considerable discomfort, to put it mildly."

Bluestocking's mouth felt dry. "At the risk of sounding cowardly, how much discomfort is involved?" She gave a thin, nervous little bark of a laugh. "More than I've suffered in the last few days?"

Jasmina smiled sadly. "Nobody's really told you exactly what's involved, have they?" When Bluestocking shook her head, Jasmina leaned toward her and murmured, "I know this is frightening." Then she told what was coming, and Bluestocking paled.

They pushed and elbowed and shoved their way through the press, still close to Aton and the others. "Is this why Brighana's people have left us alone?" Bluestocking said. "I've not seen many of them lately. I can't believe that Brighana has suddenly decided that the tiger will sing in perfect harmony with the field mouse."

"I think," Jasmina said, "that they are biding their time to see what we intend. They can't touch us today." She grasped Bluestocking by the elbows, her fingers digging into Bluestocking's arms, so fiercely that Bluestocking almost cried out. Her breath smelt of an upset stomach. "You know that you're their last chance, Bluestocking. If you are not sincere about this you might as well slip away now and leave these people to their fate."

I'd last two minutes, Bluestocking thought, *before one of Brighana's crew slit my throat. And that's if I'm lucky.* And there was her promise to Kyr. *I won't leave you to this thing's mercies, my love.*

"Penitence is the key." Jasmina took Bluestocking's face between her hands and stared deep into Bluestocking's eyes. This close, Bluestocking could see the little red lines that made up a spider-web in one eye. "In order to survive being possessed by even a demigod, you must be worthy. Those who are not will die slowly, in agony and will bring the wrath of the gods down upon all around them."

"We don't already have the wrath of one of them?" Bluestocking asked.

"This isn't a joking matter," Jasmina scolded her.

"I'm not joking," Bluestocking said, and added, "We're dead tomorrow, anyway. Let's go down fighting."

"Good girl!" Jasmina hugged her.

"Come on," Bluestocking said huskily. "Let's get this done, for better or worse."

The others ahead of them slowed. "We're at the edge of Gallows Square," Lexi said and squeezed Bluestocking's hand. "Godspeed, friend."

Bluestocking heard the same murmuring that she had noticed at the previous Retribution, but now it seemed to her fevered mind that there was an ominous undertone to it. Burning brands had been pushed into their holders and into whatever gaps there were in the dry stone walls. Bluestocking wasn't sure why they were needed so early in the day. *Unless this is going to last until late,* she thought. She wasn't sure whether she wanted it over quickly or not.

The Square was rapidly filling with people clambering onto their seats, and between the jostling crowd, vendors with trays full of sweetmeats veered. Bluestocking's stomach grumbled, and as if hearing it, Aton said wryly, "I wouldn't eat any of these things. I've heard that they are often laced with herbs and spices that cause visions."

"The walls up there," Jasmina pointed, "will protect the Queen from behind."

"Won't that pen them in as well, though?"

Jasmina smiled and whispered, "You didn't see Cas, did you, talking to some men?" When Bluestocking shook her head, Jasmina added, "He's had them putting a few bricks in a pile, so that should we have to fall back, we can jump over. And yes, someone will be perched atop the wall, keeping an eye out to make sure no one climbs up from the outside."

Wedged between Aton and Jasmina, Bluestocking looked around. Behind her sat most of their party, and at the very back, the rest of the royal family of Whiterock. Lexi waved at her as if they were two school friends out on an excursion.

"Look over there," Aton hissed.

She followed his pointing finger and saw the King and Myleetra sat on either side of Brighana. The alternative royalty were in turn surrounded by courtiers and guards. The party was of such a mish-mash in appearance that it was clear that they were more Brighana's men than they were the King's, recruited at random solely to serve the demigod's whims.

The demigod's form flickered backwards and forwards between its different forms, but even if it were to continue to look like Kyr, Bluestocking would no longer think of it as her old lover. *Kyr is dead,* she kept reminding herself. *Or as good as dead.*

As though sensing her scrutiny, Brighana turned and gazed at Bluestocking, who felt the full weight of the demigod's attention for the first time. It rolled over her and almost drowned her beneath it. She felt herself suffocating, crushed beneath the weight of a whole world.

"Bluestocking!" She became aware that someone was shaking her. Turned to look at the stranger, who gradually, as memory returned, she realised was Jasmina. The older woman looked close to panic, but her worry lines gradually eased, as Bluestocking returned to normality. "I thought that it had snared you there, for a few moments."

"It –" Bluestocking's voice was a rasp. She cleared her throat. "It nearly did. I've never had a staring competition with a demigod before." She added, "I don't recommend it."

Jasmina laughed dutifully, if hollowly. "Just keep looking at the rest of the crowd, at the stars, anywhere except in their direction. Things will get interesting soon enough."

The rows of benches seemed to rise all around her, and she shrank back.

"Courage," Jasmina whispered. Bluestocking nodded, as the other woman took her hand and squeezed it. "Our friend the priestess awaits us. Let's not keep her out in the open for longer than we need to. Come!"

They forced their way a step at a time toward the stage at the front. Several of the priestesses from the Queen's party were there, as well as several others. Amongst the latter, Bluestocking recognized three or four witches, cronies of Myleetra's that she had seen at various gatherings.

"Bluestocking!" A voice, clearly magically amplified, called through the mob, and they halted, still several spans short of the stage. Princess Lexi waved from midway between her mother and where Bluestocking stood. "I wanted to wish you good luck," she said, "and to show Brighana's rebels that there is still resistance to their uprising from the *legitimate* government."

She walked side by side with Bluestocking up the steps to the stage, and the low growl of several thousand voices murmuring and muttering spread around the Square.

"Where is Brighana?" Bluestocking whispered. "Still where it was?"

"Still up there at the back. Follow my eyes. I'm damned if I'll give that creature the satisfaction of seeing me point or nod toward it."

Bluestocking followed her gaze. The King and Myleetra sat on either side of the demigod, whose very shape flickered and whirled in the noon-day sunlight. *You don't need to point or nod, little one,* the thoughts rumbled in her head. She swallowed.

You can read my thoughts? If it could, then they were lost, surely…

There was no answer, and Bluestocking risked a glance behind her. A priestess of some minor cult stood close by. Her eyes were glazed, and Bluestocking relaxed slightly. *Parlour tricks,* she thought disgustedly. *I thought you were a demigod?*

"Is the penitent here?" The older priestesses from their party down in the caves called. "If so, let her step forward." It was purely a ceremonial request.

Bluestocking complied.

"Who are you?" The young caramel-coloured priestess called, setting the scene as they had agreed in the caves.

"I am known as Bluestocking," she cried out at the top of her voice. "But my real name is Blue. I am a name-changer. I am a heretic."

Chapter 21

A stunned silence fell and rippled around the square from the stage to settle like a cloak across the assembled multitude. Blue could hear the drumbeat of her pulse and felt giddy with tension. The silence stretched and stretched. Blue felt that if a leaf had dropped, the dull thud of its landing would have reverberated around the amphitheatre.

Inevitably, it was Brighana that shattered the tableau. It stood to its full height as the shadows lengthened in the late afternoon sunshine. "What nonsense is this?"

For the first time, Blue noticed the various gods and demigods that had assembled on top of the walls around the square. *Vultures, waiting for the feast,* she thought. She swallowed. *I hope mine isn't the corpse they're waiting for.*

"Stone her!" A man bellowed from near the back, and another cried, "Foreign bitch!"

No words passed between Brighana and the assembled deities, including those that lurked at the edge of the crowd. Brighana said no more then but instead sat down. The shouting men immediately went quiet as well.

Still, the damage had been done. Where before there had been almost a holiday mood amongst the crowd, now it felt as if it could turn ugly at any moment. The young black priestess stepped hesitantly to the edge of the stage, though when she cried out, "We are congregated here in the presence of the gods!" her voice rang out loud and clear. She beckoned Blue and asked her, "Why are you here?"

"I humbly abase myself," Blue said. "I am ashamed and sorry for what I have done. I have come to offer myself to the Gods, for their forgiveness or for their Retribution."

At the older priestess' nod Blue slowly, deliberately stepped toward the woman, who stood by a seat similar to that which had been used on Visohn the last time she had been here. Her feet felt like lead, and she swallowed nausea. *Please, don't let me be sick.*

"If you lie, or omit anything significant– and the Gods will decide what is significant–" the priestess said, "then you will die in such horror, that no heretic will ever again indulge in frivolity at the expense of the Gods."

"I understand," Blue said. They clamped her into the seat, shackling her round the waist, pressing her hands above her, palms crossed and outstretched.

The young priestess came to stand beside Blue. "I will pray to the Gods for your survival," she whispered.

An old priestess, one of Evi's cronies, said as she tightened the last strap, "May the Gods treat you as you deserve." She offered Blue the ghost of a smile.

Lexi squeezed her shoulder. "Be brave," she said. "This is more about theatre than religion. We must show the mob that you are truly contrite, that even on this day, when pain fades like the mist, heretics will suffer."

A fat man came and stood at the end of the stage as the Square began to fill with those latecomers who had heard the rumour of a Retribution.

"Gather now and witness a penitent woman confess. She risks The Gods' Retribution for her sins, in order to cleanse her soul of her evil blasphemy," the crier bellowed from his stand, his voice not as loud as the last time he had stood up here. Blue wondered whether the magic was not being used today.

The axeman joined them on stage, carrying a bottle containing an evil-looking dark brown liquid. When he unstoppered it the smell, even from several paces away, made her gag.

Even if your silly little scheme succeeds, Brighana's voice echoed in her head, *what god will bother to possess a nothing like you? They know that for two powers to fight here will only increase the people's suffering. They'll accept the situation for what it is.*

"And they're not suffering under you?" Blue whispered.

The axeman grinned and passed the open bottle to the old priestess. Even she lifted an eyebrow. "Tilt your head back, young woman," she said. "Or we'll have to force it back." Blue did as she was told and tried not to think of what was coming; instead she gazed at a cloud that swam across the sky, separate from the others. *A little like me,* she thought.

"Open wider," the priestess said. "That's good. Now, may the gods have mercy upon you, you brave, foolish child."

The liquid touched the back of her throat; it felt like they had drained every cess-pit in Whiterock and boiled the contents down to a concentrate, then mixed them with fish innards and the remains of quick-limed corpses. Hands gripped her jaws and forced her mouth closed. "No need to fret, young lady," a man's voice said, and Blue saw that it was the axeman. He smiled sadly, and keeping one hand on her jaw, she felt the other stroke her throat, so that she could do nothing but swallow. As soon as she did, he stroked her throat once more, then released his hold, and she straightened her head.

She could feel the passage of the foulbane down her gullet and down toward her stomach. "Gaaagh!" she croaked. "That is absolutely disgusting! It's –"

"Foul?" the axe man asked innocently and gave her a sheepish grin. "Sorry. Not much levity up here and what there is, is gallows humour. We take our comedy where we can."

"Silence!" the priestess hissed. "This is not the time for chit-chat!"

"Sorry," the axeman said but gave Blue a wink. She smiled as best she could.

"Are you ready to confess your sins, young woman?" The old priestess shouted the question for the benefit of the audience.

"I am," Blue replied, as loudly as she could. The foulbane was settling in her stomach like a big, black oily weight. Every time she changed position it sloshed. *Did I swallow a gallon of the stuff, rather than just a few drops?* Blue wondered.

"What is your name?" the priestess cried.

"Blue." She paused and added, "When I came here, and for a long time before that, I told everyone that I met that my name was Bluestocking."

There were gasps from the crowd and mutterings. Someone screamed.

"Quiet!" the priestess cried. The crowd fell obediently silent. "This is a woman who has offered herself up voluntarlly to the mercy of the Gods! *Show respect!*" She turned back to Blue. "Why did you come here? Was it to taunt us with your apostasy? Or to spread the taint of heresy?"

"Why did I come to the Silk Palace? Why, simply to translate the scrolls of Presimionari."

The priestess paused. "And why was that so important?"

Blue nodded. "For the glory of the Gods."

"Those same Gods you rejected?"

Blue said, "I never meant to reject the Gods! It was a silly game that got out of hand, and then...I wanted to make amends...." she trailed off, and when she resumed, she seemed to have changed the subject. "When I first went to Ravlatt, I was a half a thousand leagues or more from the village in Eastern Province where I grew up. No one there knew me. The Sisters of Beatitude were so pleased with my winning entrance to the University– the first student ever from the area– not for themselves, but for the greater glory of the panoply that they worshipped, that they paid a fortune for that coach ride for me. But though they paid a prince's ransom, sitting inside would have cost even more."

The crowd, the fear, all faded to nothing, as she lost herself in the past. "It was so cold that day, if you touched the metal door handles your hand would stick to the metal. You'd lose your skin ripping it off. Snowflakes danced on the wind, and you could open your mouth, and let them sit on your tongue, and the coolness was like the most refreshing mint you've ever tasted. I thought I was the only person catching the coach, and wrapping my sleeve around the handle, I let myself into the carriage. I sat in there for several minutes on my own, and thinking I'd gotten away with a cheap ride, I was just about to doze off when the door opened, and this fussy little man entered. Every slightest little thing was a drama. Anyone else would have minded their own business," she said, remembering sitting on the seat with her eyes apparently closed but open enough to feel his eyes drilling into her.

"I suppose you're a freewoman?" he said in a little sneer that said he supposed quite the opposite.

"Oh, yes," I replied. "As a joke and so as not to be thrown out of the carriage and onto the roof, I told the stick-like old man that my name was Bluestocking. And he was happy to share his compartment on that long and otherwise lonely journey with a pretty, but respectable, student of restricted means. It was a joke, and no one would ever know." She paused.

She could feel the sullen heaviness of the foulbane swirling and churning in the pit of her stomach. "Imagine my heart stopping shock– I still remember a Retribution against one of our locals when I was a child–" she said, with a shudder, "when the old man turned out to be an admissions clerk at the University. I never did find out what freakish chance had first of all led him to Eastern Province and then even more outlandishly taken him back on the same coach as me, but I had to go through with the charade. I *became* Bluestocking."

Someone in the crowd shouted, "Filthy pervert!"

The older priestess stepped forward, and shouted, "Silence!" As the crowd fell quiet, Blue swallowed, licked her lips and resumed. "Once I was admitted, I never saw him again. But by then it was too late. Others had heard me utter my false name. But none of the Gods struck me down. As the days turned to weeks, I became more comfortable living a lie. I knew that at the end of three years, I'd have to return to the nunnery and resume my old life, but meanwhile, Ravlatt felt more like the real world and Eastern Province simply an imaginary realm. Weeks turned to months, and my tutors looked on me with," she smiled ruefully, "grudging approval. I grew into my role. Months became years, and they asked me to stay on and take the doctorate. By the time I tackled the Tablet of Zadre for the examination, Bluestocking felt more real than Blue."

She stopped, then said, "I stayed long past the time when I was supposed to return to The Sisters of Beatitude to devote my talents to the glory of The Order. I supplemented my meagre stipend from the University by freelance translation, and all the while, the weight of my name and repute spread, all across the land, even westward to Whiterock, and no one ever connected it with a simple little slave from Eastern Province."

Blue licked her lips and tilted her head toward a jug of water that rested on a table near the side of the stage. The priestess shook her head.

Blue said, "One day a nun wandered onto campus and had the luck or misfortune, dependent on your point of view, to find me without even having to look for me. She didn't even have to ask anyone if they knew of a slave called Blue." She stopped. The stage was heaving in a remarkable impersonation of a boat at sea caught in a sudden squall.

"Go on," the priestess said gently but firmly, "expel the poison from your body." She didn't seem to have noticed the stage moving.

"If Sister Ida was shocked by my prosperity she didn't show it, though I was so stunned at seeing her that I wouldn't have noticed even if she had."

She said, after taking a deep breath, and swallowing several times; "I managed to stumble out an explanation for why I hadn't returned, and some nonsense that involved me working as a seamstress to pay my fees. Sister Ida seemed to accept it, but now all my security had evaporated like dew off the grass, and I couldn't get away fast enough."

She squinted at the priestess, who was suddenly out of focus. "By then, of course, I'd already committed myself to coming to Whiterock, so as long as I could elude her for a few more days, I had a chance but only a slim one."

She said, "And there you have it. My guilty secret." She felt tears track down her cheeks from relief at the lifting from her shoulders of a terrible and ever-growing weight. "I'm sorry," she said to Kyr, who she couldn't see through the tears. "I'm sorry for putting you in danger every day. I'm sorry," she said to the crowd and to the gods.

"Very touching!" Myleetra shouted from the other side of the square. Her voice carried so clearly that Blue guessed that she was being used by Brighana; "It doesn't change the fact that she is a runaway slave and a liar who's fooled us all and abused our hospitality!" She turned to the men around her and asked, her voice still echoing unnaturally, "Our God speaks through me! What other sentence can be passed on such a heretic but death?"

As the crowd's muttering began to swell in volume, the old priestess cried out, "You presume to speak for all the Gods?"

"And you presume to question a God?" Brighana's roar was so loud that Blue thought her eardrums would burst.

The crowd and the exchange seemed to recede; Blue seemed to be standing at the end of an immensely long tunnel. She felt watched from the shadows. Watched and judged.

Her gullet began to burn. She looked down and was sure that she saw smoke rising from her chest. *Oh,* she thought, *I'm catching fire from within.* She wanted a drink desperately, more than she'd ever wanted anything, and then the burning turned to a terrible itch in her oesophagus, and she understood why she was manacled; if she hadn't been, she would have torn her chest open with her bare hands and nails.

Her stomach seemed to bubble, as if the foulbane would explode out of her body of its own volition. *I've done everything you asked of me,* she wanted to scream at the presences in the tunnel. *What more could I have said?* Then the liquid forced its way back up her oesophagus, and she opened her mouth– but not quickly enough– and the burning liquid forced its way out of her nose as well as her mouth.

She leaned forward in the chair and spewed a gout of black liquid onto the floor of the stage. In time to the sudden cheers from the crowd, the priestess rang a small bell. "See how the true penitent confesses her sins! The foulbane has taken the poison of her lies from her body, and the Gods have spared her life!"

Blue passed out.

***

Somewhere in the darkness, a drum began to beat. A single pounding pulse that symbolised a god's heartbeat, there were fully fifteen seconds between each beat that reverberated in the echoing silence between.

Blue somehow knew that there were thousands sitting behind, on either side, and in front of her, but she could have been alone; there seemed no one else in the world. Even though she squeezed Aton and Jasmina's hands in hers, it didn't help ease the crushing awe and isolation. As her fear crescendoed to near panic, she prayed; to Nangharai, to the ugly little gargoyle god that she worshipped as a child, to the god of the monkeys that had sat on the roof of the monastery, to any and every god familiar and unfamiliar that she could think of – bar one. Praying to Brighana would be too much.

A second drum began to beat in counterpoint. Minutes later, a third, between the first and second drums. Soon, the whole world seemed to shrink to those pounding pulses. They obliterated all thought – even her mumbled prayers lapsed into incoherent pleas to get her through the ceremony.

In the darkness, revealed as though a curtain were drawn back, a light became visible in the distance. Blue fell toward it. As if they had read her mind, someone nearby said, "They have lit a bonfire on the hill to guide the Gods from Mount Halkyan. Tonight, *all* the Gods walk abroad on the earth."

"But surely that was yesterday?" a voice said.

"Time flows differently for the divine," a woman's voice said.

The fire grew bigger as if it was coming closer, or she was zooming in on it. Soon it filled the whole horizon, and its heat grew stronger and fiercer until Blue shrank back from it, fearing she would be burnt. The fire now occupied the one side of the square where no seats had been placed.

In front of the very front bench, in an empty square of space several spans across, rows of black lacquer trays that reflected the flames of the bonfire had appeared seemingly from nowhere. The reflections flickered and rippled in the breeze, and Blue saw that the ripple was due to the trays being filled with water. Again the voice of someone reading her mind. "The water is intended for travellers to drink. But if you are thirsty, the penitent pilgrim is also allowed to slake their thirst."

Finally something like a thought rose from deep within her, though to call it a thought was to dignify it beyond all proportion, for it was no more than an animal recognition that she was penitent, and that she had come on a pilgrimage of sorts, a pilgrimage to knowledge, in her desire to translate the scrolls. Blue was desert dry. She could have been reciting her prayers for hours, so furry were her lips and her palate. Releasing Aton and Jasmina's hands, she clambered over the benches, ignoring the muttered curses of those she trod upon, until she stood in the square of space. Looking back, she saw a ghostly nimbus around Aton and Jasmina's heads. She had the impression that her friends were only occasionally themselves, but at other times were akin to masks for the Gods, such as used by actors in a play. Putting it out of her mind, she picked up a tray slightly larger than her two cupped hands, and holding it by diagonal opposite corners, used a third corner as a funnel to tip the water into her mouth.

"Don't drink it all," a man's voice said, and she stopped, leaving a little thin film of water across the floor of the tray.

"The Gods are coming!" another man cried.

Out of the flames, shapes began to break away, giant sparks leaping from the fire into the world. Most were man shaped, but some were like animals, a few like strange human/animal hybrids, and one or two were shaped like nothing that a mortal eye could comprehend.

One of the shapes came closer and peered at Blue. She felt her chest tighten, and held her breath. The shape walked, no, moved away– it had nothing like legs with which to walk.

Until now, Blue had been paralyzed, but she managed to scramble back into the rows of seats, someone reluctantly making space for her with a muttered curse.

Another shape came closer, this one a giant woman with four legs and so bloated that she reminded Blue of the great female wrestlers of Irringhani, each weighing almost as much as a horse. She peered at Blue, who felt her mind suddenly gripped. She floated into the air at the Goddess' beckoning. When the Goddess examined her, Blue felt much as a fly might under a scholar's looking-glass. "So you are the Apostate," the voice reverberated through Blue's skull. "Do you know who I am?"

Blue sat paralysed in mid-air, unable even to breathe, let alone speak.

"I am Rackalantm," the Goddess said. "Well Apostate, have you nothing to say?"

The pressure eased on Blue's windpipe, and she gasped, "I have never claimed not to believe in the Gods, Almighty One."

"You believe a Goddess can be mistaken, then? Or that I lie?"

Blue suddenly felt a huge pain stabbing into every orifice, huge fiery pokers that threatened to burst her cheeks apart and leave her bleeding and broken. She spat the scream through the pain. "Never! I would never claim to understand divinity!"

A new voice: "Often divine humour thinks it amusing to torture someone in front of a lover, to flush the true target out." The Prince strode forward without hesitation, a smile on his face. At first she thought that another God had put him on like a cloak, but the pallor of his features showed his true feelings; he was barely keeping his terror under control. "I believe your true quarrel is with me, or with the god who is my patron."

My Lord, no! She wanted to cry. *You must not do this!*

"Did you hear that, little mortal?" The goddess' chuckle was so loud it threatened to shake Blue's brains from her head. "This lordling claims he loves you, despite servicing another each night. He gasps her name as an endearment, lest he forgets who she is. What can a Prince know of love, whose bed is rented out like a whore's in the name of patriotism?"

"I admit the charge, but even a whore like me," Cas said the last two words with a mocking smile, "can sometimes fall victim to the heart." The Prince added, "If you want sport you fat hag, why don't you put her down and start on your real target? Or is picking a fight with someone who isn't terrified of you too much for you?"

"You will regret that insult when the sun rises tomorrow, little man," Rackalantm's voice almost broke Blue's eardrums. She stamped a foot, and the earth vibrated.

All at once, Blue sat on the ground, although her landing was as gentle as a feather falling to earth. She could move again, although it was only to shake with relief. She sat on the ground with her knees drawn up and her arms wrapped around them. After a few moments, she looked around.

In the guttering light left by the fire and the brands that had burnt almost down to the walls, she saw that most of the crowd had left, the last dregs filing out in a semi-orderly fashion. There was only a little of the pushing and cursing that seemed to be common to every gathering in Whiterock. The crowd was entirely mortal; the assorted visiting deities had gone already. Blue wondered where Brighana had got to and shivered. *I must have been a sitting target. Why didn't it attack me? Of course, it's still the last day – or is it? Wasn't it days ago?*

She looked back and saw that the trays had vanished as mysteriously as they had appeared. She shivered. *This stinks of old magic,* she thought. She disliked things that could not be explained. Even magic normally had constraints. What had happened earlier seemed entirely too arbitrary for her taste.

The princesses and Queen Ana stood in a clump, surrounded by their little retinue of courtiers and remaining priests, with the air of people who didn't know what to do now that the party had ended. Jasmina and Aton pushed their way toward her, but Prince Cas was already beside her. He leaned over and offered his hand. She took it, and he pulled her to her feet. She caught a flicker of a frown on Cavi's face, and thought, *I wonder how much of that conversation with Rackalantm she heard? Not that any of it was true. Surely? Surely?*

She pushed the thought from her mind, and muttered, "Thank you."

"My pleasure," he said lightly, then murmured, "About what Rackalantm said..."

"It was just mischief-making, wasn't it?" she said, equally lightly. 'Though the last thing I would have thought you wanted was to make an enemy of a God."

"I'll just pray extra hard to my patron," he said.

Whichever deity that is, she thought. "Should we stay here or go elsewhere?' She mused, "Which is safer? How long do we have before the truce ends?"

"Until daylight," Jasmina said. 'We should get out of here now. We're boxed in."

"She's right," Aton said. "There's only the one exit."

Joining up with the Queen and princesses, they made their way out. At least, that's what she thought they were doing, but time seemed to be snaking backwards and forward upon itself, devouring its own tail in an orgy of self-consumption.

One moment, she was leaving the square, the next, she was still sitting in her chains surrounded by a pool of what she supposed must be foulbane. *Oh,* she thought. *It didn't work.*

"How long?" she croaked, and someone tipped a little water into her mouth, but she seemed to have lost control of her lips. Most of it spilled out again, down her chin and tunic.

"A few hundred heartbeats," the young priestess said. "You were babbling away in a foreign tongue, and you vomited and then you slumped with your chin on your chest."

Someone unshackled her wrists, waist and ankles and propped her up as she toppled forward in her seat. "It didn't work," she whispered sadly, repeating it over and over again.

"Hush, it doesn't matter," the old priestess said, patting Blue's arm gently. Blue could sense the woman's disappointment, even though she couldn't see her– as Blue rested against the old woman so her vision was blocked by the woman's body, she could feel it through the priestess' shoulder.

How? Blue suddenly wondered. She sat upright, pulling away from the older woman, feeling momentary strength suddenly surge through her. She felt ravenously hungry. She ripped a splinter up from the wood of the stage, and began to nibble on it. It was poor fare, almost tasteless, but it would have to do until she could find something better.

The square was suddenly incredibly bright. She could see every cobble, every brick in the walls, could even see where one of the roots of the Gallows Tree was poking out of one of the walls. She should be afraid. Somewhere within her, there was a small voice, gibbering with terror. *Who are you?* she thought, and knew instantly.

Nangharai, come all the way from Ravlatt.

The Silk Palace

Chapter 22

Blue looked down at her hands; she could see every pore in her skin. *At least I can look down,* she thought. *I still have some control, more so than Kyr seems to over her own body.* She turned her head experimentally; it moved as she wanted. *How much of what I know is what I know, and how much is what Nangharai would have me believe?* She knew the answer instantly; she knew everything that the god knew. *This is more symbiosis than possession. Assuming that it's true,* she thought, and decided that if it wasn't, she would never know anyway. *You might as well accept what seems real as real.* She tried to get her head to spin round and round as she'd once seen a magician do on stage. She said, "Ow!" *Maybe not.*

"Be careful," the priestess said, interrupting her musings. "Don't spend all day dreaming. Just because The Gods are forbidden to harm mortals today, you're not necessarily safe. That's one reason that Brighana's been recruiting followers as fast as it can. *They* can hurt you with impunity."

"So why not do it before?" Blue asked, and as Nangharai, knew the answer; *if **we** cannot see the future clearly, what chance does an upstart power have? Brighana wanted to see how this turned out.*

Blue looked up and saw Brighana standing by the entrance to the square, ringed by a motley gang of thugs who were idly threatening passers-by or gesticulating at one another. Jasmina, the priestess, and the crier and axeman– both of whom looked stunned– gathered round Blue to form a human shield.

"What is it?" Blue asked them. "What's wrong?"

"You," Jasmina said, her eyes open so wide that she looked like a night-dweller from the far south, her eyes like saucers. "Your face, it keeps changing– first a young woman, then an old one, then a man, then a child..." she shuddered. "You're changing so fast that I feel giddy. There's a strange smell, as well. Like pine needles and wood smoke."

All the time Blue had kept watch on Brighana. As Blue said, "Has anyone got food?" Kyr waved a hand carelessly, and someone to Blue's right shrieked, "Look out!"

A dozen scrabbling hands bundled Blue to safety. Where she had just been standing, a pile of fallen rubble from the wall behind the stage marked the spot. Somewhere in the distance of her mind, Blue was aware of a score of nicks and grazes. "Of course," she said serenely to Jasmina, "Should a wall happen to collapse, that would be unfortunate. But such things happen to mortals, even those possessed by a God." She smiled at them all. Then she let her smile drop and whispered into Kyr's ear, throwing her voice so that no one else could hear it; "You already tried that once, but now you try to arrange a second, identical accident. For one who has designs on Godhood, that shows a sad lack of creativity, don't you think?" At Kyr's lack of an answer, she continued. "When Presimonari fed the first pig on the pears from the forbidden orchard and then slaughtered it for his dinner, we told him at the time that he should have burnt the offal, rather than feeding it to the scavengers. Look at what one of those grubbing little beasts turned into. This shabby behaviour is no more than we would expect from a being that is trying to ascend to realms that it has no right to."

"I have as much right to be here as you have, you worn-out old husk," Kyr's voice whispered in Blue's ear. "I am simply trying to be merciful. I could as easily do this–" Kyr waved a hand, and the old priestess screamed and exploded into flame, falling toward Blue. Just in time, those around Blue pulled her out of the way of the poor woman.

"You dare to take mortal life, on today of all days?" Blue felt a sliver of Nangharai's horror at such a deeply unnatural act. Nangharai couldn't understand all the reasons any more than as Blue she could understand what made the stars in the night sky shine down on the land. But Blue felt Nangharai's visceral reaction to the act, and the strength of that fury made her feel literally queasy. Blue hissed in fury, "If you are foolish enough to try a third attack on me, the rest of the gods will fall upon you like that masonry did. Have no doubt about it, my loathsome little renegade."

"Strong words for a foreign interloper," Kyr hissed. "Why don't you crawl back to your boring temples in the distant east you beetle-browed old crone? And take your wearisome little hand puppet with you, back to where she belongs. With a bunch of dried up old women, who'll never know what it is to *live*." As the demigod reverted to her divine manifestation, those nearest Kyr edged away. Although they couldn't hear what was going on, they knew something significant was happening.

"That you say such a thing shows that you're worried," Blue said serenely.

"Well, why don't you show me what you can do?" Kyr sneered. "If you're going to talk me to death, I don't see why you came all the way from that dull little city of yours."

"I will act but when I choose, not at your convenience, upstart. You forget that I know how destructive it is to dwell in a mortal." Blue smiled coldly. "Especially one that doesn't want to be used. Even simply possessing her works that mortal frame far too hard– harder than she's able to take– even for a short time."

"You shouldn't worry about a mortal," Kyr said, and the words made Blue shiver inside. "They're just disposable mayflies."

"Worrying about them is exactly what you should do," Blue said. "As a divine, I'm obliged to care for my host. You should remember that, if you have aspirations; privilege brings with it responsibility." Blue smiled at the anxious looks from the others and mimed that she was talking to Kyr. They seemed to understand. "You're ageing that poor girl by hours every second that you possess her. My host won't be used up as fast." She added, "The moon will fade from sight as the day passes. Your strength will wane with the passing of the moon. I'll be ready for the opportunity when it arrives."

***

"Follow me," Blue said to the others. "I know somewhere that's as safe as anywhere." Jasmina, Aton, the women of the Royal Family and Cas fell into step behind her. There were as many priests and priestesses from various cults as before; although one had deserted and the older woman had perished, a couple of others had swollen their ranks.

"This Brighana will be even worse for the other churches than the Church of Brighannon was for alternative worship," Blue heard one old man mutter to another. "I've no idea whether this chit and her God are good or evil in the long run, but at the moment, my enemy's enemy is my friend."

Quite right, Blue thought and watching his eyes widen, gave him a wink and a smile. "Have you got any food?" she mouthed, watching with glee his shocked look at the whisper seeming to come from nowhere.

She could read his thoughts: *Gods are supposed to live on fresh air, or divine food, or something like that.*

"I could eat a horse," she added.

They probably had twice as many soldiers and militia as well, so that though their tiny army numbered less than a hundred, at least it was visible opposition.

Word of her hunger spread with wildfire speed; Hands thrust their way in entreaty, offering bread, meat, fruit or vegetables, either wrapped in little muslin cloths or clutched in the hands themselves. As she took each one with a smile, or a nod, or a few words of thanks, Blue said to Jasmina, "We must make sure that we give the cloths back." Seeing the older woman's puzzled look, Blue summoned Aton with a nod. "Get the priest or someone to make a note of their names," she said. "Many of these people can ill-afford to spare a cloth."

"They might also ill-afford to give their names," Aton growled. "What if we lose? A whole book of names of our benefactors."

"Nonsense!" Blue snorted. "We aren't going to lose."

"You can see into the future?" Aton asked, looking hopeful.

"I can," Blue said, closing the subject. At the moment, she could see so many futures. They ran across one another like currents in an estuary. In one, she was lifted atop shoulders, a sword in Kyr's lifeless body. In another, she lay dead at Brighana's many feet. In a third, they both lay dead. And they changed slightly all the time, so that in the end she tuned them out, or they would have driven her literally to distraction.

She led the motley little band through streets that seemed to be as packed with horse and eagle-headed demigods as it was with ordinary people. *How many of these things were here before?* Blue wondered. Some of them had been here all along, but beyond mortal man's vision. She knew that Nangharai's real shape defied even human imagination– let alone description– the greater the god's power, the less anthropomorphic it remained. In time Brighana would cast off Kyr's burnt-out body and emerge chrysalis-like, as something stranger still. Meanwhile the more human demigods mingled with mortals, and the stranger ones kept to themselves as much as possible, lest they seared the eyeballs of any native unlucky enough to glimpse them. Several of the gods and powers cast sidelong looks at Blue as she strode through the streets.

The group descended the steps, accompanied by something that looked like a cross between a fish and a grasshopper. Blue turned to it.

"You can tell Brighana that I've gone to the Silk caves. It'll save you having to traipse through the streets with us."

Blue walked on and abruptly stopped as a blast of something poisonous sprayed across the street in a long line of flame, blackening the far wall and singeing her eyebrows. She peered around the doorway as something long and caterpillar-like scuttled down the stairs to the floor below.

Blue turned around, guided by Nangharai's extra senses. "You'll have to do better than a firespitter!" she called, allowing Kyr to catch them up. The demigod seemed to have allowed the slave to repossess her body, but Blue knew that it was an illusion. Brighana was as watchful as a guard dog hunkered down in its kennel. A false step would bring the thing snarling to the fore, and the merest hint that Brighana's control was really threatened would mean the demigod wouldn't hesitate to banish the illusion of Kyr's return. Blue called, "Firespitters can't burn me, although you could have hurt lots of innocent bystanders."

"I don't know what you're talking about," Kyr called back. "Though if one of my more...over-zealous acolytes had tried something, of course they'd have made sure there was no mortal around." She yawned. "Forgive me if I don't join you while you lurk in one of these wet, gloomy holes in the ground, but I've had a long night."

"Yes, go and torture a few more unfortunates, and get your strength back," Blue said. "It's what you do best. In fact, it's all you can do, isn't it? That's how they managed to imprison you: So busy gorging yourself on pain that you allowed a handful of mortals and a dead god to catch you unawares." She grinned at Kyr's black look. "Wasn't I meant to know that? I've been around longer than you, since before we dreamed mortals up, when we roamed the earth alone. One gets to hear many interesting things, even when one lives a half a thousand leagues away." She added, "Run off to bed, little upstart, away from peril!"

"Perhaps I'll stay," Kyr snapped. Brighana flickered into existence and vanished again. Blue wondered what danger the demigod had sensed, but not even Nangharai could shed light on the question. *This is not my land,* the thought came; *they're not my people.*

"Are you sure?" Blue mocked. "You dare hang round here on your own, without your mob of bum-lickers? Careful, there's no one here to protect you." She raised a hand, as if to strike the other avatar and grinned at the upstart's scowl, as it flinched. "There's no one around to witness an accident," she whispered, ostentatiously looking round at her followers and feeling a wild elation coursing through her veins. *It's scared. It's scared of* ***us****! Why?*

"You wouldn't dare!" Kyr hissed. "The pantheon would know!"

Of course we wouldn't dare, Blue thought, but said, "Perhaps the other gods might view it as a divine form of pest control." *Keep it disoriented,* she thought. *Don't give it time to think, to work out that in an open fight, you probably couldn't beat it.* Nanagharai's own consideration for Blue's body compared to Brighana's disdain for Kyr was probably her greatest weakness. "Why not just have a fight here– just the two of us?" Blue leered and ostentatiously glanced at her own supporters, convincing Kyr that a fair fight was the last thing she planned.

"Tomorrow," Kyr replied, standing motionless, as they left.

They wended their way through streets even noisier and more crowded than normal, fighting the buffeting. Blue was acutely aware of every assassin's blade that might lurk on each street corner, but was able to ease her little band around the threats as they passed without them even noticing the danger.

Only once did an assassin come into the open; someone fired a crossbow from a roof. Blue sensed it at the last moment and slowing the world around her, stepped out of the bolt's trajectory. When the others squawked, she hushed them. "Don't let them distract or separate us," she soothed.

***

"Are you sure you won't join us?" Blue asked with a huge grin. All her confidence came from Nangharai's presence. Were the god not possessing her, she would be cowering in a doorway. *You'd better make sure that we defeat it,* she thought, for Nangharai's benefit. *Or there'll be such a reckoning that I'll wish the foulbane* ***had*** *killed me.*

"Positive," Kyr said from the entrance to the caves and raised an eyebrow. Blue wondered how obvious her thoughts were, then knew as if the question had actually been answered, *Not at all.* Nangharai thought. *Only you and I can read each other's thoughts, just as Brighana and Kyr are open to one another.*

She led the others down the corridor until they rounded the corner. She beckoned to Cas. *Time to rally our people,* she thought. *Let's start with Cas.* "I'll say this quietly," she said. "I don't know how much of what we discuss can be heard by our friend out there. It may be the mother and father of all lies, but it's clever, too."

He frowned. "What do you mean?"

"Halarbur still lives. And there was no massacre of your men down on the plain. That was all illusion. It entranced us all. Even the little bit of despair it was able to make you and the others feel was like a snatched sweetmeat to it and worth the minimal effort."

"Halarbur lives!" Cas stood straighter and seemed to draw fresh energy from nowhere. "Where is he? What is he doing?"

"If I conjured an image, it would draw Brighana's attention to where he is," Kyr said. "He's posed as a merchant and with another man, brought two rope-ladders up via the air-bags. They've found a deserted corner of the walls where the beast swept through on its rampage, and no one's thought to station new guards in the chaos. They lowered the ladders to your countrymen, who are climbing them while Halarbur keeps watch. Pray to every God that you can think of that their luck holds, and no one observes what's going on, or those troops climbing the ladders will plunge to their death."

Cas stared at her. "That's why you've been so calm, so confident," he breathed, a grin splitting his face.

"Let's wait here," Blue told him and the others. "If we take it in turns guarding each other, those not on guard can rest. I think we all need a few hours, don't you?"

"What?" Cas said, "You're just going to sit here?"

"For the moment, yes," Blue said. "The prohibition on harming mortals works both ways. I can no more harm Kyr than she can hurt me for the rest of the day. In fact, she's less scrupulous than I am– today is more dangerous for me than tomorrow. Then I'll be able to defend myself." She patted his shoulder and said to Cavi, "That was a maternal pat. Unless you're jealous of a goddess?" At least the aspect of one. She still hadn't quite worked it out yet, but Blue knew that it was only part of Nangharai possessing her– the part that would do some good. For all the gods bickered amongst themselves, they knew incipient danger when it was in their midst, and Brighana's escape from captivity, especially now when the moon was full, was potentially dangerous, in ways that Blue couldn't yet fully work out.

I would probably have to study divine politics for a year to get to the bottom of it, and I don't have time. Best to just count my blessings that someone at least is in sympathy with us.

One thing Blue did understand was that Brighana drew strength from the moon. It was close to some cult's actual representation of a moon god and so at the moment could gain strength faster than at any other time.

So the gods of Whiterock had held back and waited to see what would happen, and as they had hoped, Nangharai had come a-visiting. *So that if Nangharai loses, they can disown the outsider God,* Blue thought. *And if she wins, they're doubtless hoping that she'll return to Ravlatt.* For a moment, Blue was uncertain whether her divine partner intended to stay or go. *This is the best way to let the local Gods remain– unsure of my eventual intent.*

Cavi smiled thinly. "All the stories I've heard involve the gods being jealous of mortals, but I'm sure that either way the mortal rarely comes out well. So I wouldn't dream of envying you."

Blue left her with her simmering anger and strolled deep into the caves, past outlying scout spiders and the gatherers working with the webs. They seemed completely unaffected by the chaos outside. Blue asked one of them, "Do you even know that it's Last Day?"

He looked up from his delicate, gentle work with the web and the length of wood. "Oh, yes. But it doesn't matter down here, where days and nights are all the same, and we need no more fear the sun than the sleet and snow. Welcome, to you, Mother."

"You know who I am?" *If you do, tell me, please. I'm not sure myself.*

"I know what you are, if not who. I see two legs where most men would only see arms, eight altogether, and a shimmering presence as if in some ways, you're actually made up of spiders. I suspect you have different names in different places. But here, you'll be Our Lady of the Spiders. See, they come to you."

Nangharai had faded into the background of Blue's mind, or perhaps she had simply grown so used to the goddess that she no longer registered the other's presence most of the time. But Nangharai returned as soon as she sensed Blue's shock at the long columns of spiders crawling toward her, over rocks, and down walls. She didn't need to actually tell Blue not to be afraid. There was no need. Instead, Blue simply felt at ease and comfortable with the little beasts. She held out her hands, and several of them clambered into her open palms. The ones she didn't need, she tilted her hands and allowed them to feel a portion of the goddess' gratitude– but only a portion, for full exposure to her feelings would have vapourized them as if they'd climbed into the sun– she allowed the ones that Nangharai did not need to climb out again over the waiting forms of their comrades.

"Thank you," she said, both to them and to the gatherer. She tilted her face back and allowed the spiders that remained to climb out of her palms and up her arms, across her collar bones and up, over the mini-mountain range of her throat and chin, to wait, quivering with tiny anticipation, on the edge of her mouth.

Sensing Blue's increasing distress, Nangharai shared with her. Just as Blue needed food, so did Nangharai. In this case, the tiny souls of each spider, willingly going to merge with their god in an act of altruistic immolation. Mortal food, Blue realized, would have fortified her, but Nangharai would have been weakened– perhaps fatally, in light of the coming conflict.

Blue gave the mental equivalent of a shrug. *So be it.* She sensed Nanagharai's gratitude and tried not to think about the tickling of hundreds of tiny legs clambering into her open mouth and filling it. She tried to ignore the feeling as she swallowed them alive and opened her mouth to allow the next wave to climb in.

The gatherer smiled. "Blessings be with you, Lady. I hope your day goes well. It isn't often we can help you– rather than the other way around– even if it's only something as little as offering a roof over your head and food to you and your followers."

Blue swallowed the last mouthful, smiled and nodded her thanks. "It's time I withdrew and let this mortal catch a few hours respite."

Chapter 23

After she awoke, Blue wondered how much of what she had just dreamt was real— drawn from the deepest recesses of Nangharai's memories— and how much was genuine dream. Much of what little she could remember seemed to relate to the Scrolls, although much of it was a distortion of what she had translated. She dreamed of the Creation Myth of Whiterock, as outlined in some of the Scrolls, and of Tizas' story, which now she thought about it, seemed remarkably similar to parts of Kyr's life. She also dreamed of the final battle between one of the gods, now as long-forgotten to most of the people of Whiterock as if it had been obliterated deliberately from their pantheon and a vast insect-like presence that Blue knew with the logic of the dreamer was Brighana. A battle that took place within the ribcage of a skeleton that was actually the Northern and Southern Spine.

She dreamed too of a young power, ambitious, and ruthless. However much its cruelty was deliberate malice and how much its innate nature, it seemed wrong to chain it within rocks, away from either of its sources of nourishment – people or the moon – for year upon year, decade upon decade, decade turning to century to millennia to aeons, until the power was twisted as much by its perpetual confinement, futile attempts to escape and even greater punishment, as by its own nature.

When she awoke, she felt as if she'd caught up on every minute of sleep that she had missed since arriving. For the first time in months, she felt at peace. *Whether I live or die,* she thought, *I will have tried to do some good.* She knew somehow that such equilibrium was rare and always transitory. *In an hour, I'll probably be as miserable as at any time in my life.* The merest fraction of Nangharai's presence seeped back into her. She knew, as Nangharai knew, that Brighana was not so gentle in the way it treated Kyr.

She climbed to her feet and venturing into the caves, found a pool. She'd brought a small leather pouch with her, which she filled. Water dripped from it as she walked back to the mouth of the cave.

Lexi sat there, propped up against the wall, watching the tunnel outside it. She was so lost in thought that she started when Blue offered her the pouch.

"You should drink," Blue said. "Your dying of thirst does us no good."

Lexi said, opening words harsh in the silence, "I didn't want to leave while I—" and shrugged her shoulders to finish the sentence. But she took the pouch at Blue's urging and drained it.

"You can't bring her back," Blue said. "And you needn't kill yourself as penance."

"Evi was horrible to me when we were little," Lexi said sadly, "and as we got older, she simply ignored me. She never got any nicer." Her eyes watered a little. "But I miss her so terribly now. Big, strong Evi. She always knew what to do." Her face twisted for a second. "I think that lost my mind for a little while. The poets call love a madness, but to do what I did..."

Blue said nothing but simply wiped her hand across Lexi's forehead, easing some the pain, and the princess's features smoothed a little. She sighed.

"Sleep for a little while," Blue said a few moments later, and Lexi crawled over to lie beside her mother, next to the priestess. Jasmina and the score of other women and men who'd accompanied them down here, slept further on in. At the mouth of the tunnels the soldiers and militia loyal to them stood guard. Blue knew how much their battered self-esteem needed to feel that they were doing something useful, to atone for their failures. She wished she had the strength to ease all of their minds as she had Lexi's, but she had to save her energy.

Between the soldiers and this little group were those torn between wanting to be near their Queen and not wanting to go too far into the caves– the priests and scholars who were uncomfortable being so close to another God: Her.

She looked across at the others, those nearest her and watched them. Cas slept curled around Cavi as if to protect her. Blue watched them. Now she could see through Nangharai's eyes; she could read his aura and realized that she'd been too harsh on him, too quick to apply her own prejudices. He was a good man. Cavi was more brittle, but Blue now understood why. It was Cavi who awoke and gave Blue a little half-smile tinged with fear.

"Good afternoon," Blue said quietly and smiled. "You slept well, by the look of it."

Cavi nodded and half-wriggled in Cas' grip, then gave up. "I don't want to wake him," she explained, keeping her voice low as well.

Blue said, "Yes, let him sleep. He took the first shift on guard." She added, "You needed never to have feared me when I was first here. I know your love for him was what filled you with fear, but I never felt anything for him but exasperated affection."

Cavi half-nodded, as bemused at being so spoken to by a god's aspect as by the revelation itself. "It was what I thought he felt for you that worried me more. I know now," she admitted reluctantly, "that you were not the real cause of my anger, but rather it was more how I felt about myself and him."

"You couldn't believe such a man would love you."

Cavi nodded. "I never expected to feel so strongly. Before he arrived, I thought it just an alliance. Then I saw him, and..." she struggled to find the right words.

Blue completed the sentence, "You wanted to own him, to make him yours."

Cavi said sheepishly, "I wanted the same thing as what my parents had."

"What they had took years of work," Blue pointed out. "Whatever happens though, if we all survive, you need have no fear. I will be gone or dead, so you won't need to worry."

"You don't know?" Cavi was shocked. "I thought the gods omnipotent and all-seeing. Even the future...so I thought." She eased herself a little from under Cas.

Blue laughed. "We are as bound by fate and the rules of life as you are. It's difficult to explain: Imagine the most complex board game that you can– then try to explain it to a baby, and you have the situation we have here. I can see simple things some way into the future. For example, I can see you eventually wriggle so that he will topple over onto you, but that's like you being able to judge direction and distance. I can see us leaving here. But what happens then is subject to so many others with the same powers as I that I simply can't tell." Blue thought it best not to tell Cavi of the tumbling cascade of different, sometimes contradictory images that ran through her mind, presenting a churning maelstrom of outcomes that changed almost by the second.

She said, echoing what she guessed were Cavi's thoughts, "No, it doesn't seem very useful, does it?" She laughed at the look of horror and fear that galloped across the princess' face. "Don't worry, I can't read your every thought. Just the obvious ones, such as what was shown by your sceptical expression when we were talking." She laughed and touched Cavi's arm. "Shall I do something useful, and take a look outside? Without actually going anywhere," she added with a grin at Cavi's widening eyes.

She leaned back and closed her eyes and letting her attention drift said in a lightly sing-song lilt: "The crowds are still milling around throughout the palace. There's bunting and confetti everywhere, and most people are happy. Everyone's heard stories about what's happened today, and many have seen Brighana's attacks or the Retribution. But most of the stories have been distorted or wildly exaggerated. Take Voduh the carpenter. He's talking in a tavern about how he'd heard the foreigner grew a second head."

She concluded, "But most people are only slightly more scared now than they normally are on Last Day. It's always unsettling to have such powerful strangers around, after all. A few people– who didn't actually witness the goings-on– don't believe any of it."

"What about Brighana?" Cavi said, "What's it doing?"

"The usual Brighana things," Blue said, her tone hardening, "It can't directly hurt mortals, so its cronies are dragging unfortunates off the street. It's behaviour that didn't endear it to the other divines when it was free. At the time we couldn't kill it, but now it's so closely linked to a mortal, it's vulnerable..."

Blue trailed off, because she knew as Nangharai did that Brighana's vulnerability was linked to Kyr's mortality. *There are so many things that seem obvious now. So many things that they should have thought through, that they must have and should have known, but didn't. This is how it is to be less than a God. What seems obvious afterwards is confused, murky and unclear at the time.*

Brighana could survive Kyr dying a natural death, but should she be suddenly killed– accidentally or deliberately– Brighana would not survive the shock. It had underpinned Nangharai's whole desperate gamble– desperate because now Nangharai was as vulnerable as Brighana to sudden death.

***

When the group began to stir, Blue knelt by the still-recumbent Queen, who opened her eyes and smiled wanly up at her. Sleep didn't seem to have done her as much good as the others.

Blue said, "We should go and show our faces. I could go by myself, but I think it does little good to split our meagre forces in two."

"I agree. For better or worse, I think our fates are bound together."

"We'll get him back." Blue placed her hand on the Queen's arm. "By this time tomorrow, you'll be back at your husband's side."

"Really?" Ana said.

"Of course," Blue said, fingers crossed behind her back.

Outside, beneath the starry sky, an almost summer breeze had sprung up, blowing the fragrances of the festival– spices, sweat, and the odd not-quite-right-odour of the natural whiff of gods in a confined space– across the city; together with those of burning wood, dust from ruined buildings, and charred flesh.

The crowds were as dense as ever but Blue felt a difference, which for a moment, she struggled to identify. *It feels like people have grown sick of the situation. They want this settled, one way or another.* It was their collective impatience that she could sense.

The party climbed back up through the levels, taking a rambling route that allowed them to meet as many people as possible and show them that they were well. Again, a few braver souls offered them pleas for success, but others scowled and even cursed them. One man spat. "Even if you could defeat the mighty Brighana, you won't. And what's to become of the people killed in the meantime?"

But most simply looked stolidly blank. *If they don't make a decision, then they can't make the wrong one, and can't be punished for it,* Blue thought. *Who can blame them?*

They passed an odd-shaped little building, and Blue pointed at it. "What's that?" Some of the priests and priestesses looked uncomfortable, but she persisted. Blue studied it. *It's a tiny little church with skulls embedded in the walls, hundreds– no, thousands– of them.* The building seemed vaguely familiar, and looking up she saw that the structure was shaped like a rib-cage. *Well, well,* she thought and, her curiosity piqued, said, "Let's take a look around. We'll only be a few minutes. Come on!" Ignoring the half-hearted protests of the others, she strode to the door and poked her head around it.

The whole church was made of bones. Arm bones made up the architraves, a shinbone was the edge of the wall, and row after row of skulls stared back at her. A skeleton stood watching the bodies lying on the altar. When he turned, Blue saw that he had male genitalia. Looking through Nanagharai's eyes, she saw that he was a man painted with a spell-suffused paint that rendered him invisible and was painted over with a skeleton from white paint mixed with human bone taken from the walls. The effect was good enough to have fooled Blue and presumably had the same effect on his congregation. "Welcome to the Bone Church," he said in a deep voice.

"More material for the walls?" She pointed at the bodies.

The priest didn't answer directly but said instead, "When they knew their appointed day to join the Dead God grew closer, they came and lay upon the floor here and fasted. Now they are so weak, their spirits will soon be with the Dead God."

"The Dead God doesn't walk with the others?"

"The Dead God is dead," he said. "How can he? His frame has passed to another plane, a more exalted one than this vale of tears. But he has left his legacy; we give our bodies to his memory when our time is come and then follow his path, to join him."

Over the next few minutes, Blue tried to prise information from the priest, to find out what part (if any) it had played in Brighana's defeat, but every question she asked him was either ignored or deflected with euphemisms so vague as to be meaningless. Blue wondered if he didn't know or whether he even wished to know.

It seemed to Blue to be a very unsatisfactory religion, but at least she'd found out who the Dead God was. She'd heard him mentioned often enough. She guessed he'd suffered complete dissolution, the same fate that faced the loser now. Wondered too, whether this battle had been fought before– but with different names and whether she and Kyr were simply new names for Ralac and the Dead God.

Nangharai either knew nothing of what had transpired millennia before or was not prepared to share her knowledge, which Blue thought significant in itself. Either way, the silence from the God in her skull was deafening. Muttering her frustration, she left.

***

The others looked relieved when she re-emerged, blinking after the gloom. "Come along," the Queen muttered. At Blue's surprised look, she made a gesture of bemused defiance. "I'm just tired of sitting around," she explained. "If we're going to die or win then so be it, but I really don't enjoy having time to contemplate my possible imminent demise." She stomped off in the lead.

"What was the matter with them?" Blue said. "When I went in there some of them looked as I'd just farted in the Queen's ear."

Jasmina gave a nervous laugh. "Would you believe me if I said I really didn't know? I think it's just that sitting outside the Bone Church while you play tourist is a little ...odd."

"Oh?" *Do tell,* Blue thought, and waited.

Sometimes saying nothing made people want to fill the unforgiving silence. So, as they resumed strolling through the streets, Jasmina continued, "The acolytes of the Dead God are considered a little strange. They laugh too much, or in the wrong places in a conversation or stare at you a little too intently." At Blue's raised eyebrow, she added, "They have bad luck, too. Nothing spectacular, but always niggling little ailments, unfortunate accidents, and never, ever bet on the same cockerel or dog as them. It's sure to lose, usually fatally."

"Hmm," Blue said. "And none of this strikes you as in any way odd?"

Jasmina shrugged and spread her hands. "What's odd around here? That's just the way things have always been."

Blue nodded, understanding dawning. "That's probably how, with the founding of the Church of Brighannon and the gradual loss of memory of the truth about what happened, Brighana began its long, slow escape."

"The Dead God was involved with Brighana?" Jasmina squinted in disbelief.

Blue smiled. "Brighana's revenge; wait several millennia, until even those who worship the Dead God have all but forgotten why, and no one else knows or cares. Find a weak link, someone who can found a new church based on lies and distortions. And then, brick by brick, worshipper by worshipper, year by year, dismantle everything that the winning church represented, and little by little, rewrite history. Use the few adherents of the Church of Brighannon to gain a few more. Somehow inveigle the Royal Family into the ranks of your devotees. And when the time is right, claw back just enough power to be able to scheme for when the moment is right, when there is a full moon at the very New Year and invite a talented but foolish young girl to be your dupe."

"You weren't to know," Jasmina said and patted her arm.

"That wasn't how Brighana seemed to see it, when I freed it," Blue said.

Jasmina said, "Maybe they didn't do everything that they were supposed to do or started to show it less respect than it deserved. You've seen how dangerous the gods can be when they feel they've been slighted. Or maybe Redoutifalia's forebears rewrote things so they got more power than they should have. Things don't always go as they should have for mortals, so maybe it's the same for powers and demigods. Maybe there's something higher even than the Gods that we know nothing about, but whose whims can affect deities, just as they scupper all our plans." Jasmina smiled at Blue's raised eyebrow. "You never knew I was such a theologian, did you?"

"Milady, some church or other lost a rare resource when you decided to embrace a husband instead." Blue laughed. "Anyway, something didn't go as it should have. I was supposed to summon it tomorrow."

"On First Day?" Jasmina said. "When the Gods are returning to Mount Halkyon?"

"I think so," Blue said. "It fits, doesn't it?" She turned away from Jasmina's stunned expression and said quietly, "Well, we're here."

***

Looking out, Blue saw from the palace walls the camp fires of the two besieging armies settled on either side of the rock. She reached out with her mind and saw the results of the isolated little skirmishes that had nagged on all day. The soldier of the Western Alliance, a young boy hanging onto life as best he could, even as his life fled with his blood through the untended wound to his femoral artery; the captain of the Imperial Guard, who sobbed as he cradled the body of a dead youth– his lover. Blue could feel the captain's pain and bitterness that the young man had insisted on coming with him, for death or glory. Small things in the scheme of things– except to those involved or those left behind.

From out here on the wall, outwardly the Royal Quarters were unchanged, but there was an entirely different aura about the rooms now. Death and despair hung heavy in the air.

They marched through the doors to the chambers unhindered, through to the banqueting hall where Blue had dined on the first night, following an invisible trail of corruption. There were hundreds upon hundreds of revellers munching on chicken legs or downing glasses of wine with reckless abandon.

"They must have wrung the neck of every fowl in the Kingdom," Lexi muttered and grabbed a glass of wine from a passing waiter.

The crowd parted as they passed through the doorway into the throne room.

The King stood to one side, exhaustion etching dark lines as deep as cuts into his white face. He swayed from time to time and gripped the arm of the chair for support but stayed on his feet. Blue could see it was a point of principle that he didn't give way.

Kyr stood in front of Blue, the multi-faced shape of Brighana flickering in and out of sight.

"You look tired, Kyr," Blue said.

Kyr laughed, but the buzzing undertone made people look up and then away. "Playing tricks, Nangharai? You don't fool me."

"Which of you don't I fool? Certainly not you, Kyr. Brighana's done that already. Take a look in the mirror."

Kyr did so, touching her hair. She smiled. "I look wonderful."

"Now take away the glamour, Brighana– if you dare. I don't think you will."

"And leave her vulnerable to possession?"

"I can't possess her against her will, remember? Or do you fear that she'll voluntarily ask something else to possess her?"

"Don't talk about me as if I'm not here!" Kyr shouted and amplified by Brighana's power, the force of her voice made the room shake; a line of plaster rained from the ceiling.

"Take a look," Blue urged.

Kyr did so, and as the glamour faded, she gasped.

"See the grey hair," Blue said relentlessly. "See the wrinkles, the lines. Is that what you want? Ageing hours in seconds, days in minutes. I guess that you have maybe a week to live before you die of old age, worn out like an over-used shoe, worn through to nothing."

"NO!" Kyr screamed, the glamour returning, and the mirror shattered. She turned. "Enough talk!"

The look in her eyes was that of a stranger, and Blue withdrew quickly.

***

Up here in the open the crowds were a little thinner, the jostling not so bad, the noise a little less and the smells of spices and alcohol, incense and body odour, all not quite so overpowering. But there was the scent of something else on the wind; divine expectation. It wasn't every night the gods, demigods and powers of Whiterock and its neighbours had such a show laid on. "More like every few hundred years," Blue muttered.

"What?" Lexi called, from just behind her shoulder, the only one to have been paying attention– or the only person rude enough to admit it.

"First day tomorrow," Blue said.

"Yes, an extra day every four years. It's a shame the Gods don't always stay for the extra day. Sometimes they do, sometimes they don't. Oh…" She trailed off, and said sheepishly, "You know all that."

"Don't worry," Blue said. "Talk as much as you want. Only men stay silent until they have knowledge to impart. We women talk for fun, remember?' She said, leaning closer, "You know how often there's a full moon on First Day?"

Lexi shook her head. "But I bet you do," she said, with a grim chuckle.

"Once every two hundred and ninety-two years. This will be the three-thousand seven-hundred and ninety sixth year after Brighana's banishment. The thirteenth time its aspect day, full moon, has fallen on the very start of a new fourth year. Think that's significant?"

Lexi nodded.

"You're right," Blue said, and aspect or not, the sight of the bloated silver-white disk shining sinister, pregnant with menace in a clear spring sky, made her shiver involuntarily.

The bell began to ring, "Midnight!" someone shouted, as the second chime tolled.

"It's almost over," the Priestess said. "No more waiting."

Blue nodded, searching for Kyr, who she was sure, was nearby, but hidden from her gaze by a growing power, nearly as great, perhaps greater than her own.

"Ten!" The crowd shouted, then "eight!" Someone else shouted, "nine!" to cackles of laughter before the count resumed, with "seven!"

From out of the darkness to their right, the clock tower chimed. Blue counted. *Midnight.* Then she thought, *And? We've had demigods and powers walking among us all day. What difference does it make now?*

The last chime faded away, and the bell-tower exploded.

Chapter 24

Chunks of masonry flew outward over the streets to parabola onto the screaming crowd below. One somersaulting piece impaled a woman's back; another decapitated a child that was being hauled away by a mother who was herself pelleted with fragments. Larger pieces fell straight down, burying those directly beneath the tower.

Only Nangharai's strength pumping through Blue's body until she thought her veins would burst kept the ring formed by Cas and the others on their feet while the panicked crowd surged first one way then another.

Blue managed to conjure a protective shield glowing above their heads. She pointed at a cloven-hoofed bearded giant watching the pandemonium with curiosity but no terror. "Keep us near that demigod!" She guessed that the thunderbolt had come from the other side of him and hoped that he would act as a barrier. She allowed a little more of Nangharai's presence to seep into her, and now stood almost a full head taller than her mortal height. "Get those people away!" she urged Lexi and Cavi.

Brighana towered over its mortal followers now. It made it easier to fight it, now that it no longer bothered wearing Kyr's face. "To the death, then," she said, and before Brighana could reply, Blue fled, scattering friend and foe like yarrow stalks cast from a soothsayer's palms.

As she ran from the walkway, the merest tendril of Nangharai's attention caught the King arguing with one of Brighana's followers; "There'll be no fighting between mortals while they sort it out." The right side of his mouth wasn't working properly, but what he said was still understandable.

"Really?" the thug, emboldened by his new-found sense of freedom, sneered.

"Really," the King said, leaning into the other man, shoulder against shoulder, chest to chest. The thug's eyes opened wider, and then they dulled, and he leaned forward onto the King's shoulder. The King shrugged him off, and the other man slumped to the ground. "Anyone else feel that I no longer speak for *all* the gods?" Redoutifalia said, wiping the blade of his knife.

No one argued.

Ducking and weaving between the now thinner crowds– some people had gone early to bed, extra holy day or not– while concentrating on weaving a shadow web round herself, Blue knew that the King had signed his own death warrant if Brighana prevailed. It was one more reason to make sure her enemy didn't.

She bumped against someone's shoulder and sent them flying, but there was no time to apologize. Instead she concentrated on hiding her true form from whatever she'd buffeted. Just in case it was one of Brighana's followers, and they raised the alarm.

She ran hard, until she reached Gallows Square. Even on holy days, few people gathered here; there were simply too many memories, too many reminders of misdeeds and pain. In the small hours, like now, it was a moon-lit sepulchre. Visohn's skeleton, picked clean by the carrion-eaters of Whiterock, fluttered in the breeze. Other, older mementos of past retributions added their rattles to the chorus. Even here, the smell of incense and bonfires, smoke blown on the wind, was all-pervading.

She got her breath back. Blue knew she would suffer the consequences later. Her aching muscles were an invoice of exertion that could be deferred, but sooner or later there would be a reckoning. The less she allowed her body to be normal, the worse the reckoning would be.

A narrow alleyway ran from one side of the square through to a smaller square. Drawing on Nangharai's strength, Blue carefully, quickly but quietly ripped stone after stone from the wall, while keeping as quiet as possible. Stealth was needed now, not speed or strength.

Soon she'd torn the wall down from both sides, making the alleyway into a cul-de-sac. She looked around the square. *Good, no one there.* She stepped back about three paces from the mouth of the blocked alleyway, then a fourth and allowed the shadows she'd woven about herself to slip so that Brighana might see her. Reaching the blockage, she quickly gathered them back about her. She ran back to the square, weaving through the shadows again. With a little luck, Brighana would think that she'd grown careless and allowed them to slip.

She crept to a corner and waited.

Not for long. Brighana tore into the Square, a juggernaut of chiaroscuro in the moonlight, heading straight for the alleyway. Even before Brighana had reached its entrance, Blue slipped from the shadows. Brighana's momentum carried it to the foot of the pile of rubble.

Blue had drawn further on Nangharai's strength, felt the thunderbolt building within her. Learned men had said in the past that balefire was but a pale imitation of the bolts that the gods could unleash. Blue felt the power that could be allowed to dissipate or be used like a wasp's sting– if the wasp were the size of a continent. She allowed Nangharai to channel the energy until in the shadows her arm glowed red then white, until at the end her arm was blue. There was no noise audible to human ears, but Blue heard a strangled scream like a boiling kettle.

As Blue threw the balefire Brighana changed back to Kyr, mortal sized again, and some vestigial trace of love for her made Blue's hand twitch a fraction. It was enough. The bolt, flung slightly off the centre of Brighana's much bigger body, flew just past her head, close enough that it would have warmed the slave's face for her. The pile of rubble exploded into a million fragments.

A grin spread across Kyr's face, and she reverted to Brighana's form, but Blue hadn't waited to see her foe gloat. She was off, running, back across the Square and into a maze of twisting alleyways, running for her life, the hunter now the hunted.

She'd used up all of her energy with that one blast. It would have been a killer bolt had she not missed. She cursed herself as she wove shadows about her again. One moment of weakness and all her good work undone. A shout from one side told her that her camouflage wasn't working as well as before. That or Brighana's followers had obtained a seeking-spell of some kind, perhaps set to her aura.

She needed time to allow her strength to return and the power to unleash another bolt to build. Meantime, she ran like the wind and tried to shelter in shadows of her own devising. And ran headlong into a cul-de-sac. She cursed and threw herself up the wall, which probably saved her life.

The thunderbolt scorched her foot, and she screamed but managed to hang onto the top of the wall and pull herself over.

She landed awkwardly and fell face down in a bed of scented herbs. Clambering to her feet, she looked around at a small stone courtyard. A noise behind sounded as if Brighana was clearing the wall, so she threw herself at a small white door to her right into a stone-floored kitchen. She guessed it was the quarters of a senior royal servant and hobbled through.

Ahead of her was the front door. She needed time to think. Keep running and risk running headlong into Brighana's followers or try to crawl off into a lair to recover? She tugged the door. It was locked.

"Boo!" said a familiar voice from behind her.

Blue shut her eyes and rested her head against the door. "Don't hurt me, please," she allowed her voice to quaver, to hide what she was doing.

"Ready to die?" Kyr asked. Only the note of gloating revealed Brighana's presence.

"No," Blue said and yanked the now unlocked door open.

She almost made it, but her world ended in a pain that was as if she'd been dropped in balefire. It ran up her nerve endings and forced her mouth open in a soundless scream and prised her clenched fists apart but still there was no escaping the overwhelming agony– it went on and on and on and on and on and on and on and on and on and on– until finally there was nothing.

***

Blue lay still. Insofar as she could think at all, she guessed that she lay close to death. For better or worse, Brighana had used two much smaller bolts – though they had been, combined, deadly enough.

She drifted on a sea of nothingness; her mind, together with Nangharai's, seemed to have been blasted clear of her body. *This must be what the seers mean when they talk of impending death.* Voices drifted on the breeze like the susurrus of leaves in the summer then drew away. The sweetest smell she had ever known lifted her spirit higher. Light stronger yet softer than sunlight was everywhere. If she had a body, she was floating clear of it, as she had floated in the warm-water lake of her childhood, but there was no stench of sulphur as had accompanied that experience. It was literally heavenly. All that she needed to make it perfect was Kyr.

Kyr: She needed to be with someone called Kyr to make it perfect.

It's not time to die just yet, little one, the voice in her head said gentle as a mother's croon, yet reverberating through every part of her. But it too faltered, and Blue knew that Nangharai was fighting for her existence as much as Blue, for all the apparent peace she felt.

Looking down, Blue saw a woman's body, lying spread-eagled. The woman's hair formed an exploded halo that stood out in all directions. From the scorch marks on the face, Blue guessed that she had been hit by something very like balefire. The body lay still for what might have been seconds– or hours. There was no reference for time. Blue tried to move, but the body refused to respond. She might as well have been embedded in the earth. Suddenly, her body arced in agony, balefire scorching the flesh from her bones.

So why do I look untouched, as if I'm only sleeping? The truth dawned. *Because this is unreal.* Nangharai, badly hurt herself, was letting the truth seep into her consciousness as slowly as counting out grains of sand. She had been hurt; this wasn't her body she was looking at, but a portrait, painted with all the flattery of a portraitist smoothing over his subject's warts and misshapen features. Another grain of sand passed, and she realized; *I'm dead.*

Then how do I see this? She felt panic grip her. Another grain; *We're in the walls. Nangharai? You too? Of course. If we were joined, and I was killed, you would be too. So how am I able to think?*

Another grain; the awful agony of Nangharai ripping her consciousness free of her dying body in the most appalling agony, fractions of a hundredth of a heartbeat before death rode her down and with Brighana's gloating laughter echoing in both the worlds of flesh and ghosts, being allowed to escape because Brighana wanted more than death for them both.

Nangharai had been allowed to flee to the nearest solid object. A stone wall. Because Brighana wanted them to spend an eternity trapped in the rocks beneath The Silk Palace. The beaten god had been allowed to flee with her mortal passenger into the wall and from there into the very stone of Whiterock.

Show me what is happening, Blue begged silently. *Yes, I'm sure. No matter how bad it is, it can't be worse than not knowing.*

So Nangharai showed her. Showed her the King's family in chains forced to kiss Kyr's feet, to couple with beggars and lepers and to be beaten by those they had condemned as criminals when they ruled. All for Brighana's amusement, only Prince Cas spared, under arrest, but treated well for the moment because Brighana wished it so. Myleetra's severed head on a pole in Gallows Square, imbued with a ghastly half-life, still babbling like a broken-down oracle at passers-by. Blue watched as the ruins where Brighana had rampaged fell around the ears of the enslaved masses. One brave man whose resistance was punished even more heavily because he had abused Kyr when she was a slave was forced to eat himself, limb by limb. He had gnawed his arm away up to the elbow and was being kept alive by Brighana, or the shock would have surely killed him. Many of the dead had been resurrected as hollow men to serve Brighana. They manned the battlements in an eerie parody of the troops who had stood guard there when Blue arrived. Now the gliders stood unmanned, the airbag baskets empty. A few brave soldiers fought against the hollow men. Blue knew that they fought only until Brighana turned its attention back to them, at which time they were doomed.

Only the caves were not under Brighana's control. Its forces were camped outside the mouth of the caves, and a few brave mortals in Brighana's army ventured in on guerrilla raids.

Blue watched the spiders bite, and the men stamp down cursing, crushing them. The priests, now unlikely warriors, fought but were forced back slowly, steadily, until in only days there would be nowhere for them to fall back to.

Show me my body. No more grains of truth rationed out.

What was left of her lay in an alley. Rats had gnawed at her and given up, for the balefire had poisoned her flesh. The lump that was her body was barely recognizable as human at all, let alone as a woman called Blue. The arms were twisted up in an attempt at defence, legs curled up, face blasted away, so that all that showed through the blackened flesh were teeth.

Without warning, as if all the gods had tilted both heaven and earth Nangharai's presence seemed to vanish, and her mind fell back to earth. If she could have screamed, she would have.

She felt a touch on her dead body, something feather-light on her face. A voice said, not unkindly, "It is you, isn't it? Nangharai, even dead, there's an aura about you. No way anyone would ever mistake you for any young girl." Aton leaned down. "So this is what it's come to: Lying dead in a doorway!" She felt the warmth of his breath and smelt a trace of stale beer. And incredibly, a single tear.

"I'm hurt, too," he whispered. "I stole a beer to dull the stench of slaughter. It's like a butcher's shop out there; they're all hacking and maiming one another like they've gone mad with blood-lust. Men are hacking up women and children as well as each other. Yet in all the carnage, some miserable wretch *still* objected to me stealing his cup, and I took a sword-cut to my ribs." His grim laugh turned into a cough.

"You spared my life when you could have taken it, back in them caves." he said, though he must have been talking to himself. "So I can't leave you here. I'll drag you somewhere, give you a decent internment. Even before that, I liked you, but it was the caves, girl, and what came afterwards that made me see you for what you were; brave to the point of stupidity!" He sniffed and wiped his hand on his sleeve. "I had half a mind when I found a load of valuables in an empty house to just leave Whiterock, but you changed it."

From around the corner, Jasmina slid along the wall. Her face seemed to have collapsed in on itself, and she had aged twenty years overnight. *How can I see her when I have no eyes?* Blue wondered, then thought, *What's left of Nangharai's omniscience, I suppose.*

"She failed, then," Jasmina said, bitterness burning her voice.

"Aye."

Jasmina stood next to the stone wall that Nangharai had fled into. She produced a knife. "Might as well slit our veins open and let it drip on the ground," she said. She bit her lip, then said, "I might as well have killed her. I stuffed her head full of nonsense, convinced her she could fight." She straightened slightly and said sadly, "I'm sorry, girl. Sorry for my silly husband, sorry for everything." She wiped her eyes.

Aton looked at her but said nothing.

Blue knew that a vital moment had arrived, that Nangharai, able to see a little way into the future had waited for this moment, saving the last of her strength. The fate of the whole world rested on the next few moments. "Jas-min-a." Somehow, Nangharai and Blue managed to drive the air through the grinning teeth.

"What was that?" Aton said, shifting his weight.

Blue drew the last of her strength. "Help…me…please."

"Blue?" Jasmina straightened. "It's a trick!" She tried to pull Aton back.

He sat propped in the doorway, looking down at her, disheveled, unshaven, his stubble red-gold against his white face. He was quiet for a moment then said, "Can you see this, Blue? No? It's a knife, sanctified I guess, as it was on an altar." He chuckled. "Shocked are you? Don't be. I'm just a man, with all our faults, no hero, me, I'm afraid. Now, I'm cutting my hand, and now," Blue felt something cold on her palm, "I'll cut yours too. Mingle the blood, and here goes…" He recited some words in a dialect that Blue would have known, normally, but she didn't have the energy to translate.

Nothing happened. The screams went on. No, not quite nothing. Her hearing had grown stronger, just a little, and she could hear a woman sobbing monotonously, as if her heart would break. She managed to turn her head, and the sound was like gates opening on a grave. "The…penitent…woman," she managed to rasp out. "You said. That. You were sorry. Help me now."

"How?" With Nangharai's help, Blue could see despair eating the woman like a cancer.

"I'm trapped. In the walls." It was so tiring. Blue had thought that when she was dead, there would be an end to fatigue.

"You want us to get you out?" Jasmina licked her lips, and Blue guessed that she had an idea already.

"The penitent woman...offers herself...to the gods." She tried to draw breath, and it sounded like a death rattle. "Do you want to live?"

"Not particularly." Jasmina shrugged and stared straight at Blue. "How?"

"Take...my place."

"What?" Jasmina stepped back. "You want me to carry that god in my head? End up like Kyr?" She shook her head. "No. No!"

"Not...like that...take my place...in the walls."

Panic filled Jasmina's eyes. "I can't."

"Please."

Jasmina shook her head again. "I'm sorry. I'm not brave, not like you are."

"Not brave...either."

Aton interrupted. "You can't ask her to...wall herself up!"

"Please," Blue implored. "Or all for nothing."

Jasmina stepped slowly toward the wall. "Will this hurt?" She tried to smile, but all that happened was a twisted grimace. "I'm not really very brave, you see."

"Bravest...of us all," Blue whispered.

"No, I'm really, really not. But I feel so alone without my Ari. You never knew the nice side of him, you see. Or how sweet he was when we were first wed."

"Press yourself...against the wall."

Jasmina pressed herself as she was told.

"Renounce...the world...and ask...to come in."

Jasmina said the words, and the world tilted again, but it felt as if Blue were being turned inside out. Then she was looking out at a wall and at the same time watching Jasmina from her dead body. "Oh my," she said, but it was Jasmina whose mouth uttered the words. And then Blue felt Jasmina growing younger, and her face melting into someone else's features, and then as Blue fell toward her, she realized that the features were hers. Before she could say, "Oh, my," again, she could sense Jasmina in the stone, in the rocks. Her own legs gave way, and she slumped to the ground.

Chapter 25

As the seconds passed, Blue lay on the ground, gradually feeling her way back to the world around her; first her face, then the stone cobbles and then across to the rocks in the walls, where she could sense Jasmina.

I want you to do something for me, Jasmina thought. *In return for me allowing you use of my body.*

What is it?

Put me in your body.

But I'm dead! Jasmina, there's no trick ending for both of us. There wouldn't even be one for me, but for Brighana's need to gloat.

All the more reason then, Jasmina thought, *to end this misery. Even while I was still in the flesh, I knew what I really wanted, but I couldn't admit it even to myself.*

Blue nodded, tears stinging her eyes.

Then end it for me now, Jasmina pleaded. *Because I can't bear to be trapped in here if you fail. Better I die hoping that you'll succeed and make sense of Arial's death. But even if you do succeed, I've no desire to live on in here. End it now. Please?*

All this took less than two heartbeats. Eyes still closed, she concentrated on sharing with Jasmina her gratitude and pushing Blue's dead body against the wall, channeled Jasmina's spirit back into the dying young woman. There was a momentary spasm, a whisper of, "Thank you." Then Blue/Jasmina was still.

Then slowly and guiltily, the new Blue turned to Aton. "Time to go," she said, her voice sounding strange in her own ears, more Jasmina than hers, but a mix of both.

"Where's Jasmina..." He looked down at the corpse that had been Blue, then at her. "You swapped... you're starting to look like her." Anger thickened his voice. "Why did you have to take her body? Couldn't you have restored Blue?"

Blue shook her head. "The body was too far gone. I can make this woman– who *is* alive– younger and stronger, but I cannot revive the dead. That is beyond me and beyond Brighana, in truth. What that *thing* does is not to restore life but rather pervert death, which is part of the process– the ending– of life." She sighed. "I'm sorry. We will not be the only people warped or even killed by this creature's schemes."

Her senses already keener now, she felt a little tickle. A single silk spider wobbled on unsteady legs across her palm. Perhaps shielded by the folds of her cloak, it had been spared the brunt of the blast, and then crawled across to find its mistress' new body. Blue felt its shock and pain and allowed her own to mingle with it. "Go home," she whispered. "Bring the others." It staggered across the ground and vanished from sight.

"Stay here," Blue murmured to Aton. "Your job is done. Rest, get better and leave as soon as you can."

"Normally I wouldn't argue with that," Aton said dryly, "but I don't think I'm going to be going anywhere while these madmen roam the city. And I don't like leaving a slip of a girl to her own devices, even a divine slip."

"Stay here or I'll put you to sleep."

"Yes, my goddess." He grinned weakly.

She gave him a little peck on the cheek out of affection, and he looked stunned. "You're a good man sometimes, despite the mean front you present to the world," she said.

He looked sheepish and touched his cheekbone. "I'm not entirely sure I like you knowing me so well," he said, but she was already gone.

Blue crawled along the street at barely a snail's pace to start with. Gradually she quickened. After about a half-furlong, she saw a line trailing across the street. "Spiders," she muttered. When they came closer, she saw that they were silk spiders, scouts from the topmost caves and therefore the nearest. "I need your help, little ones," she whispered. "I'm sorry it has to be this way." *No!* Bluestocking thought, but obeyed Nangharai's insistent pleas. Again, she opened her mouth, and the spiders marched on tiny feet up her arm, across her shoulder and into her mouth. "This is no way for a goddess to go into battle," Blue said and stood up on legs still only a little stronger than those of a new-born foal but growing stronger by the second.

At first she still tottered, but as the sky lightened, she felt her strength return faster and faster until she was almost fully recovered. Her thoughts became clearer and sharper, and she realized too, that the god was not simply just making Jasmina stronger but was actually restoring her youth.

Blue gained the impression that although she was still linked to the goddess, there was a different quality to Nangharai's thoughts since her old body had died. After a while, Blue decided that it felt as if the goddess was almost distracted. *But what can be more important than this?*

As Blue approached the palace, piles of bodies lined the streets like cattle carcasses in a slaughter yard. "Brighana," she muttered, "you always were stupid, despite your power. What will you do when you've killed them all?" She knew the answer to that, and it made her even more determined to stop it. "Even if you drain the life from this place there's no way out for you from here. No more feeding grounds in other countries."

"We'll see," Kyr's voice whispered, as if she were stood right next to Blue.

"You've learnt ventriloquism," Blue said. "Now come out, if you dare."

"All in good time, pretty one," Kyr's voice took on the buzzing note of Brighana. Blue guessed that it was playing games with her to keep her off-balance. She drew herself upright. Half an hour earlier, she had felt close to death. Now she felt ready for anything. *The spiders made a noble gesture,* Nangharai thought. *They gave their lives for a greater cause, willingly and deliberately.*

What can a spider know of causes? Blue wondered. Then she knew, as Nangharai shared with her; Our Lady of the Spiders is the essence of the spiders themselves.

She reached out with her mind and found the soldiers guarding the King. No hollow men or villains, but ordinary, decent men but scared, who would rise up if they saw the chance. Reaching out, she sang them a silent lullaby, and their eyelids drooped. *Come,* she called to Redoutifalia, but had no time to see whether he obeyed.

She rounded the corner and stopped, watching a scene that sickened her, even though she would have thought herself immune to revulsion by now. Brighana hunched over something, and Blue saw a man drop, blood fountaining from his jugular as Brighana's claws scooped out his innards.

To one side, a long line of terrified men and women were each held captive by a pair of grey-skinned men. Some of Brighana's army looked almost normal, except for their red-rimmed eyes and vacuous gazes, but others were covered with carbuncles and sores, and many were as twisted as witch-hazel trees. The captive twitched one last time, and was still.

Even as Brighana moved onto its next victim, the pile of steaming intestines from its earlier prey began to turn grey and stretched plopping and oozing like volcanic mud. A limb extended from the pile, then another. The first turned slowly into an arm, the second into a leg. On the other side of the lump, the same thing happened. Finally, from a third side, a shorter squarer lump stretched out to form a head. While the intestines were re-shaping into another carbuncle-covered grey-man, the original corpse from which it had grown had turned fully grey but was now climbing shakily to his feet.

Two soldiers from each body, Blue thought. *There's a twisted logic to Brighana's love of slaughter. It's breeding an army of the dead. They won't need feeding, and it will have complete dominion over them.* She realized that this was as surprising to Nangharai as to her. *Does this mean that the scrolls omitted something? Or has Brighana learned a new trick? The thought was chilling.* "Hopefully, they can be killed again." She didn't realize that she had whispered the words aloud until Brighana stopped and sniffed the air.

Shouts echoed down the street, and people moved away from a fresh disturbance coming from the far side of the pile of bodies. Her jaw dropped, just for a moment. "So *that* was why you were so distracted," she muttered as western Alliance swordsmen laid into Brighana's forces with more vigor than skill. Completing a triangle of corpses and two sets of attackers were soldiers of the Empire.

Nangharai's chuckle echoed through her skull. *Even Gods have limits. Though to mortals they seem omnipotent. But we were near death and needed to shield two different nexi from an enemy's attention– that would tax any divine.*

Sharing Nangharai's memories now that the God was fully with her again, Blue could barely imagine the skill that it must have taken to have flown at night, balefire burners searing the darkness like beacons. Luck, complacency on the part of Brighana's followers and manipulation by Nangharai had shielded them from discovery.

The westerners who had flown up in the night by airbags pirated from the ground station had gathered to one side of the fortress, just as Imperial troops had been mustered on the other side of it. Nangharai had given each force's leader the idea of blocking off the alleyways around their bridgehead with rubble. When they were ready Nangharai let them know that now was the time to attack. They fell on the locals from different directions, each force a thousand strong and unaware of the other.

Almost without Blue realizing it, Nangharai drew a bundle of *something* from elsewhere out into the world and as it became balefire cast it at Brighana.

Later, Blue understood that had Nangharai not acted instinctively, some noise or movement would probably have alerted Brighana. Instead she caught it by surprise, the balefire-bolt flying at her enemy.

But she had sacrificed accuracy for haste. The bolt caught Brighana's head, but it was a glancing blow, and while the demigod spun away screaming, a sudden plague of boils that afflicted Blue proved that her enemy wasn't dead yet. The corpse that Brighana had been revivifying sizzled and hissed, then melted to nothing in the space of seconds.

Taking a deep breath Blue reached back into the other place. While the first time it had been like plunging her hand into warm water, now it felt more as if she were trying to push it through molasses. *We're letting it slip away!*

Meanwhile the grey men had tuned to face her, holding their struggling captives as shields. *If I use bale-fire on the enemy,* she thought, *I'll slaughter hundreds of innocent people, which makes me no better than Brighana.*

And while we ponder the consequences that's exactly what the monster wants, Nangharai responded. *We spend our time fighting our way through walls of enemy bodies or descend to its level. No one said that war presented easy choices, mortal child.*

"Blue?" Cas shouted. Armoured, sword in hand, he was surrounded by fifty to a hundred Whiterock militia, similarly armed. "Is that you? You look more like Jasmina..."

"It's a long story," Blue said, pitching her voice so that only he could hear her.

Cas grinned at her. "We've managed to gather some supporters. All that these men needed was a cause to rally round. Now, how can we help?"

"Hold..." she cried and cast the grey men's captives into a deep slumber. They slumped, which actually made the grey men's task easier, for they now held inert lumps, rather than squirming captives. "Kill the grey men," she called. "Try to hurt the locals as little as possible, but don't be hostage to sympathy. Your countrymen are over there," she added, indicating where the Imperial troops were.

He nodded and shouted to his men, "Two of us to each grey man! Work in pairs!" He clambered up onto a ledge, dodging an arrow. "Imperial troops, to me!" he bellowed, and a cheer went up from his countrymen.

The Whiterock militia waded gleefully into a massed sword fight with ranks of the grey men. With a part of her mind, Blue noticed that even when an enemy soldier lost an arm or a leg to a hacking sword, little blood flowed.

Unlike their people, who bled as freely as any other mortal.

We're making slow progress, she thought. *And sacrificing too many men.*

While the mortals are helping, Nangharai replied, *the real fight is up to us.*

Blue reached again into the other place, and this time drew a smaller bundle of the other-stuff that metamorphosed into balefire. But rather than throwing it, she smeared it over her arms and legs. She caught a startled glance from Cas. "I can tolerate it for a while," she shouted. "But after a time, my skin will burn like any mortal's."

She looked up and saw Cavi and Lexi wade from the side into the brawl with the grey-men. Both wore light armour and wielded what for men would be shorter, lighter training swords. Blue clenched a fist in exultation; both princesses were each accompanied by a handful of guards and civilians with weapons. Lexi shouted, "Yoo-hoo!" When Blue looked over, two of Lexi's men were tossing the princess a shield. Blue had to stop herself from laughing out loud at the way the princess could barely lift it.

Another hundred heartbeats wasted day dreaming, she thought and stepped forward, toward the advancing grey men. Blue ran to one side of the street to ensure that the wall was to her back– the last thing she wanted was to burn one of her own people, or worse, to be caught between grey-men attacking her from both sides– and picked up a sword lying on the ground. She searched around, and grabbed a shield, pushing the loops up over her wrist and almost up to her elbow so that she could still use her left hand– although it was extremely awkward, hampered as she was by the shield.

When she reached her first opponent, she parried its sword thrust easily enough and reaching around the hostage, grabbed its flesh near the collarbone. The animated corpse jumped as if stung and immediately started to sizzle. The eeriest thing about the whole encounter was how quiet it was. Apart from a grunt when she had touched it, neither of them had said anything. There was none of the shouting of the battles between the ordinary soldiers.

It released its hostage and clutched at where she had grabbed it. She had no time to waste finishing it off but instead pushed through to the next one. This time the grey man managed to push the hostage at her, and she felt the stench of scorching flesh and heard a scream from him as the pain woke him from his spell-induced slumber.

She pushed on, using all her strength to shove the grey-man back against his next fellow, where both were attacked by Whiterock militia who waded into the fight with yells and war-chants in contrast to the silent enemy.

Blue spent the next few minutes fending off a stream of curses that Brighana and its army of turncoat witches and wizards hurled at her with manic intensity. The latest one manifested itself as a small rain-cloud that dumped its contents on Blue in seconds, accompanied by bolts of lightning that fizzed harmlessly against Blue. *Harmless at the moment, but am I going to be sore afterwards when Nangharai stops blocking the sensation,* Blue thought. She grinned. *At least now I half-believe there might be an afterwards.*

"Militiamen!" Cas bellowed. "With me! To the lady!"

No, Blue urged him. *Your men will get burnt.*

Cas shook his head. "Doesn't matter!" He led by example, hacking with his broadsword, moving diagonally to Blue's path to form a buffer against reinforcements.

Blue continued shoving her way through the grey-men, trying not to touch the hostages but not flinching from burning them where she had to grip the enemy, the screams that followed indicating where she touched living flesh.

The sleep-spell was starting to wear off, and Blue could see some of the victims struggling against their captors. Cavi saw it too, and she shouted, 'People of Whiterock! If you don't have a sword or axe, use a knife on their arms or their legs! If you have no weapons, just bite them! Whatever you can do, anything helps your countrymen!"

"Pay them no mind!" Someone with a local accent shouted back from behind enemy lines, then cried out. Blue glanced up from gripping a grey-man's thigh with her balefire coated hands and saw a man topple from a wall, a crossbow bolt in his eye.

As if the shooting had given others ideas, more bolts flew in both directions. Blue heard Lexi shout, "Fire into the air! Try not to hurt our own, but if in doubt, just shoot!"

On command, dozens of bolts flew up in a fairly flat arc of twenty or thirty degrees from horizontal past the front lines, toward the side wall where Blue was pushing her way through. Most pinged harmlessly off armour, but several screams showed where hostages had been hit, and several grey-men slumped.

Blue felt for Brighana's presence and felt it pulling away from her, now more than one alley away. She redoubled her efforts; drawing again on Nangharai's reserves, she set up a field of repulsion for some thirty lengths around her, which took much effort and a few seconds but which paid off spectacularly.

All around her grey-men who pushed toward her suddenly shoved in exactly the opposite direction as the conjuration took effect. They scattered the grey-men behind them and their hostages in a tangle of arms, legs and suddenly freed captives. The harder they tried to get near to her, the more they moved away.

Such a spell had to levy a price; Blue could barely hold her shield up, and her left leg dragged as she and the little bubble of chaos around her crab-raced along the street.

Blue's little phalanx of protectors had veered toward her, and she hissed, 'Fight parallel to me!"

The battle resumed, but Blue had had vital seconds to clear the lines of Brighana's defenders and reach the end of the street. The next one was clear, and for a moment, Blue thought that she had lost Brighana. But as she rounded the next corner, she stepped over a man who was lying groaning in the street.

Her step saved her; she stumbled and the weight of her shield dragged her to one side. The balefire bolt shot past her hair, missing by the merest fraction. She felt the heat and sickness of its passage raise blisters on her temple and smelled the singeing of a lock of hair. She cursed, pulling the shield round in front of her. A second bolt struck moments later, but in its haste to create another bolt, Brighana had had to throw a weaker one, and it splattered against the shield, merely eating slightly at the fabric.

Take your time, Blue told herself. Using Nangharai's knowledge, she cursed Brighana with a bout of dysentery, and while the enemy was laughing at her naivety ("You can't make a god sick, stupid,") she caused a wall to collapse on the distracted Brighana. As the demigod was digging itself out, she drew another bolt from the elsewhere-place and moulded it as best she could one handed. A third bolt caught the edge of

Blue's shield and deflected onto a nearby wall. With a crack, plaster fell away; the smell of burning once again filling the air.

Blue hurled her own bolt with as little movement as possible beforehand. It worked, for she appeared to catch Brighana by surprise, catching it squarely in the forehead, and its shape wavered while blue rings of sparking power spun up and down around the demigod. It stood motionless for a moment, Kyr's skin boiling and bubbling horribly, chunks of flesh falling away in liquid, melting gobbets before she reverted back to Brighana's form.

Blue stood momentarily paralyzed by the horror of what was happening to Kyr, biting on one of her knuckles. But prompted by Nangharai's urging, *magic will not do it– you must use balefire or some other means of killing mortals,* Blue reached again into the other place, and before Brighana could reappear, Blue gathered one last surge of energy, which she hurled at Brighana with all her strength.

Blue thought that the huge shape would topple, but it was Kyr that now stood amid the rubble, shaking her head as more flesh peeled away, her hair smoldering. She screamed, but even as Blue's heart went out to her, she ran from the street. "You need more than that if you want to kill me!" The familiar voice drifted back on the breeze.

Blue grimaced, but ran after her. *She should be dead,* Blue thought. *Neither mortal nor demigod should be able to withstand that much balefire. Who knows where she could be drawing that kind of power from?* For a half-second, Blue allowed herself to hope. Maybe Brighana was gone, but Kyr survived and fled in panic.

They ran toward the Northern end of the castle, toward Mount Halkyon. Kyr was pulling away. Blue felt the stitch in her side and pulled up.

Then the running figure stopped. Ahead of her sat a dozen or more of the delta-winged gliders that Whiterock patrols used to scour the skies. Now they sat untended.

But separating Kyr from her prize was a huge spider's-web made up of spiders. Tens of thousands of them, wriggling and writhing in a desperate struggle to stay linked.

Kyr backed away, then saw Blue walking towards her. Blue tried to allow herself to relax, to fill with power for a thunderbolt, but little came. "Too soon for that," she muttered. "The well has almost run dry."

The half-light to the east told Blue that sunrise wasn't far away.

In backing away, Kyr actually touched the web. She screamed and jumped back from it and began frantically brushing herself down. "Go on, my little beauties," Blue whispered. The spiders had reacted as they would to a hostile intruder in the caves. She allowed a couple of others who were running toward Brighana to instead climb onto her palm and popped them into her pocket.

Kyr rippled into Brighana and back again, and her whole body pulsed with a dark red, then orange glow that seared the eyeballs. Then Kyr, to the watching Blue's horror, ran toward the edge of the lane and ran through the edge of the web. Screaming in agony, she grabbed a hang-glider and launched herself into space.

Chapter 26

For a moment, time froze. Blue saw Brighana's hands scrabbling to get a grip on the handlebar of the glider, Kyr leaning forward, stomach across the central bar, struggling to control it, below her the patchwork of different-shaded green fields.

Beyond Kyr, a line of dots marked the reinforcements arriving from the Empire, a column that stretched all the way to the frontier. Through Nangharai's near-omniscience, Blue knew that a similar line stretched toward the different territories of the Alliance. Blue squinted into the rising sun, a part of her mind noting the fluffy clouds to the south where the rain wall should have been. *Should have been?* She thought, *They've seduced me into thinking that their iron grip of the weather is natural!*

"Well, go after her," someone said, and Blue turned to see the young black priestess watching her. One eye was covered with a makeshift dressing, and her robes were torn. But she looked exultant. "You could hear that the spiders bit the abomination. You can tell how strong their venom is, by the fact that even she screamed. The pain must have been incredible. But she'll recover, if you don't hurry. You'll have only ten or twenty minutes, before she– it recuperates."

"Go after her?" Blue whispered, horrified. "I can't!"

"You must," the priestess urged. "These people are relying on you. They'll suffer if you let it return to take revenge. Or imagine what it will do out in the wider world."

Meanwhile, Nangharai was also urging her to grab a glider. She cried, "I can't! I'm terrified of heights."

"You're a god," the priestess said.

"You know better than that," Blue snapped. "I'm a god's avatar, but I can die and take Nangharai with me. I nearly did before."

"Only if you fall," the Priestess said. "And you won't."

"How simple you make it sound," Blue said, shaking her head. She looked down. Her feet seemed to move of their own volition. She looked up again, and the priestess had vanished. Blue wondered if she had ever been there. She stopped, then took another half-step, but she was having difficulty breathing, and her heart was beating so fast she thought it might burst from her chest. "I can't do this." Her voice was almost strangled by fear.

You must. Nangharai's voice was clear in her head. *Else countless people will have died for naught. I could make you, but that would require me taking control of you. You would be merely a puppet, and scarred for life. And I would be no better than Brighana.*

"What if I asked you to take me over?"

*Still I would have to make your body do things. It's better that you **want** to. I can steer you, guide you as a teacher shows a novice, but you must provide the will.*

Blue tottered toward the gliders parked in their racks, all sharp lines and predatory shape in metal and cloth. She clumsily took one from the rack by its crossbar, banging it against the rail that contained it. "It's so light," she whispered aloud. "How can this possibly hold me?" It thrummed with magic, and that gave her the answer.

It's silk. Nangharai's thoughts in her head sounded equally amused and annoyed. *We don't have time for lectures. Do you trust me? Would I let harm befall you?*

Blue shook her head. She knew that Nangharai wouldn't hurt her, but was the god omnipotent? She climbed onto the parapet, shaking with terror. *If I fall now...*"How do I fly this thing?" she asked of the world in general, and one of the attendants nearby who had arrived to find his workplace in chaos told her how to lean, climb, and manoeuvre, his face blank. Blue wondered how much he would remember of his mind being picked up by a god on a whim, then put back. *Hurry!* Nangharai urged.

"Take my hands," she whispered. Her mouth was so dry; she could barely utter the words. "Theory's fine, but I have no experience."

I will, but not your feet. ***You*** *must leap. Hurry! Before it's too late.*

Blue shut her eyes. Her knees almost gave way beneath her, but then she stepped back, took a little run and launched herself off the edge.

***

Clinging onto the crossbar so hard she felt it splinter, she plummeted ground-ward. She screamed, trying to force her terror out through her mouth, rather than her bottom. She screamed and screamed again. The wind roared through her hair, and the pressure built until she thought her eardrums would burst. Her stomach felt as if it might void its contents, but hanging on took part of her attention, and shifting her hands clumsily along the bar took more, so that her panic gradually dissipated.

She leaned back on the crossbar, Nangharai's invisible hands cupping round her like a girdle. It was maddeningly slow, but she finally stabilised the wobbling glider and eased it onto a level course.

She made herself open her eyes. To her right, the east, the light on the land was a spreading stain rolling infinitesimally slowly toward her, lighting up a varied green board of fields and hedges, with home far beyond the horizon. She was almost starting to enjoy the spectacle, but that was as much avoiding the thought of what was sure to follow, when she reached the ground. Nangharai gave her night-eyes, and she saw, far below, Kyr's glider sailing across the massed ranks of the besieging armies. Arrows flashed harmlessly by it, its speed taking it past trigger-happy sentries.

I'm just guiding you, Nangharai thought. *Now you must take the next step. It's getting away. Draw in the wings– I'll show you how– and put the dart into a dive.*

The icy knot of fear in her guts was back again at the thought. She clamped down it, or she would never see home again. Home. Longing rose up through the fear like a bubble from the depths, and she almost welcomed it. She leaned back as instructed.

Brighana has grown complacent. It thinks you would never dare follow it, and it knows I would not seize you and make you my puppet. See?

As Blue leaned back, furling the wings with little levers on the crossbar that led to a host of tiny wires which tipped the nose forward, she saw that Brighana was circling back over the besieging forces and drawing their fire. *Its hurling sickness-spells down onto them,* Nangharai thought, *and feeding off their pain.* Most of the arrows that were on target were so weakened by the climb that if they hit Brighana, they simply bounced harmlessly off it, as it weaved lazily back and forth in a figure of eight.

She steepened the dive at Nangharai's urging, and the wind pushed at her face, drawing her lips back in a rictus, pushing at the flesh of her cheeks so that they rippled and flattening her hair against her head. She would have screamed in exultation, but the air was forced back into her every time she tried to exhale.

The enemy dart drew closer, closer by the second.

Blue saw an amorphous shadow closing on Kyr's glider. Even if she had wanted to, she couldn't have shouted a warning for the air was still being forced back into her.

Kyr banked to the left. Not enough; an elemental snapped hold of her leg, and her scream shattered the silence. A moment later there was a flash which lit up the elemental in a harsh blue halo. Another scream echoed the first, and the elemental released its prey and fell to the ground.

Kyr's glider wobbled and weaved in a lazy circle, one wing now tipped upwards at one end, where the struts had severed with the impact of the collision. Blue could see Kyr wrestling with the glider for control, and then the demigod fell like a stone, by some fluke, toward what seemed to be the only space in the massed ranks of soldiers now completely around Whiterock.

Blue leaned back further, and as the glider's dive grew ever steeper until it was almost vertical, it shook and rattled. A tree that started out as a little dot grew with each passing second until it filled her vision. Blue leaned slightly to avoid it. Then the ground rushed up, and almost too late, she tilted forward to pull the wing's nose up before the ground hit her with a mighty blow that knocked the breath from her.

For a few moments, she lay dazed. But even winded, she knew she had little time. Staggering to her feet, she looked around. She wiped her nose, which was still bleeding– together with her ears– from working so many spells in such a brief time. She was bruised and cut from the landing as well. About twenty yards away, Kyr had climbed to her feet and was lurching toward her, looking as battered as Blue felt. Several Alliance soldiers approached, but Kyr waved a hand, and several of them fell to their knees, clutching at their chests, screaming as they tried to rip their own hearts out with their bare hands. "Stay back!" Blue screamed at them. "Leave this to me!"

Instinct warned her, and Blue threw herself to one side. She felt the heat of the bolt on her face as it passed. The effort of throwing herself around wrenched a groan from her, but there was no time to lose. She rolled side over side on the ground, which probably saved her life; another bolt grazed her ribs, but most of its energy was dissipated into the ground, which erupted in a burst of grass and soil.

Gritting her teeth, Blue rolled to her feet in one almost-fluid movement, a flailing arm ruining the elegance of it. Even though the near-miss made her side feel as if it had been set alight, the bolt wasn't as strong as the one that Brighana had hit her with before, up on the rock. "You're weakening!" she cried and fired one back, but thought, *you should've waited, you had more time*. She'd lost her composure and rushed it.

"*That* wasn't strong enough to harm me," Brighana taunted as the bolt sailed past, but the demigod was fizzing in and out of sight, and smaller now, not much taller than a big man. "Hand-to-hand," Kyr said and blew Blue a kiss. Her face was leprous-scarred now; and lacy ribbons of skin hung from her arms, but still Blue ached to hold her and to stroke her. "To the death, darling."

"I don't want to," Blue said, panting. "But you're not Kyr anymore. You're a chrysalis carrying a wasp larvae that's eating it from inside." She flung another bolt, but there was almost no energy left, and it merely fizzed and sizzled harmlessly against Kyr's flesh. Her response only made Blue's skin tingle.

"You say the sweetest things," Kyr mocked, but clearly realizing that she had almost exhausted magic, tore her tattered blouse off. As Blue hesitated she crowed; "I can still stop you with sex anytime, can't I?" She leaned toward Blue. "Come lie with me, one last time." She cupped her breasts. "Kiss them, darling." She laughed coarsely and stepped out of her leggings, fondling herself. Blue was shocked at the bouillabaisse of emotions that her lover could arouse in her; pity that even now Kyr was using sex as a weapon, revulsion at the cheap theatrics. But above all, shock at the heat that she felt rising within her, even now, even in these circumstances. Several of the watching soldiers whistled and cat-called, but fell silent as Kyr waved a hand. Somewhere, a lone soldier screamed, then sobbed. Blue wondered what the demigod had done to him, but forced herself to concentrate. She knew that it was foolish, but still even now she wanted Kyr.

"Of course," Kyr said. "If you get bored with me, now I can become anyone." The prince stood in front of her, still naked, his penis rising slowly. "Would you like to try someone else?"

Blue shook her head. "Nangharai said that you were stupid. You almost had me, then, but you lost just when you might have won."

Kyr suddenly became a half-rotted lump of flesh, the way she should have looked if the balefire bolts had taken their effect the way they were supposed to, and then Kyr stood before her again, miraculously whole again. "You see?" Kyr breathed. "It's not all bad, darling, being joined like this. It's saved me more than once."

Blue shook her head, her face a-flame, but her eyes locked on Kyr's. "For its own selfish purposes," she said. "Not out of any wish to benefit you." She didn't know how much of Kyr was still there beyond the residual amorality.

Kyr said, "Come and lie with me, and I'll snap your neck with my hands, if I don't break your back with my thighs."

"To the death, you said," Blue sneered, surreptitiously taking from her pocket the knife Aton had given her and palming it. "Are you going to talk me to death?"

For reply, Kyr aimed a kick at her head, so hard that Blue heard the kneecap crack with the effort. Blue drew her head back out of reach, but close enough that she could smell the slave-girl's feet and leaping closer, grabbed left-handed at Kyr's hair. She caught a handful, and Kyr shrieked and ripped her head away, so hard that it tore several strands out, but amidst the blood, Blue still had hold of some.

Another spider dropped from her wrist onto Kyr's shoulder. It was one of the smallest, most venomous ones, a juvenile warrior. A second one followed it.

Blue twisted, just dodging the raking nails that hissed past her face. "Nasty!" She panted, trying to get Kyr's throat exposed, but instead Kyr bit her wrist through to the bone, then screamed at the balefire coating that had already started to burn Blue's palms and was increasing in intensity with each second.

Blue also screamed as the blood spurted but held on, though every instinct, every muscle and fiber clamored at her to let go.

Then Kyr screamed again and released Blue's wrist. "Get them off me! Get them off!" She shrieked, slapping her shoulder. For a moment she was Brighana, again, but it was even smaller now, no bigger than Kyr. Blue saw her opportunity and plunged the knife hilt-deep into Kyr's chest, straight into the heart.

For a moment, time seemed to stop. Kyr looked at Blue with mouth agape. Her mouth puckered. "You…" she didn't finish the sentence. Blue stepped back, wary of another trick. But the glamour was fading by the second from Kyr's eyes. Tinder dry gray streaks seamed her hair, and together with the age crinkling Kyr's face, it all convinced Blue that this was real.

"Water!" Blue screamed at an Imperial officer. "Throw me a flask, now!" She caught the flask and poured some over her hands, rinsing the balefire off them. When they stopped stinging, she knelt.

"Always loved you," Kyr said weakly. Blue scooped her up into her arms and pressed her lips to Kyr's. If she could have, she would have blown life back into Kyr's mouth, but she knew that wasn't possible. The taste of blood was too strong.

"Done it, then," Kyr said when they ended the kiss and broke apart. "Well done, my love. You did right by me."

Blue shook her head, tears staining Kyr's face. "I didn't want to."

"*I* wanted you to," Kyr whispered. "Deep down inside. The power was nice at first, but it wasn't right, and I soon got bored with being able to hurt people who had wronged me. And after a while, I realized that who could compare that with the power that I had, that of being able to make you happy?" She laughed, mocking herself, Blue guessed. "All that flowery, romantic poetry stuff," Kyr breathed. "Who would have thought that I'd end up mouthing all the same rubbish as those soppy poets?" She coughed, and a thin stream of blood trickled down her chin. Blue wiped it away. Kyr whispered, "I've had more lovers than I can count, although love didn't figure for most of them. But I can't think when else I was as happy as with you."

"I've never loved anyone else," Blue said. "I never will love anyone else."

"Hush," Kyr whispered. "*Never* and *ever* are short words but an awful long time. The best way to remember me is to live long, and tell everyone you can about me."

"I'll do that," Blue promised. "I'll sing your name to the very highest point of the sky. As long as I live, I'll tell anyone who'll listen– and those who won't– about you."

"Then I won't be dead, will I?" Kyr whispered and coughed up more blood. Her eyes were dulling by the second, and she said weakly. "As long as you remember me, and tell others about me, I live on through you."

"I never stopped loving you," Blue said, "at any time in all this, despite everything that happened."

"I love you too," Kyr gasped, "and I did from the first second that I saw you." Her voice was now so faint that Blue could barely hear her. Blue leaned closer to catch what she said. "Always have. Never doubt it..." her voice faded, and so did the life in her eyes.

"Never did," Blue said and continued to hold Kyr until the slave stiffened and then went limp in her arms. She was still holding her when thirty or more gliders from Whiterock landed an hour later, each carrying a soldier lying alongside the pilot.

Chapter 27

It was early afternoon when Blue again set foot in the square in front of the Silk Palace.

When the Whiterock militia had finally accepted that she was no threat, they advanced– still cautiously– and surrounded her. Even in her grief Blue had noticed how the lances had quivered with the fear of the soldiers holding them.

"You'll accompany us," the leader said, his voice harsh with fear, "please."

Blue wiped the snot from her nose. "Lower your weapons." Her voice was nasal and shook too but from barely controlled grief and rage at the waste of life. Life had been cheap in Ravlatt but not as cheap as it had seemed here in the last few days, and besides, years in the cloistered halls of the University had softened her. "And I will."

The officer had signalled his men, who slowly lowered their lances and crossbows. Blue admired their bravery in even considering taking her on. *Something's stiffened their spines in the last few hours. Unless all they needed was time to regroup. Was everything I did, everything I suffered, all unnecessary?* She knew otherwise.

By contrast, both Alliance and Imperial troops had kept running long after they had scattered, clearing a huge space around the combatants and had shown no stomach to return.

"Leave the corpse where it is," the Whiterock patrol's leader ordered his men.

He flinched as Blue said, "I don't think so." Maybe it was the fury in her eyes that scared him. She had managed to rouse that much emotion at least.

The officer shrugged. "Cover the body with whatever rocks we can lay our hands on, lads." The patrol built an impromptu cairn, and she tried to think of something to say to mark Kyr's passing, but no words would come.

The soldiers from Whiterock then insisted on escorting her back the long way around the rock, though she was unsure whether they wanted to parade her as prisoner or saviour. Nor did she care. With Kyr dead and Nangharai gone– it had retreated as soon as Brighana truly died– nothing mattered very much. Blue was a hollowed-out gourd; inside, where there should have been regret and fear of her eventual fate, she felt nothing at all.

They'd marched with three men on each side of her, past the troops from the Karnaki Empire who were pulling tent-pegs hurriedly from the ground, collapsing tents, stowing them on pack-mules, and kicking earth over fires. None of the soldiers who had besieged the castle in the name of the safety of Prince Cas would meet their gazes, and several made warding signs as if they believed that Blue and the Whiterock soldiers were evil spirits.

Later, they passed a few remaining soldiers of the Western Alliance who even as they passed were melting away.

"Where are they going?" she'd asked, but there was no great interest in the question, just mild curiosity. "Retreating?"

"Run off with their tails between their legs," the patrol leader had said gleefully. "They both got such a savaging from up top that none of them wanted to stay around for more, especially when you and the false god appeared down here."

How quickly history is re-written, she thought. *Already Brighana is a 'false' god.*

They reached the launch site for the balloons, and when they climbed aboard Blue slumped in the foot of the basket. Someone had scooped out her innards of all thought, all feeling, all humanity, leaving her merely empty, so much so that she was no longer scared of flying. Whether she had simply reached a point when she couldn't be any more terrified, or whether it was a legacy of Nangharai's presence, she no longer had that bowel-melting fear of falling.

More guards met them at the air-bag station and saluted her. "If they're going to hang me, at least they're doing it with respect," she muttered out of the side of her mouth to a soldier. "Gallows humour," she said by way of an explanation, but he merely looked at her blankly, and she shrugged.

They marched her back through the portcullis, but she stopped to watch the on-going repairs. Bricks and masonry lay everywhere, and dust clogged the air. The guards hovered, anxiously. "His Majesty is waiting," their leader said.

"He can wait," Blue said, watching the ruin of Myleetra's head still mounted on the wall. "Why?" Blue said, still moved by pity for the witch.

"We needed someone naive, someone young," Myleetra croaked, "who could be guided along the path we wanted. Someone malleable, but who had to be gifted. Even with our help, translating the Scrolls of Presimionari wouldn't be an easy task. When we heard of a talented scholar, who had translated the Tablet of Zalte for her doctorate, the choice was obvious." She added, "We hadn't considered that though you were young, you might conceal within that diffident exterior of yours a heart of iron. Nor did we think that you might be *so* talented that you could succeed in the space of a few weeks where others had failed over months, even if those others were hampered by not having Brighana's help."

She closed her eyes. "Worse, you had to shout about it. Why did you have to announce it to the whole world? That realization panicked us, though it was Daragel who tried to kill you."

"Just so he would have the pretext of protecting the Princess to give him reason to invade."

Myleetra nodded. This time she was silent for so long, that Blue thought she'd passed out, but then she whispered, "Of course, you're young. We hadn't thought of that either; that it might have become a labor of love."

Myleetra's face puckered, and Blue realized that she was trying to cry, but couldn't. *They've done something to her eyes,* she thought.

"The King's wizards will keep me alive as a warning to those who plot against the King." Myleetra opened her eyes, begging Blue silently, *kill me, please. Have mercy.*

Blue turned away, ashamed that she couldn't bring herself to do it.

They resumed their march through the Palace, strangers turning to stare at her without recognition. Eventually they reached the throne room, and her guards ushered Blue in.

The King sat on his throne, looking shrunken and shriveled compared to the giant of only weeks earlier. He stared at her. When the guards had left, he said, "I should have you executed and thrown into a pit of lime for your part in the last few days."

Blue stared at him, the sheer injustice of his comments finally filling her with some semblance of emotion. She thought, *Executed for what? For staying, and fighting the demigod that your family have used for your own ends for who knows how many generations? For saving you as you licked its feet?* Instead she said, "Is that why you had me trudge around the rock. I wondered why– it would have been as easy to have come up the side I landed on. It was to give you time to re-establish yourself." She shrugged, sitting on the floor. "How do you know that doing so won't call the wrath of Nangharai down upon you?" She stared at him. "Are you ready to take the risk, so soon after all that's happened?" She kept staring until he looked away.

He spluttered, but Blue ignored him, instead glancing at the queen, who watched them with the trace of a smile. Blue rolled her eyes, and Ana looked away, hand over her mouth. When she was satisfied that the King had exhausted his indignation, Blue looked around the court. From behind the throne, the priestesses watched her with awe and other emotions she couldn't quite define.

Blue beckoned Lexi, and the princess approached her slowly. "Still friends?" Blue asked, and Lexi nodded. "Then let your pain go," Blue said. "You can't bring her back."

"I know," Lexi said, her eyes brimming. "But it's hard to say it out loud."

"You'll have no peace until you do," Blue said.

Lexi nodded. "Father," she called, and the King broke off his muttered conversation with one of his courtiers. "I have something to say," Lexi continued. When she was sure she had his complete attention, she said, "I– that is– I—" She stopped and took a deep breath. "It was I who killed Evi. I meant the bomb for someone else, but I was responsible."

The King stared at her in horrified silence. "Who? Who was it intended for?" Lexi turned and fled from the room as he shouted, "Who did you intend to kill?" He turned to Blue. "You knew?"

Blue nodded. "Of course I did. You think a mortal could keep that from a god?" She drew herself up to her full height, and a tiny residue of Nangharai that she hadn't realized remained showed itself. Her reversion to her divine form of earlier was so sudden that the King looked away. When he looked back and spoke, his voice quavered. "We must suppress this."

Blue nodded. "I agree– but the price of my silence is a royal pardon for *all* crimes committed here." Her voice brooked no argument.

"Some are difficult to swallow," he said.

"*All* of them."

The King stared into space. Even without divine sight, Blue could see him wrestling with the question. Finally he sighed. "Agreed."

Blue left the throne room without waiting to be dismissed, offering no farewell.

***

"What do you want?" the guard snapped. He clearly hadn't seen Blue before or didn't recognize her from her time as an avatar.

I need your help for a few more moments, Blue thought. *Hopefully for one last time.*

She felt again that vast, benevolent presence. *You only have to ask,* Nangharai thought. Blue could feel the smile in her voice.

Blue waved the guard away, and he silently obeyed. She marched through the empty rooms until she came to the ante-room where Prince Cas and Princess Cavi sat in awkward silence. Cavi jumped to her feet, while Cas sat looking sheepishly at his.

"Would you excuse us for a few moments?" Blue asked Cas with a smile. She ignored Cavi's spluttering and beckoned the princess. Cavi followed her to the bedroom.

"I'm supposed to leave today, according to your earlier proclamation banishing me," Blue said, "but as a courtesy, I thought I'd let you know that I've decided to stay an extra night."

"Why should I care?" Cavi said. "You can obviously do as you wish."

"As I said, courtesy, foolish girl! Something you should learn if you wish your marriage to be anything but a sham and your children to inherit the throne. I'd have thought that the last few days might have taught you that you rule with both divine and the people's consent."

"Who are you to tell me–" Cavi's hand flew to her mouth, her eyes wide.

"I—" Blue drew herself up to her full height and beyond, until she stood over nine feet tall, and her voice shook ceremonial plates off the wall, "—am Bluenangharaistocking, avatar of a goddess, *at least* equal to a king, and with a LOT more power!" To illustrate the point she turned the bedposts into miniature fountains which sprayed the bedroom, then changed them back again. Cavi stared at her and swallowed audibly. Blue leaned toward the princess and murmured. "Normally I wouldn't be so crass, but it seemed necessary." She fluttered her fingers; the vast hall appeared in microcosm in a corner of the room. "My name has been registered in the Great Hall of Names." Unseen hands lifted her name crystal up a wall of hand-high niches tens of hundreds of thousands high by as many wide, as far as the eye could see, all the name-stones that had ever been, were and would ever be, its progress marked by a thousand-strong unseen choir.

Looks good, doesn't it? Nangharai's whisper echoed in her mind. *Something like this always impresses the suggestible.*

It's not really like that? Blue wondered.

Nangharai's chuckle threatened to shake Blue's brains loose. *Not even our avatars are capable of comprehending how much grander, but also just how truly strange the reality would appear to a mortal mind. It would be too much, even for an avatar like you.*

Turning her attention back to Cavi, Blue said, "I have more power than you could ever dream of, Highness, but to the outside world, I shall simply remain Bluestocking, or Blue to my friends. After all, what does a name matter?"

And with that last, small, simple declaration, Nangharai thought, *the first cracks in this great monolith of a society appear unheralded.*

Blue wondered at the glee in the thought; then remembered that one of Nangharai's aspects was that of the Trickster God.

Cavi opened her mouth to speak, but Blue forestalled her. "Lexi will not want to be around the Prince and you: too many memories. She was only ever a threat to your happiness in her own fantasies." *Not strictly true,* she thought, *but never mind.* "Treat her kindly, and eventually you'll all look back at this with the peace that time brings."

Cavi stared at her, swallowed, and said in a husky voice, "May I go now?"

Blue smiled. "Go prepare for your wedding. Say goodbye to Cas for me and give Lexi my love."

***

The walk back to her quarters was a lonely trudge. She was surprised to find her few belongings untouched, as if she had been gone minutes- not days.

When Nangharai retreated, Blue felt that awful hollowness again. She wondered whether it was something the few avatars that there had been over the eons had had to learn to deal with. The gods were so vast, that even their small presence that they allowed to inhabit humanity would stretch the avatar, in the same way that a woman must stretch to carry a child. *Strange,* she thought, *that I should equate gods with children.*

She kept expecting to feel Kyr's touch, or to hear her voice or smell her musky fragrance. But when she finally accepted that none of these things were going to happen, only then did she lay on her bed. It took almost an hour for the tears to come, but when they did, it was as if a dam had burst inside her. She cried and cried, until her throat was sore, her nose felt stuffed and her eyes stung.

Then she slept.

***

At some point in the night she awoke and lay awake for a time. She wondered what it was that had woken her. In her dream, she had been buried in a mud-slide so vast that it had shaken the very earth, and none of the people in her dream– some old friends from the nunnery and Ravlatt, some people from Whiterock– had been able to dig her out.

She kicked back the thin sheet and eventually drifted back to sleep.

***

The next morning, she packed her meager belongings; her notes, scribbled on various pieces of parchment, a wooden hair-grip that Kyr had tied her hair back with when she was bathing her. The sight of it brought a dull ache back, but she packed it anyway. *I might have to pin my hair back,* she thought, knowing full well that she was being less than fully honest with herself. It was almost the only tangible memento of Kyr. *They say that time heals all ills,* she thought. *I hope that they're right, whoever* ***they*** *are.*

Most of her clothes were dirty or torn, and she reflected ruefully that she should have created herself some finery while she had almost unlimited magical powers, but somehow she suspected that there might have been consequences to that. One thing that she had learned in Whiterock was that nothing was ever easy or straightforward where magic was concerned, at least for her. *Perhaps others find it easier,* she thought.

Somehow these rooms had become almost home. She had filled them with her presence, and they seemed to have shrunk when she finished packing. Without looking back, she pulled the door closed behind her and set off for the air-bag station.

She paused when she had handed over the money for the fare but only for a moment. She had faced worse than sitting in a basket, watching the ground slowly come closer. As a distraction, she studied the rain-belt marching steadily north and wondered when she would cross it. "One thing's sure," she said to the merchant who stood next in line to her.

"Milady?" he said quizzically in a thick Alliance accent, and she realized with a rush of joy that he had no idea who she was. *Somehow not having the whole of the world watching is immensely satisfying,* she thought. *I've had enough of notoriety, for the moment.* "The one thing that's sure is that some point we're going to get wet today. That rain will stop for nothing." *How quickly life returns to normal.* It felt good to know that the sun still moved around the earth and that the gods would walk amongst men again next year. "Life goes on," she said, so quietly that no one else could hear.

As she clambered in, the merchant offering a helping hand that she declined with a smile, she noticed that the rain-belt was less symmetrical, less assured in its progress than when she'd watched its irrevocable march before. Clearly the King had lost enough of his wizards to affect his control of Whiterock's weather and that pleased her even more. *Life goes on, but Redoutifalia's benevolent tyranny has been forced to ease a little.*

On the ground, Blue stepped unsteadily from the basket. The attendant met her and handed her a set of reins, as she had been promised that he would. Blue stroked Fourposter's head. The fat little pony, which seemed to have gained even more weight while he had been left alone, nuzzled her, looking as usual, for food. "Sorry, sweetheart," she murmured, "I left without having breakfast."

"Milady," a familiar voice called. Blue looked around, and Aton raised his hand in greeting. "Which way do you go?"

Blue smiled. "I suspect we are headed in different directions," she said.

"So which way are you going?" the peddler asked innocently.

"West," Blue said. "I've had enough of Whiterock to last a lifetime, and while the Gods have pardoned me, I don't relish wasting the time explaining to any rare soul in the Empire who recognizes me. I may feel differently in time, but for now, I'd like to travel westwards and see if these Alliance people are all as devious as Daragel."

The Silk Palace

"What a coincidence," Aton said. "I travel westwards as well. Now," he held up his hand. "If you ask me nicely, I might just keep you company part of the way, but I don't want it taken for granted."

"Why you, you..." Blue sputtered.

"And I want it clearly understood, no monkey business," Aton said.

"What do you mean?"

"I'll not be your plaything," he said solemnly, but at the sight of Blue's hanging jaw, he let out a guffaw. "Sorry. My crass humour, Milady–"

"Blue. How did you know I wouldn't turn you into a baboon for such insolence?"

"I didn't, Blue." He grinned. "I like to live a little dangerously. I thought you'd realized that." He turned serious. "But, you need not fear me."

"No, she need not," said a woman's voice, one that Blue had thought that she would never hear again.

"Jasmina!" Blue stopped, gulped and grinned. "You look well," she finished lamely. "Such finery..."

"Your friend Nangharai worked some deep magic to have me freed," Jasmina said. "It seems that in the still, small hours of First Day morning, such things may happen if one is favored by the Gods."

"As you should be," Blue said. "Without you..." *But pleased though I am to see you, why couldn't it have been Kyr who was favored by the Gods?* She knew the answer, of course: Kyr was tainted by assosciation with Brighana. The silence grew. "What will you do now?" Blue finally asked to fill it.

"The priesthood seems apt," Jasmina said. "No man will ever take Arial's place, so if I am to wed again, it might as well be to a God."

"Oh? Any particular one?"

Jasmina half-laughed, and looked down. "They corrupted Brighana's story, in making it into Brighannon's. Nonetheless, Brighannon had many, many adherents. Countless numbers of them now feel a spiritual vacuum. Perhaps a new church which recognizes the truth, and pays no adherence to any single God may help them in their time of need." She beckoned behind her, and a slave stepped forward, carrying several bundles of linen and clothes. A second one carried a sack. "I was told by those who freed me that you probably hadn't had the foresight to conjure yourself decent traveling clothes or food. So I wondered if you would consider these as a gift of the grateful populace."

Blue thought of what the populace likely really thought of her and burst out laughing. "Thank you," she said when she wound down. "They will be worn and eaten with great gratitude." She grinned at Aton. "I assume you have no problem with eating Whiterock cuisine a little longer?"

"None at all," he said. "Food's food, and if it's free, so much the better."

"I was wondering whether I could ask a favour?" Jasmina said.

"Of course!" Blue said.

"I heard you say that you were going to go west to the Alliance?" Jasmina suddenly sounded awkward, and Blue wondered why, but nodded. "I wondered whether you might be prepared to accompany another who travels in the same direction." She stepped aside, and Lexi shuffled forward, looking sheepish.

Blue hugged her fiercely, then said over her shoulder to Aton. "Don't look like that. If you travel with me, you travel with her as well."

"Be like traveling with a flock of bloody starlings," he grumbled, but it was half-hearted.

"You're marrying the Emir, after all?" Blue said.

Lexi shook her head. "I want to travel for a while before Cavi's wedding. I've agreed that I'll return, but in the meantime, Papa has sent messages to the Emir that I am ill and will be indisposed for some time even after the Emir has apologized for his invasion." She grinned. "I thought that if I'm going to have to marry one of these people, I ought to see how they live. How better than to travel incommunicado with an avatar and my bodyguard cum valet? Meet Selon." She waved forward a broad shouldered young man who vaguely resembled Prince Cas and who blushed when Blue bowed.

"So," Blue said to Aton. "We'll have company while we travel westwards."

"Not such a bad thing," he conceded at last. "Four are less likely to be attacked by bandits than two. And I'm going North– eventually." He added, "I understand there is a lost temple on the far edge of the world that has some interesting pictograms."

If he had tried, he could not have said anything more guaranteed to snare Blue's interest. She sat in the saddle, gazing at him for a long time, then nodded, so slight he might have missed it, though his shy smile said otherwise. "Come on," Blue said.

The attendants brought forward horses for Lexi and Selon, and they set off, Aton walking, Blue on Fourposter, the bulk of the vast rock on which the Silk Palace sat rising sheer behind them.

Also By Colin Harvey

Lightning Days

When British Agent Josh Cassidy is sent to Afghanistan to investigate the mystery behind photographs taken by an American satellite, he expects Afghan tribesmen, or an Al-Queda training. He doesn't expect a beautiful but mysterious Neanderthal woman.

The band of refugees that she has led into our world is strange enough, but what they are fleeing from is even stranger, and infinitely more dangerous.

Cassidy must lead a squad of human and Neanderthal troops deep into hostile territory, before the enemy can destroy not only our world, but the entire universe. And time is already running out…

Colin Harvey's short fiction has appeared in Peridot Books, The Pedestal Magazine, and Flash Me! His first novel, *Vengeance,* was published in 2001 and reprinted as a trade paperback by The Winterborn Press in 2005. His science fiction novel, Lightning Days, was published by Swimming Kangaroo Books in 2006.

His fiction can be found at: http://www.geocities.com/colin_harvey

Printed in the United States
98451LV00005B/136-147/A